FATE'S HANDS

A THREE-BOOK SHIFTER TRILOGY

BOOK ONE: THE SPARE

By

Lori Ameling

*I want to dedicate this book to my Twin sister,
who always encouraged me to go.*

Lisa

1970-2019

completed my entry-level courses for college. I want to be a doctor or something that allows me to care for others.

As soon as graduation is over, I am leaving. I have enough money saved from my job, but I must keep that hidden, or Lily will find it. God only knows what she would do with it. I worked my tail off cleaning hotel rooms for every penny I have now; the thought of her getting it makes my skin crawl.

Lily gets three hundred dollars a month to spend on frivolous things, not that she pays for her clothes or anything else like gas for her new car. I keep telling myself that I am not envious, well, a little. She gets all the love and attention while I'm not even allowed to use the front door.

That reminds me, "The Grandparents" are coming tonight for dinner. It doesn't matter anyway. It's Friday; I picked up an extra shift at the hotel. I want to say that work gave me some friends to talk to, but it doesn't. It's just me and the cleaning cart.

Every day I tell myself, soon. There is one girl I am friendly with; she is an Omega and is entirely invisible like me. We chatted every day, she was so excited when she came up to me that day, she had found her mate, on the night she was to be with him she just disappeared, and now it has been over a week and I have heard nothing, she didn't even show up for work. I tried to look around and ask a few Pack members, but I didn't want or need any extra attention; I hoped she was ok.

Thank God for my only friend, my wolf, Artemis. She is a beautiful white wolf with black tips on her paws. Her eyes are even darker than mine. She is graceful and swift. She has kept me sane growing up and motivates me when I feel like giving up.

So here I am, pushing my cleaning cart from room to room; you don't understand how nasty and dirty people can be till you work as a maid in a hotel. It truly makes me wonder what their houses look like. I knocked on the door, but there was no answer, so I hit a little louder. Nothing. I use my key and open the door just a little to say, *"Housekeeping, anyone here?"* again, nothing. So, I grabbed some supplies and entered.

The bathroom is first on the left, so I start there. I turn on the light expecting the usual carnage; I am surprised when it is neat. I clean everything and restock the extras. I then turn on the light for the main room, and I gasp; there is a naked man on the floor; he is unconscious. I sigh; just what I need, another drunk guy passed out on the floor.

I grab a towel off the cart and cover his unmentionables. Then I reach down and shake his shoulder; I see the blood running down his face. Oh, God, he is hurt! I shake him gently one more time, and he moans. *"Sir, can you hear me?"* he sighs again; he is starting to move. He rolled over on his back; I thought of going to the front desk for help. But unfortunately, I couldn't afford a cell phone so I couldn't call the front desk directly.

He is a tall, well-built guy with tan skin and darker blond hair. And when he opened his eyes, they were so unusual; they were a bright gold with a life of their own. His scent was intoxicating, a combination of the deep woods and rain. She could tell that his wolf was looking back at her too. She backed away…

"I'm sorry if I was too close; you were unconscious. Are you ok? Let me get a cold washcloth for your forehead."

Duncan woke to the sweetest voice; he almost thought he was still dreaming. Then he remembered how he ended up on the floor naked. His wolf, Apollo, assured him that he was healing—nothing to worry about.

When she returned with a cold washcloth, it took the sting out of the cut; her scent hit him. It was a strange combination of roses and peppermint. She was gorgeous, the most beautiful woman he had ever seen. Both Duncan and his wolf spoke at the same time. *"MATE!"*

At the same time, a look of horror came across her face, and she bolted out the door; Duncan could still hear her words as she ran, *"NO! Please, not now!"* Without thinking, he ran after her. He caught her just as she was heading for the back door. He wrapped his arms around her, and she started to panic. *"Shhhh, my little wolf, I will not hurt you."*

She stopped moving and was quiet; he carried her back to his room over his shoulder. Duncan noticed how small she was and that she hardly weighed anything. He could feel her breathing; it was still fast but calming down.

Spare got a pleasant view of his very nice ass. Artemis was going crazy in her head. She was so frustrated at that moment that she could have slapped her.

"Stop it, you hussy; this messes up everything."

"He is our mate! He can help us."

"Take in his scent; he isn't from our Pack."

He went inside his room and shut the door, locking it behind him. He sat her gently down on the bed and went to get a pair of his jeans. Just as he was buttoning them up, she bolted for the door. Catching her quickly, he sat down with her on his lap this time. *"Tell me, my little wolf, why are you so afraid?"*

"Please." She whimpered. *"You have to let me go; I can't stay here in this Pack anymore; you will ruin all my plans."*

10

"Calm down, little wolf, and take in my scent again."

Spare looked at him for a little bit and then sniffed his scent again. It was the same as before, but something else there too. *"OMG, you're not from this Pack."* He smiled at her, taking her all in. His wolf Apollo was doing happy circles in his head. A very smug Artemis repeatedly said, **"I told you so."** in her head.

"What is your name, my little wolf?"

"Umm, my name?"

With a chuckle, he asked her again, *"Yes, little wolf, your name."*

Hanging her head in shame, she whispered...

"My name is Spare."

His mind couldn't get around it; what kind of name was Spare? *"As in a spare tire?! That kind of spare?"*

"Yes, as in that kind of spare."

It embarrassed her, so he decided to drop it for now. *"My name is Duncan MacPatton of the Storm Crow Moon Pack."* Spare didn't know much about the Storm Crow Moon Pack, only that it is a mysterious and secretive Pack, that the Wolf King hires to hunt down criminals and rogues.

"My full name is Spare Williams of the Rising Moon Pack." When she said her name, his eyes went from golden to an almost copper color. His voice gave off a low growl when he asked... *"Williams as in Michael and Erick Williams?"*

"Yes, my father is Erick."

"I met Erick's daughter, Lilly, but there was no mention of another daughter."

"Lilly is my twin sister; there was no mention of me because I am the Spare. I don't exist to them unless they want to vent some anger or need an ego boost."

Seeing her shrug it off as if it were normal broke his heart. There were so many questions and so little time to get the answers. She isn't going to like what he was going to tell her next.

CHAPTER TWO

"*Spare, you will not like this but since you are my mate, and they know I am here. You are going to have to come with me to my Pack.*"

"*What!! No! I can't; I graduate in three months. I have money saved up to leave here and go to college. It's the only thing I have had to hold on to all these years. I promise I won't tell anyone; believe me, I have no one to tell.*"

Her pleas were breaking his heart; he had no choice. She had to come with him. There was no way he would leave his mate in this hell hole.

"*When your shift ends, we will quietly go together to your house and gather your things. Then we are heading for my Pack, where we can sort it all out. I promise.*"

Spare should be mad, but whenever she looked at him and smelled his delicious scent; she just went weak in the knees. She wanted to scream, but all she did was nod her head. It shouldn't be too hard to get her things since they will be gone; they went into town tonight for a celebration.

Spare finished her shift and returned to Duncan's room. He was carrying a backpack as he guided her to his truck. *"Ok, my little wolf; it is time to get your things, and then I will get you far away from here."*

She noticed that he was almost healed because he wasn't walking funny anymore.

They drove silently as they parked on a side street from her house. She took one look at him as she got out of the truck. He smiled wolfishly, *"Little wolf, don't make me chase you. At least not tonight."* He could see her shiver as she walked back to her house.

He knew he had lied to her when he told her she had to go with him because she knew he was there. He couldn't leave her, knowing she was living in that house with that family.

He'd finally found his mate; he wasn't letting her out of his sight ever again. They would have to do something about her name; he refused to keep calling her Spare. Her mother was a cruel bitch to give her that name.

Spare grabbed what little stuff and money she had, angrily stuffing it into an old duffle bag. Lastly, she held max, her teddy bear; she had made him from all the torn-up ones Lilly had tossed away in her temper tantrums.

She snuck back out of the house. She walked up to the truck, cursing herself and this mate bond crap. She yanked open the door, got inside, and slammed it shut, just as her family pulled up into their drive. She ducked down low so they wouldn't see her, not that it mattered. They never could see her anyway.

It is a long four hundred miles when an angry she-wolf is in the truck with you. At first, he said nothing but noticed tears running down her face when he looked over at her silent figure. *"Crap,"* his wolf noted in his mind. ***"You must talk to her. We can't have our mate crying."***

"Look, I am sorry about your plans. I promise, though, to make it up to you. Your life is going to change as my Luna. My Pack is strong. We have over two thousand members. All of us are warriors; you will be safe. I will ensure you never have to be around those jerks again."

"Won't your warrior Pack be disappointed in a Luna that can't fight? I was never allowed to train."

Duncan didn't even give a second thought; it didn't matter to him, and it won't matter to his Pack either. He worried that she was so thin she needed to eat better. He

15

would take her straight to the Pack doctor for a check-up. Make sure she is ok. Then they will have breakfast and get her settled in his room.

He knew she was angry and that putting her in his room wouldn't improve things. He didn't care; he would put her where he knew she was safe. Besides, she better get used to it, knowing it will also be her bedroom.

She'd fallen asleep two hours ago when they were almost home. Ten minutes later, he pulled up to the gate as the guards waved him through. He came up to the packhouse and parked the truck. He looked over at her; she must have been exhausted to sleep so deeply.

That made Apollo happy, *"That means they must trust us a little bit."*

He decided to change his plans a little. He'd take her to his bed and let her sleep. He carried her inside the house as various Pack members stared in curiosity.

Once in his room, he laid her down on his bed, took off her shoes and jacket, and covered her up with his blankets; seeing her in his bed was very satisfying. He decided to look into her duffle bag; there wasn't much there, that was for sure. An odd-looking teddy bear, a couple of T-shirts, a pair of jeans, a couple of pairs of underwear, and a bra.

In the bottom was an envelope; he looked inside. It must be the money she had saved up. He counted it; there was over three thousand dollars in there. He went to his hidden safe and put the money in there for her. He took note of the sizes of her clothes and put them all neatly in the top drawer of his dresser.

He left her to sleep, as he mind-linked his beta Marco to meet him in his office. Marco was already there waiting for him, with a big grin. Duncan chuckled; nothing happens here that he doesn't know or find out.

"So, Duncan, did you find something interesting at the Rising 'Nasty' Moon Pack?"

"You know I did, asshole. I found my mate, and you will not believe who she is."

"Well, don't keep me waiting in suspense, drama queen; who is she?"

"She is the most beautiful creature I have ever seen. She is Spare Williams, as in the Williams of Rising Moon Pack. She is their second pup, fraternal twins. She is nothing like that skanky slut Lily. She found me knocked out on the hotel floor; she was a maid there."

"Spare? as in a spare tire? That isn't a nice name." Marco said with disgust. *"How could a mother do that to her child? Seriously this Pack is a piece of shit. Did you get any evidence before they made you?"*

17

"I assume they made you because you were knocked out; that was taking a big chance. They must not have known exactly who you were, or this entire thing would have gone way differently."

"I got some names of places to look up and names of missing girls; not all of them are wolves either; seems they like variety. They are also taking girls from human towns, not too many at a time and not at the same place."

"Maybe your Mate will know a few things?"

"I don't think so; she was living in the shadows. I doubt many Pack members even knew of her existence. You are right; it won't hurt to ask her, even though she is pissed at me."

"Oh, and pray tell why she is pissed at you? Did you use your not-so-charming charm on her, perhaps?"

"Nope, as it turns out, I ruined her plans to escape her Pack. She was saving up every penny to make her way to college. I don't know what her life was like, but I can tell you it wasn't all that good."

"She is underweight for one thing. She is as jumpy as a long-tail cat in a rocking chair factory. I can also tell you she is smart, clever, really fast, and will probably plan to escape. At least until we can show her what a Pack is really like and that she is safe."

"To be honest, I don't think her escape plan would have worked; even though they treated her the way they did, I don't think they would have liked her leaving. They would think perhaps that she knew or seen too much."

"We will take it slow, Duncan, she is going to be scared and untrusting for a while, but we will win her over. Show her she doesn't have to give up her dreams either."

Marco went off to check the border patrol, then went off to bed. Duncan sat in his office watching the fire in the fireplace, thinking of his wonderful mate, and all the things she would have to go through to be normal again.

He knew he would have to take it slow with her and earn her trust. He decided to send a couple of spies into the nasty pack to check things out, though he wasn't sure if they could get in now that he had tipped them off. That whole pack is a den of vipers, in serious need of being taken down.

As for Spare's college dreams, he had no problem helping her gain that dream. He would also have her change that name; he wouldn't let that name be a reminder of what they did to her for the rest of her life.

He texted his sister, Marnie, telling her everything and sending her Spare's sizes, asking her to get enough for possibly a few weeks until they could take her shopping.

Marnie was a very cheerful and wise nineteen-year-old she-wolf who had a mean side a mile long, especially if anyone messed with someone she cared about. Marnie texted back that she would be there tomorrow afternoon with all the things that Spare might need.

It was time for bed; he had someone bring a spare cot to his bedroom; he wasn't going to frighten her right at the start by climbing into bed with her.

Her scent hit him like a runaway train when he entered his room. His wolf wanted to mate her and mark her right now. Duncan cooled him off by reminding him they had to earn her trust first. She was sound asleep in his bed; she might not know it yet, but it would be the only bed she would be sleeping in for the rest of her life.

She was clutching that weird bear and his pillow. He would have to ask her what the deal was with that bear. The damn thing looked like it was pieced together from other stuffed toys, it reminded him of Frankenstein.

She was even more gorgeous in her sleep. Her scent took on a warmer sleepy quality, making his mouth water and his cock hard in anticipation. Letting out a sigh, this isn't going to be easy to take it slow, as he walked into his bathroom for his first of many cold showers.

CHAPTER THREE

Spare woke up feeling like she was still dreaming. The bed was warm and soft; a lingering scent drove her crazy as she rubbed her face over the pillow. She had never had a bed so comfortable before.

She came fully awake, not knowing where she was. It was then that Artemis very lazily informed her that they had spent the night in their mate's bed.

She quickly got out of bed looking around the room. It was huge; it was pretty spartan though, there was however, a couch on one side with a giant TV.

The colors were primarily blue and gray; you could tell it belonged to a man. When she turned to look at the rest of the room, she saw him asleep on a cot. He didn't look extremely comfortable; he was half hanging off it.

She silently made her way over to him. The blanket was down around his hips as he was snoring softly. She took him in; no one should look this good, his broad shoulders and dark blonde hair covering his well-muscled chest.

She followed that hair to where it disappeared under the blanket. Artemis was panting so hard that Spare started breathing harder too. His scent was so strong right here that she couldn't control her hands; she managed to stop before she almost touched him.

She turned and found another door; upon opening it, she found to her joy, a bathroom. She had to pee so bad her eyeballs were floating. She wondered what the rest of the place was like.

When she went into the bathroom, Duncan opened his eyes. He pretended to be asleep to see what she would do; he could still smell her arousal in the air.

Running his hand through his hair in frustration, mind-linking his wolf, Apollo.

"This will be the most challenging thing we have ever done."

Apollo grumpily agreed and went back to sleep.

He got up, put on some casual clothes, and waited for her to get done in the bathroom. He picked up her shoes. They had holes in the bottom, she must have patched them because there was duct tape over the holes.

He took the envelope with her money out of the safe and put it on the side table. He didn't want her to think she couldn't keep it. He went to the drawer where he put her clothes last night; nothing was remarkable about them.

She wasn't going to be happy, but there was no way his Luna would wear those clothes ever again. He stood up and went to sit on his cot, just as she was coming out of the bathroom.

They looked at each other for a bit; Spare blushed and finally looked away. She sat down on the bed, looking a little defeated.

Duncan saw this and cringed as he went and sat down on the bed beside her.

"I have ordered breakfast for us to eat in here; I hope we can talk about everything."

She was grateful for that; she didn't feel like meeting new pack members just yet. A knock came at the door, Duncan opened it, and two girls came in giggling, as they sat down the two trays loaded with food and drinks.

Spare was happy about them leaving as quickly as they came; she didn't need anyone giving her looks. She hated to be in the spotlight. It made her feel vulnerable.

She sat at the table, looking at all the food; it smelled like heaven.

"Is this all for me?"

He nodded, not knowing how to respond to that.

She wasted no time digging into the food with gusto, grabbing her fork.

Duncan watched her eat; at least she had an appetite. It did make him wonder just how terrible things were for her at that house. She would get all the food and snacks that he could give her.

"So, little wolf, tell me about that weird-looking teddy bear; what is his story?"

"His name is Max; I made him when I was six years old. Among the things they tossed away in the attic, was a sewing box along with two brand new books about sewing."

"I wasn't allowed any toys of my own; My sister, though, would throw huge tantrums and destroy her stuffed animals. So, one day, I started to collect parts out of the garbage and made max."

"Did you do anything with your family?"

"No, I had to stay out of sight; I wasn't even allowed to use the front door."

Duncan was getting increasingly pissed as this conversation progressed. He was taking a deep breath to calm himself and his wolf down.

"How about food? If you were not allowed to be around them, how did you eat?"

"When I was little, I waited for everyone to go to bed, then I would sneak down and steal some food. They never said if they noticed that things were missing, though I was punished badly when I got caught out of my room."

Ok, he would have stopped asking those questions, or he would be punching out the walls.

"I know I messed up your plans to get out of there and go to college. However, first, you can go to any college you wish and study whatever you like."

She got up and grabbed the envelope with her money inside; she handed it to him.

"Here, take this to help pay for my things, it isn't a lot, but it's something. I can also work, cleaning or cooking to earn the rest of it."

"You are not going to worry about money ever again; that money is yours to spend on anything that catches your fancy. I don't want it, and you will not try to give it to anyone in this Pack."

25

"If you do any cleaning or cooking, it will be because you want to, not because you feel like you should pay for being here. I will spoil you rotten even if you don't like it."

"My little wolf, you are my Mate, and no one will hurt you ever again; you will want for nothing."

She just stared at him with her mouth open in shock.

"You can't be my mate; claiming a mate is a bad thing in our pack, well, not every time but usually more so than not."

"What do you mean by Claiming a Mate is a bad thing?"

"Well, I only hear gossip here and there, but the last two girls that found their mates were rejected and disappeared the next day."

"Everyone said it was because of the pain of the rejection that they would come back in a while, but they never returned, and just last weekend, it happened again to two more girls and a friend of mine."

"I also heard rumors that their mates had sold them."

Duncan sat there in silence, stunned; what was going on in that Pack? Could they all be slime balls? Were the males rejecting their mates to make money?

"Spare, I want you to know that that is not normal behavior for mates; a mate is your other half. To be cherished and loved forever. It's a gift from the moon goddess."

"One more thing, I want you to choose another name besides Spare; I will not have that insult slapped in your face whenever someone speaks your name."

"I don't know a name to choose to be honest."

"It will come to you, don't worry, you have lots of time. My sister Marnie will be here soon; I'm sure she has new clothes for you and all kinds of things; she loves shopping."

"You two can come up with a name or perhaps you should ask Artemis. Just for today and tomorrow, I want you to relax and pamper yourself. When Marnie gets here, do whatever girls do when they are together."

"Umm, Duncan I don't really know what girls do when they are together. Other than a work acquaintance. My only faithful friend is my wolf Artemis."

At the mention of her wolf, Apollo perked up and started to tell Duncan what questions to ask them.

"What does your wolf look like? Can you shift?"

"Do you want me to show you?"

Duncan nodded his head; the fact that she would show him meant that at least she had a little trust in him.

"Ok but turn around. I have never been naked in front of anyone before."

Duncan turned around; he heard a soft woof behind him after a bit. He turned around to see the most beautiful wolf he had ever seen. She was snowy white with tiny black tips on her paws. She had even darker eyes than Spare did.

Apollo was dancing around in his head, excited. Artemis just sat and stared at him like she was sizing him up.

Duncan quickly got undressed and shifted into Apollo. He had to remind him to go slow. Apollo was huge next to her. He was a golden wolf with glowing amber eyes. Apollo got down into a laying position so as not to intimidate Artemis.

Artemis gave out an excited little bark and went to Apollo, rubbing herself all over him; Apollo laid there smugly. Duncan felt his joy and was happy for him. Apollo spoke to Duncan.

"You will have yours soon, too; we have to gain her trust; she has been through too much. She needs time to heal."

Artemis then grabbed Duncan's shirt and walked to the bathroom. Spare came out shortly afterward; Apollo was still there waiting for her.

She reached out a hand to scratch him behind his ear. Apollo looked like an idiot with his tongue hanging off to his side.

"You're very handsome, Apollo, thank you."

With that, Duncan stood before her once again, naked. She quickly turned her head but not before she got a little peek at him and blushed. Duncan was happy, almost giddy; He loved her in his shirt; it came down almost to her knees... **"She is ours, Apollo."**

"Nothing will take her from us. Not even her."

CHAPTER FOUR

As Duncan came out of his thoughts, there was a knock at the door and his sister shouting for them to open it before an accident happened of massive proportions.

He opened the door as his sister came tumbling inside, carrying bags and boxes of every shape and size.

"I see you went shopping, Marnie."

Marnie laughed, *"There is more coming; I sent Marco to bring up the rest."*

"Marnie, I said just enough till I can take her shopping; this looks like you bought out every store."

"Oh, stop being a drama queen and start helping me."

Duncan started unloading Marnie and putting it all down in the middle of the floor, just as Marco came in the room looking like a pack mule. He went straight to where Duncan put the other things and dumped them into the pile.

Marco mind-linked to Duncan, *"If you know what is good for you, you will run away fast. I have three sisters. Remember, I have seen this before. Trust me; you don't want to stay. They will make you do things no man should ever have to do."*

Marco then turned on his heels and ran from the room.

Duncan looked at Spare. She looked confused; he walked over and took her by the hand.

"Spare, this is my little sister Marnie; Marnie, this is my mate, and our Luna Spare."

Marnie started to jump up and down in excitement, *"Sweet, sassy molasses! You did find your mate."*

Duncan leaned in and kissed Spare on the top of her head.

"I'm going to leave now; I got some work to do. You two have fun."

"Oh, and maybe Marnie can help you come up with a new name. I meant it when I said I don't want you to remember all that bullshit every time someone says your name."

With a very graceful bow, he left the room.

Marnie went and sat down on the bed, taking Spare with her.

"We are going to be really good friends; I can just tell those kind of things. We will talk as we walk and get to know each other better."

She started to pull things out of the bags; she had shampoo, conditioner, body wash, and body lotion before she knew it. She had everything that a girl could want in the toiletry department.

Marnie was a whirlwind of energy. Now, she took out sundresses, jeans, T-shirts, sweatpants, and sweatshirts, Pjs, nightgowns, bras, underwear, and quite a few items she was sure were nothing but string. Any items she was unsure about, Marnie just put in the closet anyway.

"Ok, now we will pamper you, give you a makeover, and everything."

She ran into the bathroom and started the bath. Spare could smell all the stuff she was using. It was very potent. Marnie came out and saw Spare wrinkling her nose up at the smell.

"I know; I put too much of it in the bath, damn stuff smelled like a French whore house on Friday night. Don't worry I started a new one."

"Ok, the bath is ready now." Spare went into the bathroom and started to take off her clothes when she heard Marnie gasp. Spare knew what she was looking at and turned to hide them.

They stared at each other for a little bit, and then Marnie launched herself at Spare, hugging her. Marnie was crying and saying she was sorry over and over.

Spare pulled back, looking at Marnie's tear-stained face.

"I never want to hear you say sorry ever again; what was done was not done by you. Never say you're sorry for the shit other assholes do."

Marnie hugged her again and let Spare get into the bath.

"Now, I want you to relax and try all the bath scents. I'll be back in half an hour."

Soon as Marnie closed the door, she mind-linked Duncan.

"Did you know about all those scars on her back and legs?"

"Marnie, what the hell are you talking about?"

"Duncan, she has long scars across her back and upper thighs; she also looks like she hasn't eaten a healthy meal in a long, long time. Why is her name Spare?"

Marnie waited for Duncan to answer. Instead, the bedroom door opened, and a furious Duncan stood. He moved past Marnie on his way to the bathroom; Marnie grabbed him and pulled him back.

"If you go in there all angry while she is naked in the tub, you will never get her to trust you. The bathtub is where a woman is most vulnerable. So, slow your roll and go back to your Alpha chores."

Duncan looked at Marnie a while longer till he calmed down.

"Alright, I will leave, but I want to know everything she tells you, got it?"

Marnie nodded her head and shoved him out into the hall, closing and locking the door behind him.

Lily walked in a fit of anger through the halls of Her High School; no matter where she looked, she couldn't find The Spare anywhere, and neither could any of her friends.

Oh, that little bitch will pay for this; how dare she not show up to school; she was supposed to give Lily the answers for the test. If she didn't pass this one, she might have to take summer classes; there was no way she would suffer that humiliation again.

There was no choice; she told her friends to tell the teacher that she was sick and went home. She stormed out of the school, stomping her feet in four-inch heels. She got to her brand-new BMW and peeled rubber out of the parking lot. She was heading like a missile straight to her home.

Lily stormed red-faced into her house, her mother, Joanne, stopping her.

"What the hell are you doing home? You are supposed to be knee-deep in exams right now."

"Mommy, that little bitch never showed up to give me the answers; I had to tell them I was sick so I could come home."

Her mother hissed in anger. Storming off to the attic to teach The Spare another lesson, she better be dead. It was the only excuse she would take; even then, she might still use the whip on her.

When they got to the attic door, Joanne used her key and unlocked the door. They were met with silence; turning on the light, they looked around. The room was empty. From the looks of it, she packed her shit and left.

Joanne became furious, pushing over the dresser, which smashed to pieces on impact with the floor. How could that little bitch do this? How dare she think she could leave.

"What do we do now, Mom?

"We find the bitch and beat her back into submission again. I'll contact your father and tell him to get his ass home. She knows too much; we can't let her leave pack territory."

Joanne pushed Lily out of the house.

"Go and start looking for the little bitch, and when school is out, get your friends to help you. I'm going straight to Alpha Michael and informing him what is happening."

Lily drove off, unsure where to look; it's not like The Spare hung out anywhere she liked to go. She then got an idea, which is rare for her.

She heard a rumor that the little bitch had a job at a local hotel; now she must figure out which one and start asking questions. To be honest, deep down, she hoped that Spare did escape.

Spare was now dressed in comfortable jeans and a soft T-shirt. Marnie had been doing her hair, trying out makeup and lotions, and they were eating pizza during all this. She now knew what it was like to be one of the barbie heads that little girls play with.

"Marnie, what should I call myself? I don't want this name even though it is all I have known."

"Well, is there another name you have always liked? You could try it on for a while and see if it works for you, what does your wolf say?"

Spare mind-linked Artemis, **"Well do you have any ideas?"**

Artemis was quiet for a while, and then she said, **"Adira."** *(a- deer- a)*

"Artemis says, Adira, I like it."

"Very well, I name thee Adira Marie MacPatton; I gave you my middle name as sisters. Now we can share it."

Marnie mind-linked Duncan and told him the name they decided on so he could get all the paperwork taken care of.

Duncan said the name; he and his wolf both agreed it was the right choice, a beautiful one. A perfect name for his ideal mate.

As evening set, Duncan escorted the ladies to dinner; this would be Adira's first time eating with others of this size of a group, so he stayed as close as she would allow him to be. He never wants her to feel alone or not welcome ever again.

He couldn't believe his eyes when she came down with his sister. Was it possible for her to be any more beautiful? It was getting harder to resist her. He reached for her hand, and she gave it quickly, which pleased Duncan. No one will ever hurt her again; I will rip them to shreds if they try.

He escorted her to their table and began introducing her to his Beta Marco and a few of the elders sitting with them. Everyone was happy about Duncan finding his mate, and they warmly welcomed Adira.

He watched her as he could see her visibly become more comfortable. She even was smiling while they were finishing dessert.

CHAPTER FIVE

It was chaos when Erick got home. His brother, the Alpha, yelled out orders to various Pack members. His wife was crying in the corner, and his daughter was nowhere in sight.

He looked at his brother, He had plans for that little bitch, and now they are all gone. Not to mention the repercussions should she start flapping her lips to the right people. He wasn't too worried about her talking; for one thing, who would she tell? She knows no one.

Nobody in the Pack would help her. So how did she escape, and where does that bitch Spare hiding? One thing is for sure if he finds her, her days as a spare are gone.

Lily came through the door; she went straight to the Alpha. Sigh, he knew his brother fucked his daughter regularly. He wasn't sure how that would end; if it continued much longer, he would end it himself.

"Alpha, I didn't find her anywhere; however, I found out where she was working, and they told me that she ended her shift early and left with a man. The name of the Hotel is Ridgewood Inn, she was getting paid regularly, and none of us knew."

Alpha Michael let out an angry growl, *"Ridgewood is where we left that piece of shit, spy. Do you suppose that they knew each other? Maybe he somehow found out what family she is from and decided to take her."*

Alpha Michael was furious; his plans for that girl would make him a lot of money. Virgin werewolves were rare; soon as he had one in his sights, she got claimed and sold as used goods. He must get that little bitch back. Even if she were used goods by now, he was sure he could find another way for her to earn him some money.

He was already aware that his Pack was under investigation; not like any of those morons would find anything, they never do, or they can be bought. There was always at least one corrupt slime ball in every group.

I want that little bitch back and locked in my packhouse. Once she is there, she won't leave; if she is still a virgin, he will sell her to the highest bidder; if she isn't pure, he could have some fun with his niece. Not like he hasn't had enough pleasure with her sister.

One of his enforcers ran in, *"We have a last name, Alpha; it is MacPatton."* *"Did you activate the tracking tracer on her yet?"* Michael sometimes felt he had nothing but morons as pack members.

"Yes, it is beeping at a distance of at least four hundred and thirty miles to the north of us. The GPS will be up and running within the hour."

So, the little bitch has found a way out, not for long, though; soon, he will have her back and make her regret ever thinking of going. Soon.

Duncan sat in a chair at the pack hospital, waiting to see what the Doc said about her health. He thought it would be a quick check up, but he had been waiting for two hours now. Just as he was about to go in there to ensure all was ok, the nurse came out to ask Duncan to follow her.

He thought that he would see Adira. Instead, she had brought him to the doctor's office. He started to get worried when he sat down, thinking of why he was there, and none were good.

The Doc looked at his Alpha's worried face, *"I am sorry for keeping you waiting; we had to run all kinds of tests* since she has never had a check-up. I called you here because of the nature of my findings. The young lady has been through a lot; she is underweight; she has several bones that have been broken but haven't been properly healed."

"The most disturbing thing we found, though, was this," he handed Duncan a small clear container with a small device. "That was implanted in the back of her neck; It is a tracking device."

"Not to mention all the scars on her body; her wolf should have healed those without leaving any scars. That tells me that either her wolf is too weak, or they were given wolfsbane to make them weak."

"She is a strong-minded young lady; however she may start showing signs of PTSD. How bad it will get is unknown at this time. We won't know until she shows symptoms, so it's a waiting game. "

"With that all being said, this is what I want to be done. First, she needs to eat not just junk food but also real food; I want her to start eating three times a day with snacks. Also, I am sending her home with vitamins and a lotion for her scars it is to be applied twice a day for two weeks; it should help loosen them up, so she isn't so stiff."

He handed Duncan another bottle. "These are for when she has a panic attack; they are quick acting. Also, if she wants, I can set her up with our Pack psych. Doctor. She will find her *methods to cope with the emotional scars. I also wish to tell you that you could help her more with the mate bond if you were mated. However, it's best to let her go at her pace."*

Duncan was beyond pissed; what had those pigs done to her? How much had she suffered? He will ensure they don't get away with anything; if he must, he will just wipe out the whole Pack and be done with them.

"Now follow me, and I will take you to her so you can go home. Also, we might have to have her return to reset the bones that are not healing properly. It is also best if she shifts a little more and goes for runs, not long ones at first; go slow and build them up in strength."

"Some of the blood tests won't come back for a couple of days; I will inform you if there is anything of concern in them."

"Oh, I more thing. We are unsure about this; I just wanted you to know that when the wolves are abused, it sometimes throws their systems out of sync. She may come into heat soon."

When they stopped in the hall, they were in front of Adira's exam room. The Doc gestured for him to go in as he went down the aisle.

Duncan peeked a little through the door first, and what he saw made him mad. How had he missed all of this? He mind-linked Marco, ***"Come to the pack hospital NOW!"***

Duncan paced outside the exam room door as Marco came running to him. Marco took one look at his friend and knew he wouldn't like what was coming. First, though, he had to calm his Alpha down before he started destroying things.

Adira was dressed and was waiting for Duncan to get her out of here. They were all truly kind to her, but she hated hospitals primarily because of the smell. She wondered what was taking so long for him to come.

A full-length mirror was on the wall as she looked at herself. You wouldn't know it was her, even if you compared the before and after pictures.

At first, Adira wanted to escape from here and continue with her original plan. Now, she decided she might try it out for a bit. Her mate is friendly and is some unbelievably delicious eye candy; his scent drives her crazy; he also seems like a perfect guy. She can't trust him too much just yet; she remembered the last lesson she learned by trusting a seemingly good guy. That won't ever happen again, ever.

Duncan showed Marco the tracking device and he swore several exceptionally long curse words. *"Who the fuck are we dealing with here?"*

"I have some idea Marco but nothing solid yet. I have a job for you; I want you to take this tracker further north from here,

about another two hundred miles. Can you cover that kind of
ground on your motorcycle?"

"Yeah, it will be a cold ride, but I can make good time;
where am I taking it?"

"You are going up to Cold Mountain Pack territory. You
will meet an old friend from the military; he will know what to
do with it. His name is Jack; he is a werebear."

Marco smiled. Taking this tracker to Jack was the best
idea ever.

With that, Marco took the tracker and ran out of the
hospital. Getting that tracker as far away as possible, let
them track that shit into werebear territory, see how far
they get.

CHAPTER SIX

Jack Dawson, Leader of the Cold Mountain Pack, a large group of werebears, that were also bikers. He sat just outside the forest, waiting for Duncan's Beta. When Duncan told him everything was going on with that stupid pack, he wanted to run down there and wipe them all out. Putting a tracker on a female, there are only one, maybe two reasons that someone would do that; neither of them were good.

Jack could hear a bike coming off, perhaps two or three miles away. He hoped that those damn fleabags would come here looking for her. He'd show them what bears could do to weak wolves. First, though, he would lead them on a merry chase smack dab into the middle of his territory.

He also sent two of his best hunter-trackers to Duncan to help patrol his borders if they wanted a war. He was sick of shifters of all kinds, doing this kind of crap. There is at least one in every type of were species, and he'd personally wiped out another werebear pack last month; they were running drugs and kidnapping young human children.

The sound of a motorbike approaching him took him from his thoughts as he watched Beta Marco pull up to him.

"Hey, Marco, long time no see." He held out his hand to hand him the tracker.

"Jack, I didn't know it was you personally, to whom I was handing it off."

"Yeah, it's me, alright. You better get going; you don't want to hang around here too long if they are already looking for her."

With a salute, Marco was gone again.

"Well, I better get going if I want this plan to work," Jack said to nobody as he disappeared back into the forest.

Duncan took Adira out for dinner; she chose pizza. They sat together in a small booth, waiting for their pizza to arrive.

Adira thought this place smelled like heaven; she was all but drooling in anticipation. She looked at Duncan. He was so handsome; she couldn't get enough of looking at him and realized she was starting to trust him. He never criticized her or was violent. He was patient with her.

Mate bond or not, she wanted to know what it was like to kiss him. What if he thinks she is one of those kind of slutty girls and decides to cast her aside?

Artemis growled in her head, *"Will you stop that crap, every time you start to doubt yourself or run yourself down, it is just another win for them."*

" We decided that no matter how bad it gets, we will never give them anything for free. If they want to take it from us, we fight; if they want us to do something, we do the opposite."

" Remember, Adira; we are beautiful, smart, and strong. Our mate loves us as we are and is willing to take on all our shit. If that isn't love, Adira, then what the hell is?"

Adira's eyes started to tear up as she mentally hugged her wolf. *"I remember Artemis, I remember. I love you, Artemis."*

Duncan was looking at Adira, she was starting to cry, and he had no idea why. He could tell she was talking to her wolf, but he had no idea what was said. They were not fully mated yet, so he had no way of speaking to Artemis.

That was when his wolf jumped in, *"Maybe you can't, but I can."* Adira was doubting herself, and Artemis was setting her straight."

"Apollo, come on, what else did she say? What is making her cry? Why did she doubt herself?"

"She is crying because she is happy with what her wolf said to her. As for what made her doubt in the first place, Artemis won't tell me; she says it's a female thing."

With that, Apollo went back to sleep. Duncan decided to take a chance and put his arm around her in comfort. She didn't try to move away; she moved closer.

She rested her sweet head on his shoulder, and he was almost lost in her warmth and scent. Thank God the pizza came then; he watched Adira eating the pizza and was glad that getting her to eat wasn't going to be a big problem.

She had finished half the large pizza before he finished his; she looked at that last piece with almost a predatory smile. Duncan looked into her eyes and realized that it was Artemis. He chuckled and slid it over to her; she gave him a thousand-watt smile and the last slice disappeared quickly.

"Artemis?" Duncan asked.

"Yes, Alpha mate?"

"Why are you here instead of Adira?"

"It is a pretty long explanation. Are you sure you want to hear it?"

"Yes, we have plenty of time."

"It all started when we were very young; the neglect and abuse she was going through, I knew I couldn't leave her to deal with it alone."

"I asked the Moon Goddess to help me find a way to help her. The Goddess answered by allowing me to take Adira away from the pain by bringing her into my special world. She built a doorway so I could go through the door and bring her to my side whenever Adira was in trouble."

"We were ten years old when we learned to shift."

"That is where she is now; the pizza brought back a bad memory; she started to panic, so she went to my place, and I came to hers."

"Why did pizza trigger a memory.?"

"Are you sure you want to know; it will make you angry.?"

"Tell me everything, Artemis. Please."

"That piece of crap, Alpha has a talent for knowing when she-wolves shift for their first time. That's how he knows when they are ripe for the picking. He knew that we had shifted early; he came the next night. He said he was proud of the little spare; he rewarded us with pizza and soda. We hadn't eaten in three days, so without thought, we started eating."

"It was poison; he put it on the pizza it was wolfsbane. He started laughing when Adira started to get sick. He said it was for the best, can't have your wolf running away with you now, can we.!"

"I believe that they poisoned us at least a couple of more times; it was always at random. It ended when Adira got a job at the hotel, we couldn't afford much, but we managed to buy our food. That was almost a year ago when we couldn't afford a lot of food, Adira would get off work early, and we would hunt in the forest."

"Every penny we made that didn't go for food or personal things, went into the box where we hid it for our escape after graduation."

"Then, while cleaning rooms, we find ourselves a naked Alpha, and Poof, all our plans get changed, not that I mind even a little bit. I am happy it turned out this way; I wasn't sure if we could get away far enough without them finding us. I know those bastards put a *tracking device on us, so I am glad the Goddess stepped in and changed our plans."*

"I must go now; I am tired after eating all that pizza."

With that, Artemis was gone, and Adira was back. He took one look at her pale face, knowing it was time to get her home.

"Come on, my little wolf, it is time we head home to our beds."

Once they were out in the parking lot, Adira pulled him back before getting into his truck. Duncan looked at her but couldn't understand her thinking; her eyes were heated.

She reached up and pulled his head down for a kiss. It turned heated instantly as Duncan took over. He had her backed up against his truck door, he started to kiss her neck, and her scent hit him like a speeding train; he knew he had to stop himself; otherwise, he would take her right here, right now.

She made a low moan as he parted them and carried her to the passenger side, setting her on the seat and putting her seat belt on. He managed to get himself under control by practically running his way to the driver's side. Thinking that he will be in trouble if she goes into heat early. He isn't a saint; no way would he be able to resist her in that state.

They drove off to go home; Adira liked its sound (home), his home and now mine. Knowing she could give him her trust, she decided to tell Duncan everything. Everything about the Rising Moon pack and where he can get the proof he has been looking for. With that last thought, she fell asleep with a happy sigh on her lips.

CHAPTER SEVEN

Alpha Michael was waiting for the exact location to ping off the tracker. One of his enforcers placed a map down on the table and started to put little pins in it for the various pings on the system.

When they were done, they sat down and studied it; *"This one here is the base, that is her home. Then there was one at the school, one at the library, and the next when she worked at the hotel. This is where it gets a little odd."*

"After her shift at the hotel, she came home for a bit; we assumed she was packing. Then she was moved to a northbound vehicle. They stopped four hundred and twelve miles north of here, there is a pack called The Storm Crow Pack there."

Alpha Michael let out a growl of anger, *"That is the pack the spy was from; the last name is MacPatton."*

"Did you get anything other than his name and pack?"
"No, Alpha. We did not, just what you already know. We went

back the next morning, but he was already gone. He paid for everything in cash; there wasn't a paper trail to follow."

"Sir, if I may continue with the timeline."

"Yes, by all means, continue."

"Well, as you can see here, she was there for almost two days, then she is on the road again, going another 230 miles north. She hasn't moved since."

"Alpha Michael, we don't know what is up there; if it's a pack, it is off the grid or very small. Perhaps they didn't want to keep her in their pack, not wanting any trouble, and decided that she should go deep into the north woods to hide with some of her friends, or perhaps she is alone. It would make sense, especially since they wouldn't know we had the tracker."

"He knew that we had enough information to find out where he came from, so he couldn't keep her in his pack; he knew we would look for her there."

Alpha Michael smiled, *"Well, the jokes on him, we will skip over his pack and go straight for the girl. Whoever is there with her, kill them. He sent all six of his enforcers fully armed to go pick up his niece."*

Jack and his pack warriors were ready to go, waiting for the guests of honor to show for the party. His boys have been itching for a bit of fun, and I can't think of anything funnier than chasing stupid fleabags through the forest.

He could hear the car engines about two miles away now; all the werebears were excited. They were shifted into their bears, except Jack and his third Morgan. Jack and Morgan waited at the gate that signified where his territory began. The cars pulled up to the gate, arrogantly yelling they knew they had a girl that was missing from their pack.

What a bunch of idiots, so arrogant that they didn't even bother to take a sniff. They just assumed that they were human. Jack smiled at them and said they were welcome to come in and look for her. Just like that, they went inside the gates.

"Talk about stupid; it almost takes the fun out of it. It's more like we are making mercy killings for mother nature. Stupid fleabags."

"Remember to link everyone, and I want one left alive. I do not care which one. The rest you can have some fun with but kill them when you are done."

After all, it wouldn't be fun if no one was left to tell the tale. All he had to do was make that messenger believe he had the girl, and they would keep trying to get her, giving Duncan more time to get things sorted.

Not to mention more fun for the guys and less of an army to send Duncan's way if they ever figure it out. As soon as the cars were out of sight, Jack and Morgan shifted into grizzly bears and were off to start the fun.

Duncan got a message from Jack, saying that the Rising Moon pack was a bunch of stupid fleabags and that the plan was in motion. That gave him some breathing room and time to contact some other friends and contact the King.

After that, Adira told him everything and where he could get proof. He was furious that she had gone through all that; he wondered what else they had planned for her.

He also wondered if this pack participated in the international mob scene. They sure fit the bill. Evil bastards should all get a silver rod shoved up their asses.

He looked over at Adira; she was so gorgeous, wow, and that kiss the other night. His wolf was practically purring if that was even possible. Marnie had just left after watching a movie with Adira; all she left behind was Cheeto dust on his pillow in the shape of her hand. He laughed at that; she always did things to make you laugh or bug the crap out of you.

"Adira, how about you and I go for a run? Nothing too intense, more like a little run and then a stroll. There is a place I want to take you to."

He decided to make it a picnic; he mind-linked with Marco and told him his plans. Marco loved the idea and agreed to have all they needed at the cave waiting for them.

The walk to the caves was only about two miles, and though the trail wasn't easily marked, Duncan knew the way. Only a few of his pack members go here anymore. He doubted that even some of the younger generation knew about it anymore.

They walked along as Duncan told her about his pack's history; she reached out and grabbed his hand. He didn't make a big deal about it; he held her hand tighter. This made his wolf dance in circles, ***"Apollo, stop that. You're going to make us both dizzy."***

"Duncan, you know what this means; they like us and are starting to trust us."

Duncan didn't bother to answer captain obvious. He looked down at her; she seemed relaxed and happy as the sun shone through the trees around her. When they were almost there, he brought out a blindfold. She looked at him in skepticism; there was fear in her eyes for an instant.

Duncan stopped her from panicking, *"Adira; it is a surprise, that is why I have the blindfold, don't worry, I won't let anything happen to you. We can leave the blindfold out of it, however if you prefer we can walk in backwards."*

Adira started laughing, turning around so he could put on the blindfold. He took her hands and gently guided her through the last part of the trail. When they were at their destination, he took off the blindfold; as she opened her eyes, he could tell she loved what she was seeing.

Adira was in complete awe. She couldn't believe that something this beautiful existed; it wasn't a cave but a stone formation around a waterfall and what looked like a natural garden. When they walked inside, she noticed an open tent. A giant picnic basket was sitting on a fancy rug; next to the basket was a massive chest.

The tent looked like something out of a romance novel. It was all white, and there were curtains tied back.

Though it was early fall, and the leaves were changing inside the enclosure, there was a slight breeze, and the air was warm.

"I know you're wondering why it is warmer here than outside. There are a few thermal pockets in this area that are still active. Also, there is the legend of a witch who once lived here."

They went into the tent to see what had been left for them. Inside the chest were blankets, pillows, towels, swimming suits, and a change of clothes. The picnic basket was loaded with all kinds of things, sandwiches, snacks, fruit, brownies, fried chicken, and salad with dressing.

"Well, would you like to try out the water? it's warm." He reached down into the chest, pulling their swimsuits and towels from the trunk. Adira was excited. She always wanted to learn to swim it always looked like fun.

"You will have to teach me to swim; I have never been in the water before."

They walked down to the pool formed by the waterfall, taking her hand. The water felt fantastic, and it was pure. There wasn't any muck or cloudiness to it. She felt Duncan's hand's warmth, which gave her confidence to go deeper into the pool.

Before she even realized it, she was up to her chest in the water, as it surrounded her. She felt refreshed as Duncan pulled her closer to him. His warmth was terrific next to the cool of the water. She relaxed and gave her trust to him. She knew that his arms would always be there for her in that moment.

CHAPTER EIGHT

Alpha Michael met with his brother at their second packhouse, the first house was for show, where the family lives, and all looks fine and dandy. That was for when they would have official visitors.

The second packhouse was their playhouse, where all the buying and selling of young females were taking place. It also served as their whore house. They also made drug deals as well as ran guns across state lines. They were well on their way to being noticed by the international league of the Mob. They even had a few of the Mob bosses here for parties.

The hottest thing happening now is selling young female wolves in heat. They would find their mates; the mates, in turn, get to have their first mating. One of the cruelest things was the fact they didn't mark them. Then they would slip a drug into their system and wait. This causes the females to go into heat a few days or weeks later. Of course, the females go to their mates when this happens, and instead of getting the heat taken care of and being marked and bonded, they are sold that night to the highest bidder.

By the time the females are sold, they are so far into the thrall of heat that they are almost insane, thus making them a really good fuck.

Unfortunately, a few commit suicide, but there are always more. Most of the time, the females are broken inside because of how the mate bond gets broken. It makes it easier to keep selling them. They keep going into heat until they get pregnant.

This brings them to another part of their "what they like to call the factory." The pregnant females are put into individual cages until they give birth, then the babies are sold on the black market. Some females are then put back into the prostitution part of their organization, while others must be disposed of.

They also have a branch only for human girls, and young children that are to be sold on the black market.

They are also starting another branch with young boys, it is just a starter program right now, but it shows some significant profits. They are making a huge profit, with last year's profits alone, close to two billion and this year promises to be even more profitable.

He had been thinking of new ways to advertise his merchandise; his cousin had created a national and international catalog. So buyers could see their variety of selections. Also, they can learn when auctions will be held. Of course, everything has a code name. That is how it keeps going; for instance, he thought himself clever when he listed girls under eighteen as calves, girls under 12 are lambs, and females above 18 are sows.

Most of the profits go into an offshore account; Michael was sure that his brother and his family would be pissed if they knew what name he put it in. After all, he didn't lie to them; he put it in their daughter's name. Just not the one they wanted it to be in.

That is the other reason he had to get that little bitch back; he needed to have her digitally fingerprinted so he would have them on file for the opening and transferring the funds into another secret account that only he knew of. Of course, he would leave his brother something much smaller than expected.

On the other hand, his niece Lily is particularly useful, especially on the nights he gets stuck in the other packhouse. Mostly though, she brings him a lot of human girls as well. He wasn't expecting to hear from his enforcers for a few more hours, but he was getting impatient.

So, he asked his brother if he wanted to sample one or two new girls to pass the time.

When the six enforcers for the Rising Moon Pack stopped at a dead-end gravel road, they knew it wasn't a good thing. Humans always thought they were clever; as it turned out, they'd managed to get one over on them this time.

They got out of their cars, *"We will shift here and hunt down some stupid humans; let's show them what they are messing with. Play with them for a bit first before you finish them. Remember, keep one alive; we need to know where they keep the girl."*

Just as they were about to shift, one of the enforcers sniffed the air. He went pale and tapped on the shoulder of his partner. He told him to take a sniff. When his partner did, his face turned pale too. They both went to their leader, Benny.

"Sir, I think we are in over our heads here. We need to get out of here now." However, the wind had shifted in another direction; their leader sniffed the air and caught nothing of interest.

"If you two idiots are done fooling around and can stop acting like stupid little girls, we can have some fun before we get the girl; the scanner says she is nearby."

The two enforcers looked at each other, knowing; that just as the tires on their vehicles started blowing out, one of the enforcers yelled, *"SNIPER!!"* as they all dove for cover.

They heard thunderous growls from around them, some close, others in the distance. Then came the chopping of teeth. A loud clacking noise was sending fear down the spines of the enforcers. It was coming from everywhere at once. Just then, the wind shifted again, and this time, all the enforcers picked up the scent, swearing when they recognized the smell drifting toward them…*"It's a Sleuth of Werebears!"*

Alpha Michael was at the warehouse when one of his enforcers approached him. *"Sir, we have a late-night delivery."* *"Delivery? We don't have any scheduled for tonight."* They walked out to the loading dock area just as a semi-backed up to the door.

His men inspected the two pine crates; one could be a coffin; the other was a giant cube. They forklifted them to the floor in front of the Alpha. They were shrink-wrapped and nailed shut. FRAGILE was written on top of the crates in big words: FRAGILE. The boys thought that was funny, *"Hey, it's just like The Christmas Movie. Frageeelee."*

A big envelope was also taped to the side of one of the crates. So they took it off and handed it to the Alpha. Then they started to open the crates and popped the lids off with crowbars, and then it was just silence. Both enforcers closest to the containers began vomiting.

Inside the coffin-shaped one were four of what was left of the enforcers he sent after the girl.

When Alpha Michael looked inside, he saw something from a horror movie. The heads were removed, and their hands, feet, legs, and arms were gone. The torsos were tied together in a bundle. There wasn't any blood; where the holy hell was their blood!!

They all stood there in silence when they heard muffled groans from the cube-shaped crate. This one was also labeled Fragile, but no one was making jokes this time.

They opened the crate this time with some reservation; once the lid was off, it was a different story, although just as bad in its way. In the middle of the crate were the last two enforcers, one alive and the other dead.

His alive enforcer was hogtied up, so his ass was in the air. Sticking out of his ass was the head of the dead enforcer. They shoved it up in him face first. Though they didn't drain the blood, the smell coming from the crate was overwhelming.

Alpha Michael let his men tend to the living enforcer. He was so filled with rage that he couldn't see straight. He yelled out for all his enforcers to meet in the morning. They were going to pay for this, girl, or no girl. Should they find her, though, his plans for her have changed; she wasn't going to be sold off. He would put her in the pit and make her wish she stayed the spare.

Then Michael remembered that the prince was coming next week to pick up Spare; he'd already paid two million in advance. The shit would hit the fan if he didn't get that little bitch back. Of course, the deal was that she had to be a virgin, but there are ways around that.

He then found himself a corner and opened the envelope, inside was a simple note.

"Going to have to do better than that, ass sniffers."

CHAPTER NINE

Maybe it was the whole mate bond thing; she didn't know. It felt like they were connected somehow. It felt more profound than just love alone. Adira was getting comfortable with Duncan; she never thought she would ever be able to trust anyone again.

She was on her back, floating in the water with his arms under her. It felt wonderful to be honest, she was comfortable and calm. She managed to swim a little on her own. Once he was confident that she at least knew the basics of swimming, they got out of the water.

She sat on the bank's edge with her feet swaying in the water as she became lost in thought. So many memories, so much pain, so much betrayal. Why? she never wanted anything more than their love. She wanted a family. When she started sneaking out and following her father and uncle, she wasn't sure what she would find. It was far worse than she ever thought it was.

When the family would go on vacations, she would go down to her father's office and look for stuff; she found plenty of bills of sale, documents, fake visas, bank account records, and account books for profit and loss.

She also found another account book separate from the others, she wasn't an accounting genius, but she could tell that her father was keeping this book to keep track of the money he was stealing from their businesses.

Wonder if Uncle Alpha knew about that? Not that she was going to tell him. Neither of them liked each other, so it's a good bet that Uncle is doing the same thing to dear ole Dad.

She drifted off to other memories, where she and another girl were playing together in the woods, and Uncle Alpha came up behind them. He just stood there and watched them; it gave them both the creeps. Finally, Cathy's mother called out for her, and she never saw her again.

A week after Cathy went missing, a note was taped to her attic door. She remembered it word for word........

{I Don't Ever Want You to Play in The Woods Again.}

The note wasn't signed, but she knew who it was from. She never went to that spot again, but she needed the woods again when Artemis showed up. She would always wait till the end of her shift at the hotel and run into the woods behind it. It wasn't that much, but it was enough to get them through some nasty stuff.

Adira noticed she was shaking and had trouble breathing; she couldn't get enough air. The world around her started to dim as she could hear the voices and all the terrible things they were saying to her. She could hear Duncan screaming her name off in the distance, and then it was all gone.

She was back in her room in the attic, tied to a support beam, and being beaten by her father because she got caught using the downstairs bathroom.

Duncan was in a panic; she was fine for one moment, and then she went quiet. The next thing he knew, she was screaming "NO! NO! NO! NO! NO! NO!" over and over. He picked her up and carried her to the tent as he held her yelling her name repeatedly, hoping she would return from her nightmare.

He saw the scars on her back and legs; he wished he could have been there for her so none of this would have happened. He could not because he was not. He will do or give her anything she needs to get through this; for now, he will just hold her tight until she wakes.

He laid her down on the rug, using the blankets and pillows made her a bed. He then went to the sides of the tent and shut the curtains, so she would be surrounded by white when she woke up. He lovingly put her down right in the middle of the bed he made, then cuddled up next to her and gathered her into his arms. He was falling asleep as close as he could get to her.

An hour later, Duncan woke to the sound of Marco in his head; Marco was waiting outside for him. He slowly disentangled himself from her body and went to meet his Beta. When he stepped outside the tent, he gave Marco an angry stare. Marco held up his hands in surrender.

Mind linking him so there would be no noise to disturb his Luna…

"I have a message from Jack. He says that enforcers were sent into his territory. Jack and his Sleuth of Bears took care of them easily and sent a rather nasty message back, daring Alpha Michael to send more."

"They still believe that Adira is with them in their territory as far as he knows. He said he will play as long as you want him to."

"He also said he can be on the move at a moment's notice if needed. All you have to do is give the word."

"That is good, Marco; send this message back to him. Tell him he can play as long as he wants; just let me

know when he gets bored with it, and I will change it up for him."

"Also, Marco, I need a favor; Adira had a bad PTSD attack. I don't want to move her through the forest and wake her. Can you bring one of those futon mattresses here and some extra blankets? Ask the Pack cook if she can send along some of her homemade herbal tea."

"I will keep her here overnight and possibly most of tomorrow."

"The Doc warned me about this; I think just keeping her here away from everything for a little bit might help her sort some of it out."

"I can't believe that those flea-bitten mongrels did the things they were doing to her, not to mention all that shit they were dishing out in their pack."

"You stay here; I will make sure you have all you need, keep her here a couple of days while the weather is good. Give her time to be with you and maybe heal her heart a little."

"Then you can come back and declare her your Luna. The pack has waited a long time for its Luna; I can tell you they are all happy with you both."

"Don't worry about pack business; I will take care of it until you come back, and I will mind link you to any developments and problems."

"Now go back to our Luna; I will be back shortly with everything you're going to need."

Duncan pulled back the curtain and just looked lovingly at his Luna. She was so beautiful in her sleep; he could see she was sleeping peacefully now. He lay back beside her and fell into the content sleep of a happy wolf.

The following day Adira woke up to the most beautiful warmth, Duncan's scent hit her, and she snuggled in closer to him. He, in turn, held her tighter.

Duncan had been awake when he felt her awaken; he was surprised when she snuggled deeper into his arms. Mated or not, he would die happy if he were to die right now. When he heard her soft breathing turn back into sleep, he gently got up and went to see what Marco had sent him.

When he opened the curtain, what he saw made his jaw drop; how did he manage this without waking us up? Then it dawned on him; Marco went to the pack mages and asked for help.

There was a small cabin not more than twenty feet from their tent. He went inside, and it was a cozy, inviting little house. The kitchen was old-fashioned but workable;

there was a table with two chairs; on the other side of the room was a couch and two end tables with oil lamps. A fireplace adorned the other wall, complete with wood.

He entered the bedroom and realized that Adira would love this room; it was old-fashioned in decor, and the bed looked like a big fluffy cloud. He opened an adjoining door, and it was a bathroom.

The door on the other side was a massive closet with some of their clothes in it and more blankets and towels. There was a note on the bed; he picked it up and read it.

Dear Alpha Duncan,

We wish to inform you as of this moment you are on vacation for the next several days; this cabin is magically built. Everything you need or want is here for you. Just think it and it is yours. Enjoy and bring back our Luna.

Your faithful,
Mages.

Duncan shook his head; he had two elder mages who lived with them in their retirement. They were a couple, going on fifty years now. Mathew and Cheryl. He will have to create a lovely thank you gift for them.

He returned to their tent; Adira was awake and sitting up; he looked at her...."*Are you ok?*"

"*Yeah, I am sorry about that yesterday.*"

"Do not say you're sorry ever again. You will have these for a while, and I will help you get through them. See what my two mages did for us in the night."

CHAPTER TEN

Alpha Michael sat at the desk in his office, surrounded by his enforcers. He was not happy about how things turned out. His enforcers kept their distance, not wanting to be a target of his anger. Some even had daughters they needed to protect. Soon there would not be any females left in the pack.

"So, now we know that the pack we are dealing with are those nasty werebears. I don't mind saying that I don't like dealing with those assholes. They can't be bribed or negotiated with; they only understand one thing, fighting. They are not only really good at it, but they also enjoy it."

"Do we have any information on them at all?" Everyone shook their heads," *Nothing Alpha other than they are a rather large clan, and they all looked like bikers. Their territory is massive, though it's primarily mountain range."*

"Has that tracker moved out of the territory yet?"

"Not really, Alpha; it did go into a small town about a mile on the north side of their borders; it is now back in the middle of their territory. They are keeping her in the center of their territory, probably at their packhouse or whatever those smelly bastards call it."

"Is there any more information on the wolf pack that MacPatton is from.?"

"No, Alpha, they are a pretty secluded pack; they like to keep to themselves. Those that do travel out of the group are exceptionally tight-lipped."

Alpha Michael ran his hand through his greasy hair with a sigh, thinking things through. Something inside his head was going off in alarm; no matter how he tried, he couldn't pinpoint the problem.

"Ok, listen up, here is what we will do; I want the three best hunter-trackers we got to go to the werebear territory; they will sneak in and do some spying, if at all possible, get the female out."

"I also want two other hunter-trackers to go to the Storm Crow Moon pack and do some recon; I want to know how big the pack is, how big their territory is. Gather any information you can, no matter how small it is. Don't engage with them if you can get away with it."

"Both teams will have two days to gather info, be back here in two days no matter what. Now GO!"

Alpha Michael was starting to sweat it out, and he hated that more than anything else. Prince Adam will not be happy when he finds out about this. Still, if he can get that little bitch back before he gets here, all will be well.

Alpha Michael motioned for one of his men to come to him, *"I want you to start checking out Storm Crow. Tell me anything you can find and use the royal contacts if you must. Something about all this isn't sitting too well with me."*

"As you wish, Alpha."

"Tell no one you are doing this; I think we have a spy in our ranks."

Lily was throwing another of her famous spoiled rotten temper tantrums at home. She was pissed when her mother told her she would be punished for not keeping better tabs on the Spare. Alpha Michael sentenced her to two weeks of cleaning the cages at the warehouse. Lily would also be sleeping on a cot in one of the back rooms, as added punishment.

She didn't know that Alpha Michael was giving her as a reward to the wolf or the wolves that brought back Spare. Not as a mate or wife, just a couple of nights of fun.

If she gets pregnant, she will be living in one of those cages she will be cleaning.

Lily decided she wasn't going to be the cleaning maid. Thinking that this is how she will be treated after all she has done for that bastard. Then she will repay it in kind; she overheard them talking about the pack up north, which sent back all his enforcer's inboxes.

Perhaps they would be interested in some information and where the locations of the Alpha's favorite factories are. She looked at the backpack she had taken with her everywhere. That should at least buy her a ticket out of this hell hole.

It contained all the information she would need, including pictures, things she copied off his computer at the factory, a logbook, and security camera footage on DVDs. She made sure to cover her tracks; they won't even realize that it was missing until it's too late. She started doing this as an insurance policy; she realized how terrible things were by watching some of the footage, and that was when she realized that he was going to toss her in with the rest of them.

She also found recorded camera footage of her dad and Alpha doing despicable things to break in the new girls. It made her want to vomit when she saw what her dad liked doing. She realized her role in it all and wanted to curl up and die; she was such an idiot.

She packed her suitcases and gathered up all the money she could get and more from her mother's purse. She took one last look around her room, only to realize how empty her life was.

Perhaps Spare wasn't as stupid as she thought she was after all, she escaped from this miserable excuse for a Pack. Lily wondered if she would ever see Spare again, not that she thought she deserved to be in Spare's life. It was just a thought, nothing more.

She put it all in her vehicle; her stupid mother thought that she was happy about going to live in that hell hole of a warehouse. The longer her stupid mother thinks all is well, the further she will get away.

When she left, she made sure her mother watched as she went in the direction that was to the warehouses. Once convinced no one was watching, she turned another corner and headed to the freeway.

Prince Adam Antonio Ryes Mason Breckenburg of the High Moon pack of High Garden Castle sat in his study, tapping his fingers on his desk in agitation. He was so close now to his goal he could taste it. That moron Alpha Michael was lying to him. Why he was lying to him, he couldn't guess.

He better not mess it up; he wanted that girl because she was pure. Also, she would be his and only his. No more of these court whores trying to get in his pants because they want money and power. He wanted someone who would only be his, someone he could easily manipulate.

He wanted a showpiece, and he wanted her enslaved. He could continue with the natural things he liked doing while the world looked on at the happy royal couple. She was perfect for this in many ways. Mostly, they could not find any information on her besides what he was putting out.

He had rooms designed just for her. She, of course, wouldn't be able to leave these rooms, at least not until she earned his trust. So he bought everything she might need or want. He was willing to give her anything she desired except her freedom.

He knew that going this route to get her was wrong; he was out of options because his father would force him to marry some stupid half-wit, horse faced princess. Not that he minded stupid in his women, he did want them to be pretty, though.

He couldn't stand that idea at all. He wanted a girl who was for him and only him; Alpha Michael better not mess this up. He needed everything as he wanted it because he could control it all; he didn't intend to do anything with her. She would have his heirs, and that would be all he needed from her. He would be free to play as he saw fit.

He wished he had never met Alpha Michael; something about that Alpha never sat well with him. The problem was that he couldn't get rid of his need for sex with younger males. The second he told that shady Alpha what he liked, he was in this position, if he just kept his mouth shut. Alpha Michael decided to open a branch in his factory because of the prince's need for young males.

Another thing he didn't want his father to find out. Not that his father cared if he were gay, his father would be insane with anger if he knew about his habit. His father hated men and women who liked children that way—no telling what he would do to him if he found out.

His father would give everything to his little brother, Alex. He laughed because he knew his brother wanted nothing to do with the crown. He would murder the perfect little brat before he ever had a chance to wear the crown if he had to. Though he wasn't worried about that happening, his brother was odd. He disapproved of the habits of the Royal court.

He had his wife and children and his own life, and his father would try to force the issue, but he had a feeling that it would be the last anyone would hear from his saintly brother.

If his father didn't want to disown him, he would make sure he suffered for the rest of his life. He would find the worst of them all, an ugly shrew of a princess that no one wanted.

Suppose his father doesn't find out, at least not in time. He will secretly marry the girl and introduce her to the royal court and his father. His father will want to know all about her, but there won't be anything to find. The girl didn't exist anywhere.

Alpha Michael threatened him one night by telling his father all about him; Adam wasn't intimidated as Michael had hoped. Instead, he found himself on the other side of the coin. The prince told Michael that if he thought about doing that, then he would expose everything, but he would also skin him alive and feed his dick to the royal pigs.

If he lost that girl, though, there wouldn't be enough time to find another; that is when he got the idea to start looking for another now. It's always good to have a backup plan.

CHAPTER ELEVEN

$\mathcal{D}$uncan and Adira looked over the little cabin in awe. Adira thought it was the best thing she had ever seen. It had everything they could ever need and it had a warm and cozy feeling. It made her feel safe. She blushed a little when she saw the bedroom, knowing they would share it. Surprisingly, sharing a bed with Duncan didn't bother her at all.

Every time they touched, there would be these little tingles along her skin; she found that she liked them. They made her think of things she only read in her romance novels. She enjoyed his kissing; it made her weak in the knees and hot at her core. His scent, though, is what drove her crazy.

She felt safe when he had her in his arms; she wanted to kiss him again and maybe more if Artemis had her way. Artemis has been quiet about pushing Adira, giving her more time to get used to new things. All this freedom without having to be sneaky about it was sometimes overwhelming. Lately, she was looking less and less over her shoulder or thinking things were a trap.

She looked at Duncan as he was making a fire in the hearth. She watched as his muscles moved under his shirt; he was so handsome that there wasn't one thing she could find at fault with him. She walked over to where he was and wanted to touch him; Artemis nudged her in reassurance.

"It's ok; He is our mate. He will not harm us or reject our affections."

Adira tentatively reached her hand out and touched his shoulder.

It was the lightest of touches, but Duncan could feel it to his toes. He closed his eyes, relishing the feeling that she trusted enough to touch him. He had to calm down Apollo, telling him to take it easy and let her dictate how much and how far.

Duncan did reach up to his shoulder and touched her hand; there were the sparks that drove him crazy, he took a deep breath, they stood there like that in silence for a little while. Then she did something that surprised him; she moved forward till the front of her body was utterly touching his back; she wrapped her arms around him and stayed like that for another long while.

She showed him her trust and was willing to move things up another notch. Duncan knew he had to go slow, but this show of confidence made him happy.

He turned into her hug, so they faced each other; he wrapped his arms around her in another hug. The sparks ignited, and she let out a little moan of pleasure; it was almost his undoing. He pulled back slowly and returned to get a fire going.

Adira stood there for a bit, unsure of what just happened but decided she liked it.

Duncan decided to make some conversation to keep things toned down.

"So, my little wolf, how did you get wolfsbane in your system?"

"I am not sure when it first happened; I think it was gradual so that I wouldn't notice. It was in the food I was stealing from the kitchen. I knew that it had become too easy. One night though, it became really awful for Artemis; I stopped going to the kitchen for food after that."

" When I went to school, I would get us breakfast and lunch, there at least I would eat my meals knowing they were safe."

"When I was old enough, I got a job at the hotel where we met. At first, it didn't pay much because I wasn't given many

hours; it was enough to get us some food. As I got older, I was given more hours; I was able to keep us fed and save up for college."

"Artemis and I pretended to still be weak; we never shifted unless we needed to and never where they could see us. Staying away from Alpha Michael wasn't easy; he is a creeper. I learned he didn't like the end of town where I worked; the woods behind that hotel were rarely used, and if it was it was only by lower-ranking wolves."

"He rented rooms there and I made sure that I was never around for him to see me. He would always have a girl with him and sometimes my father too. They would drink tons of terrible-smelling alcohol; whatever it was, it came in jars like the one you can things in."

"One night, just as I was almost done with my shift, they called the desk and requested more towels and sheets. Sally, was coming in for her shift and she got the honors, I was curious though and went with her."

She knocked on the door, "Housekeeping." She didn't say it too loudly; I don't think she wanted them to hear her; it is hotel policy that if you request service and don't answer the door, then that service can be denied."

Duncan could see she was starting to shake and tense up; he put his arms around her and sat her on the couch on his lap. She didn't say anything, just leaned back into him like she wanted him to keep her safe as she told the story.

Unfortunately, I heard *"Come IN!"* I ducked behind her cleaning cart as she opened the door, I was still able to have a fairly unobstructed view, I know that I was being stupid. Uncle Michael was smirking as he reached out for the towels, looking down at his crotch where a girl was sucking on him. He said in a growl *"I will need extra towels for after."*

"Too bad you are not working tomorrow morning, then you would have the pleasure of picking up all these towels; I bet you would smell and lick them. I know it is part of the benefits program for hotel workers."

When my drunk father tried to rip open the top of her uniform, the things he was saying to her were horrid and nasty. She got away and I managed to stay out of sight as we ran to the front desk, reporting their behavior to the clerk. One good thing came out of it: The Alpha and my father were never allowed in again because that hotel is mainly for humans.

Still, I never fully slept in my room ever again after that.

Duncan just held her in his arms; she leaned into him again, resting her head on his chest. He tilted her chin to look him in the eye, *"I promise that you will never be in that kind of situation ever again, I would kill to protect you."* He bent down and kissed her lightly on the lips.

It wasn't meant to be passionate, only to show her that he would protect her always. The fire inside them both took it as an invitation. As she responded, he made the kiss more intense, and she started moaning in pleasure. He pulled back from the kiss before it got out of hand. If that were to happen again, he wasn't sure he would be strong enough to resist the temptation.

She moved and lay down on the couch with her head in his lap while he stroked her hair absentmindedly.

He thought back to his meeting with the King…

"*Duncan, if you can find me proof, definitive proof. I will give you full carte blanch' over their punishment, so as long as you let not one guilty party left alive. Except for the leaders of this shit organization, I want you to bring them before me so I can punish them personally. As for the innocent, bring them to my territory, then burn that whole area to the ground."*

At first, he thought that the king's orders were a bit harsh; but the more he found out, though, the more he thought about it, it isn't a big enough punishment.

He looked down at his mate; he loved the name that her wolf gave her. He thought they should go for a run together tomorrow, so Apollo and Artemis could get to know each other better. He told Apollo not to do anything stupid and scare them away.

Apollo spoke up..."*My mate is not scarred as yours is; Adira took the brunt of the abuse, so Artemis didn't go crazy. I think that was their goal, to make Artemis lose her sanity, thus influencing Adira to do their bidding.*"

"*It's a shitty thing to do; if you make your wolf go crazy, they will start killing anything, and everything, or commit suicide. Then they try to poison her with wolfsbane to weaken them both, makes me think this isn't their first time doing this sort of thing.*"

Both Duncan and Apollo had to stop for a deep calming breath because they were starting to get killing mad. He hoped the King was sadistic with their punishment, and he also hoped that the King would let him help or at the very least watch.

CHAPTER TWELVE

Alpha Michael went down to the basement in warehouse five to check on the pregnant females; he had two specials to check on.

Sometimes other packs would come to him because their wives could not give them pups. So, he would loan out a girl for a while till she was pregnant, then she would be put in one of the special secluded rooms till she gave birth.

When he got down to the cages, he noticed that they were not clean and that his niece was nowhere in sight. He was instantly enraged; how dare she defy him. The specials he was supposed to check on were all forgotten, as he made his way to his brother's packhouse to teach his niece a lesson.

When he arrived, he could hear yelling coming from inside. His brother and his stupid mate were fighting. They were always fighting these days; Joann didn't know about the business that was going on, which caused problems for Erick because he was always gone.

Joann was no innocent; she was a stupid and nasty bitch; she didn't know about the details of the business because of her flapping mouth. If she wasn't talking about something, she was thinking of talking about something. He didn't know how his brother put up with it.

When he got to the door, he just went right on inside. His brother hated when he did that; that was why he never stopped doing it.

He realized the fight was about Lily; she wasn't home, nor was she at the warehouse, where she was supposed to be.

"Where is she, Joann, she isn't here, and she is not at the warehouse, then where is she?"

"I watched her pack her things; then she drove off toward the warehouses."

"You were supposed to go with her and drive her vehicle back here. Not just let her drive off trusting that she would go where you want her to, you dumb twit."

"Well, maybe if you were home more often, these problems would not come to fruition."

On and on they went, and it was starting to give him a migraine. He decided to put an end to it.

"WHERE THE HELL IS SHE?!!"

His yell finally got through to the both of them, and they stared in fear at him. He laughed; they both looked like they had dropped a load in their pants.

"We don't know, Alpha."

"Then why are you here yelling at each other and not going out to find her?"

"Both of you just go find her or don't bother to come back if you don't. Cause I can tell you; no one will go looking or even care if you two are missing."

They ran around like chickens with their heads cut off, till finally they grabbed what they needed and left. Michael just sat there for a minute, holding his head. Pulling out his phone, he contacted another one of his enforcers and sent him on his way to find the bitch Lily.

Lily had driven the four hundred and some miles to the gate, where she was sitting in her car, waiting to see if anyone would come out to talk to her. It had been well over an hour, until she finally got out of the car and yelled into the silent woods.

"Hello, anyone there? If you are listening, I have information, pictures, and camera footage of the Rising Moon pack that would interest you."

Her response was just the wind and the trees moving; she couldn't even get a scent of anything to know if someone was close. With a sigh, she went back and sat in her car. It was twilight now, and the air was getting cold. She always hated this time of day; it wasn't a day or a night. It always brought back the bad memories.

Even with her enhanced vision, it was hard to see; too many shadows were dancing in the dim light. She was exhausted, coming off that mindless rush you get with fear and anger.

She started to go to sleep; she forced herself back to stay awake. Just as she was about to give in, there was movement outside her car. Something big was sniffing her out. She sat perfectly still, not moving a muscle.

She thought she was going insane; maybe she was just overtired and stressed. She started laughing; Goldie locks is about to get eaten by the three bears.

Suddenly the door to her car was ripped off, and an excessively big man reached in with a syringe; she backed away as far as she could with a look of absolute terror.

She started babbling, *"No, please, not again, please, I will be good. I won't tell, I promise, please don't, not again, please no, no"* She was in a catatonic state, rocking back and forth in the back seat of her car.

Geesh, one of the Jacks' men, said, *"I feel bad to knock her out, but at the same time, I think maybe I would be doing her a favor. Is there anyone in that pack that isn't fucked up?"*

"Just do it and be done with it, so we can get her out of here, hide the damn car and all the evidence that it was here."

One stayed behind to get rid of the evidence of her being there, and the other carried the female back to their Den. Once the other one was done with the car, he carried all the female's bags back to his leader's office. Swearing all the way, why do females always pack so much shit.

Alpha Michael looked around at his brother's house; he was so pissed that he had destroyed almost everything. He was fairly sure he was going insane. His wolf had had gone quiet a long time ago, unable to abide by things that Michael loved doing.

He felt empty inside all the time now, which made him angrier. He always had a punching bag, though, so it wasn't bad. Laughing to himself, he had over five hundred punching bags. He walked out of the house, leaving the door wide open.

Making a memo to himself for the next time he visits relatives; he must have a full gas can in the car and a box of matches.

When Michael returned to the warehouse to do his daily check ins and inventory, his Beta stopped him. We have another delivery from those stinking asshole bears. Michael sighed; idiots surrounded him. *"Fine, let's see whatever creative shit they sent us back this time."*

Again, the delivery truck was different; the driver was human and had already been paid. He had no idea what it was he was delivering. The driver drove off after unloading. There, in front of him, sat three small crates. Having his men open them, he already knew what was in them.

Again, his men returned to him in pieces, all the arms in one crate, legs in the other, and the heads in the third; he didn't care to know where the rest of them were.

As before, there was a note for him to open and read.

He grabbed it and went to his office; the next thing his men heard was a roaring growl that shook the walls. Michael sat down at his desk and opened the note.

Dear Idiot fleabags,

You failed yet again, so why not try one more time. No need to be shy, it is silly to let your mangy fur hold you back. You know what they say, the third time is a charm.

Best Regards,
The Smartass Bear clan.

He was so pissed he let out another roar, balling up the note and whipping it at the door. Then he destroyed his office, ripping off the door and tossing it down the stairs.

Hearing this, Alpha Michael's Beta decided it was best to lock all the doors that led to the females. You can't make money with damaged goods. He had learned that lesson the last time the Alpha went off the deep end. He ended up having to get rid of the bodies of six females, good ones too.

After Michael's Beta took care of the crates and bodies, he locked the Alpha in the warehouse, knowing that the Alpha had a stash of moonshine in his office. The Alpha will get drunk and pass out somewhere in the warehouse for me to find in the morning.

"Sigh, the Alpha was starting to be a pain in the ass." He said to no one as he got into his car."

Jack looked at all the evidence that the female had brought to them. Duncan will go crazy when he sees all this; there is enough to hang them twice. It was so much worse than either of them thought; that pig of an Alpha needed to die slowly while hanging by his balls over hot coals.

As for the female, he knew enough about her to see that she was one of Duncan's mate abusers. That little scene in her car made him think there was more to that story. For now, he put her in one of their guest rooms under lock, key, and guards.

Great, just what he needed; helping Duncan always was an adventure. This, though, was a complication neither of them had foreseen.

After those three very stupid spies were dispatched, he felt he could leave long enough to tell Duncan about this development personally.

Maybe he would have an idea about what to do with their new guest. God, I hope she isn't one of those screechers, they drive me batty.

CHAPTER THIRTEEN

$\mathcal{D}$uncan and Adira were out for a run, her wolf Artemis was beautiful and fast, and Apollo was utterly smitten. They played, hunted, and ran races with each other. They even took a nap together under the bows of a pine tree. Duncan thought back to when they woke up this morning.

Another kiss, this one was a lot hotter than the other two; Duncan could sense her need building up inside her; it would be just a matter of a little more time.

They were heading back to their cabin when both wolves sensed they were being watched.

Duncan mind-linked Marco his location and what was going on. Then Apollo mind-linked Artemis telling her to pretend to be oblivious of the watcher. When he said run, she was to run to their cabin. There were protection barriers in place that would keep her safe.

Marco was the master of stealth; he mind-linked Duncan to tell him he was stalking the sniper; the sniper was using his scope to watch them. He was also downwind from him; he smelled like one of those Rising Moon bastards.

Duncan heard a loud snarl and choking sounds coming from the trees ahead. Duncan took off to the sounds of the fight and the smell of blood.

Duncan managed to get there in time, mind linking Marco killed him. *"We need some questions answered, so we keep this one alive for now."*

"Alpha, we already have one in custody; I was on my way to find you when you mind-linked me. This piece of shit was aiming his rifle at our Luna."

Looking down at the spy with a malicious smirk and a low growl to his voice…*"Oh, well then, it looks like your luck has run out then."* The spy had a look of total horror on his face, as the Alpha reached down and tore his head clean off.

Marco sniffed the air, *"Duncan, do you smell something off about these guys?"* Duncan sniffed the air, *"Yes, it is there, faint, but it is there."* Then it dawned on Duncan, *"This guy was a shifter; he was born with a wolf, but there was no wolf present in him now."*

"Duncan, I don't like this, for someone to lose their wolf. They must do something so horrible that their wolf leaves them or dies. What kind of fucked up shit are they into in that pack?"

"I don't know, Marco, we will find out; whatever is going on there, must be stopped."

Duncan turned around; he sensed something coming at them from the opposite direction. He recognized the scent and calmed back down.

"Perhaps I can be of some assistance in the information department."

As Jack Dawson walked out of the shadows.

Erick and Joann returned home without their daughter, Lily. Their house looked like a bomb had gone off; both knew who to thank for this mess. Erick went to his hidden wall safe; with a sigh of relief, all the money and account books were there.

Thanking what gods may be that his brother had never caught him siphoning money, which he had been doing for years, he wasn't stupid he knew his brother was never going to fully share, so he took what he thought was his share anyway.

"Erick, we can't stay here; we must pack what we can and go as far away as possible. We can always go to High Garden and seek an audience with the prince; he could protect us from that insane mess you call a brother."

Erick looked at Joann for a bit, thinking that once they got the help they needed, he would make sure his mate came up missing. She was grinding his nerves to a pulp; whatever he saw in her was gone.

It probably had something to do with the night his wolf left him. Since then, he'd lost his ability to give a shit. He felt no attraction to her; his need to kill was becoming more intense, and almost impossible at times to resist since he had lost his wolf.

"Yes, let's get our stuff and go to High Garden; we will find a small place to live while waiting for the prince to grant us an audience."

Joann was sick of her husband. He was a fantastic mate, till that fateful night when she was about to give birth to Lily, when he brought in another child. Right there in the birthing room. He wanted her to raise his bastard; he asked her this as she screamed in pain. Now he doesn't even feel like her mate; it was like something died in him.

It doesn't matter, though. As soon as they are in High Garden, she would go alone straight to the Prince to request her own audience. She was also going to visit one of the local herbalists to get poison to put her husband out of his misery and hers.

They packed everything they would need; plus a few things they could sell at a pawnshop for more money. They hurried to their car and were gone before anyone was the wiser.

They might have changed their plans if they knew the Alpha had a spy watching them. As soon as they were in the distance, the Alpha's spy came out of the shadows, already reporting what he had seen.

Adira stood behind Duncan; she was unsure who had just joined them; he was huge. At least 6'7 and all muscle, he had a deep voice. He kept looking at her, but she kept hiding behind Duncan.

Duncan knew that Adira was learning to trust people and that meeting a giant like Jack was intimidating for her.

Duncan reached behind his back and grabbed her hand; he pulled her out in front of him, wrapping his arms around her like a shield.

"Adira, this is a good friend of mine, Jack Dawson. He is a Werebear. He's big and intimidating, but don't let that fool you; he is a sweet fuzzy teddy bear on the inside."

Jack gave Duncan a look that said he would get even later. Duncan laughed.

"Hello there, Adira; I am Jack Dawson, Leader of the Stone Mountain Clan of Werebears. We will also accept the term Pack. Let me know if you ever need to slap this idiot around. I will come over and fix his attitude up really nice for you." Then he gave a courtly bow, which made Duncan roll his eyes.

This did seem to make Adira a bit more comfortable as she relaxed in Duncan's arms. Jack was staring at Adira; Duncan let out a warning growl. Jack put both of his hands in the air and backed away. *"I am sorry about that; it's just that she is a twin, and her twin looks nothing like her."*

Adira stiffened up again but asked, *"You have met my sister, Lily?"*

"Yes, she is at my Clan house until I decide what to do with her. She came to us with all kinds of information. That is why I am here; you are going to want to know what she had to tell us, and I have a video to show you as well."

He held up what looked like a backpack; then, Adira let out a slight hiss. *"That backpack belongs to Lily; she never goes anywhere without it, not even in the house."*

Once I show you what is in here, you will know why she never went anywhere without it.

Duncan gestured for Jack and Marco to follow them back to the magical house; it was the perfect place for privacy. He had a feeling what he was about to find out was going to take him beyond killing mad. Duncan also hoped it wouldn't hurt Adira anymore, she is strong, but still, you can only take so many punches.

Lily woke up in a strange room; she looked around. It was a nice size room and was a little spartan, though. Then, she realized she was wearing an oversized shirt that smelled oddly good.

She got off the bed and explored the room; there was a huge bathroom. It had a shower, tub, and everything else you could want in a bathroom. She looked in the empty closet and drawers but didn't find any of her things.

She went to open the door to go out, but it was locked. She could break it down if it were a standard door, but the damn thing look liked it came out of an old prison movie.

"Hello?! Anyone?"

She sat there on the edge of her bed for what seemed forever, till the door opened and a colossal biker guy came in carrying a food tray. Another brought in her bag that had her clothes in it. She tried to talk to them, but they acted like she wasn't there.

She sat down and looked over the food: bacon, eggs, toast with jam, and orange slices. On the side was a cup of coffee and a glass of chocolate milk. She thought that it was a little odd, chocolate milk. She was starving, so she began eating the food. It tasted like heaven.

She lay down on the bed, feeling tired after eating everything and she even drank the chocolate milk. As she was drifting off, she yelled to her wolf, ***"Zinnia...They drugged us!"*** As she was drifting into unconsciousness, she said three words..."*Damn I knew it was that chocolate milk!*"

CHAPTER FOURTEEN

Alpha Michael woke up face down on a loading ramp in his warehouse. The place was quiet; it was still too early for his type of business to start. He didn't remember much about last night; he'd never used to have hangovers. That is the fault of his stupid wolf being gone.

He had to be born with a coward for a wolf, constantly nagging for him to change and stop hurting our mate. Finally, one night, his wolf went silent and never spoke again. It was only a matter of time before Michael couldn't feel its presence.

His pack didn't know his wolf was gone entirely, though he suspected several of his enforcers were suffering from the same condition. The werebears must have found them not much of a challenge. We are just a bunch of worthless humans. Michael started laughing at that irony.

He got up and went to his office to make some coffee; he mind-linked his asshole of a Beta that he was up and sober again. He waited for his Beta to answer, then went to the bathroom to wash off some of the dirt and crud from last night.

When he looked up in the mirror, it wasn't his face staring back at him; it was the face of his wolf. He was shocked; how was this possible?

"I am here to warn you; the goddess sent me here for one final message. You are to stop all this abusive dark shit that you like so much; then, you will make it right again. Then and only then can I return to you. You have till the next full moon."

Michael scoffed at his wolf's message. *"There is no chance of me stopping now, you idiot. I'm getting way too much money and fun; it doesn't matter anymore to me what you say."*

Just as the words left his mouth, a loud growl was heard, then the terms, *"Till the next full moon."*

Michael sat at his desk drinking his coffee, waiting for his Beta to let him out. His Beta is getting increasingly defiant. If he takes it too far, he will have to replace him.

Duncan sat listening to all the stuff Jack had found; it was enough evidence to hang them all twice. He looked over at Adira. She held her own so far, occasionally adding a few details she remembered.

Jack looked over at the two of them; he was happy his friend had found his mate. It was then that he caught Adira's scent again.

"Duncan, I would like to know if it will be alright to get some DNA from Adira.?"

"Why do you want it?"

"It is just a hunch; if I'm wrong, then no harm, no foul, but if I'm right, then I think it will prove that Adira and Lily are not full sisters, definitely not twins."

Both Adira and Duncan stared at Jack. They were not saying anything.

"Jack, are you saying that I am not a twin? How is that possible?"

"I am not sure, Luna Adira; I can tell you that there are some big family differences when I take in the scents of you and your sister. It makes me think that you two only share a father."

Duncan put his arm around Adira for comfort while kissing her on top of the head. He couldn't help thinking, how did this pack end up so messed up?

Marco spoke up.*" I don't think they will stop trying to get our Luna; we should let the mages see if they can extend the magic on this little house. Just for a couple of weeks, we caught their assassins quickly. This time, I will go and interrogate the one we have in custody and see what answers he can give us."*

"Marco, we tried to question the two we kept alive; we got nothing out of them."

"Jack, if you like, you can come with me; I can show you how to get a wolf to talk."

With that, Jack and Marco left, and Marco mind-linked to Duncan, informing him that he would keep the link open during the interrogation, so if Duncan wanted to know anything, Marco could get the answer for him.

Adira was still sitting in Duncan's lap, with his arms wrapped around her. Thinking about all the information she had just heard gave her mixed emotions. Could Lily be so messed up because she was abused too? Why does Alpha Michael want her back so badly?"

She was so lost in thought that she didn't even know when Duncan carried her to their bedroom. She finally came out of her thoughts as Duncan sat down on the bed with her still in his lap. He started kissing her neck, right where he would mark her.

She couldn't help it. She let out a moan of pleasure.

She whispered into his ear, *"Duncan, I want you to make me yours; I want you to mark me. I don't know why I feel that it is so urgent that you do so; I just know that I want it."*

"Adira," he whispered her name, sending tingles down her spine and straight to her core.

"Are you sure, my little wolf? Once it is done, it can't be undone. There will be no me without you, no you without me."

"I know what I want and won't regret it; I want to be yours. I need to be yours just as I need to breathe air. I want you in my mind; I want to be in yours. Please, Duncan, fill this emptiness inside me with your love."

Duncan was lost; there was no way to resist this kind of temptation, nor did he want to.

"Ok, we will take it slow, and if you want to stop, we will stop."

She pulled his head down for a deep passionate kiss; no more talking. Duncan removed his clothes a little at a time while she watched.

He watched her eyes go from that warm coffee color to deep black. Her wolf was here with her. That brought out Apollo; he didn't take over. He was just blended with Duncan.

"Adira, I want you to take your clothes off slowly for me; let me see you uncover that gorgeous body, one piece at a time."

Adira felt her panties getting wet, Duncan's voice was a low deep growl, and his scent was everywhere, driving her crazy. She was getting so hot; it was too much. She had to have him end this painful pleasure she was feeling; it was urgent. She wasn't sure what was wrong with her.

"Duncan, I need you right now".... Duncan could smell her arousal, and then he smelt something else. Oh, god, she is going into heat!

He quickly mind-linked Marco, telling him that Adira was in heat and that he was to keep every male away. Marco linked back that he would keep them away; he also said that the mages would be there in two hours at sunset to lengthen the time in the cabin. I will warn them not to bother you.

Duncan wanted her first experience to be a slow and romantic thing; Adira was going crazy. He went into the bathroom as Adira moaned his name. He can't take her like this; it is too fast. He is going to have to slow things down.

He filled the tub with ice-cold water and added all the ice he could find. He ran into the bedroom and scooped her up.

"Adira, listen to me; you are going into heat. You are not in control of your body; you will get pregnant if you mate during the heat. Is this what you want right now?"

"I only want what is best for you; if you can tell me that this is what you genuinely want, I will. We will take another route if there is a doubt in your pretty mind. I will do all I can to get you through this; I must know your answer. I will put you in the ice bath to calm the heat and clear your mind so you can reach your true answer."

Lily sat in her room; there was nothing to do but stare at the walls. She couldn't even look out the windows; they were boarded over.

She'd been feeling agitated and uncomfortable all afternoon; she no longer was being drugged, though she wouldn't mind if they did right now. The room seemed to get hotter and hotter with no end in sight.

Then, she realized what was going on; oh, my goddess, I'm going into heat. She realized she couldn't take her daily potion keeping her heat at bay since she had been here.

She went to the bathroom and ran an ice-cold bath. This is going to turn into a nightmare. She had managed to suppress her heat for two years now; she knew that the Alpha was waiting for it, and she wasn't going to give it to him, not after what he had done to her and the one she loved.

This one would be bad; she had suppressed it for too long, and her poor wolf rolled around in agony. ***"Hang in there Zinnia; I will get us through this."***

CHAPTER FIFTEEN

$\mathcal{D}$uncan mind-linked the pack doctor to see if there was anything that he could give her to get rid of the heat.

The Doc mind-linked back, *"I will be there shortly, I have her blood tests back, and there is something you need to know. I will also bring an antidote."*

Duncan became alarmed, antidote! *"What do you mean, Doc, by antidote?"*

"It's alright, Alpha. We discovered it in time. As soon as your Beta gets back with one of the elders and shows me the way, I will be there. Alpha, don't sexually engage with her; it will only make things worse."

Duncan returned to the bathroom to add more ice; Adira was moaning and rolling around as the ice melted more. It was good that the ice maker was magically made, or he would be in big trouble right now.

Finally, Duncan heard a knock at the bathroom door; he yanked it open; there stood the doctor and the elder

Healer, Sarah. She pushed past them both and shut the door leaving them in the bedroom.

The doctor explained to the Alpha what is going on and what must be done to save the Luna.

Adira stared at the woman and let out a cry of pain. *"Luna, my name is Sarah. I am a pack healer; I will help you through this. It is not the heat, but rather the result of a poison that slowly entered your bloodstream; once it was there, it would build up for years till the third year of the poisoning."*

"Then it will cause your body to go into a false heat; this heat is far worse than the normal version. If it weren't for your mate putting you in this ice bath, you would be going insane with need. It wouldn't matter who you were with; it would never be enough."

"The Drug is called Aphrodite's Kiss. It is banned just about everywhere. In all the shifter packs, it is punishable by death if you use it on a female."

Sarah started to roll herbs between her palms and let the leaves hit the water. *"These will help ease the burning pain; the antidote, I am afraid to say, this will be a painful experience."*

Adira began to cry, *"I can't get away from them. It doesn't matter how far I go; they always will find a way to hurt me."*

Duncan was smashing things left and right as Marco tried to calm him down. He was saying words and breaking at the same time.

"HOW COULD…SMASH!!!!, I'M GOING TO KILL.....SMASH!!! THEY ARE GOING TO......SMASH!!!!, DIE!!!!!!....SMASH!!!"

After a bit, Marco managed to get him to settle down.

"Those bastards, after all the shit she had to go through, they go and do this to her. It wasn't a spur-of-the-moment thing either; they planned this shit out for the long haul."

"How is she ever going to trust anyone ever again? She just got out of that hell hole and was starting to learn to trust and enjoy things without fear of repercussions. Now she has to go through more pain."

It was then that Duncan heard his mate crying; it sent him over the edge and into a killing thrall. He went outside, shifted into Apollo, and just ran. Marco went after him. Marco also mind-linked Marnie and told her to get to the cabin as fast as possible and bring comfort food and anything she could think of that might help. He also told Marnie to call Jack Dawson back here to help with Duncan.

Jack was about five miles out of Duncan's borders when he got a phone call from Duncan's sister. He pulled the bike to the side of the road and answered the call.

Jack quickly turned around sending gravel flying everywhere, he had to find Duncan; if he were to go into a killing frenzy, it would be a fight to calm him down. He must calm him down even if it meant he had to beat it out of him; that pretty little mate of his needed him.

Adira was calming down a little, the herbs were helping a more and the pain was a becoming more manageable. Sarah held her hand and added more spices, making things more comfortable.

"We will wait a little longer for the herbs to take more effect, then I am afraid we will have to give you the antidote."

"I don't understand, Sarah; how could they poison Artemis and me? We were cautious what we ate or drank; none of our food or drink came from them."

"I am afraid, Luna, that the poison is designed to go on your skin. It could be put in your body wash, shampoo, body lotion, hair gel, etc. It is odorless so that you wouldn't have sniffed it out either."

Adira groaned, *"I didn't guard that stuff all that well, I didn't think they would mess with that."*

Another knock at the bathroom door; Marnie asked, *"Hey, can I come in to help too?"* Adira smiled and nodded. Marnie wasted no time; she came straight to Adira, holding a popsicle out for her to eat; it did help a little. *"I also have ice cream too, as well as all things chocolate."*

Jack and Marco managed to corner an outraged Apollo; It was all Apollo. Both knew their only chance was to talk Apollo into letting go of his control, so they could speak to Duncan.

Jack decided to wait before he shifted; getting Apollo calmed down was the priority here; shifting into his bear could be seen as a threat, and Apollo would attack.

Marco was sitting in his wolf form, as close to Apollo as he would let him. Then Marco did something almost comical; he started to roll around on the ground with his tongue hanging out like an idiot.

Apollo seemed to calm down upon watching Marco; he sat down with his back facing Marco and Jack. When Jack came over to his other side and sat down next to him, they stayed that way in silence.

Mind linking to Apollo… *"You know, Apollo; your mate needs you at her side right now. This is too horrible for her to suffer through it alone, she needs your help, with you she will go through this with less pain."*

Apollo mind-linked him directly when Jack felt something he never thought he would with his friend.

"You're a great friend Jack; I will be letting Duncan come back; it was stupid of me to react that way; I couldn't stand to hear them in so much pain anymore; I had to do something to make it right again. If that meant

going to that poor excuse of a pack and ripping them all to shreds, then so be it."

Apollo turned and ran back to the cabin, to his mate. Marco and Jack are right behind him.

Duncan shifted just outside the cabin as Marco and Jack did the same; caches of clothes were hidden in the trees. Once they were dressed, they entered the cabin. It was quiet. The Doc came up to them holding a nasty-looking potion in a small flask.

"The Luna has been informed of what is to come; before I give this to her, I want you to know that you can't have any more outbursts like you just did. She needs you to be with her through this; you are her anchor."

"Duncan looked at the Doc and then hung his head; I won't be doing that again, so you don't have to worry anymore. The fact that you have known me since I was a Pup means I will forget about the tone you used with your Alpha."

Duncan held his hand; *"I am sorry, Doc, I'm still coming down from the thrall."*

The Doctor smiled, *"I understand it all, Duncan; I would have done the same thing if this happened to my Betty. Let's get this over with; it will be a long night. Come on, lads, let's go save our Luna."*

Everyone was in the bedroom waiting for Duncan; he requested a minute alone with Adira.

Duncan sat on the edge of the tub, holding Adira's hand. *"You know that I would never hurt you, that this has to be done to purge your system of the poison. I will be here every moment with you."* Adira reached up and touched Duncan's cheek wiping away a tear. To think that this big strong Alpha wolf would shed tears for her, was the greatest gift he had ever given her.

He lifted her out of the tub and into a towel and quickly dried her off; he didn't want to touch her more than he had to. One lingering touch could cause her to go right back into heat. He then wrapped her in a soft blanket and carried her to their bed.

The Doctor wasted no time; he uncorked the little flask and poured it down Adira's throat. At first, Adira didn't feel anything, and then she started to feel cold. Then it turned to freezing. Her teeth were chattering as Duncan held her tight to him in their bed. Duncan felt Apollo adding his body heat to Duncan's. It seemed to help take off the bitter edge of the cold.

Then, Adira's body almost came off the bed as she arched, screaming in pain, every muscle in her body cramped simultaneously. Apollo started to go nuts, yelling to Duncan, *"Mark her now!!!!!"*

"Have you gone crazy, Apollo? I can't mark her now. What would it do to her."

MARK HER NOW! WE ARE GOING TO LOSE THEM!

"Listen to me, Duncan. We can be linked together; you and I can take on some of pain."

Duncan didn't waste any more time; he put his mouth on her neck and bit down hard. He was joining them together forever. He wasn't going to lose her, not now, not ever.

CHAPTER SIXTEEN

Lily was in so much pain; the ice water wasn't enough, and her wolf had gone quiet. There was a knock at the bathroom door; she sat in the tub, hugging her knees.

There was more knocking, this time, more frantic. Lily didn't hear it anymore. She was in the throes of pain, screaming and scratching at herself, trying to get it to stop. The door shattered as two of her guards entered the room.

"What is wrong with her?"

Sam looked at the little she-wolf; she was clearly in pain, almost insane with it. The worst of it was all the blood from her trying to scratch it out.

She looked up at Sam, *"Please. Leave. I can't. Take much. More."*

"What do you need?"

"Ice"

Sam looked to his partner, *"Go get as much Ice as you can find, send someone out to get more."* His partner took off at a run. Sam sat on the edge of the tub, he wanted to help, but he was afraid that touching her would make it worse.

"Do you know what wrong, little wolf?"
"Yes"
"Well, are you going to tell me?"
"No"
"There is no point in being stubborn; you need help. So come clean. Are you on drugs or something?"
"No."
"Little one, I can't help you if I don't know what is happening. So spill it already."

"I'm not going to tell a bunch of idiot werebears about personal female stuff."
"Oh my, I think I know what is going on; you're in heat, aren't you?"
She gave him what he was sure was her best death glare, which told him he had a bingo. *"What needs to be done? You need more ice to cool down; what else?"*
"There is nothing else you can do; I need my mate for this."
"Tell me where I can find him, and I will bring him to you."
"He is dead."

At that moment, the other guard brought in several buckets of ice. *"I emptied the ice machine, it is making more, and I sent Mika and two others out to get what they could find."*

"Good, now go to the forest spring and bring back some ice-cold water," Sam emptied the Ice into the bath, and the little wolf calmed down some. Handing the buckets back to the other guard with instructions to keep gathering them.

Sam also brought the shower curtain out at an angle, so no one would be able to see her. It was giving her some sense of privacy anyway. Poor little thing must be mortified.

He also brought out all the softest towels he could find, not that there was much in the way of soft in this house. Sam had to contact his Leader and tell him what was happening with their guest. This was some crazy shit—it is a good thing that she is a wolf, and not a bear. Otherwise, we would have males in here hanging from the rafters.

He stepped out of the bathroom, mind-linking Jack.

Marco and Jack were sitting on the little cabin's porch, both disheartened. *"What kind of messed up piece of the shit pack is this? How do you get so bad that your wolves leave? What makes someone do that?"*

Jack ran his hand through his hair, *"I don't know if there is a good reason for that. There is no excuse for it. They are pure evil. At first, I thought we'd mess around with them and piss them off slightly."*

"Now I am declaring war. I will report to the King tomorrow and ask to be the enforcer and executioner. I know it is Duncan's Job, but he can't leave Adira, and I would never ask him. I am free now; my boys have been itching for a good fight. I always take care of my boys."

"No one should ever suffer like that, I told Sam to take care of Lily the best he could, and Duncan sent one of his elder healers and a mage to help. Let's hope that we can all get this mess sorted."

"Jack, don't forget that Duncan will want a piece of that shit pie too."

"Oh, he will have his Alpha size share. You see, I forgot to get him a present for his birthday. This year, I will give him his very own punching bag, The Alpha Michael Punching Bag, a top-of-the-line model. The perfect gift for those friends with a more eccentric kind of taste, Duncan will love it."

"Maybe pick one up for me too? Since finding out about all this crap, all I have wanted to do was play beat up the asshole."

"*This brings me to another thing, Jack; once we clean the house, so to speak, what are we going to do with all the victims?*"

"*Marco, I don't know yet. I feel there are many more victims than we suspect.*"

Jack stood up and stretched, "*Well, I will go home and get ready for my audience with the King. See how my guest is doing; see if any of my guys are mortified yet.*"

"*Yeah, I got pack business to finish up and a prisoner to interrogate. Duncan's sister Marnie is here now, and she will help them as much as she can. The Doc and the mages will all be coming and going. It will take as much of the load off of me as possible; our Luna is top priority.*"

Right then, they heard a gut-wrenching scream coming from inside. Both Marco and Jack were sad and angry at the same time. Marco looked at Jack..."*Promise me that you make it hurt before you kill them.*" Jack nodded and faded into the forest, just as Marco silently shifted into wolf form and ran off into the woods. In the distance, Marco let out a single howl for his Luna.

Erick Williams had the perfect plan to rid himself of his mate once and for all. He went to an herbalist for the perfect poison. It kills in about an hour, an hour of agony but the ideal thing about it is it takes away your ability to speak.

Now all he had to do was get it into her food or wine at dinner, and bingo, he could be the merry widower.

Joann Williams just returned from an awfully expensive Herbalist; the poison she bought killed the victim in about an hour; it is a slow and painful death. It takes away your ability to speak or call for help. Now all she had to do was bake that idiot his favorite cherry pie, and just like that, she would play the merry widower role.

When Erick entered their tiny apartment door, he could smell his favorite dessert, Cherry Pie.

Joann came out of the kitchen wearing an apron, *"Hello Erick; the Masons have invited us out for dinner tonight; I made you your favorite Pie. I noticed how stressed you had been lately with everything, and I thought you would like to have your favorite dessert."*

"I will have it ready for tonight, wine, pie, and candlelight when we get home. Just the two of us, like it used to be."

Erick thought, well, how about that? She did a splendid job planning her own murder. Perfect.

The prince was at his favorite resort; he had to stay away from the royal court. He found out yesterday that his father was investigating Rising Moon. He hoped to the goddess that he was kept out of it, no telling what his father would do if he found out his role in it all.

He was not a fool; he knew what his father would do, if he knew that he participated in the activities of Rising Moon and was one of its biggest founders.

He did have some money tucked away for a rainy day; it wouldn't be enough to get far. He felt no money would be enough to help him hide from his father's wrath.

He knew he must let Spare go and get rid of any evidence that would tie him to any of this. It is the only way for him to come out of this smelling like a rose. Even if he must marry the ugly princess, he can still have his side action. He contacted his spy within Rising Moon; he will take care of the evidence and put it all on Alpha Michael. He also informed his spy to get the formula for Aphrodite's Kiss. That will come in handy for future profits.

It could help with future endeavors or blackmail; nothing like a little hot sex in kinky ways to make a person pay up. He sat and pondered more ways he could use the drug. Maybe he could use it on the horse-face princess to make her more palatable.

He wished his father had died when his mother died; no, he had to continue for the kingdom. Now he felt he had to make more plans to become King sooner than later. As for his stupid brother, he didn't want anything to do with the crown, so it shouldn't be a problem, but if he changed his mind, he would have to come up with a solution to get rid of him.

His father cut his brother out of everything, dear old Dad gave him some of their mother's money, and then Adam just disappeared from all eyes of the world. If he knows what is good for him, he will stay where he is.

Chapter Seventeen

$\mathcal{D}$uncan bit down hard, tasting his Adira's blood; instantly, he could feel all of her pain; it was unbearable. He called out to Apollo for help. Instead, he got Artemis surrounding him with warmth, as he passed out.

Adira was floating on a wave of pain; she couldn't escape it. She felt so alone, as she was floating in this sea of torment. She could hear Duncan in the darkness but couldn't make out what was said. She lay on the dark ground hugging her knees, and that was when she felt light by her side; she looked up, and there was Artemis, wrapping herself around Adira.

Adira could hear her heartbeat; the pain became less as she listened. There was a lonely-sounding howl in the distance; it was getting closer and closer. Adira wasn't afraid of the cry; she thought it sounded beautiful and made her feel calm and warm inside.

With each howl, the pain lessened more.

"Adira?"

"Yes, Artemis?"

"Open your eyes."

"There isn't anything to see but inky blackness."

"No, little one, look around you, it is no longer dark."

Adira opened her eyes; she was in the most beautiful of places, tiny fairy lights were dancing lazily around, and a gentle wind carried the scent of the blooming flowers. A little brook ran through the middle, giving the sound of moving water to the music of the singing birds.

The sky was the brightest blue, and the sun's rays danced in and out of the little clouds. Then she saw a man and a wolf standing side by side. Looking at them in the distance, Artemis danced around Adira's feet and then took off at a run towards their two visitors. Adira couldn't help herself. She took off running too.

The closer she got, the more she realized who the visitors were, Duncan and Apollo. She ran even faster until finally, she leaped into Duncan's arms, laughing in complete happiness. The pain was all forgotten, as Duncan twirled her around and around.

Once their joy subsided a little, Adira asked Artemis. *"Where are we, Arty?"*

"We are in my realm, little one. This is where I stay when I am apart from you."

"You couldn't take any more of the pain; I think whoever gave us that poison meant to kill us eventually. Duncan and Apollo saved you by marking you, that gave me the power to bring everyone here. We will all be here till the sun rises again. Then we go home; we have to follow the rules of the Goddess, though. I will explain that later and don't be alarmed if time moves slower here than out there."

"Now we play, relax and then teach each other." Artemis backed away and then came at Adira at a run, knocking her down. Adira was laughing so hard; Artemis used her snout and teeth to tickle her.

Duncan was laughing at them as Apollo tackled him; the next thing he knew, Apollo was doing the same thing to him; all you could hear were giggles and playful growls.

Erick was excited with anticipation all through dinner with the Masons. He was the perfect gentleman, he thought; he was funny and the life of the dinner party. The Masons thought he was a bit creepy; his sense of humor was a bit too dark.

Joann was quiet; she barely spoke more than five words all night. She laughed at his horrible jokes, which encouraged his overconfident attitude.

They were pleased when the evening ended, and it was time for them to part ways. They said their goodbyes, and they sighed in relief when they got into their car.

Erick and Joann drove home in silence; it wasn't unusual for them. It was how they preferred it. When they reached their place, Joann jumped out of the car.

"I will get us a bottle of our favorite wine; remember the one we drank at our wedding? I will get everything set up for just the two of us."

When Erick entered their tiny dining room, it was lit with candles; Joann was waiting for him in one of the chairs; she was wearing the red silk teddy he loved. He had to admit that she still had a great body, even now.

She got up with the bottle of wine and handed it to him; She kissed him. *"Why don't you pour us each a glass while I get the pie for us to enjoy."*

He watched as she entered the kitchen; he poured them each a glass and then added the poison to hers. She came in with the pie, this time only wearing an apron. She smirked at him as she sat his piece in front of him. Together they toasted each other, she drank all her wine in one gulp, and he smiled.

He picked up his fork and ate his piece of pie plus another in anticipation of waiting for the poison to kick in. It didn't take long, and she was doubled over in pain, rolling on the floor in agony. When the poison hit him, he started laughing; the pain was horrible; he had joined Joann on the floor withering in the same hell he put her in.

She saw him fall, and though she was in terrible pain, she laughed maniacally.

By morning both were dead; their bodies lay there for weeks stinking with decay, until the landlady found them because they were late on their rent.

When Jack returned to their Den house, his second came to him to report on the she-wolf.

"She had a rough time for a while there, now she is sleeping normally, and her heat is all but gone now."

"Thank you for taking care of it, Sam; it couldn't have been easy." Sam laughed; it was NO dang picnic, let me tell you!"

"On a more serious note, what do you plan to do with her, Jack. I know she isn't innocent, but I feel there is more to her story than meets the eye."

"I know, Sam, many things are finally adding up, but so many questions remain unanswered."

"Have her ready to go in the morning; I want her hands bound; I want her to know she still has to face the consequences for her part in all this."

"I will take her to the King and see if she has any more information to tell us. I will let him decide her fate."

When Jack got to his room, he sat on the end of his bed in sheer exhaustion, running his fingers through his hair. His thoughts went to the things he found out about the royal house. He found it strange that the prince was off on some island, when he was scheduled to complete his Royal Guard duties.

Something isn't in the picture fully yet, and he was determined to find it. There is no way that Alpha Michael could have come up with the money to fund such an operation on this big of a scale.

He hoped to find the Alpha's account books, the real ones this time. Find out who is all tied to this. Every pack, every human, everywhere. He wanted to find all the other pack members of Rising Moon. To see how far the abuse goes, he had a feeling he wasn't going to like the answer.

Alpha Michael was in his apartments in the second-packhouse, playing nice with some big-time drug dealers interested in Aphrodite's Kiss. How to mix it for both shifters and humans.

Alpha Michael realized that tomorrow night was the full moon that his wolf had mentioned. He wondered if anything would happen. Probably not, his wolf was always a righteous prick and a coward.

Michael smiled in the darkness, thinking of his father, and wondering what he would think of what Michael did to his pack. He could still hear him yelling at him, **((What did you do this time. I simply don't understand what is wrong with you, boy.))**

His guests enjoyed themselves with a couple of his females, demonstrating how the drug works with various female species. He will know their decision in the morning. The prince decided to play the cowardly role and backed out of his deal, he didn't get refunded what he paid upfront, but Michael wasn't going to get any more money from him either.

Now that his search for that little bitch wasn't so urgent, he could take his time to get revenge. Fucking Werebear's, they messed everything up by getting involved. It doesn't matter anymore because he now knows where that stupid female is hiding. They thought they were so clever; I will show them how to be sneaky and clever.

I should know; I have pulled the wool over many inspector's eyes. Not to mention that I have kept this operation going without any shifter enforcers being aware. This is my time, and I will not lay down like some dog and let them ruin it for me.

Speaking into the darkness of his room...."*The Game is up, assholes, time for round two.*"

CHAPTER EIGHTEEN

Duncan, Apollo, Adira, and Artemis were finally played out; they sat in silence, watching the clouds roll by. Artemis let out a contented sigh, *"Well, everyone, I think it is time I explain how we get home."*

Everyone looked at Artemis; they knew she'd kept that information for later.

"We have to mate. Apollo, and I, Adira, and Duncan. In the traditional way that Goddess had designed."

"Adira, you will go off with Duncan when you find a spot you like; run, and Duncan will give chase. Once he catches you, I think you have the idea."

"Apollo and I will do the same thing somewhere else. We will continue until the third and final climax. Once that has happened, we will merge again and return to your realm. Whole again."

Adira was red as a tomato; she sensed that Artemis wasn't telling the whole truth; she'd left something out.

"Artemis, what are you not telling us.?"

Artemis looked around at everyone and sighed. *"I was hoping I wouldn't have to get to this part till we are on the other side; I suppose I should tell it all; just don't get mad at me, Adira."*

"ARTEMIS, OUT WITH IT."

"OOOK, fine. If we mate here in this realm, we will become pregnant; there is no way out of it. I know that I didn't think things through before; I was so concerned with the thought of losing you that I did the only thing I could think of to keep you alive, which was bringing you here."

"Oh, Arty, it's ok. You worried me there for a bit; I thought we had to sacrifice something to leave. I want to mate with Duncan; I am a little scared by it, but mostly because it is the unknown. I don't mind having Duncan's pups. I planned to wait for a little before taking that step; if it is to be now then that is fine to."

"After all, Artemis, we will still have to make a sacrifice; I believe the Goddess wants us to spill our virgin blood. Eww, forget I said that. It did not come out right."

Duncan didn't think Adira could get any redder, but she did. She was beautiful as a ripe strawberry.

Artemis didn't say anything more. Instead, she took off in a full-out run into the nearby forest. Apollo looked stunned for a second and then bolted off after her. She was leaving Duncan and Adira alone.

Duncan just sat there for a moment with a pleased, stupid-looking smile.

"Well, little wolf, are you going to run? I will give you a head start."

He was so excited that he felt like a young pup, staring at the Christmas tree, waiting to open the presents.

Before Duncan realized it, she was off and running; he could hear her laughter in the distance. He counted to five and took off after her.

They ended up in a field of flowers, flowers of every kind. The scent they gave off was Adira's and his, depending on which way the breeze was blowing. The fairy lights seemed brighter here; they gave off a soft glow mixed with the sunlight.

Duncan finally caught up and pounced, grabbing her around her waist and pulling her down on top of him into the flowers. *"Hello, my little wolf."* was all that was said as he pulled her head down to kiss her.

At first, it was playful, but then it became a heated passion; they tried to get their clothes off while still kissing. Neither wanting to let go of the other, a back-and-forth war of the lips as they finally achieved their goal, they were finally wholly naked. It only fueled their frenzy into something wild and primal.

One couldn't tell where one began or the other ended. Duncan couldn't get enough! Her scent was a drug he would gladly stay addicted to forever; her body was incredible, her milky white skin so soft and responsive to his every touch.

Adira couldn't get enough; his body was that of a god. His skin was a soft covering over a hard muscled body. His scent drove her higher and higher. His lips and nibbling teeth on her breast drove her insane. She could feel his manhood long and hard against her leg; now, there was a big bad wolf.

Duncan flipped them so he was on top, his weight encompassed her, and she felt safe and surrounded by his love for her. He started to kiss and lick his way down her body; he lingered over her belly button, licking, moving lower and lower until he teased her petals with his tongue. When he found her little bundle of nerves, he sucked on it, driving her to a new level of ecstasy as she arched her back in intense pleasure.

His low growls of pleasure were vibrating in her most sensitive places. Making it impossible even to think. He moved, so he was kneeling between her thighs; he positioned himself at her opening, then moved his body so it was entirely on top of her, whispering in her ear, *"Ready or not, here I come."*

With one swift thrust, he was in her all the way; she screamed in pleasure and pain. He stayed still inside her for a while so her body could adjust to his size, then he began to move out and back in slowly; she wrapped herself around him, holding on tight.

He began thrusting faster until she was mindless with pleasure, her nails raking down his back. He was kissing her deeply while she moaned into his mouth. He was so far up in her that it felt like he was touching her belly button. Just when Adira didn't think she could take anymore, she climaxed with a scream of his name and took him with her over the edge of pleasure and beyond.

Just as she was coming down from her climax, she reached up and bit him where his neck met his shoulder; they both climaxed again as he screamed her name, repeatedly, emptying his hot seed deep inside her.

Apollo chased Artemis through the forest; he would catch up to her, rubbing herself all over him, swishing her tail in his face, and take off again.

This continued for hours until they both fell into the age-old need for mating.

Adira lay exhausted on top of Duncan's chest; she didn't think it possible that they were able to do it again so soon. Duncan moved to sit up, holding her to him. Their skin was cooling in the breeze of the clearing. Duncan looked around and then smiled.

In one swift movement, he had her in his arms and started to walk in the direction of the trees. They walked for a while; Adira kissed Duncan everywhere she could reach him; she left marks all over him from her perch in his arms, claiming her territory.

Adira wasn't paying attention to the surrounding area; it was too late when she heard Duncan giggle as she felt herself flying through the air and then landing in a big splash of warm water.

She came up laughing when she stood up. Drops of water glittered in the rays of the sunset as they ran lovingly down her body. Duncan stared at her like a wolf that had just captured his prey. He started to walk into the pool of water with a purpose. Adira just laughed and swam away, splashing him as she went.

He gave her a predatory smile as he dove in after her. She avoided him for a while, mostly because he enjoyed the chase and her laughter. He was so happy that she was receptive to his love after all the crap she'd been through.

He let her control the situation a little longer, then he dived deep into the pool and came up right under her. She flew backward into the water as he caught her, wasting no time; he took her mouth in a desperately heated kiss, her lips already swollen from their previous lovemaking.

He backed her up slowly till they were at a rocky pool wall; He clasped both of her hands above her head and she wrapped her legs around him, with one forceful thrust he drove himself home; he pounded into her repeatedly as she was screaming his name; he growled when they came again.

He should have been exhausted, but he found he couldn't get enough of her. He smiled into her neck, giving her yet another mark; he will always want more of her.

Just as he was thinking of going for one more, there were two big splashes from the other side of the forest pool. Artemis and Apollo were swimming over to them; both looked incredibly happy.

"Well, is everyone ready to go home now?" Artemis asked happily and a little smugly.

Everyone reluctantly nodded.

They swam to the pool's center, then the full moon rose into the night, casting a light on them as the water began to swirl under them. They were caught in the whirlpool and merged wolves to become human werewolves. Then they knew no more.

When Duncan woke up to the sun rays of high noon coming in the window, he looked down into his arms at Adira lovingly.

He then called Apollo to see if they were all back where they belonged. Apollo answered sleepily and grumpily, *"Yes, I am here, now let me sleep."*

Duncan laid back down and lost himself, thinking of what he'd just experienced. It felt like a dream though he knew it was not; then he looked at Adira. Could she be carrying his pup already?

When he heard a laugh inside his mind, it was Artemis!!! ***"What the hell? How are you in my mind just as if you were Apollo?"***

She laughed again. *"**Silly male, we four are joined together now. I can be in you, and Apollo can be in Adira, or both wolves can join with one. There are a lot of combinations. I don't know everything about it yet.**"*

"To answer your question, yes, we carry our pup."

CHAPTER NINETEEN

Jack Dawson was like any other werebear. He preferred the deep woods. He didn't go into the bigger cities and towns. He kept to the smaller towns if he needed something; he would venture out if it were needed to the bigger cities but he preferred to stay within his realm.

Ordering online was his thing; they kept apartments in different little towns to stay in if there was a need when traveling. Each apartment was fully furnished, had internet, and television to keep up with the times. Werebears never stayed in hotels. Too many people, too many smells associated with people.

He looked over at the she-wolf sitting next to him in his jeep. Her hands were bound in front of her, and she sat with resolve; it was like she was going to her executioner. Maybe she was, she had done some pretty nasty things, some of which he believed she might have been tricked into at first; that didn't explain her later actions, though.

He didn't talk to her; he felt no need to do so. If his silence added some anxiety to her punishment, so be it.

They arrived in good time; two of the Kings guards and a servant met them at the back entrance. The guards took the female, and the servant took the one bag that Jack allowed him to touch. He would not see the female again till the morning when the King would sentence her.

Once inside, one of the king's servants motioned for Jack to follow him to the king's private chambers. Once there, he bowed and sat next to the King by a large fireplace.

"Now, Jack, please show me the evidence and tell me all that you know. I will go to the female personally to gain the rest of the information; I will find it if she has any more."

Jack flinched a little; the King has a unique ability to look into your heart and soul. It can be very invasive and can even be very painful if it is met with resistance.

Jack began with the physical evidence, and then they talked for two long hours before the King was satisfied that he had enough evidence to clean out the Rising Moon Pack.

"Your Highness, I have to say that there is a lot more to the situation than meets the eye; I still think that Alpha Michael had or still has a benefactor. "

"I looked over the financials from before; there was no way he could get something this complex and lucrative off the ground, not without an original loan or at the very least a partnership with a wealthier person."

"Jack, I want to tell you this again, so we are very clear on this. I want every guilty party punished in that pack, those who knew but did nothing; I want those who did the smallest things right up to the ring leaders. I want you to bring that Alpha Michael shit smear directly before me, unharmed."

"Yes, my King, it will be done as ordered. What of the innocent?"

"If there is any, escort them here, or if there is another pack they wish to go to, then take them there."

"Now, if you will excuse me, Jack, I have to talk to that she-wolf and see if we can get some more answers."

Lily was taken to a small cell. The guards pulled her inside, put her suitcase at her feet, and locked her in the room.

The room consisted of a small bed, big enough for one person, a small dresser, and a mirror. There was one small shelf under the barred window. The glass in the window was milky, it would let light in, but you couldn't see out of it. Everything was grey. The floor was made of some kind of hard stone of a slightly darker grey.

When she sat down on the bed, she had a feeling she was going to be here a long time. She started to put the things she was allowed to bring away with a sigh. There was a hook on the back of the door; besides the small dresser, there was nowhere else to put clothing. Not that she was allowed to bring a lot with her anyway.

When she opened the top dresser drawer, she found two towels, two washcloths, three candles, and a candle holder. Nothing to light the candles with, though. Once she was done, she kept the suitcase under the bed for extra storage. She sat down on the bed with nothing else to do. She noted that the room had no light source other than the window.

She heard the key in the lock and stood up; a tiny older woman came. She carried a tray with a cup of tea, a bowl of soup, and a sandwich. She placed it on her bed and pointed to the candle.

"The candle will be lit once every night; you will only be given the three candles to last you for the month; you will live in the dark if you run out."

The older woman opened the door and slammed it behind her; Lily could hear the key in the lock; she looked down at the food with a sigh.

She went to the door and knocked on it; another key in the lock and a guard came inside.

"I was just wondering about using the bathroom.?"

The guard looked at her without emotion on his face. He said, *"Eat first."* without letting her say anything more; he was back on his side of the door, locking it.

She sat down to eat with a sigh, finally noticing that they didn't give her any utensils to eat with.

The spy sat down in the woods just outside of the borders of Alpha Duncan's Pack territory. He was waiting for the informer to meet him. He almost got caught once when he got a little too close. He always got the creeps here; this pack is always on alert and always persistent in the knowledge of their surroundings. One missed step and he will have to explain much more than he wanted to.

The informer, well, not an informer, more like they were holding his son hostage for a little while. He didn't hear the guy come up next to him; the informer was silent as a ghost.

"I don't have anything to report other than something is going on with the werebears. Their leader is a good friend of our Alpha. He has been here twice. Usually, he doesn't travel this far south of his clan. Unless it is important."

"The female you seek is with our Alpha. No one in the pack has seen either one for almost a week now." Marco the Beta is doing all the work for the Alpha in his absence."

"That is all I have for now." Then he disappeared into the forest as silent as he came.

The spy didn't waste any time getting out of there. The informer was on the verge of deciding between saving his son and loyalty to his Alpha and pack. He knew that the informer would become more defiant; his son was always in trouble, and that is how they found out about his father; the kid was always blabbering away about everything and anything.

If they kill the kid, they lose the father. However, they could only use the kid for so long. If the father starts to suspect that his son is not in danger and that he is the mastermind who thought all this up, then the father will no longer be under our control.

As it was already, he suspected that the informer was holding back information, only telling them enough to be interested and not enough to do any damage. Alpha Michael isn't going to be happy about this. He had a feeling that his next orders regarding the informer are going to be to kill him.

The guard kept his promise when Lily was done eating and took her to the toilet. That is what it was a small hole in the wall, with a curtain for a door, no sink—nothing but a toilet and a lightbulb on the ceiling with a string.

One small toilet paper roll sat on the floor next to the toilet. The curtain didn't go down to the floor; she could see the guard's boots on the other side. Mortified, she did her business as quickly as possible and then informed the guard that she was done.

She thought she was going back to the room when she was done. Instead, the guard brought her to a double door, he knocked once, and the doors opened, inside was another guard. This one looked at her in pity. She held her head up higher. She didn't need anyone's pity.

The guard brought her into a big circular room made of stone, there were windows, but there wasn't any glass in them, just long white with gold trim curtains. The only thing in the room were two chairs facing each other in the center of the room; a massive fire roared in the fireplace on the other end of the room.

There was another door opposite the one she came through; the guard sat her down in one of the chairs, and vines came out of nowhere, restraining her to the chair so she couldn't move.

She sat straight like a lady; she was determined not to show the fear she was feeling; she didn't have much of anything left. They'd taken everything they could from her; all she had left was her defiance to live, no matter what. No one will take that away from her or her wolf, Zinnia.

Zinnia had been quiet of late; they both were resigned to the fact that it was time to tell everything and let the chips fall where they may; she knew she was messed up and did some terrible things; Zinnia went crazy there for a while after they killed their mates, Leo, and his wolf Zack.

She started to tear up again and forced it back; the guard had left, and she was alone in this room; the only sounds that could be heard were the cracks and pops of the fireplace. She closed her eyes and waited for whatever this was to begin.

CHAPTER TWENTY

$\mathcal{D}$uncan and Adira moved back into the packhouse after Adira's Luna ceremony. Duncan had felt a little uneasy all day; it was as if he was being watched, yet there wasn't anyone there. It was setting Apollo off too, making him uneasy as well.

Duncan mind-linked his second Marco, *"Could you come up to the office for a few?"*

Duncan went out into the hall to meet Marco. He still couldn't shake the feeling of being watched, which meant it was also here in the hall. What the holy hell was going on, he only felt like this when he was hunting Rouge wolves, when they were lying in wait for him.

As Marco came up the stairs, Duncan mind-linked him again, *"Act normal. Do you feel like you are being watched?"*

"Yes, I thought it was just me."

"We need to have our security system checked to see if someone has hacked it."

"Marco, check everything to do with our security but keep a low profile while doing it if you can. I don't want to spook our peeping tom."

Closing the link, they walked off in different directions; Duncan went to his bedroom to see if there was a camera; if there was, it wasn't part of the security system; it was the peeping tom. Not only that, but that would also mean that their little peeping tom was part of the pack.

Suppose the system has been hacked; that is one thing. If cameras are in places that never should have them, that can only mean one thing; as he thought before, they have a traitor.

He entered their bedroom; he made it look like he was looking for something he had forgotten. It didn't take long to find it; the camera had a full view of the bedroom. He went to the dresser, grabbed his keys, and left the room, Mind linking Marco with what he found.

Marco and Duncan went outside to discuss this latest development and find out who did this; the spy had to be found. Duncan wasn't going to tolerate his privacy being invaded, let alone Adira's privacy, God, how long had that camera been in there? He didn't think too long because he would have noticed it before.

Lily sat in the chair waiting; she was sure it was intentional; she didn't care anymore; in truth she had stopped caring long ago. She has for years vented her anger on her parents, the pieces of shit that they are. Betrayers.

She heard a faint click, and the King walked into the room; she wasn't expecting the King to show up. She didn't feel she was worthy of that, some lower-ranking official perhaps but not the King.

He sat in the other chair facing her; he didn't say anything, just looked into her eyes. She started to feel like she was sleeping; she was still awake but distant; her wolf Zinnia, came to the front pushing Lily away to protect her and take the punishment.

That is when she heard the King's mind speaking to her and her wolf.

"Alright, it is time to share everything; I want the whole story. I will know if you hold back or lie, and there will be lots of pain if you do."

Zinnia moved in front of Lily and started telling everything, telling all their secrets..."*My name is Zinnia, I am the wolf to Lily. We were born to that piece of shit pack, Rising Moon. My human Lily didn't have a chance, and neither did her half-sister Spare; their father had bartered them away the day they were born.*"

"*At first, things were good; it wasn't until we shifted our first time that things went from ok to bad and then a shit storm of pain. When the Alpha took an interest in Lily, that piece of shit took a fourteen-year-old girl and forced her to do disgusting sexual things with him.*"

"*I got sick of it, I bit him, and we were punished for it, five lashes for our first offense. It wasn't our last. When Alpha shit discovered that pain was no longer a good way to control us, he moved on to her friends.*"

"*He started slowly; he would send her pictures of them in their bedroom; twice he sent us pictures of them in the shower. It was plain to see that he would do something to them if we didn't do what he wanted.*"

"*He started stalking all of us; he would watch outside the windows at school. He would be there to pick them up from school; their parents thought the Alpha was kind enough to take time out of his busy day to ensure the girls got home safely.*"

"He made me want to vomit. I told my parents, but they said it was an honor to be chosen by the Alpha."

"Lily took the brunt of the crap of what he did to us, we did everything we were supposed to, and he still hurt our friends. Lily changed after discovering that he used her to capture her friend Anne; he flaunted it in front of us and tied us to a chair to make us watch what they did to her. They are so sick they called what they did that night Anne's breaking in the ceremony."

"Lily was never the same again; she wouldn't even talk to me anymore. She was always angry and hateful. She tortured Spare something terrible. She did that because it seemed like no one bothered her. Lily stopped when she found out what was going on with Spare."

"I couldn't reach her for a long time, not until we found our mates Leo and Zach. Leo was a Beta. He was almost done with his training and visiting from the North Moon Pack. We had to keep everything a secret; it worked for about six months. Leo was done with training and was summoned home; we would go together."

"I would be free of my pack and join his. It was the only happy time in our life. I didn't know that we were being spied on; when they told Alpha Michael what we were planning, He went crazy. They barged into our room *and shot us both with a dart gun the next thing we knew. We on woke up naked, tied to chairs in an empty room."*

"Alpha Michael came in with two others; they circled Leo, but Leo and Zach did not cave into their intimidation: they..."

The King let her rest for a minute, *"They what? Zinnia. What did they do?"*

Lily and Zinnia doubled over in pain, *"Please don't make us live it."*

"I am sorry, but I told you at the beginning that you have to tell me everything. So, you will have to relive this memory one more time. I have to know everything."

"He couldn't fight back; they kept punching and kicking him. We both tried to shift, but we couldn't. Then Alpha Michael took a small Knife and said that because Leo looked at what wasn't his, he would no longer see anything again, HE TOOK OUT HIS FUCKING EYES, HIS BEAUTIFUL EYES........"

Lily started talking, almost whispering, *"Then his lips and tongue because he kissed me, then his ears because he listened to me, then his hands because he touched me. Finally, they cut off his genitals because he fucked me. I kept screaming at them to stop. It was as if I wasn't even in the room."*

"Every time they cut off one of his parts, they would throw it at my feet."

"When he was done, Alpha Michael gagged me and turned my chair to face what was left of my lovely Leo. They left the room as I watched Leo bleed to death. I was in that room alone with him for two days."

"They came to get me the third day and brought me to some kind of exam room, it looked like a lab or something it wasn't the pack hospital."

"They found out that I was pregnant with twins, then they...they...took them out of me and put them in jars to study. Then Alpha Michael had them take out my womb so I could not have any more pups."

"Once they let us go, we couldn't feel anything anymore, nothing we were nothing. Alpha Michael had us do things; we did them without any emotions. He would rape us; we didn't care anymore. He destroyed everything that we were. He took everything we had."

"All that we had left to hang on to is our rage and the empty blackness that consumed us."

"He would have us find virgins for him, most of the time in our pack, but he was running short, so he sent us off to see find more in other packs or even rogues when we could find one."

"I always found a way to defy him, though, when it came to the children or babies. He gave me a baby to deliver to this pedophile scientist, who got off on experimenting on babies. I stopped at another pack and dropped the baby off in the night."

"He would force me to deliver drugs and guns to humans once in a while; he would send me as a reward to his men if they did a good job."

"When the Prince would visit, I was his toy slave. I would have to wear this outfit he brought with him: a silver mini skirt, no panties, and I had tousled silver pasties. He would drop things, so I had to expose myself for him to pick them up."

"I had to stand by the bed holding a towel while he fucked all the little girls and boys. He would get excited when they brought him, little boys..."

The King shouted......*"STOP!"*

"Zinnia, tell me about this prince; who is he? What is his name?"

Lily was gone; only Zinnia was there; there was no deceit in her voice, nothing held back.

"Are you sure you want me to answer that?"

"NOW!"

"It was your son, Prince Adam. He is the only benefactor of the whole operation, anything and everything that needs approval must go through Prince Adam."

CHApTER TWENTY-ONE

Adira was told that her sister was only her half-sister on her father's side. Lily was her half-sister; that explains a lot. Lily left the pack, and now she is before the King for trial and punishment. Part of Adira felt sorry for Lily; she never really had anyone. Sure, she did some terrible things, and now she will have to pay for them.

Adira just couldn't hate her, not that Lily ever gave her a reason not to hate her. She saw Lily once walking alone in the park. Adira couldn't get that image out of her mind; Lily looked full of despair and alone. Adira knew that this was Lily's true face. Since that day, Adira could never entirely hate her sister, Lily.

They were now hearing from Duncan, news from the Royal press. Her father and Joann killed each other with poison, what a fitting death; they died as they lived. Still, perhaps they got off just a bit too easy. It's for the best, though; those two might have found a way to escape punishment. They were now dead and gone. Adira decided to look no more at those memories. They took all they would get; she wouldn't give them anymore.

She wondered what punishment would be given to Lily, perhaps not death, but it is up to the King. Some of her actions led to other people's deaths. She decided to let those memories go; whatever happens to Lily now is no longer in her hands.

Duncan asked her if she wanted a say in what Lily's punishment would be, and she decided that it was best to leave it up to the King. There was a lot to Lily's story that she didn't know, and to determine her punishment was wrong because she would be prejudiced and unfair.

Adira decided that everything that had happened to her before she found Duncan on the hotel floor; was just a nightmare that would fade with time and be erased by the love in her new life.

She did feel uneasy, though; she was waiting for the other shoe to drop. If she knew anything, it was this, Alpha Michael must be punished and killed. Death was his only ending. Otherwise, he could come back and do even more evil than before. Not to mention those in the pack that liked to participate in the Alpha's sins.

She was a little down when she thought of all the potential victims and deaths of innocent lives. How many will go unaccounted and forgotten? How many are nameless and will never be found? When all this is finally over, and the evil is removed forever, she must do something as a memorial to all those unknown lost souls.

Tears began to run down her cheeks; she felt a hand catching her tears.

"My little wolf, why are you crying? I never want to see anything but happy tears in your eyes. What has gotten you so upset?"

"Alpha Michael has a lot to answer for; what could make someone so evil? There are so many bad wolves in our pack. Some knew, including myself and did nothing; some did nothing because they tried to keep their pups out of the Alpha's clutches. I don't understand how he gets away with it, I lived in that hell hole of a pack, and I still don't understand it all."

"Maybe if I would have tried harder or did something, anything, someone might be living a normal life right now."

"Little Wolf, you will not take responsibility for not speaking up, you were one of his victims, never say that you feel guilty for not doing more. If you did you would either be amongst the poor girls that got caught or dead."

Adira leaned into Duncan with a sigh, *"I was thinking of all those poor children and women, how many victims will be left unknown, lost. I want to design a memorial for all of them, so they are not forgotten. Perhaps choose a day to dedicate it to them, so no one ever forgets them or what was done."*

Duncan looked at her and kissed her on her nose. He whispered her name...*"Adira, you are the single most beautiful being on this planet; just when I think I have seen all the rays of your light, you shine even brighter than before."*

"I Love You, my little wolf, for all eternity."

" I love you, Duncan, my handsome naked knight. Thank you for being passed out on the floor of the last room I had to clean."

After the session with Lily Williams, the King sat at his desk. After learning about his son Adam's involvement, he was worn down and tired. He rested his head on his arms and started to weep.

If there was evidence to back up what Lily told him, he would have to order the execution of his son. How could Adam, the only son he had left that wanted anything to do with the royal court, could have done this, molesting and raping children? Investing Royal money into that evil business, to get it started no less. Had he raised him to be so cruel?

The King howled in pain; it could be heard throughout the kingdom and felt in every heart of every wolf within a hundred-mile radius.

Jack and the Kings guards arrived at the Kings chamber door simultaneously. Jack knocked.

"Your Highness, are you alright?" "Can we come in?"

"I am fine; I wish to be left alone tonight."

"Jack come to me first thing in the morning; I have a task for you."

"As you wish, my King."

With that, the guards went back to their duties, and Jack, with one last look at the door, turned and went back to bed. They were leaving the King alone so he can deal with the grief and anger.

Just before he went to bed, The King called for his captain of the Guards.

"I want you to take six other guards with you and bring my son back to me; I want him under guard and locked in his room. I don't wish for you to use the velvet glove either, make him as uncomfortable as you wish, I will give you further instructions once this mission is done."

The captain said nothing, simply nodded, turned, and left to do his task as ordered.

Marco gathered all the recording equipment he found around the packhouse and outside. He called two of their best trackers to look at the items; they picked up a faint scent on several of the items. They left Marco with their plan to sniff out the spy.

Now, all we must do is be patient and wait. See what the trackers find out. They were to be as silent about it as possible; they will find the culprit and then tell the Alpha who it was; from there, Duncan would decide how to deal with them.

Marco was pissed that they did that right under his nose. It had to be someone with a higher rank in the pack; otherwise, someone would have questioned their presence in the packhouse and on the Alpha's floor.

Everyone was going after the Alpha of Rising Moon, but Marco felt that Alpha Michael's Beta was just as much to blame.

The Beta would know everything his Alpha was doing; it was his job to assist and help the Alpha run his pack and allow the Alpha to achieve his goals and dreams.

In Marco's eyes, the Beta was just as guilty as the Alpha, if not more so; it is the Beta's job to assist. That meant that the Beta was the one finding him new avenues and women to abuse.

Alpha Michael has pissed yet again; being pissed was becoming his natural state lately; nothing was going the way he wanted.

Two of the females in his pack that were marked to be taken, have come up missing. It was suspected that they had run away the night before.

His drug suppliers were running short of the things they needed to continue and wouldn't be able to make the deadline. His drug handlers are insisting on raising their pay. His Beta has been ignoring him; he will have the shit beaten out of him when he sees him again.

Those stinking Werebears took a shipment of Aphrodite's Kiss worth Seven hundred and fifty thousand dollars; God only knows where it ended. Knowing those assholes, they probably drank it, thinking it was some sort of fancy wine.

Three more of his enforcers came back, this time in garbage cans. Damn, those Bears are a fucking pain in the ass.

Michael has heard nothing from the prince; he knew that the prince wouldn't betray him. Not after all the blackmail material he had on him, all he had to do was tell the Prince that he was going to go to daddy and he would have total control.

His brother and sister-in-law killed each other, they were always stupid, but he really underestimated their stupidity. He found out that his brother was taking money from the business; and transferring it to an untraceable account. Sixteen million gone.

No one knows where Lily took off to; knowing that bitch she is probably spreading her legs for those disgusting Werebears. She will keep her ugly, little mouth shut if she knows what's good for her.

Then there was Spare; she made him think she was hiding out with the Bears; instead, she spread her legs for the King's Hound, Alpha Duncan. Now she is the Luna of his pack, making it harder for Michael to get to her. He will get her, though. Make no mistake, that little bitch will pay for what she has done to him.

Soon he will have her; he must be patient and bide his time.

She is going to pay and pay hard.

CHAPTER TWENTY-TWO

Lily was in another room. It wasn't much different than the last, only this one also had a small bathroom attached, and everything was done in every shade of Tan. None of her things were given back to her. With nothing to do, she just lay on the bed and waited. Zinnia wrapped herself around Lily; they were both resigned to their fate.

They were both hoping for a death sentence. It was no more than they deserved, and it would mean they could be with Leo and Zach again. Without them, there wasn't any point in living, every day is just pain.

Just as she was about to drift off to sleep, the door opened to reveal one of the King's guards. Thinking to each other, well, this is it.

Her hands were bound before her as they walked down the empty corridors to the King's court chambers. Those they did meet would avert their eyes away, saying nothing.

The doors opened, and before her was the King on his throne, Jack Dawson, and the panel of elders. The only person not in place was her representative, every trial had the defendant's representative, yet hers was empty. Not that she expected any, but she thought there might be someone.

In the center of the room stood a huge male in an executioner's robe and cowl. He held a very sharp silver sword; it shined in the light like a bright beacon of death.

Lily walked into the room, curtsied to the King, and nodded to the elders in respect. She stood in her circle on the floor. She stood straight and silent. Then the King did something she never thought would happen; he stood up and walked to the place where her representative would stand. He gave up his right to sentence Lily or have any say in the prosecutorial proceedings.

Those in the common's balcony all gasped. (The commons balcony is where everyday citizens could watch the proceedings of the court.)

The King spoke to the whole room, not just the elder council.

"I come before you today not as the King but as this woman's representative. I do this because I am the only witness to the truth of her story and because there isn't anyone left to stand here on her behalf."

175

"I have given all of you the interrogation record, my notes, and evidence against her actions. As her representative, it is my duty to point out the reasons for her actions. I ask that you consider the abuse she suffered and the horrible way she lost her mate and pups."

"She willingly did terrible things; most of the time she didn't have any control of what she was being forced to do, there were a few times though when she was so enraged that she did things willingly."

"She had no guidance to tell her otherwise. Once her mate was killed in that horrible manner, her pups ripped out of her body and her wolf also had left her for a time in pain. Thus, she did things out of anger and pain that she may have not normally done."

"None of these things can say that the actions of her choices were not hers; she chose to do what she did. For this, she will have to be punished, abused or not. All that I ask is that you take the sentence of Death off the table."

With that, the King went to stand next to Lily, as is his place as the representative at the time of sentencing. The council of elders got up and went into the side chambers to discuss the case and punishment.

The King was compassionate for what she had been through; no one should have had to suffer as she has. Understanding why doesn't change the fact that the crimes were committed, nor does it excuse the severity of those crimes.

He had to admit that she stood strong and ready for what was to come; she was sorry for what she had done, but she understood what is done, is done; there is no going back. If she was to die for what she had done, she was at least ready to face it. He wondered how she would face a sentence other than death, though.

Lily was surprised when the King stepped in to be her representative; she wasn't exactly his friend when she delivered the news of his son. She wasn't a good person, and she had been through some tough crap. She was sorry for those she hurt who didn't deserve it, especially Spare.

The only family she had left, perhaps Spare could forgive her one day. What is done is done. There is no going back, only forward to wherever or whatever that may be. The room was as silent as the grave; no one spoke as they read about her and the things she went through. The council of elders has been out now for over an hour.

Lily went inside herself to be with Zinnia; they both sat together, watching the sunset in Zinnia's world. Zinnia looked at Lily, now comes the night, my little one. Perhaps it will rise with a few stars to light our way.

The King watched the she-wolf as she went inside herself to be with her wolf. He usually would not allow for such a thing, since he was her representative and no one else could say no, he let it be. Let her have a little time with the only being who understands her completely.

Just as the King was getting a bit tired of waiting, the council of elders came out of their chambers to tell them of the charges, verdict, and punishment.

Everyone in the Kings Court Room stood waiting for the sentence to be handed down to the accused.

"We, the Council of Elders, recognize this as a unique and tragic case. How do you punish someone who has been punished all their life, then to commit other crimes for which they were predisposed to do, with only the teachings of their own experience to rely on."

"How do we judge someone who has already faced the executioner?"

"Still the crimes were committed, as to her admission she willingly committed some of these crimes knowing they were wrong."

"It is for this reason we sentence you, Lily Williams of the Rising Moon Pack, to a year of servitude for every person that you were directly responsible for causing their death and a half of a year for every person you were responsible for hurting indirectly."

"As there is no way for us to be sure of the exact numbers, we have decided that since you have been alive for 19 almost 20 years, you will serve 20 years plus an extra 5. Your sentence will start at sunrise tomorrow morning. You will start as the official floor scrubber, from sunrise to sunset."

"You will not talk to anyone; if you must converse, then nod your head. You will be given your daily instructions by the King's personal butler in written form. No one will be allowed to talk to you or touch you any-way. Penalty for talking to someone is death; penalty for anyone talking to you will be their death."

"At the end of the 25 years, you will be given a choice to continue as a servant of higher standing, or be allowed to leave as you are, with the same things you came here with."

Lily said nothing as she was escorted out of the room; they led her to the same room she spent the night before. On the bed was a napkin; she opened it, it was a sandwich and an apple for her dinner. On the back of the door, she noticed two uniforms hanging. She was tired, and there was soon going to be no light as the sun was setting; she ate her dinner and laid down on the bed to sleep.

Duncan and Adira got a summons from the King; it didn't say why, only that they were to come within the week. Duncan wasn't concerned, but Adira was a nervous wreck. He held her in his arms as she rested the back of her head on his chest.

"Listen, my little wolf, there is nothing to fear; the King is a good man. I think he wants to meet the girl that was named Spare. I also think he is calling his closest friends for support; he has a terrible choice to make about his son."

"We will spend the weekend there, possibly the week, so you don't have to pack everything you own. Once we get there, I will have a little surprise for you. Now get ready. We leave in an hour."

The Spy waited for his informant to come, and once again, the bastard snuck upon him.

"Well, you said you have information; what is it?"

"If I tell you this, can you promise that you will not hurt or kill the Luna?"

"I promise that I won't hurt or kill your Luna."

"Duncan and Adira are going to the royal gardens to answer the King's summons; they will be taking the car and are

heavily guarded. They will be staying for the weekend. You may have the chance you are looking for. They will not be so closed off or guarded as heavily if you go there. They will not be taking the same route home; I don't know what that is going to be."

"Now, are you going to free my son?"

"He will be free if this turns out for our benefit; if not, then perhaps another arrangement could be made."

The Spy looked around, and that damn informer was gone again. *"I've got to find out how he does that."* As for not hurting or killing Luna, he told the truth on that. He wasn't going to be the one to hurt her or kill her. That job belonged to his Alpha.

CHAPTER TWENTY-THREE

The informer was coming out of the woods to the back of the Packhouse when a shadow moved into the light. It was the Beta Marco.

"Hello Nolan, out for a run?"

"Hey there, Marco. Yeah, I was out for a run."

"You are going to be busy tomorrow, I know as gamma, you oversee the training, and you decide who is going to be doing what and all that; I am sending you four new wolves who need some training. Is it ok to send them?"

"Yeah, it's good, Beta Marco. I have room in the intermediate class if that will suit their needs."

"Thank you, Gamma Nolan, it helps out a lot. Well, see you around then." Marco nodded and went off into the woods; Nolan assumed he was off for his daily run along the border as part of his duties.

Marco stood just inside the tree line, watching the Gamma go into the packhouse. He now knew who their traitor was. He turned and with a heavy heart, headed into the woods to trace Nolan's trail, to see where he met his spy. Just before he shifted, he mind-linked Duncan to tell him who their traitor was and not to trust him.

Alpha Michael listened to his spy report, thinking that this was the perfect time. He was going to get her himself, no more bumbling idiots. He's going to send a team in to get her too, he will use them as bait for his distraction.

They will keep them focused on them, while no one would be looking for him. They wouldn't even think to go looking for him there, thinking that he would want to avoid areas where he could be captured.

He will have his revenge on the whole lot of them, starting with their Luna. He has a special room all made up just for her, her special room, and he spared no expense. After all, she is a Luna, and protocol has to be maintained, don't want them to think he didn't have any manners.

Once he had her, no one was going to find her, they would come here looking, but she won't be here, and neither would he. They are going to the honeymoon cabin, where he took only his special girls.

He will, after all, need a stress reliever, it has been a very busy week for him. It ended today when he had to kill his Beta. The fool thought that I had gone too far and was putting everyone in danger of discovery, he thought he could take my place.

Well, surprise, I got him first. Poison and women are the best ways to kill a male. Too bad his Beta never learned that lesson.

He was no fool, as soon as he heard about Lily being before the King, he knew that little bitch would spill her guts out. He would have his fun at the honeymoon cabin with his little Spare. When he was done with her, he would hang her from the hooks in the rafters like a trophy for all to see, then he would take his money, and go where no one would find him.

This time when he starts up the business again, he will make sure there are no loose ends left to take care of or any Kings to answer to.

The Prince was enjoying his afternoon bath, he was being washed by two beautiful maids. Music was playing softly in the background. Another maid was feeding him fruit and dates, she would place them between her breasts, and he would have to go in to get them.

They were all laughing, as another servant served them wine. The prince had the servant put a small amount of Aphrodite's tears into the bottle, the young maids were getting quite heated, it was wonderful. He will have them all over and over tonight.

It had been a good day for the prince, until he heard the noise of boots hitting stone. In marched his father's Captain and six of his best warriors. They wasted no time, the girls scattered as the warriors grabbed him out of his bath, dragging him naked and dripping through the halls of the Prince's Summer House.

They tied him up and gagged him, tossed him into the back of a van, and drove off to the airport.

The prince was frantic with fear, he wasn't sure if this was about his involvement with that pack or something else, perhaps a military coup. At least he hoped that this was a takeover, it had to be, his is father would never hurt him like this, he would yell at him and take away perhaps a toy or two, but that was it.

Then it hit him, they were kidnapping me to make sure that I marry that dog faced princess. That would be a fitting punishment, after all. He smiled at that thought, it didn't matter anymore if he had to marry that ugly bitch.

He was going to have his own special place soon, that he could visit any time he wished, so he could enjoy his dirty little desires.

He tried to shift into his wolf, but nothing happened; that was when he noticed that he was bound with silver cords wrapped in cloth. It won't burn him, but he won't be shifting into his wolf again till they are removed.

Didn't matter anyway, his wolf had been refusing him lately and had gone silent, he always was a coward and a bit crazy.

He cursed the Captain from the back of the van, vowing that the Captain of the guard would be the first to go when he becomes King.

Adira was in awe of the Royal Gardens; you would think it would be part of a big city. Instead, it was at the base of two mountains, there was a castle, but it blended in with the rock and trees.

Other houses surrounded it, some as large as packhouses, three or four stories high. Then there were others that were smaller and blended in with the wild of the mountains.

There was a smaller human city about four miles from here, the city called this place the resort. She gave a giggle when she heard that if they only knew. The city, though, was a lovely kind of city, well taken care of and its residents seemed happy enough.

They were also incredibly grateful for the resort because they donate money to the town when it is in need. They also sponsor programs for children and teenagers for schooling. They are also responsible for the well-equipped hospital.

As they got closer to the castle, Adira realized it was much bigger than it looked. Perhaps it was an illusion that made it look smaller. Most of the place was carved from the surrounding stone of the mountain. As they went up the final drive, Adira saw why it was called "Royal Gardens" it was nothing but flowers, mostly roses of every kind everywhere. It was beautiful and breathtaking.

When they pulled up to the main entrance, six servants and four guards greeted them.

Duncan held out his hand for Adira to take; he led them up to the servants, all lined up for inspection. Adira wasn't used to this sort of thing; she greeted them by asking them questions and shaking their hands.

When they went into the castle, the servants all scrambled to get their things to their room. They were happy because they usually did not get the nice ones. Usually, all they would get were the demanding snobs.

No one realized they had a watcher in the shadows at that moment, watching and waiting.

The Gamma, now Beta of Rising Moon Pack, was getting worried and frustrated. Since the Alpha went off to god knows where, they have had constant attacks on all their shipments going in and out. It was those damn Werebears; they were nothing but a bunch of smartass assholes.

They never attacked the same place twice. He even made his routes random daily, still, the bastards found them. It was getting out of hand; with the Alpha gone, he was unsure how to manage it. So he decided that they were going to go into shut down for a couple of days.

Lock the whole place down; everyone will be locked either in the packhouse or the warehouse. Two females are about to give birth, and the midwife is missing. The high-end clients were no longer coming in after hearing about that stupid bitch's trial.

Not to mention the highlight of his hell week, their Luna hung herself from the fourth-floor window. That was a mess to clean up; over half a dozen pack members were witnesses. He had to make up a story, saying that it was just a sick joke.

He wasn't sure how many bought the story, but he knew they wouldn't ask too many questions. They knew what happened in this pack if you went sniffing around.

Whatever the Alpha was up to, he better get it done quickly, or he isn't going to have a pack to come back to. Already he had noticed that a few of the innocent families had left in the night.

You can't have them all leaving, they wouldn't have a source in which to use for their inventory. He had the enforcers going around the pack houses, warning them not to leave, if they do, they will all end up missing. Fights are breaking out amongst all pack members; it is a very tight rope they are all dancing on.

CHAPTER TWENTY-FOUR

The Prince was getting a little worried, usually, when his father sent guards to fetch him, he was always waiting for him to come through the door and pounce on him, yelling and screaming.

This time there was nothing, they walked him down a silent and empty hall. When they reached his room, they tossed him in and locked the door. He wasn't worried about being locked in he had plenty of other ways to get out of this room.

He walked to his closet and put on one of his more formal uniforms. He then went to the other side of the room, where a secret panel was hidden, that led out to the gardens. He snickered as he crossed the room, when he got to the panel, however, it didn't open. No matter, he went to the trap door by his bed, it was sealed shut.

With a little bit of unease, he went to his balcony, when he opened the doors, he was met with bars. He sat down on his bed, this time, he felt fear creeping up his spine. Something was wrong, perhaps it was a military coup after all. He won't know till he visits his father if they let him see his father.

He remembered that he'd left his laptop in his adjoining study, he opened the door and found the room was empty. Literally empty, there was nothing, just open room, and empty bookshelves, even the curtains were gone. He rushed over to the bookcase in the middle and moved it away from the wall, he then tapped the hidden panel to find his safe.

He opened it, and to his horror, there was nothing inside. He cursed and kicked the bookcase till he calmed down. He went over to the bell pull and gave it a tug, but nothing. He did it again, again nothing. Usually, when he tugged on it, a servant came running to do his bidding. Now only silence.

He started to throw a fit, smashing things left and right. Completely destroyed an old priceless table and chair set. When he was done, he listened to see if anyone was coming, there was only silence.

That was when he noticed an envelope on the floor by the door, it was an official invitation with his name written on it. It was his father's handwriting, he opened it. All that was in there was a simple invite, he was to dine with his father in his private rooms at 7pm in two night's time.

He went over to the bar area to get a drink, he looked through all the shelves and storage closet, nothing, not a single drop of anything.

Well, I guess the cat's out of the bag now, he is going to have me marry that dog faced princess. I will probably be under lock and key till we have at least our first child. He couldn't wait to be King and rid of all this nonsense. Perhaps it is time that dear old dad met with a tragic accident.

He had been planning it for years now, he even had three plans to do it. Then he remembered that those plans were on his laptop. Shit........

Duncan was asked to go to the King in his private chambers as soon as he arrived. When he got there, he wasn't surprised to see Jack there too. He gave Jack a hug in greeting, and they sat down with their longtime friend and King.

They were worried about him, he looked sick, tired, and older. His son was killing him from the inside out. He greeted them, but then he went silent again. Both Duncan and Jack looked at each other in concern.

"Your Highness, please talk to us, tell us what has you so troubled?"

"As you already know, it is my son that grieves me so. What have I done to make him hate me so much? I already was dealing with heartache when I learned what he had done. Then this morning, before my son arrived, I looked through his laptop. He has plans, yes, more than one plan, to kill me off."

"He wrote it all down as if it was nothing more than another chore he would have to take care of. It was in so much detail, two of the plans were almost flawless, he would have gotten away with it for sure. He was just waiting for the right time, waiting for the right opportunity."

"Then I find out that the money he used to invest in that horrible pack operation, came from the peoples' coffers. He stole the peoples' money, to open a business that would rape, torture, kill innocent children and women. Even grown men. They thought of humans as no more than tissue paper, to be used and disposed of. They don't think much about our species either."

The King went quiet again, then he grabbed his head and began to yell out in a voice that was filled with pain.

"MY SON, MY SON DID THIS. MY SON WANTS ME DEAD, MY FUCKING SON IS A MONSTER, MY SON, MY SON.......WHY?"

"I LOVE YOU, MY SON...... MY SON, WHY?.....WHY?...."

The king let out a howl of rage and sorrow, shifted into a huge golden wolf, taking off an jumping out the window, into the last rays of the sunset. Duncan and Jack shifted and went after him. When they cleared the window, they noticed two other rather large wolves going after the king. They realized that it was two of the Kings personal guard.

Adira was sitting in her very fancy room, enjoying some alone time to just be at peace and talk with Artemis about their pup. She was also worried about the King after hearing of the prince's betrayal, she didn't know the details, but it couldn't be good if it involved Rising Moon.

She heard the most painfully sad howl she had ever heard. She could feel the pain, it had to be the king, only he is powerful enough to project that so strongly.

She was just thinking of going to the balcony to see if everything was ok, when the doors to the balcony burst open, and there stood a beautiful golden wolf, the look in its blue eyes made her heartache for him.

She wasn't sure what he wanted till he padded over to her and laid his head in her lap, whimpering. She pet his head slowly to comfort him. Why he came here, she didn't know, she hadn't even been introduced yet. She let him stay there, softly petting his fur till she felt him calm.

It was then that two more wolves jumped into the room, followed by her mate and a big grizzly bear. Duncan went into the other room and came back wearing pants. He mind-linked Adira, asking if she was ok.

"I am fine, Duncan, but why is the King and his wolf seeking comfort on my lap?"

"Perhaps because you have a very nice lap."

Adira gave him a dirty look, "Really Duncan, jokes are a bit out of place at the moment."

"I don't know why he came here, perhaps he needed a safe place to let go of his sorrow. You project that you know, you and Artemis both do, now that you are with pup, it is even more intense. Either way, do you mind if he stays there for a little while?"

"Of course not Duncan, he can stay as long as he needs to."

With that, Adira slid off the chair and unto the floor, as the King wrapped himself around her, keeping his head on her lap, falling asleep.

The two guards mind-linked Duncan, telling him that it is the first time since he found out about his son, that he has slept. Without waking the King, Duncan put pillows and blankets on the floor so Adira would be more comfortable. Adira mind-linked them all at once, using her Luna abilities.

"I don't care what he has to do today; cancel it, furthermore, I would like for you to bring in food and some herbal tea. Oh, one more thing, the only naked wolf allowed in my room is my mate. So bring the king some clothes, please."

Jack being the smartass that he is, mind-linked back.

"Well, I know that you said no naked wolves, but how do you feel about naked Bears?"

"If you parade around my room naked, Jack Dawson, I will find a way to shave both you and your Bear bald."

Duncan started laughing as all the males exited the room, the guards assumed position outside the door, and Duncan and Jack went off to get the things that The Luna asked for.

Adira looked down at the King with a sigh, *"The world is an unfair, nasty place sometimes. I am so sorry about your son. If you like, we will name you our child's godfather, that way you can visit and play all you want. No strings attached."*

She started to hum a song; she wasn't even aware she knew. It was somewhere over the rainbow. As she continued, the King's breathing became deeper as he went further into sleep.

Lily was cleaning the steps and sidewalks of the main entry courtyard when she saw movement out of the corner of her vision. When she turned fully to get a better look, whatever it was, it was already gone. She shook her head at the feeling, it felt like Alpha Michael's presence for a second.

It was that same creepy feeling she would get when he would watch her and her friends play in the forest.

He would haunt her day and night till she was dead. Letting it go, thinking it was just a figment of her imagination, she went back to her sweeping.

CHAPTER TWENTY-FIVE

The prince lay on his bed in his room, it was getting late, and still, no one came in. He was getting hungry; he gave a sigh at his discomfort. He got up to bang on his door again when he heard the most painful howl, he knew in an instant that it was his father.

Good, he thought. At least he wasn't the only unhappy wolf in this castle. Still, that howl made him feel worried. What was going to happen to him? What kind of punishment was his father going to inflict on him? His wolf let out a whimper inside him and then went silent again.

Just as he was about to bang on the door again, two guards came in with a tray. They sat it on the floor and locked the door again. When the prince lifted the lid covering the food, he grimaced. It was two slices of plain bread and a cup of water. That was when he felt things might be worse than he originally thought they would be.

Still, though he won't be treated like the others that get caught, there won't be a public trial or punishment for him. It will all be done under the table, to save face for the royal family. That was always his ace in the hole. Whenever he would get into trouble he would play the Royal card, either buy his way out or intimidate them into silence.

Well, if his Dad found his laptop and his financial records, then as the King, he would be pissed. This means that the elder council has also seen all the evidence. Shit, I am screwed this time. Better get used to the horse faced princess, he had a feeling that his days of fun were over.

They will have a big fancy Royal wedding to distract the people about their prince's dirty deeds. He will get married and must start a family as soon as possible, while he is being watched day and night.

As far as the plans on his laptop to kill his father, he will just say he was thinking about writing a book about a king killer. He would never hurt his father; how could they think such a thing........The Prince started laughing and couldn't stop.

Marco and two of his most trusted hunters were waiting at the spy's meeting place. Marco had already put Nolan in the dungeon, he then had Nolan text the spy, saying that he had more information for him and to meet at their normal spot.

The fact that this wolf called himself a spy was a joke. They could hear him a mile away, and he stunk of drugs, sweat, and sex. It was enough to make all three of them want to vomit. Marco decided that the first thing this guy was going to get in the dungeon, was a much-needed bath, sort of like a bath anyway.

When the spy reached the meeting spot, they all surrounded him. The spy was surprised at their presence, geesh, what an idiot. They were not even really hiding from him. What kind of wolves do they have in that pack?

They tossed him onto his stomach, bound his feet to his hands and a rope around all of it, and proceeded to drag him out of the woods on his stomach. When his little girl screaming got too much, they stopped long enough to gag him.

They decided to drag him, because not one of them wanted that stench close to them. Perhaps some dirt and leaves from the forest floor will help to improve his smell.

The King woke up in a bunch of soft blankets on a floor, whose floor? There was soft morning light coming in from the open balcony, a gentle breeze moved the curtains. There was the scent of blossoms everywhere, it was coming from outside.

"If you are awake, your highness, there are clothes for you on the bed. Please put them on and join me for some breakfast."

Normally he would be a little put out if someone ordered him around, but this voice was soft, and it was more like a request than an order. He put on his clothes and stopped for a minute. He didn't remember the night before, he, ummm, didn't sleep with someone, did he?"

His wolf started to laugh, something he hadn't heard in a long time.

"No, we did not sleep with someone last night, not like you are thinking anyway. We found refuge in our grief."

He went out on the balcony, and there at a table was a lovely young she wolf and then it dawned on him. Even though he had yet to meet her, this had to be Duncan's Luna, Adira. The female that was once named Spare.

He sat down and just looked out at the fall gardens; his heart still heavy. The sun had come out from behind the clouds and the air though crisp was refreshing.

She handed him a cup of tea and served him a plate of food. It was pancakes, sausages with a side of bacon, and scrambled eggs. It smelled heavenly.

When he tasted them, he was surprised. They were delicious, lately his doctor has been giving the cook instructions, and his food has been a little lacking.

"This is wonderful, Luna Adira."

"Thank you, I asked your cook for the use of her kitchen, so I could make you breakfast."

"I know you have some serious and terrible choices to make today. I also think that for just this little moment in time, you could just be you and relax. I know that is hard and that this timing might be off, I do not think so, though. This is what you need, to get back your strength."

"What is it you think I need, some really good food? To make all this better?"

"No, your highness. You need to feel again, the sunshine on your face, the smell of the blossoms in the air, and the taste of good food. I suspect that you have not allowed yourself even the simplest of pleasures for a very long time."

"Once everything happens today, the world will be dark again. I want you to remember this moment and what I tell you."

"Oh, and what might that be? Just be happy, dance around, and chase rainbows?"

"No, your highness, all I ask of you, is to remember to just breathe."

He looked at Adira speechless as tears formed in his eyes, *"How did you know?"*

She looked at him with a look that said she did not understand.

"Those were the same words my wife spoke to me before she left this world to be with the Goddess."

"When things for me got really bad, or I was starving as a young pup, I would cling to those words, I would tell myself, Just breathe Spare, just breathe; you know things will work out, and I would go on."

The King stared at her and then said...

"How in all that is good and holy, did that dark shit hole of a pack ever give way to such a bright and beautiful light?"

They sat there in happy silence and sunshine, as the King and his Wolf prepared themselves for what was to come.

Before he left, she stopped him.

"Your Highness, do your heart some good, don't manage matters today alone. Let this burden be carried by more than

just you alone. Tonight, you dine for the last time with your son, and then tomorrow, he will face the council alone for judgement."

"Don't discuss anything that has anything to do with this trial, just for this last time, be father and son. It won't be easy, but if you manage to do it, you will not regret it."

Once the King had left, Duncan came in and sat down where the King just was sitting. He looked at Adira in wonder.

"Do you know what the King just told me in the hallway?"

"He took me by the shoulders and said that if I ever hurt you or make you cry, he will come himself, and personally beat the living shit right out of me. Then he is going to take you back here and make you his queen."

"Then he said that we are now family, that you are to be called Lady Adira the Luna of Storm Crow Moon pack and of Crystal Moon Pack, it is the King's birth pack. Our pups will be his grandchildren. Not only in name but in an official compacity. He said he wants at least six."

"What did you two discuss in here anyway? Whatever it was must have been epic."

"Duncan, we didn't discuss anything other than the truth."

Duncan went over to her and knelt down on one knee in front of her, I wanted to do this as soon as we got here, out in the gardens, but things happened.

"Will you, Adira Spare Williams MacPatton, be not only my Mate but also my Wife?"

He opened a little blue box, inside was a gold ring, in the center of the band were two hearts holding a diamond in the middle of them. Like the love that their hearts share, brilliant and bright.

She jumped into his arms, knocking him on the floor, and started to kiss his face frantically while giggling at the same time, saying *"Yes"* over and over in between kisses.

Things quickly became heated, and they both lost their sense of time and space. Duncan made love to his Lady right there on the balcony floor in the spotlight of the sun.

Everyone in the gardens and that side of the castle heard their joyous cries of pleasure, including one angry Alpha Michael hiding in the shadows, waiting for the right time. He was sickened and enraged at hearing Spare's cries of pleasure.

He wondered why his men were not creating the distraction they were sent to do. They need to hurry up, he wasn't going to stand listening to this again.

CHAPTER TWENTY-SIX

Jack Dawson watched from the shadows of a doorway, watching two men who had been asking all day how to get into the castle. Seriously, killing these two idiots felt like he would be doing their species a favor. He was astonished at their stupidity; they did not even bother to be quiet about what they wanted.

The Morons even asked if there was a secret way into the Lady's quarters. He shook his head; how could Rising Moon do all this evil crap and not get caught? Did we kill the only smart ones when they came into our territory? Seriously, how did they do it?

Yesterday, two more; were caught trying to climb into a window on the castle's east side. The dumbasses managed to climb into the guard barracks. They were promptly taken care of and questioned.

They squealed like little girls, easily giving away their plan and that there were two others as well. They also blurted out that one other spy was working secretly on his own.

Jack waited for the two morons to walk past him; when they did, he broke the neck of the first one instantly. The other started running; Jack shifted into his bear and chased the screaming idiot for two hours, it would have been a lot sooner, but he was getting some exercise and having a bit of fun before finally ending it.

Jack had a feeling that the spy was not exactly a spy, he was the real threat instead, and these idiots were just a distraction. They all smelled like they were from Rising Moon. So, they were not hired out from another pack. That means their targets had to be Lady Adira and Duncan. He headed back to the castle to find Duncan and share his ideas on how to handle this.

Marco stood over Gamma Nolan with his arms crossed and an angry face. Nolan had seen better days, his face was swollen, and he could not see out one eye. He now knew what a punching bag felt like.

"Nolan Ex Gamma of the Storm Crow Moon Pack, you will tell me everything you said to that piece of smelly shit spy; you will also explain yourself and why you betrayed our pack. I

better like your answers, or you are going to die an excruciating death."

Nolan spit out a wad of blood and teeth before speaking,

"Marco, please, they have my son. He has been into drugs for a while now; no matter what I said or did made no difference; they would kill him if I did not tell them what they needed to know."

"I told them nothing of importance; everything I said to that spy was already common knowledge in the Pack. There were cameras placed, but I didn't send them any footage; I told them there was a problem that I had to fix."

"Why didn't you come to me or the Alpha, Nolan?"

"I was ashamed of him and myself for what I let my son do to me. He has used up all his mother's money; he continues to ask for more. I said no; finally, I did not have it. I guess that was when he went over to that Rising Moon pack; Please punish me as you see fit; I understand the rules and the punishments for breaking them."

"Tell me everything you told them, even if you thought it was of no importance."

It was a long night for ex-gamma Nolan; he told them everything in the end. As for the spy, Marco was leaving him for the Alpha to take care of. Marco hoped it was sooner than later; the guy was stinking up the dungeon even after they hosed him down.

Marco called Duncan immediately, telling him everything he found out and what he was doing with the prisoners until Duncan returned to the pack.

He also told Duncan they opened the trunk when they found the spy's vehicle and found two incredibly young, frightened girls around seven years old. He sent them to the pack doctor and was in the process of finding their parents.

Duncan told Marco what he wanted to be done with the spy. As for gamma Nolan, he is to stay in the dungeon; he will be given one healthy meal a day and water twice a day. As for the rest, he can sleep in his cell like any other prisoner. No one is to speak to him. Nolan can stay there till we find his son, and then they can switch places.

The prince quickly dressed in his royal ceremonial attire; it was never a good idea to keep a King waiting. It does not matter if he was your father. Three guards then came and marched him to his father's private rooms.

When the Prince knocked on the door, his father answered, *"Come in, Adam."*

He cheered when he heard those words; his father was an old fool. All he had to do now was play nice and charm his father once more. Then everything will just get swept under the rug. He will have to do some stupid community service crap to make his family look good and then he could go back to playing again.

He smiled as he opened the door; his father sat at the end of the dining table with an expression that Adam did not understand. It gave him the chills. The look he had when he made a difficult decision, and the answer wasn't going to be one that anyone wanted. He shrugged it off as not eating much the last couple of days.

"Come and sit down, my son; you must be starving now. I have taken the liberty of ordering your favorite dishes. There is also your favorite wine, and the kitchen took the time to make two of your favorite desserts."

Adam was so happy he could burst, food, real food. He wasted no time and began eating like it was a mission. His father slightly smiled while he watched his son enjoy the meal.

The King watched his son in disappointment; he just went right into eating and didn't ask about his predicament or what punishment awaited him. Sadly, he concluded that his son must be insane; it did run in the family, though distant. He even had given his son a look, his son did not seem to react.

He still remembered the day that Adam was born, his first time riding a bike, learning to read, his first shift into his wolf, and even potty training. He was very stubborn with that one. The King decided to smile and pretended that this was just an ordinary dinner with his son.

Even if it were the last dinner, he would ever have with his son. He still had his youngest son, but what good would it do? His youngest wanted nothing to do with him or the crown. He will not even answer his letters or inquiries about his grandchildren.

Deciding to leave those thoughts behind and try to enjoy the evening, without the cloud of death looming in the air.

"So Adam, perhaps after dessert, you can play the piano for me; I love to hear you play. It relaxes me. Then perhaps I can read to you like I used to and discuss the topic afterward; I would love to hear you give your opinion one more time."

As Adam thought, he would have to play nice and smile, dance a merry tune for his father, listen to his boring stories, and then all this stuff will disappear in the morning, and he would have a mild reprimand and could go back to making his all his plans come to fruition.

"Sure, father, I would love to. Sounds like fun."

The night went well. They laughed and talked, and Adam played four songs on the Piano. They had wine and cigars. They had black forest cake with coffee; the night went on for hours. They went through old photo albums and talked about their fun memories together.

At midnight, there was a knock at the door; the guard took the prince back to his room. Adam looked at his father and hugged him.

"I knew you would understand, Dad. I will take the punishment and marry the princess, and all will be fine once again."

The King smiled back, *"I will love you, son. Always and forever."*

Then Adam happily left his father, not knowing it was for the last time.

The Werebear clan got the word from their leader Jack, it was time to clean house on that Rising shit Moon pack. They were to go to the factory and warehouses first. Kill anyone found to be guilty and free the innocent, taking them to three different pack hospitals.

From there, the victims would get all the physical and mental help they needed, and they could start the process of finding temporary homes till their families could be located.

If any of the victims decide to just run for some reason, track them down quietly and see if they need medical attention. If they seem all right, let them run. Any of the girls who come to you for help, give them any support within your power to do so.

"Remember, they have been traumatized repeatedly, so some might not exactly have all their fries with their happy meal. Treat them gently even if they go wild on your ass, restrain them only if you absolutely must, till the pack hospital can safely deal with them."

"Then we will go to both Pack houses and the remaining residences of the pack and clean it all out. When all houses are empty, they are to light the whole thing on fire and let it burn to the ground."

They were also to burn the forest surrounding the pack territory within a five-mile radius. For the burning, they will use a spelled fire called Ghost Flame. It burns hot, fast, and best of all, humans cannot see it. So, the fire department will not show up to ruin the party.

Once it was done, they were to return to their clan house; if they wanted to, they could take in some of the refugees, till the King could find places for them all. *"Ensure they are mentally normal, ask Hilda, the elder, to scan them for any lies."*

"If anyone steps out of line, you have permission to kill them on the spot. Make sure that you tell them that. It might help keep things calmer and under better control."

"The King wants you to find as many of the head pack members involved and behead them. He wants you to send the heads to him and let the bodies burn. However, if that piece of crap Alpha happens to be home, he will be taken before the King. The King wants no harm to him and wants him fit for trial and punishment."

"Rising Moon Pack will no longer exist, all records of it will be taken from the books, and there will be a royal order that no one will ever speak of the pack again. The grounds will be tainted, so no other pack or humans will use it in the future."

After everyone was briefed on the plan, Sam, a particularly good smartass, stood up on a table and said in a sing-song voice.

"Look out, big bad wolves; we will huff and puff till your houses all burn down."

CHAPTER TWENTY-SEVEN

Adira sat quietly in her room; with a sigh, she thought of what things would have been like if she had never found Duncan. She doubted she would still be alive or wished she were dead anyway. It amazed her how fast things moved along and look where she is now compared to where she started.

Still, who would have thought that the road would lead here? It was a dark and gloomy day outside. Perfect for how she was feeling about the upcoming event of the day. It was not going to be pleasant, and she didn't relish the part she had to play.

The prince did make his bed; now, he will have to sleep forever in it. The saddest thing was all the victims he would leave in his wake. The poor King must be facing this not only as The King but also as a father. It must be tearing his heart in two.

She had also learned that the King was going to have to face some sort of punishment as well; she wondered what it was and prayed it wasn't too horrible of thing to do, when he must already face the death of his son. Still, he was in council with all the elders yesterday, and when he came out, he was pale and would not speak to anyone.

A servant awakened the prince; she was a cute little thing dressed in black. She put the tray down at the table in front of him; he slapped her butt as she tried to get out of the way. He giggled at her "You're going to have to get faster than that if you want to get away from me."

She kept her face void of expression and said nothing. She opened the door so the King's butler could come in; he carried garments for the prince. He said not one word as he dealt with his bath and helped get him ready, ensuring that the prince was dressed adequately in his formal black uniform. The butler walked out when he was done without showing any respect, not a nod or a bow.

Adam swore under his breath, that stuffy old codger, he will be the first to go when I am a king. That old fool had seen too many of Adam's sins, always looking down his nose at him. He was always trying to warn his father about what he liked to do. Father would brush it aside. He would always take his side, though, and the old codger would just keep at it, like an old dog with a bone.

217

Prince Adam looked outside; it was a dark, cold, dismal late fall day. The rain was removing the last of the fall leaves. It was positively gloomy, perfect weather for him to bend the knee to repent his sins. They were all such dull and useless fools; his father was the King of Fools. When you least expect it, I will kill you all in your sleep.

The prince looked at the garments but did not give them much more thought. The somber look will only help in his defense; if they believe he has learned his lesson, then all the better. He would be the picture of the most perfectly pious of princes. He did notice that none of his royal decorations were on his uniform. Probably part of his punishment to try to humiliate him.

After the Prince was finished getting ready and had eaten, he was left alone for about half an hour. Then two guards dressed in their finest escorted him out of the room; the prince walked in his most high and mighty walk, ready to look down his nose at anyone they would pass.

Head held high in the air, he had perfected the walk and was proud of himself. He did wonder why the halls were so empty. Asking one of his guards, they told him that the king thought it was best to close the court and send everyone home during this time.

He thought that that was clever of his father, that way, there would be no witnesses to this farce of a trial. They will think he got his just punishment, and that is that.

When the two guards stopped in front of the black and silver double doors of the High Council, Prince Adam was taken aback a little; why were they taking him here instead of the royal throne room. He felt a little bit of anxiety standing in front of these doors.

When they opened the doors, the room was filled with all the High Council members, something the prince had never seen except for pictures in books about war. The guards took him to the circle in the center of the room where he was supposed to stand.

He looked around, but his father, The King, was not in the room. His chair stood empty. He looked all around, but to his horror, the only other person on the floor standing was the executioner; Adam couldn't see his face. A heavy cowl covered it. Then under the cowl, he wore a long black robe.

"Prince Adam ...."

Adam was bored hearing his name and all his titles, blah blah blah blah…He rolled his eyes in annoyance. It was not until the end that he wasn't sure he heard what the Head Council said...there was no way he heard that right.

"................................*you stand before us accused of treason, misappropriation of money from the people's treasury, for which you used in a variety of criminal acts, murder of several young men and boys, conspiracy to murder the King, sexual acts with minors, and unlawful selling of forbidden drugs.*

"Prince Adam, how do you plead?"

The prince just stood there speechless; he looked again for his father, still, there was nothing but an empty chair.

"High Council, I request a representative to stand with me, as is my right."

"Very well, we searched and searched. However, no one wanted the job until finally one person agreed to do it."

The Council Member waved his hand as the double doors opened again; Lady Adira was standing on the other side, dressed in a simple white gown adorned with gold.

The little bitch that caused all this to happen to him. He wanted to beat her senseless and rip out her heart. How dare this little nobody come to his defense dressed like this.

She walked up to him, stopping just outside his marked circle where his representative would stand on the floor before the High Council to plead his case for the defendant.

"All I ask of you, members of the High Council, is that you do not make Prince Adams's execution a public spectacle, not for the Prince's sake but the King's."

After saying those words, she turned and left, not looking back. Her head held high as she walked back out like a queen.

The prince stood in his circle, enraged; he tried to go after Lady Adira. Calling her filthy names, the guards restrained him and held him in place, facing the Council again. As if remembering he had to be perfect, he stopped resisting the guards and stood up tall, looking at the council members as if they were beneath him.

"It is the ruling of the High Council Court that you will be taken from this room and executed in the King's private garden. There will be three appointed witnesses to your execution. These witnesses have been ordered to not speak of any of this after this day."

"As is also law, if the pup commits a crime, the father or mother must also pay for their failure not to teach the pup the right way. Therefore, the King's punishment has already been decided and will commence at the time of your death."

"You will be buried where your head falls, with no marker. Also, your name will be removed from all documents, census records, and history books. Nothing of yours will be left; all will be burned."

"Your mother's bank account and any money allocated to you will now help the victims you left behind and also give restitution to the families of those you murdered."

"There will be a royal decree throughout the pack lands that your name is never to be spoken again, nor used to name any children born after your death."

"This judgment is made upon this day in the year of the of our Lord 2021. May he show you mercy as you go to your final judgement."

"Guards take the condemned to the executioner."

Adam was in absolute terror and shock; his father was supposed to get him out of this. Where is he?

"NO, NO, NO, THIS IS NOT HOW IT IS SUPPOSED TO GO; YOU ARE TO LET ME GO THIS INSTANT.!!"

Adam was screaming like a mad man as they dragged him out of the hall, calling everyone every bad name ever created.

"You will all pay for this; how dare you treat me like this; I am your Crown Prince; unhand me this instant.!!!!"

His screams became whimpers, till finally, he lost his voice entirely. He had pissed himself in fear; the servants had lined the hall one at a time. They turned their backs to him in silence, while the guards dragged the prince to the king's garden and his death.

They placed his head on the chopping block and held him down as the executioner raised his sword; it gleamed dully in the grimness of the day. It shook just a little as it was held high, and then, in one final swoosh, the blade swung down, taking the prince's life. His head rolled down along the wall under a small oak tree.

The three witnesses, Duncan, Jack, and Adira, stood silently, heads bowed in the gloom of the falling rain; the council members stood in front of the executioner. There were servants already digging a hole for the grave in the muddy, cold ground.

Your Highness, our King, you have completed your punishment. You are free from any guilt now. The three witnesses gasped in unison as the executioner took off his cowl, and there in the falling icy rain with empty eyes stood the King. They could see that his wolf was there, giving his friend strength both looked like they would fall.

He threw the sword into the distance as he fell to his knees; he let out a loud painful howl that could be heard throughout the kingdom. The Council members hung their heads in sorrow. Duncan, Jack, and Adria knelt beside him as their King and held their friend as he deeply grieved in the cold falling rain.

Chapter Twenty-Eight

No one knew just how big a clan of bears was; in the Werebear world, you are not born the leader. You must fight for it. Jack had beaten every one of his male clan members who challenged him, over seventeen of them to become the leader.

He now had an entire clan of seven hundred male clan members and about three hundred families with cubs. All are loyal to him—something in the Werebear world that was unheard of and the first of its kind. Though Jack ruled with strict rules, he was fair and was always willing to listen.

Werebears are usually solitary creatures; there are family units, and sometimes, up to three families in the same community. To have a clan, though, is not only rare but, if not ruled with reason and fairness, could become dangerous. Why? Because male Werebears like to fight. As a rule, they are primarily solitary beings; some, even when they mate, leave their female. However, that is becoming a rare practice anymore.

Right now, three hundred and sixty of the clan's best warriors surround the Rising Moon Pack. The three hundred and sixty warriors were split up into three groups of one hundred and twenty; in each group were two warriors that were recorders. They will record everything they find; one will take still pictures, and the other will take video. They will also take recorded statements of the victims and witnesses, if any.

One group was to take over the warehouse, the next the factory, and the third the packhouses; when each group had completed their assigned tasks, they would meet up with the others. They had several vans, and each van had two medics and one nurse to take care of any victims in bad shape, as well as two buses to transport victims and innocent pack members.

When the first group surrounded the warehouse, though heavily guarded, the werebears took them down without too much of a fight. They rounded up the ones that were in charge and killed the rest.

What they found made them sick; it was all set up to ship live animals. Behind the six locked doors, they found all the females in locked cages. Females of every age and species. It looked like the human ones suffered the most. They got them out first to the medics.

The females could not even sit up; the cells were lined with straw and looked like they hadn't been cleaned in weeks. The smell was beyond terrible. When they tried to open the cells to get the females out, they would move as far away from them in the cage as possible. They would whimper in fear, and some yelled, *"NO, NO, NO!"* repeatedly.

After a little while, they realized they were not there to hurt them and were carried out to the vans; some were as young as five. It was hard for them to keep their anger in check. They were all close to a killing rage; the only thing keeping them in check was the scared and hopeless faces of the females.

There was one six-year-old who was in a corner cage. There was not much light there, but they could see her bruised and swollen face. She would not come out for anyone. They were about to go in and get her by force when one of the older warriors got an idea.

He shifted into his grizzly bear form and slowly walked up to the cage; he stood outside it where she could see him and did a funny little dance. She giggled but was still too scared to come out. So the werebear made a whimpering sound and laid his head just inside the cage. He pretended to go to sleep and started to snore.

The little female slowly made her way to the end of the cage and gently touched the bear's nose. He licked her face, and she giggled some more. After a little while, the bear came out to the medic van, and clinging to his back was the little female. After giving her off to the medic, he shifted back to human. He put his dog tags from the military around the little girl's neck.

He turned to the medic; I will be her family if no one can find her family. Either way, I will make sure she is never again hurt by anyone ever again. He turned and left. The little female clutched his tags in her hand.

The factories were worse; there were no young children here, the youngest being thirteen. The women were in three categories; each section had its caretakers that recorded everything on clipboards; it was like working in a zoo.

There were guardrooms where they found all kinds of footage and records about what was expected and what was done to all the females that came in, how far along the process they were and if they were going to be trouble, and so on.

The images of them herding the females into cages and rooms as if they were nothing but cattle, some of the records were about, how to make them comply in some nasty ways to achieve that goal; it read like some sort of instruction manual.

The werebears were so disgusted that they rounded up every worker in the place, stripped them naked, and forced them into one of the train cars waiting to be loaded, locking them inside.

Several of the pieces of shit tried to bribe them with the use of the women, telling them they could do whatever they wanted to them; the warriors pulled those that made the offers out to the side, and beat the crap out of them before making them join their fellow pieces of shit in the rail car again.

Every room was its own nightmare. The section labeled new arrivals was a small cold room made of metal when they opened the door. It was, to their horror, a meat locker; the females in here were hanging by hooks in the ceiling by their tied hands.

Six warriors went in and started to remove the females from the hooks. They would walk up to a female, wrap a warm blanket around her, remove them from the hooks, untie them, and carry them to the medics.

The human females were the worst of them all; their bodies simply couldn't take the same abuse as the shifter females, so they had to remove them first. Six did not make it; they died in the medic van. There were no records of their names or where they were taken from. The medics did everything they could to save them, including trying to turn them, but there was too much damage done.

The following section was named, Ready to Process. Inside it was a spacious room, with no windows. All the females in here had dog collars that were electronically attached to their necks; if they passed the censors in the door without a guard, they would be zapped; one zap is painful, two zaps you're knocked out, and three zaps, you are dead.

The guards made sure that every female was zapped twice. So anyone who tried to escape would die; twenty-two females had passed already. Their bodies were taken away and burned. The thirty-four other females just sat around on the floor, with dead eyes of the beaten down. In the four corners of the room were buckets for them to relieve themselves in. They were overflowing.

The warriors destroyed the sensory system and took all the females. They looked like they had not had a good meal in years, not to mention the dark circles around their eyes—the raw skin on their necks, hands, and feet where they had been chained before.

The last room was the worst, but they soon found out that there was yet one more room. The third room was more like a hall of jail cells. There were eight rooms in total; each cell had a sign above its door; the first one said it would take three. Each door sign was more vulgar than the one before.

A female is chained to the wall in each cell by a silver collar around their neck. The collars were lined with silk so they would not burn the females but it made sure that none of them could shift or use any shifters' abilities. Just before the door at the end of the hall was a vast closet; it contained a variety of skimpy dresses and other things such as shoes and cheap jewelry.

When they came to the door at the end of the hall, it was a solid silver coated door, and it was locked. Good thing that werebears don't have the same problems that werewolves do with silver.

Two of the warriors had no problem, ripping the door right off its hinges, lock, and all. Then they went into the next and final room; above each of the cages was a clipboard, each labeled **breeder one, breeder two, and so on till it reached six.**

In six of the ten cages were females in various stages of pregnancy; one was going into labor. They, of course, got her out first. These females were the most haunted looking and beaten down out of all the ones they had come across; two of the warriors that were helping, had to leave to blow off some anger because they wanted to kill the bastards.

Finally, all the females were removed, and those that could move on their own were loaded into buses and taken to safe houses and other packs. Those that were worse off were taken to various pack hospitals. The unfortunate few that had lost their minds entirely, had been taken to pack homes where they could be treated and cared for with the hope that they would someday recover.

When they were done, and all the victims had been taken care of and removed from the pack lands, all the warriors got together to decide what to do with the rail car full of all the miserable pieces of shit. There were many ideas, but they all agreed on one solution since they needed to join up with the other groups, they wanted them to pay with their lives, they also wanted it to be as painful as possible, time was not on their side.

The warriors gathered around the rail car, there was shouting and banging heard from inside, but no one seemed strong enough to break out, which showed everyone just how pathetic this pack had become. Did any of them have their wolves anymore?

Three warriors stood by the exit door, three more were on the car's roof, and each was standing at a small air vent.

Each warrior poured five gallons of gasoline down the vent; when the cans were empty, they tossed a lit torch down the hole and jumped off the roof. The screams were terrible the smell was worse. In about ten minutes, everything went silent.

The rail car's walls started to turn reddish as it was getting hotter and hotter and made popping noises from the heat. They watched and made sure no one survived; time was running out, and it was time to go.

The warriors turned and left, not bothering to look back, most of them feeling that they had let the bastards get off too easy.

CHAPTER TWENTY-NINE

The warriors surrounded the pack grounds; they gathered everyone they could find, from the very old to the teenagers.

A warrior stood before them..."Do you know what has been happening in this pack, in the buildings two miles away on your pack lands?"

To the warrior's disgust, almost all of them raised their hands—only the very old and some younger teenagers didn't raise their hands. The warriors took the ones who did not know to another house under guard. The others looked around at each other.

"Tell us, pack members, where is your leader? Where is your Alpha?"

"Do you even know who is in charge right now?"

One of the females looked at another male in fear, but she spoke up anyway.

"Alpha Michael has been gone for some time now; no one knows where he is or when he will return. The Beta is dead, killed by the Alpha. We are unsure who or where the next ones in charge are."

"We all knew terrible things were going on; the Alpha and Beta threatened us all; if we talked or tried to leave, they would hunt us down and kill our whole family and our neighbor's family. At first, no one took it seriously, but then whole families started to come up missing."

"At first, we thought they had just left in the night, and it was an empty threat until the Davis's family left. They went after them, when they brought them back, they were all executed before us, then they did the same to their neighbor's family."

"We were too afraid after that; he had eyes everywhere. If we complained, our pups would go missing, especially if they were young or female."

"We all had to keep ourselves from under the Alpha's radar. He made examples of some of the elders. Further, into the woods, there is a trail. You will find several bodies impaled with spears into the ground."

"There are two more places you need to know about, the orphanage and the party house. They are on the other side of the wooded area; there is a path easy enough to see and follow."

The leader of the werebear group sent twenty-five warriors to go check these houses out. Then he sent two more to find the path in the woods that led to the Elder's bodies.

The two warriors did not take long to find the path in the woods; they followed it to its end and stood in horror at what they saw. There had to be at least fifty pack members in various stages of decay, all impaled in numerous ways into the ground.

The smell was horrendous, but they could see why this spot was chosen; the trees were so thick that the wind could not move the scent around.

When the warriors got to the first house, the music was so loud you could feel the beat of the music in their bodies.

They looked at each other with a smile, time to crash the party. All twenty-five of the warriors crashed in through every entry point. In the main room were six male werewolves; they all looked to be around their early twenties. They surrounded them, tied them up, and gagged them.

"Will someone find the source of that shitty music and shut it off."

One of the warriors found the player and smashed it against the wall, silence. They started looking around; the upstairs had four bedrooms all of them were a mess. When they found the door to the basement, they found six female werewolves; they were all chained to the walls with silver chains.

All of them were in bad shape; two pleaded for them to kill them. The place was filthy and damp. One warrior for each victim; as they carried them out, the females wanted to stop when they saw the males.

Each one of the females, no matter how weak they were, managed to reject the males as their mates. The males started to roll around in pain. Each male was tied to another rope as a warrior started to drag them down the path like a chain gang.

The remaining thirteen warriors went on to the next house; this one was a little bigger and quiet. It was as if it was sleeping. They all rushed the house coming in from every entry point as they did at the party house. The ground floor was dark and empty. It looked like the setting for a school.

This time they went to the basement. First, they did not find anyone. It was just full of supplies. They went up to the first floor; it had two doors. Upon opening them, they were in the sleeping area of the male pups, and bunk beds lined the walls. In the other room, the same only was for females.

They went to wake them up but discovered they were drugged. They decided to leave them where they were while searching the rest of the house. When they got to the third floor, it was one giant room. There they were met with two males and three females. They managed to tie them up and gag them quickly.

When they looked around the room, it was lined with several cribs; there were fourteen of them, all of which had an infant pup. All the infants seem like they were drugged as well. One of the warriors called the leader and told him what was going on and that they needed more warriors to remove all the pups.

One of the warriors walked up to the tied-up pack members and spit on them.

"You guys are a special kind of evil, drugging children and infants to keep control; seriously, what big bad warriors you are."

Once everything was done, all the houses were empty. They loaded the innocent people onto a bus to be taken to another pack; the rest, such as the six young males, would be taken to the Royal Gardens to meet with the king. Six other older males were also singled out and taken with the first six.

The other pack members that knew but did nothing were to stay and watch them burn it all down. Once that is done, they will be split up and given to other packs as servants.

That was the end of the Rising Moon Pack, when they were done that night nothing was left but embers and ash.

Twelve males total now stood before Jack and Duncan, who ordered the guards to place them in the dungeons till the King decided to deal with them.

Duncan let out a sigh..."*So the Alpha is still missing, and the Beta is dead at the hands of the Alpha. We got six of the ones in charge or knew too much to be innocent. Plus those six males who were torturing their mates. So they could sell them to the Alpha.*"

"*Yeah, that sums up this shit show; what I want to know, Duncan is where Alpha asshole shitface is hiding.*"

"*We better start looking harder; I don't want that nasty turd popping out of the bowl and causing more trouble.*"

"*I will inform the King that these twelve have arrived, Jack. Why don't you go down and have a little fun with the prisoners? I have sensed for a while now that you need to let loose some of that anger.*"

"*Yeah, you're right. I think I will go down and welcome those twelve pieces of shit to the Royal Dungeons. I mean, it is only fair to them that they learn the rules and what is expected of them. Don't want them complaining that they don't know what to do."*

Duncan knocked on the Kings chamber door; the King was no longer who he once was. He was quiet and sad. He was angry at his son for doing what he did and what he had to do to stop him. He would always smile when Adira came to visit; she was getting bigger by the day and seeing her helped him forget that anger for a little while.

Duncan stopped before the King,

"Your highness, we have twelve guests in the dungeon awaiting your notice."

"Duncan, I think we will hold a public trial and execution for these twelve." I will sit as King for this trial, and all the council will also be in attendance. I want everything that they have done made public."

"I want pictures and video of it all shown at the trial. I want everyone to see why the Rising Moon pack will no longer exist. Nor will the Name be allowed for another pack to use. I want them all to see what happens when you break the laws of our world."

"I will see that it is done, your highness."

Duncan bowed and left the room. The King turned to the window with a sigh; things felt wrong with the world now; it felt empty and lifeless.

He was sure he would deal with it all and with much more attention and reason in time. He also knew that a part of him died that day and would never be the same again. Time heals all wounds; whoever said that should be flogged and locked in the darkest closet, to be forgotten.

A Small interlude set in the future

Three mages and a group of witnesses gathered around a small place in the middle of a clearing in the forest, it was spring. It was a wonderful day. The sun shined through the trees with their newly formed leaves; a gentle breeze moved playfully as everything returned to life after a harsh winter.

Before everyone was, the bodies of the six females who had died, wrapped in white silk, each lay on a bed of rose petals—each one laid at the bottom of a grave dug out carefully in the ground.

The three mages stood before them as the earth filled in around them as if it had a mind of its own. Then the mages magically erected a stone archway in the center of the gravesite. Flowers began to magically grow and cover the graves in a perfect circle.

Hanging from the archway were moonflowers in an unusual shade of lavender that changed their color as the wind would pass by. Everyone watched in awe at what was happening before their eyes.

On the top of the archway was a golden plaque. It read...Here they lay, six beautiful females. We do not know their names, families, or anything about their lives before they met a terrible fate. We named them all beautiful.

On the plaque were six words; each word was written in a different language, that read "beautiful" when translated.

The mages announced that this place would remain sacred; the flowers would bloom every year from spring to fall and sleep in the winter. If anyone needed to be reminded of this world's good, they need only come here and stand in the flowers.

No storms of nature nor hands of man can destroy this sacred site. Children may pick the flowers without harm; no adult must pick the flowers or desecrate the area; to do so is an invitation to join the dead.

Standing in the middle of the group was an older werebear named Oliver; on his shoulders was a little girl; she held on to his hands as she watched the ceremony. Around her neck, she wore Oliver's dog tags; she smiled as she watched, she was still having nightmares, but she clung to her bear with all that was in her.

Her future would be promising from now on; her big bad bear had killed all the monsters.

CHAPTER THIRTY

Adira was getting to the point that her old clothes were no longer fitting her. She had two summer dresses that she could still wear comfortably. The rest of her clothes, however, were getting too tight.

The King insisted that they stay there till the birth of their pup, and he also insisted that the royal doctor take care of Adira. She had a diet she had to follow now, not complaining; the doctor insisted that she was still underweight and needed to eat more.

He has her on all kinds of vitamins, and she is to get bed rest at least three times a day. Till she starts gaining more weight, she is allowed some short walks in the gardens of the castle. The King also insisted that she have lunch with him every day. She was starting to feel like a lazy leopard hanging in a tree with the noon sun above.

She did not mind; she knew that she and her unborn pup were helping the King through his grief. She could not help noticing since all this happened that he now looked older than he did before.

She also involved him in the design of the nursery and baby clothes and names, it made his face light up a little, and she did not mind sharing all this with him. She and Duncan both discussed it at length; He did not care. She still always informed him of everything, though. So, he has a say if he wants to jump in and add anything.

Winter arrived as the first fluffy snow fell to cover the ground last night. The palace was getting ready for the holiday season, and everything seemed to be a little lighter than before. So that at least was a plus. Though she had this feeling like she had forgotten something. It has been getting stronger. Lately, she told Duncan about it, and he, too, has been on a higher sense of alert.

Of course, he is a helicopter mate of late; it was because she was starting to show, and he jumps in when there is something that needs doing. When she thought that she was alone and wanted to do something on her own, poof, he was right there to do it for her; it was starting to get a bit annoying.

She sighed; Artemis thinks it is cute and a sign of a good father. Adira thinks that Apollo and Artemis snitch on her; that is how Duncan always seems to know where she is and what she is doing.

245

She had to admit that she liked being able to link with both their wolves and Duncan. Apollo and Artemis decided it would be funny to switch places for a day. Apollo seemed to enjoy being lazy and eating whenever he wanted.

Artemis had a blast; Apollo thought he had an excellent vacation but hated the lack of what he called "action." He said that although he loved talking to the pup and being with Adira, the rest was boring.

He could not understand why females had to take so long to decide what color the nursery walls should be, what colors for the furniture, and on and on and on. He did help Adira get another little walk in the castle, he told no one, and she finally had a little privacy.

Alpha Michael was pissed as he sat in his little cabin outside town. He had overheard what they did to all his things and businesses; how dare they. All of them would pay, including the King, if he could arrange it.

There was nothing left, he still had his one bank account, but the others were frozen. So he still had some money, enough at least to find some rogues. He is going to need them to conduct his plan for revenge. That little bitch and her pup will be the start of his new business venture.

By the time they realize she is missing, I will already have her in her new cage. Who knows, maybe he can snag a few servant girls too. His kind of business did require variety.

He will, of course, have to break her in; all the females need to be shown the rules on how to please an Alpha. The thought of what he was going to do, made him hard. He stroked himself in anticipation.

Unfortunately, the Prince was nowhere to be found; he decided he would have to let that ship sail. He was a little too demanding anyway. He decided to go down to the local pub and treat himself to a female for the night. He could not have as much fun here with the girls that he wanted, they would be missed or worse escape and he would be screwed.

Of course, every time he must curb his pleasures, it will be that little bitch's job to give them to him; he would keep a tally, so she would know how long she would have to please him.

After all, he thought that if you don't use it, you lose it. Off to find himself a piece of ass for the night; maybe he could find one that was more open to his kind of play.

Jack Dawson did not like that they could not find that piece of shit, Alpha; he couldn't shake the feeling that he didn't just escape to a tropical island. He felt the poor excuse for a living being was still hanging around. He was waiting like a snake under a rock, ready to strike.

He had already traveled to his clan to take care of things with the warriors and the extra members. Everyone was getting along nicely. They even gained two cooks, which was better than gold. They also acquired three new clan members, all-female and one little human girl named Chloe with black hair and bright blue eyes.

At first, the clan did not want her because she was human. Oliver had none of it; she was already exposed to the shifter world. Once everyone saw how Oliver was with Chloe, they decided that she should stay after all. Oliver finally had a cub that he had always wanted. No one would argue with him because no one wanted their face rearranged.

Jack still could not shake the feeling that Alpha Michael was still watching and waiting. If they can't find him soon, they will have to take extra security measures and hope he does not get through them.

Jack called his clan, asking for six warriors to come to him at the castle, under the radar as quietly as possible, and to mask their scent. He was assured that they were on their way and would be there by morning.

He was not sure where things were going but to have some of his men in places watching things. He was sure of them anyway; too many here could be bought or blackmailed for his liking.

Jack knew that Duncan was more than capable, but he was distracted for a good reason. His mate is in danger and is pregnant; Duncan is also helping and protecting the King during his time of grief. So that means that Jack must have all their butts covered.

Still, he had the feeling that something nasty was on its way. He hoped it was not with Adira; not only would Duncan go ballistic, but so will the King. One of them alone would be a handful to get under control; the two of them together would be impossible and lethal.

Still, he cannot stay here forever; he must return to his clan for a more long-term stay. Three of his best warriors were taking care of things for him; they reported back to him every other day or sooner if there was a pressing issue.

Duncan's pack and his clan had been exchanging items and people that were needed and information; they also sent some of the best healers; Jack had left the warriors he lent to Duncan. Leaving them there provided extra security.

Who would have thought that werewolves and werebears would work together as one pack?

Marco had been a tremendous help; he had also been responsible for getting the victims the help they needed and searching for their packs. The human victims were harder to track down, but most had found their way home. Some had nowhere to go; they were offered to choose which pack to reside in.

Marco made sure that all females were joining other packs or their families; both humans and shifters had everything they needed physically and mentally.

Alpha Michael had to take a late-night trip to the mountains; he stood at the edge of a cliff just after he tossed the body of a female over the edge. It was the prince that showed him this place.

He had to be more careful; it was a good thing she was one of the lower-ranking whores in town. If she had been well known, he would be in trouble right now and would have to forget his plan for revenge.

He heard rumors around town that the prince had been executed; he was never one to believe in idle gossip. Still, there were a lot of rumors. Mixing that with the fact that he cannot get a hold of Prince Adam worried him.

He was over the moon happy when he found this hiding spot; he had a perfect view of Spares' room. He did, unfortunately, have to watch her mate several times a day. She was pregnant for sure; it was out there for all to see. Soon she would be ripe for picking; he had already found himself an insider willing to look the other way for some fast cash.

It is just a matter of time before her mate slips up, and she is alone. It must be in the right place; once she is alone, he will have her, and her poor mate will be so lost without her. He laughed under his breath at that; perhaps he would send him some updates so he wouldn't feel so lonely.

Alpha Duncan does not have to worry; he will see that his little bitch will have plenty to do so she doesn't have to deal with heartbreak. His rogues were ready and waiting; the trap was set to be sprung.

All the pieces are on the board; all he must do is wait for them to make one wrong move.

CHAPTER THIRTY-ONE

Adira was sitting in the King's chambers, she was reading at first, but now she stared into the fire. The King was having nightmares, so Adira, Duncan, and the King's butler would take turns staying while he slept. The King's doctor gave him sleeping pills, but sometimes they did not work.

The King's butler was an odd fellow; he was certainly old. She found out from Duncan that his name was Alfred. He would not speak directly to her. Duncan reassured her that he was just old school. This meant he would not engage with her unless Duncan was with her and gave his permission.

He took loving care of his master, though; he gave Adira the creeps sometimes. He always had this ability to just show up out of nowhere. She supposed it was just his servant training, to be there when needed and unseen when not.

She fell asleep while on watch two nights ago, and when she awoke, she was covered by a soft blanket. She thought it was Duncan, but he had checked on her earlier when she was still awake; he hadn't come back yet because he was on patrol with Jack.

So it had to be Alfred that had done it, so he was friendly, just quiet, and took his job very seriously. On the other hand, the King's maid was nothing like the butler; she always had all the gossip about what babies were born and to whom. Death's, family drama. She was a what's what information center of the kingdom.

She was loyal to her king; she saw one of the prince's servants talking down about the king; she was on him in seconds, repeatedly hitting him with a broom till he ran off. She never saw that servant again.

Artemis was restless lately. At. First, she thought it was just the pregnancy and everything that had happened; Artemis denied it and said she was disturbed because she could feel something lurking in the shadows lately, she just could not pinpoint its smell or presence.

She heard the door click, and there stood Duncan; they only talked through mind linking when the King was sleeping.

"Are you alright, little wolf?"

"Yes, all is well here, though I am getting tired and might risk falling asleep."

"It seems the bigger my middle grows, the more tired I become."

"Would you like me to stay here while you go to bed and get some much-needed rest?"

"Don't you have other duties tonight?"

"Nope, Jack has some buddies out and about now, so I am free to stay here tonight or call for Alfred to come to sit with him while you and I go to bed."

"Do you think Alfred would mind?"

"No, he has been asking about taking more shifts so you could get more rest."

"Alright then, call Alfred, and then you can take me to our room. It will be great to sleep in your arms again."

Alfred came into the room as if on cue, doing his servant creepy thing again.

Duncan nodded to Alfred and picked up his mate, carrying her to their room. Once they were safely locked inside, Duncan ran a bath for them.

When he came back for her, he had already undressed. She started to undress, but he stopped her. *"No, my little wolf, I want that privilege for myself."*

He slowly began to undress her. He was starting with her shoes and socks. Then her shirt one button at a time.

Till finally, she was standing before him, naked as the day she was born.

"It has been a while since we had any real-time for just the two of us. Jack has given me the day off tomorrow, and you will be with me the entire day and night."

He carried her to the oversized bathtub and sat down with her in his arms; he sat her between his legs and lathered her up with soap; he took his time to make sure he got everything clean. He paused both hands over her tummy, lightly doing circles repeatedly with his hands.

She could feel his erection going up along her back; she decided that she wanted more than just a bath; with a devilish grin; she started to move her butt slowly up and down against his erection as he began to moan.

He whispered in her ear, *"You are a naughty little wolf. Would you like me to show you what happens to naughty wolves?"*

He grabbed her by her hips and lifted her so he was positioned at her entrance, feeling that she was already wet, and pushed her in one swift thrust. He let out a low growl of pleasure.

"You feel so good; I can never get enough. You drive me crazy; the more of you I have, the more I want. Apollo goes nuts when he smells your naked skin, even if your scent just lingers in a room. You're perfect in every way."

After that, he stopped talking and began moving her slowly, then faster, as both enjoyed that naked slide. He moved his knees upward, spreading her wider, holding her wet, soapy breasts.

Both were being driven mad with pleasure; water was sloshing and splashing everywhere. Till they both reached their peak, screaming each other's names. They stayed that way for a little while until they regained their senses. Duncan started to laugh. Adria looked at him, "What?"

"I was just thinking, now I have to wash you all over again."

"Well, at least we are in an enclosed room this time, so the whole castle and half the kingdom can't hear us."

"I don't know, my little wolf; I like everyone knowing that you are mine."

With those words, he entered her again; she let out a gasp; how was it possible for him to feel bigger. Then he settled himself deep within her; it was not long before they were both mindless again.

Adira and Duncan did not get much sleep that night.

The King woke up in a pool of sweat after yet another nightmare. It was the same one; he was holding his son's head as he looked up at him with empty eyes and cried out to him; he was still in his executioner's garb, still holding the sword.

"Why, father?"

Over and over, his son cried to him; he could do nothing; he could not speak, nor could he move. He could only stare at his son's headless body, while holding his sons head as it was crying out to his father.

After the first nightmare, he ordered forget-me-not seeds to plant over his son's grave for the spring. He did not give a shit about his son not having a marker of any kind, it was his garden, and if he wanted to plant flowers, he would do so wherever he wished.

Why had his son been so evil? Was it something he did or did not do? The thoughts ran around his head like a tornado, spinning out of control.

He sat up and looked around the room; Alfred, his loyal butler, was sitting in the chair. He was initially his father's butler, and now he was his. His silent rock was always waiting and willing to serve.

"Alfred?"

"Yes, your highness?"

"You can go to your room and get some sleep; I am not going back to bed anymore tonight. I will stay up and read or go through some of the invitations for the Christmas ball."

"As you wish, my King." Giving the King a bow, he left the room.

The King went through many papers at his desk and the invitations. He could not concentrate on anything, though. So he sat down by the fire with a sigh and went through a photo album. Pictures of his mate and sons filled his vision, tears ran down his face like diamonds, his wolf Arthur wrapped himself around him in solace.

"Arthur, where did it all go wrong?"

Jack was up on the wall with other guards; the moonlight was out tonight. It was giving everything a silver shine. To Jack's eye, it was almost blinding. Snow was falling, but there was not any natural accumulation.

That was coming tomorrow or the next day; they predicted a blizzard for their region. It will be a challenging time; it would be an excellent time for an attack; it would be a 50/50 gamble. Great for cover, bad for getting away.

Jack was hoping that whatever shit show was about to start would get its ass going. This waiting is a pain in the ass. Still, he felt that there was something out there. It was lingering in the shadows, waiting to pounce.

One of Jack's warriors reported that he had moved and checked it out. When he linked to Jack again, he said he was bringing him an early Christmas present. He went happily to meet him. He so loved getting Christmas presents.

Jack met his warrior at the back gardens along the wall. His warrior was there waiting for him, and he did indeed have a present for Jack, in the form of a rogue.

Chapter Thirty-Two

The King went down into the dungeons with six of his guards. He wanted answers, the answers that only come out after pain. The King wanted the truth. Why were they so bad. What would drive a male werewolf to torture his mate, to break that bond? He had seen mates reject each other for distinct reasons.

How did you get so bad that you would trade your mate for monetary gain; what kind of sick joke has this pack become? After making the mating connection, and then selling out and abusing your mate. It was a nasty crime, that could destroy the very foundation of the wolf and human connection.

This, whatever it was, was deranged. To sell young females and males for slavery was beyond his understanding and sense of right from wrong. It made him and his wolf sick and truly angry.

That gave the king and his wolf an idea; I wonder if they would piss their pants if we changed into our Lycan

261

form. His wolf chuckled; yes, let's see, I have not had that kind of fun since we were younger.

The King changed into his half-wolf half human form, to his guard's horror. He stood almost eight feet tall; golden fur covered him, his claws were all gold, and his eyes were like burning sapphires. He looked like a golden god of death.

Once he entered the main holding area, he reached out his claws, scraping them down all twelve of the metal doors where the prisoners stood; the sound was a terrible symphony of rage and the promise of pain to come, causing the smell of fear take over the air.

He let out a low growl of a voice…

"Do I smell the smell of pissed in pants?"

The Kings guards stayed in the corners and shadows, watching the ultimate Alpha's incredible power, the King of all Alphas. Thankful that that power was not directed at them.

The smell of piss and fear became so intense it burned the guard's eyes and throats. It did not matter to the King; he enjoyed a little revenge. He let out a loud growl; he ripped off the door to the first cell and stomped inside.

When he smelled the male's scent; he pulled his head back in surprise; the male did not smell like a wolf—just a man. So, there was a punishment. Good, the bastards did not deserve the gift of the Goddess.

They had to remember that they could not kill them; they had to stand trial. That did not mean he couldn't castrate them.

His mind-linked one of the guards that they would need doctors down here. He insisted that the crew had to be all-male, they were to get them as quickly as possible, along with a cleaning crew.

He wasted no time with the filthy piece of crap; he grabbed him by the neck with one huge, clawed paw, lifting him till he banged his head a little on the 9-foot ceiling. He reached out with his one long middle claw and swiped the male's cock and balls, ripping them from his body, leaving a wide-open slash in the bastard's pissy pants.

He proceeded to the other eleven cells doing the same thing to all the males; they were not males anymore. The doctors came down and were horrified at the King's work. The King stayed in his Lycan form and stomped through the castle and back into his chambers.

When he was inside and cleaned up, two council members asked for an audience with the King. They wasted no time reprimanding him for his behavior in the dungeons. The King turned on them in a fury, "YOU ARE

ALL A BUNCH OF IGNORANT, EGOTISTICAL, HIGH, AND MIGHTY JACKASSES!!!!

"DO YOU THINK THEY GAVE ANY OF THE THOUSANDS OF VICTIMS ANY MERCY OR KINDNESS? THEY TREATED THEM WORSE THAN GARBAGE.!!"

"IF YOU THINK FOR ONE SECOND I WILL BE SORRY OR FEEL ANY REGRET FOR WHAT I DID TODAY, YOU ARE SO FUCKING WRONG IT WILL MAKE YOUR HEAD SPIN.!!"

"I AM CALLING A MEETING OF ALL THE COUNCIL MEMBERS IN 15 MINUTES, THOSE WHO CHOOSE NOT TO ATTEND WILL BE TAKEN OFF THE COUNCIL AND WHIPPED TWENTY TIMES."

"ANYONE WHO HAS A PROBLEM FOR ANY REASON WITH MY ACTIONS CAN STAND IN THE CASTRATION LINE. I HAVE HAD A LOT OF PRACTICE OF LATE, AND I HAVE GOTTEN QUITE GOOD AT IT."

"NOW GET THE FUCK OUT OF MY CHAMBERS!"

The council members wasted no time running out the door.

The King marched into the high council chambers like a God of War on a rampage. Duncan, Jack, and twelve guards walked in their finest uniforms behind him.

Every council member was in attendance, even their scribes. As he took account, the hall was so silent you could hear the marching of the guards outside. No one was even moving. It was as if they were afraid even to breathe. This pleased him; good, it was time they felt the eyes of scrutiny upon them.

The King stood up before his throne council members. I have called you here for a reason; we have all been lax in our duties. We all swore an oath upon taking office that our first duty was to keep our people safe. We failed in that duty.

The guards are now handing out pictures and logs of what we have found lurking in our packs. We will be watching a movie as well. I have named the film "While we were on watch."

After everyone looked at the evidence passed around, they watched the movie. Some of the council members even vomited. When it was all done, the king looked around the hall.

"I will be putting some new rules in place, so perhaps this terrible kind of shit will never happen again."

"Rule one: Any shifter caught selling or buying males or females of any species will be castrated in public."

"Rule two: Any pack members who willfully hurt, abuse, or murder another pack member or shifter from another pack. Will be brought before the King and Council for trial."

"Rule three: If any Alpha decides he will rule his pack with fear and abuse, he will be subject to the same from the King Alpha."

"Last: From now on, a new position will be created, Investigator of pack affairs. If anyone in any pack has a complaint about those that rule them may go to or send for the Investigator with their problems."

"So that this position isn't abused, the King will hear the complaint first. If anyone tries to use the investigator for fraudulent purposes, they will be found guilty of the original complaint and punished accordingly."

"If the investigator uses their position for purposes other than what it was created to do, death is the punishment."

"Furthermore, no one is above the law. Everyone from the lowest omega to the King will be held accountable."

"This is all I have for now; I will be adding a few more as time goes on to correct any loopholes that someone may find."

"If for some reason any of you have a problem with these new rules, if there is some way you can improve upon them, come to me; if you can't because it is something that you are morally against, then please step down and give your seat to another."

"Now, will these six council members come down before me?"

He called their names as the council members happily stood before him. The King usually only called a council member down to give them a particular title or honor.

As the six stood before him, ready for their reward, the guards surrounded them. All of them were shocked and demanded to know what this was about.

The King wasted no time telling them, "You six have been charged with treason and for buying young pups for sexually deviant purposes, as well as various other crimes, which will be brought up at your trials."

The guards tied their hands behind their backs and marched them off to the dungeons.

He watched from the shadows as he had always done; there were times he was proud of himself for his loyalty. It was about time that the King cleaned his house.

Still, though, since the loss of his son, he has been around the wrong kind of weres. He will be fixing it soon, though he does not care for the Alpha he has to deal with. For him, sometimes, the ends do justify the means.

To call her Luna was a joke; to have the King give her the title of Lady was an even bigger joke. The king is still grieving and not thinking straight. So that means he must step in and take care of things for him.

She was a nice she-wolf, intelligent and considerate; after all she had to go through. For the love of the goddess, she is a low standing bastard; she should have been an omega and the lowest one at that. She had the right name the first time around, Spare.

Lilly was still feeling like the Alpha was watching her; at first, she thought it was just in her head. It had happened too many times now to be something to blow off. When she was little, he liked to stalk her as she played. He always wore a scent blocker potion that also helps you blend in with your surroundings; he bragged about it when he got it from a witch.

She always knew, though, that she and Zinnia were always sensitive to the energy of others. She felt his energy change over the last two years; that was when he realized he was losing his wolf. His power the last time felt different. When it came to her, he no longer had his wolf.

She also learned that she was like a ghost; her meals are slid under her door, and her assignments are under her door. No one paid attention to her; she even evaluated it one day. It was not till she was at the outer gates that she was stopped.

Tonight, punishment or not, she and Zinnia were going hunting.

CHAPTER THIRTY-THREE

Jack dragged the rogue to one of the dungeon's interrogation rooms. The bastard was laughing the whole time; it made Jack alarmed something was going down tonight. Whatever it was, he felt that it would be all over soon; he just hoped it did not end in death unless, of course, it was that Alpha Michael asshole.

He mind-linked Duncan to be on alert; Jack motioned the guards to come forward.

"I want three of you to stay here and take care of this piece of shit."

"Beat that smirk off this asshole's face; when he starts to sing, let me know what tune he has chosen. If it isn't anything worthy of our time, kill him slowly."

"Also if it becomes obvious that he won't be talking, kill him slowly."

Jack went to Duncan to change the guard and their tactics; someone had to be watching and found an opening. They just hoped that the plan would work this time. This cannot continue.

Duncan did one last check on Adira; she was fast asleep again in the King's chambers. He wanted to take her from here and back to the magical cabin, hide her forever—just the two of them.

He shut the door, nodding to the two guards outside. He decided she was safest with the King. Guards at all the gates, Alfred was also coming and going making sure all was well.

The King was sleeping but not under any drugs, so he would be alert and do what he needs to do if it came to that. Adira learned self-defense, but he doubted she could move very fast with her tummy. Duncan made sure she always kept a taser with her. She was to tell no one she had it.

It was a special taser he got from Jack. Duncan was not sure how it all worked, but it was effective against werewolves. If used on humans, though, it would be deadly. Duncan was not worried if she killed a male that attacked her; damn bastard should consider himself lucky that Duncan didn't get to him first.

Duncan always believed in a slow death policy; an enemy that is desperate enough would face death if necessary; they tend to stand back, though, when it's a slow, painful death over a long period of time.

He headed out to go on patrol with Jack and his warriors, wanting round up the rogues, and find that evil piece of crap Alpha, for the last time.

By the day, Adira felt bigger and more like a jelly roll, and she was not even fully rounded yet. The doctor said it would be another four months before she could hold her pup. She sat in the chair by the massive fireplace; Alfred was a dear; he brought her a soothing cup of tea and some little lemon cakes.

After Alfred cleaned up the dishes and left, she started to feel sleepy; she looked over at the King. He was getting out of bed. She did not like how she was feeling.

The King put his hand on her shoulder, "Don't worry, little one; all will be well by morning. Now sleep and be at peace. Alfred will pay for this, and Alpha Michael will soon be in pieces.

Lily and Zinnia hid in the long shadows of the night as they hunted their prey. No matter how, she would get that bastard for what he did to her and thousands like her.

She had just one wish: she had enough time before she killed him to rip off that useless excuse for a dick and shove it down his throat.

Neither one cared what their punishment would be; if they wanted to kill her and Zinnia, so be it; they were in this together. Her only regret was not telling Spare that the only reason she was mean to her was to keep her safe. That was the only reason Alpha Michael could do what he did to her, made her do the things she did.

No one could understand what it was like for them; no one knew the pain, anger, fear, and shame. Only Lily and Zinnia knew what they had done to them. If killing that miserable bastard cost them their lives, so be it; it was not like they had anything to keep them in this world anyway.

Alpha Michael waited outside a hidden side door for his informant to open it. It was his one shot at getting Adira; the rogues he hired were failing him, stupid

273

asshole werebears; they are everywhere like cockroaches. He had to change his plans once again because of them.

He decided it would not be wise to take the female out of the castle; there were just too many guards that would see him taking her away. So, he decided that poor little Spare would hang herself from the king's high tower instead.

The informant now was unlocking the door, just as a chill went down Michaels's spine. He was not sure where the feeling was coming from; he didn't like the sense that he was being stalked. The door opened, revealing the Kings own personal butler, Alfred.

He led Alpha Michael up a flight of stairs to a smaller side room and told him to wait there. He paced the room in mild panic. The butler came back with the female in his arms about fifteen minutes later. Alpha Michael smiled with glee. Finally, he would get his revenge.

The female was handed over to Alpha Michael; he then pointed to the money envelope on the table. The butler pocketed the money. "Just make sure she stays gone."

Alpha Michael nodded; that was his plan. Already the image was in his head, everyone's favorite, poor Adira swinging by her neck for all to see. Looking down at her swollen stomach, such a horror it will be with her unborn pup hanging with her.

He turned and made his way up the stairs to the Kings tower. He was laughing under his breath at this little bitch, hoping that she would wake up just as she was going over the wall.

Too bad his wolf left him; it would have made things a lot easier; though he does have some extra strength and vision, he ultimately lost his sense of smell. He suspected that soon he would lose all the other extraordinary talents. It is not going to be easy to continue with his plans now that he will be nothing but a weak human. He would find a way to deal with that, he was sure.

Best to get this done and then disappear.

Alfred got back to his Kings chambers only to find that the King was gone. He looked everywhere, but it was not in his room where he was. He had drugged him heavily; he shouldn't be moving around.

The King's pajama bottoms were on the floor by the bed, and the balcony doors were open; there just was not any way he could be out and about. Then Alfred noticed, to his horror, on the other side of the bed, almost under it, was the cup of tea Alfred had made for him.

In a little bit of a panic, Alfred opened the doors to the hall and was confronted by six of the King's guards. He turned pale, knowing that his plan had failed.

They tied him up and tossed him in a broom closet. Two guards stood outside the door.

Alfred was resigned to his fate, all this trouble over a worthless female named Spare.

The King's tower was massive; he was not sure how many guards were there. It did not matter. He had the powdered version of a new drug. It had not been tested yet; he would have free access to the tower roof if it worked. He had to throw the little pouches at their feet, and they would pass out or die; he smirked; time for the first testing.

However, when he reached the tower, there were no guards. He found this to be a bit off. Unless they abandoned their posts in their panic to catch the rogues, thinking the tower was a low-key site. He slowly made his way out the door just in case.

He dragged Adira behind him like a rag doll; she started to moan, making Alpha Michael realize that his time was running out. He pulled her to the stone arches; the arches did not have any railing; it was supposed to signify the way to God.

This little bitch would find her way alright, with a rope around her neck.

As he was halfway to the arches, that feeling of being stalked was there again, just as a dark figure moved from the shadows and into the dim light.

CHAPTER THIRTY-FOUR

$\mathcal{D}$uncan and Jack were on the outskirts of the royal gardens; with the help of the royal guards, they captured eighteen rogues. Some of the guards were still out there and would continue until they were satisfied that they got them all.

Jack was worried about what Duncan's reaction was going to be towards the King's secret plan to catch the traitor within, thus luring Alpha Michael out of the shadows. He knew if it were him, he would be beyond pissed and would take his mate out of here and never return; he also hoped that it wouldn't affect their friendship too severely.

Duncan mind-linked Adira to check on her; he was alarmed when he felt nothing. Even if she was in a profound sleep, he should feel something. This was nothing. In alarm, he mind-linked to Jack as he shifted and took off, running back to the castle.

Jack shifted and took off after Duncan. Something was not right; the plan was working, but to not feel Adira was making Duncan frantic; Jack hoped it wasn't anything serious. If Duncan were to go into a killing frenzy, it would take more than one werebear to subdue him.

They ran to the King's chambers, where Duncan last knew Adira's location. There were guards everywhere when they got there, the kings' guards. The rooms were empty. The guards were looking throughout the whole castle and grounds.

Well, that part of the plan did work, just not how they planned it, the informant was indeed flushed out, but no one expected it to be Alfred.

Apollo stopped running because Duncan was getting worked up. *"Remember, Dun; we still have the four-way connection. I need you to calm down, so I can merge with Artemis."* Duncan took a deep breath and sat down on the floor.

Duncan waited for an eternity, *"I've got them; they are on the top of the King's tower."* Duncan mind-linked Jack. As the wolf, and the bear were running to the Kings tower; along with them were twelve of the king's guards, all in wolf form.

It was quite the sight, one sizeable grizzly werebear and golden wolf with a dozen wolves, running behind them as if going to war.

Alpha Michael just stood there in silence as the figure moved closer; he could hear a whole pack of wolves howling.

For the first time in his life, he was starting to feel fear; this figure was almost eight feet tall and had all muscles on its muscles. It terrified him in ways he did not think he could handle anymore. Once the figure came into the light fully, Alpha Michael almost pissed himself.

The King was in his Lycan form, and he did not look like he came to play. Alpha Michael grabbed Spare and held her closer to him like a shield. Alpha Michael took out a silver dagger and held it to the female's throat, the king was still coming.

That was when Alpha Michael's plans all went south. The female in his arms started to fight him; he was not strong enough to hold her anymore, so he tossed her away from him. Adira hit a wall and was knocked out once again. In truth, that was not Adira at all; it was Apollo.

Alpha Michael then took a vile from his pocket and downed it in one gulp. He disappeared into thin air. He was laughing as he went. Alpha Michael knew that the King could not see or smell him. He still had to be careful because he could still hear him. Good thing he had shoes made with soles that gave off little to no sound.

If he were careful and quick, he could kill himself a King tonight. It is a better prize than that stupid female. Who knows, with that last throw, maybe he got lucky enough to have killed her anyway.

He approached the King from behind; when he was almost ready to strike, the King turned and backhanded him. He landed roughly against one of the arches, five inches more, and he would have been out the door and to his death.

He stood again, not moving too much to give away his position. He was almost close enough to plunge in the dagger; he raised it high and in a downward swing.

Duncan and Jack were racing up the stairs to the tower as they heard a god-awful roar. It shook the very stones in the walls. The King was in his Lycan form; he must be pissed off.

As they raced to the top, Duncan was frantic to find Adira. Finally, he spotted her over by the far wall. He was there by her side in an instant. She was still sleeping under whatever that old ass of a butler gave her. She had a bruise on her wrist and another on her cheek. He picked her up, so she was safe in his arms.

He mind-linked Jack, telling him that he was getting Adira to the pack doctor. As Duncan passed one of the guards coming up the stairs, he tossed Duncan a pair of pants.

He passed Adira into the arms of another guard just long enough so he could quickly put on the pants, then took Adira back and ran to the pack hospital. That is it, Duncan thought to himself; she wasn't supposed to be a part of this, he was taking her home, and they were going to stay there.

He was going to find out who thought it was part of the plan to use his mate as bait; he was beyond pissed and was going to beat the shit out of someone.

Before Alpha Michael's dagger could contact, a small female wolf came out of the shadows and knocked him.

She wasted no time in her attack; she was on him in a flash of claws and teeth. She bit down on his crotch with all her might and ripped his privates clean off, pants and all. Alpha Michael let out a scream of rage. He knew who this wolf was. He was so pissed that he did not register the pain.

"You should have stayed working on your hands and knees, you bitch. It was, after all, what you're best at doing."

The she-wolf came at Alpha Michael again, taking a chunk out of his thigh. He was bleeding heavily, but he did not care. They were all going to die tonight.

The King watched for a bit and then ran back into the fight.

"Oh, mighty King. Alpha Michael sneered; if only you knew what your son Prince Adam was up to. Perhaps you wouldn't be so cocky."

The King let out a roar, in his Lycan's voice, *"I know exactly what my son was up to and what he is doing right now. He is dead; I know this because I was the one who took his head."*

For the second time in his life, Alpha Michael knew what absolute fear felt like. Then just as the mad rush dissipated, he felt his pain and gave out a pathetic cry, rushing the king head-on; he never made it, though.

Again out of the shadows came the she-wolf; she ran straight at him, pushing him back, then she kept pushing back, repeatedly, each time taking a bite out of him till he was a bloody mess.

She was making terrible growls. Her ears were back, her tail was straight as she gave one more push, and Alpha Michael fell through the arches taking Lily and Zinnia with him.

Jack and the King were the only ones left in the King's tower. Jack broke the silence...

"I did not see things ending like this, not even close. Who would have known that the wolf had it in her."

"Is Lady Adira alright? Was their pup hurt? Is Duncan going to be mad for a long time?"

"Well, your highness, I think both Lady Adira and pup will be just fine; for how long Duncan will stay pissed, well, if it were you, how long do you think you would be.?"

The King let out a sigh, *"Yeah, I see your point."*

They both stared out into the distance enjoying the silence when they heard a slight whimpering noise. They looked at each other and ran to the ledge where Alpha Michael and Lily went.

To their amazement, there was a very naked Lily hanging on to the rocks on the side of the tower.

The King and Jack started laughing, not at Lily, just at the situation she found herself in. The King decided that he would have to do something about her sentence; he could not make her a lifetime servant after all that. He would have to find something else for her to do.

She looked up at them, *"I know I'm in a lot of trouble, and I did escape but before you punish me, do you think you can get me off the side of this tower? I hate heights, and it is getting a bit chilly in places I have not been chilly before."*

The King mind-linked anyone who would listen with a list of things that were needed and to have a dozen guards to help out. Getting a naked she-wolf off the side of the castle turned into a bigger deal than Lily wanted. It turned out half the kingdom decided they needed to see the spectacle.

After three hours, Lily was back in her room dressed and trying to forget the whole thing.

CHAPTER THIRTY-FIVE

Duncan lay in bed with Adira in his arms, guarding her like a dragon with a favorite jewel. The doctors were sure that no actual harm came to her, except a minor bump on the head and some bruises. The sleeping powder that was used was all herbal and had no ill effects on the mother or pup. They told him that she would wake up in the morning.

After bringing her back to their room, Duncan moved their bed into a corner; he put Adira on the enclosed side of the bed and then wrapped himself around her, with his back to the world as their shield.

When a servant came in to give them some early breakfast, she was greeted with an extremely low, angry growl and promptly left the room running. Anyone that came to that door that night and early morning was welcomed similarly.

Finally, the King stepped in and told everyone to stay away until they came out on their own. Jack was not going to so much as put a toe in that room, though he was sure that Duncan would let him in. He just was not sure if Duncan would let him leave in one piece.

He checked on them right after returning from the hospital; he found the bed was moved into a position that could be easily defended.

On the bed next to a sleeping Adira was a giant golden wolf, that meant nothing but business; it did not matter if you were a friend or foe. It was a kill them all and asked questions later kind of situation.

Jack did not blame Duncan one little bit; he agreed to the plan if Adira wasn't a part of it. Of course, none of them knew that the informer was Alfred; had they known that Adira would have been locked in her chambers with a dozen guards inside and a dozen more outside.

When dealing with evil, you sometimes cannot fathom how deep its roots go. In this case, it was prejudice: the oldest and easiest sin to get into the hearts of all species. No exceptions.

The King was not much better to deal with; not only did he feel terrible that Lady Adira was put in danger, but also about his lifelong-trusted servant Alfred.

He ordered that Alfred be put in the darkest dungeon hole they had. Then he appointed the guard captain to question him in any means he saw fit to get the whole story out of him.

When they were done, Alfred had done what he did because he felt Adira was not worthy of anything. That her birth was too low to be considered anything at all, and he was afraid that she would get a higher standing than just a lady.

The King ordered Alfred to be left in that dungeon hole to rot, with no food, no water. He must be left there to deteriorate when he dies until nothing is left but his bones. When he is nothing but bones, they were to gather them up and toss them willy-nilly in the forest.

As for Lily, the King decided that she would become an advocate for abused and exploited pups and human children. She would travel from pack to pack, giving information and making speeches on the subject. She would relate to everyone she met, what happened to her, the things she did under the influence of the Alpha's voice, and her actions fueled by her anger.

A guard would accompany her for her safety. Just in case, she met up with a former abuser, which would be reported to the King personally and investigated. She will do this for ten months out of the year. She will return to her room for intensive therapy for the other two.

She will continue to do this until her therapist feels she is in control of her emotions and has forgiven herself.

Duncan did not care if his behavior was rude or that he was scaring people. He, too, blamed himself for what happened; he should have been with her so that none of it would have happened.

It wasn't till around noon that Adira started to wake up. She tried to move, but a hot and heavy male wolf was lying on her. She gave out a sigh wondering why it was Apollo, and when she started to move, he let out a small whimper and started to lick her face.

"EwWwee...lick...Apollooo...lick...stop it....lick,lick....Apollo.....lick...Stop please!"

"I love you too, Apollo, but now I need a shower. Where is Duncan? Is he hiding? I don't remember anything from last night; I was drugged, and Artemis confirms it."

When she rolled over to look at Apollo, a very naked Duncan waited for her.

"Why was Apollo out and about?"

"He was so worried about you, little wolf; I was just a bit too agitated to be allowed out unchecked. So Apollo took over."

"How are you feeling, little wolf?"

"I feel a little sore in places, and my head hurts a little. Other than that, I am ok. Artemis says the pup is perfectly fine. Now, will you tell me what went on last night?"

"I will tell all after we have some breakfast or lunch; I am not sure of the time."

Duncan stuck his head out the door and caught a terrified servant girl; he very carefully told her that they needed some food and something to drink and would she please relay his message to the kitchen staff. She ran off in a hurry. Duncan watched her go; the grass did not grow under her feet.

He figured they had about half an hour or so before the food would come, just enough time to get his mate in the shower. Mind linking Apollo; *"Wow, **man, you are a slobber puss.**"* He looked at their mate's hair, sticking to the side of her face; she tried to move it away.

He started laughing, but when his mate looked at him, he could see that it was Artemis; she looked back at him like she would rip him a new one.

Duncan thought it was wise at that moment to hold back any laughter, at least until after the shower. What was the old saying, happy wife, happy life?

Alfred sat in a filthy cell; there were not any windows, bed, toilet, bucket, floor, just dirt and cold mildewy walls. The only light came in from a small slit under the door.

He could not hear anything; he didn't even think mice had found their way here. He had been here now for two days. When the door opened with an ominous creaky squeal.

The captain of the guards stood before him; it took his eyes some time to adjust to the light.

Alfred Marvin Thomas Harrington, third-generation personal servant to the Royal Family. You are, at this moment, sentenced to death. You will remain in this cell until you are dead. Alfred looked on in shock.

"He can't do this to me; I am a high servant."

"YOU ARE A TRAITOR, AND THE PUNISHMENT FOR THIS CRIME IS DEATH."

After the guard yelled at him, Alfred sat down in the dirt. The guard came in and sat something down beside him: a blanket, pillow, a bucket, one loaf of bread, and a paper cup of water.

"Listen carefully; once this door is shut, you will not come out again till you are nothing but bones."

The guard then shut the door leaving Alfred crying in the dark. He hated that stupid lowlife she-wolf; she should have never been allowed to even sit at his feet or be called a Lady. He curled up in a ball on the blanket and stared into the darkness.

The King pondered on what he was going to do with his life. He had lost his will to rule anymore. He missed his mate and his sons. He had found out that those you thought were your friends, could suddenly turn out to be traitors for the stupidest reasons.

He had to face it; he was tired. Tired inside and out, his wolf was just as tired as he, maybe more. The King decided that it was time for him to redefine his life. Since he no longer had an heir, he would have to find another who would survive the right of rule test or would have to find his true mate; he did not think that that was ever going to happen, though.

He knew the one he wanted it to be, but he knew Duncan would pass the test. That is, if he will accept the offer. Duncan was the right man for the job; his pack was proof of that. Adira would make a perfect queen. The only question is will they want to do it. If not, then who will he choose.

Jack was on his way to say goodbye; it was time for him to get back to his clan. He and his bear were getting restless from being around too many people. He could not wait for the cool green of the forest to surround him again.

His first stop was the King to ask permission. Then he is off to say goodbye to Duncan and Adira. After that, he would pick up the medical supplies the King promised and the food.

It bugged him that he had to tow his bike back and drive home, but he was going home, which was all that mattered to him right now. As long as his destination was home for good, he could suffer driving the delivery truck there.

Jack was starting to feel that restless feeling again; his bear shifters need to be out in the wide-open spaces; it may also be that he does not have a mate yet. It did not matter when he got home, and things were settled down. He was going on a walkabout.

CHAPTER THIRTY-SIX

Adira sat in their chambers, refusing to think about anything of the past. There was nothing good to dwell on in the past, so she thought up baby names; they found out they were having a boy. She still could not settle on a name just yet.

Duncan was not helping; he kept producing weird names that no kid should have to endure. His last choices consisted of Pubert, Ingleberk, Bertran, and Huckleberry. Adira knew he was just making her laugh. She even thought of choosing one of them just to mess with him for a while.

The other thoughts she was pondering were whether to stay here as Lady Adira; she just wanted to be ordinary again, raise her children away from all this court intrigue and status prejudice.

She had also been deciding on whether to see Alfred. She knew it was stupid, and it would not change anything. She just felt terrible that his sentence was so harsh. To die slowly, alone in the dark. It has been a week, and he is gone already at his age.

As stupid as it was, she needed to do this ever since she went to his quarters and found the boxes. She gathered a basket of food and other items, nothing that would aid in his escape. Well, that depended on how you looked at it. She felt that she just wanted to show him some mercy. He was an old man stuck in an old world; there were many like him. Granted, they did not try to kill anyone.

Perhaps he was dying alone and in the dark; she didn't know for sure, but she made her way to the dungeons anyway. She was hoping that they would let her in.

The guard stopped her at the gate...

"Lady Adira, what brings you to the dungeons? This is no place for a lady in your condition."

"My condition, what is it with all the male population? You make it sound like it is a disease. I'm pregnant, not made of fragile glass that I might break at the slightest whim."

"As for why I am here, I wish to see one of your prisoners."

"Which one do you wish to see, my Lady.?"

"Alfred"

The guard looked taken aback. *"That prisoner is off-limits, my lady."*

"Listen, I understand why he was sentenced to death. I understand that the king says that he has to die alone, I understand everything except one thing, why. I know his thoughts of me; what I don't understand is why he would betray his King."

"I want answers, and the only way to get them is to ask Alfred before he dies."

"Alright, my lady, under two conditions."

"1. You let me go with you as your guard."

"2. I have to inform the King."

"Fine, you can come along and inform who you will; it will not stop me from doing what I wish to do here."

Alfred sat in the darkness feeling weak and tired. He was hoping death would find him in here. He was not so sure, though. It seemed to be taking too much time; he laughed at that; he was old and close to death, yet he complained that it was taking too long.

He heard a noise or was it just another figment of his imagination? When the tiny sliver of light shined on his face, he hissed in pain. When the door was open, a figure was standing there, and he knew who it was before she even spoke one word.

"Why are you here?" he asked with a sneer.

Duncan and the King were in his chambers discussing the idea that Duncan and Adira were returning home to have their pup. When a guard, out of breath, came into the room.

"Your Highness and Alpha Duncan, I am here to inform you what Lady Adira is doing at this moment."

"She is going to visit Alfred."

"SHE IS DOING WHAT???"

Duncan and the King both raced down in a fury to the dungeons.

Adria went into the cell with a very nervous guard at her side.

"I just wanted to share some food and wine with you one last time and ask you some questions, if you are willing, that is?"

"You mean you want me to suffer even longer by eating the food and drink, stretching out my suffering time."

"No, that is not my intent at all. I thought you could have the civility you always wanted to surround you for one last time. A bit of dignity if you will."

He looked at her with one eye and then nodded his approval.

She lit some candles to give light; the room did not improve except that she could now see. She sat out what looked like a picnic, but instead of a meadow, it was more like the inside of a cave.

She poured him a plastic cup of wine and set out a plate of food before him, complete with napkin and silverware. Well, just a plastic spoon, but it would have to do; she did not want him getting any ideas. They ate in silence for a little while.

"So Alfred, why did you betray your King? It wasn't just because you felt I was unworthy of the title he gave me."

"Well, I must say I didn't think you were all that smart. I betrayed him because of the mess he made of everything; he stopped caring about things after his mate died. I started to help

out with some things, but no one else could when he had to rule."

"Then I tried to tell him what his son was up to, but he wouldn't listen. Brushing it off as rumors. When I told him that I witnessed the prince's crimes, he still wouldn't believe me."

"Then you came along, and he started to dote on you; you and Duncan were all he would talk about, he believed your story, but he wouldn't ever believe me, a faithful, loyal servant. "

" I had just had enough, that is all. Enough of commoners thinking above their stations, enough of my King not listening to me, while his son started to kill servant girls."

"Alfred, if you knew what the Prince was doing, why didn't you try to stop him yourself?"

"I am not just a servant but a high servant; to do something such as to interfere with a royal member of the house I serve, would be unthinkable."

"So you knew what was going on, and you just let it continue. Even if the King did not listen, I would have found a way to stop or expose it. By knowing and doing nothing, you're just as bad as the criminal that commits the crime."

Alfred did not say anything more after that; Adria knew that it was the end of the conversation. With the help of the guard, they picked up everything and put it all in the basket; just as they were leaving the cell, Duncan and the King came rushing in.

The guard shut the cell door as they walked away; Adira looked back once more and moved on.

Once they were clear of the dungeons, Duncan and the King stopped Adira in the walkway.

"What we're you thinking, Adira, that was taking too big of a risk. Not just for you but our pup as well!"

"That is enough of yelling at me, Duncan; I went because I needed answers, I knew that neither you nor the King would let me go. I was at minimal risk; I was with a guard. Did you not notice that there were two other guards just outside the door? I found the answer I sought and gave him the mercy that he should have been given."

"Adira, what are you talking about? What answer were you seeking, and what mercy did you give him? Feeding him and giving him wine will only prolong his misery."

"I love you, Duncan, and I also care about you, my King; if you go back to that miserable cell, you will see that I have prolonged nothing."

With that, she turned and walked away to her chambers.

Duncan asked Apollo what was going on; he did not know any more than Duncan did; Artemis wasn't talking at the moment.

The King turned and asked the guard with Adira and Alfred what was said while they were together.

"My King, they didn't talk all that much, but Alfred did tell her why he committed treason."

"Did Lady Adira give him anything to keep?"

"No, sir, they ate and drank. They talked for a little bit, and then Lady Adira decided she would not get any more information. That was when we picked up all the stuff and left. There was nothing left in the cell; I made sure of it."

The King motioned for Duncan to come with him back into the dungeon to find out what was going on with Alfred and what this was all about.

When they opened the door to Alfred's cell, he was lying in the dirt. Blood and foam came out of his mouth; his eyes were wide open, his face a look of horror. His hands were at his throat like he was trying to stop choking. However, Alfred was now quite dead.

CHAPTER THIRTY-SEVEN

𝒟uncan was a little alarmed at what Adira had done; he was not sure how to approach the subject. He was also unsure if he wanted to know—his sweet little wolf, who was all that was understanding and kind, just poisoned a man to death.

Letting out a big sigh, he opened the door to their chambers. Adira was there waiting for him; she patted the seat on the sofa next to her. She had been waiting for him and knew that he would want answers without consulting with their wolves.

He sat down on the opposite side of the sofa and patted his lap; she laid her head down where he wanted—playing lightly with her hair and tracing the outside of her ear.

"Tell me, my little wolf, why did you do it?"

"Oh, Duncan. It was his punishment for what he did. After talking with him, I realized why he was so corrupted. That is why I gave him the poison, I brought it with me, but I wasn't

sure if I would use it. He confirmed it with his answers to my questions."

"I got the poison in Alfred's room; he had two boxes. One was potions; the other was poisons. I took out the one with my name on it. "Spare."

"He had poison with your name on it. That evil old turd, I should go and kill him again."

"I think he was hoping not to use it; I think it was his backup plan should things not go the way he wanted."

"Anyone who thinks that killing someone because they are different or not high enough of a class, are unhinged. These are dangerous people. First, they start with one or two, then before you know it, entire populations."

"He knew that I was carrying our pup; he would have murdered not only me but also our pup. I didn't want to leave here, not knowing for myself that he was dead. I couldn't let him take his sweet time to do it; if he knew I had poisoned his food, he would refuse to eat."

"Enough about that evil turd; let's talk about what will be coming in two weeks."

Duncan sat in silence for a bit and decided that he liked knowing Adira had an edge if pushed too far to protect herself and her family. He wasn't sure if it would have been just Adira's life that Alfred tried taking. She might have done nothing, but even if she won't admit it to herself, he threatened their pup—something no mother will tolerate.

"Little wolf, you are not due for another month and a half; what else could there be?"

"Christmas, you silly wolf!"

"I have never had one; I was always in the attic and was not allowed to show my face. So, I want a Christmas; I want everything to do with Christmas. Everything, leave nothing out."

Duncan got a sad look on his face.

"What is it, Dun? You don't want Christmas?"

"Don't be a silly little wolf; I was sad because before all this crap started, we were starting to plan our wedding."

"I know, my love; I just thought we would do something simple and have a party or something with the pack at a later time. However, now that I think about it, I don't want to compromise. So how about we have a Christmas wedding?"

"I will have all the other Christmas celebrations I want later in the future with you and our pups."

"We will have the wedding and dinner celebration here, and then we are going home to our pack to have our party. I want to spend some time with you there and have our pup. Can't deprive the pack of its Alpha and Luna for too long."

"I am not sure what the King has in store for the future, but I know it will take him some time to set things in motion. I am taking that time to get to know and be with our pack; you barely met any of the pack members. You are their Luna, after all."

Duncan was done talking; he wanted his mate all night long. He had already ordered their dinner brought to them. He grabbed her hand and helped her stand up. Turning her around, reaching her front, he began to undo the buttons on her blouse.

She moved to help him, but he stopped her, huskily whispering in her ear…

"I want to go slow; I want this to last all night long."

His lips slowly made their way down her neck to his mark; he licked it and nipped it, driving her insane with pleasure. He held her back tightly to him and massaged her breasts; he started to suck on his mark like giving her a hickey.

She gave out a high-pitched wail and a moan as she reached her climax; she would have fallen to the floor if he hadn't held her upright.

He turned her to face him again, she started to undress him, but it wasn't fast enough. He ripped off his shirt and pants. Standing naked before her, he picked her up and carried her to the bed.

She crawled up it till she was on her hands and knees. Duncan wasted no time; he came up behind her and entered her in one slippery naked thrust. He tossed his head back and let out a howl. He was home. She was his. He was hers. Perfect.

He stood in the middle of what used to be The Rising Moon pack. Now it is nothing but burnt grass and ash. He was furious. He at first thought that piece of shit shifter packed up and left. This was different, though; this looked like annihilation.

Everything was gone; he sensed movement off to his right inside the forest line. He didn't know who it was, but he ran back to his car, driving off in a hurry. Just what he fucking needed; he has a shipment due in two weeks. He could get the females anywhere if it were for just the average pervert.

These guys were scientists and wanted shifters. They wanted werewolves, werebears, and werecats. It didn't matter. As long as they were shifters, they would pay a premium price.

He wasn't sure where to go to get more; he would have to find his initial contact, which wouldn't be easy.

This shifter was a ghost; you would not see him if he didn't want to be seen. He also knew that at least one stronger group of weres was nearby, because of all the damage done to Rising Moon.

He will have to locate that pack and send a team to harvest some of them.

When his cell went off, Jack was fueling up and getting some snacks at a gas station for the road. It was one of the guards he left at what was left of the Rising Moon pack. He reported that they had a late-night visitor. He didn't stay long enough to look at him, but they did get his license plate number.

Jack hung up; the third player has come out to play. He knew that Alpha Michael wasn't acting alone. He had the prince to finance it all, and Michael took care of acquiring the products. That left distribution of products.

Jack knew it wouldn't be easy to find the one shipping the products. They were never easy to find because of all the paperwork and programs they hide behind. With Shell companies by the time you find a location, they have already changed fake addresses, it was like a game whack a mole.

Jack hoped that this third wheel would stay away, but no such luck. When shit rolls downhill, it takes the whole outhouse with it. He would have to call in all kinds of favors to get this guy.

He would have to tell Duncan when he could, let him know that one more turd was still floating in the bowl.

Duncan had just gotten the text from Jack about the third guy involved. How was he going to tell Adira this? It's going to ruin everything. He let out a few swears into the air.

Adira came into the room with concern written all over her face.

"What is wrong, Duncan?"

"Well, I just got some bad news from Jack; he texted to tell me that there is yet another idiot to deal with. The one that took care of shipping everything and finding new clients for Alpha Michael."

"Adria didn't look happy, and that was the last thing that Duncan wanted; even Apollo was pissed. He didn't like anyone near Adira since she became pregnant, it made his wolf want to go and kill things."

"I've talked to Marco; we leave here in three days, just long enough to have our little wedding and pack up. Marco will be sending a boatload of pack warriors to escort us home. My sister is on her way here right now, so she can be part of the wedding. Then she will be with us as we travel."

"Everything is ready to go, Duncan; we have everything we need for the wedding, including the fact that I had to alter my dress."

"The King sees to all the arrangements and the license. He will have a dinner banquet in honor of our marriage; there will also be a few royals but no one else."

"The King is still paranoid about who he can and can't trust. He also says he has a surprise gift for us too. Everything is ready to go for tomorrow night."

With that all said, they cuddled each other in bed; Duncan had his hand over Adira's abdomen, protecting their pup.

"I love you, Adira."

"I love you, Duncan."

Adira put her hands over Duncan's.

"We love you, our little pup."

CHAPTER THIRTY-EIGHT

Jack made it back to his clan with all the much-needed supplies. They could get everyday things in town; getting some supplies when you are not human can be challenging. For instance, you can't find special herbs and medicines in a regular store. Bulk food is always a good thing, they could get it at a whole foods store, but it isn't the same. He even managed to bring twenty cases of jars back for their honey and maple syrup production.

They sold both honey and syrup in town; they also made jams. Jams were the werebears favorite, they never sold any of the jams, that was always primarily made for their consumption.

Did they need all these things from the King? Not really, but it was a gift. Jack never turned down presents as long as there were no strings attached. This gift was a simple thank you from the King.

Werebears tend to like things as natural as possible, they grow most of their foods and dry, freeze, or can them. Of course, they hunt and fish for their meat, do the same dry, freeze, and can that as well; what they buy is more of a luxury than a need, and those needs are well maintained. No one goes without medicine or doctors.

They even have their own modernized mill to process grains and such for several types of flour.

They don't have internet or television. Nor do they use cell phones while in clan territory. Cell phones don't work in the mountains anyway. They have a landline for several phones stationed in the houses, so they can call if needed.

They have their doctors and hospitals, and Jack ensures they have all the modern equipment and training they need and whatever supplies and medicines they request.

They also have jobs out in the human towns, such as sheriff and police officers to truck drivers. There is a wide assortment of jobs they tend to hold down; the only thing in common with them all is that werebears tend to stay in the small towns and rural areas.

Jack's clan is a bit more unusual than usual; they are a big clan, mostly grizzly, which is exceedingly rare that it is more legend and old stories than reality.

Adira stood in front of a full-size mirror, looking on in disbelief that the woman staring back at her was her. Her gown was gorgeous; it was an empire waist, and off-white with gold trim and designs. It was made as a velvet overskirt with silk and tulle. It had lots of sparkles.

Adira almost didn't wear it because she discovered the sparkle was actual diamonds. It also had a cathedral train. Her lady's maids did a fantastic job on her hair in an elaborate style of braids and curls.

A small golden crown with diamonds and sapphires attached to a long flowing lace veil was upon her head. It was perfect. She was about ready to leave to go to the waiting area at the court when a knock came at the door.

When the lady's maids opened the door, there stood the King in his finest, with a massive smile.

"Your highness, Adira gave a very graceful curtsy."

That was when she noticed what the King was holding in his hands. It was her bridal bouquet; it was beautiful with white and cream-colored roses. The roses themselves looked like the tips of their petals were dipped in gold.

"My dear girl, you look beyond amazing; I thought you would need someone to walk you down the aisle. I want to volunteer for this duty if it is alright."

"With teary eyes, she said, I would be honored to have you walk me down."

"Adira, the honor is mine, little one. Now let's get going before your very nervous Duncan explodes."

"Why would Duncan be so nervous? He knows I love him and that we are forever."

"All males, whether they know it or not, think that their brides love them, and it is a sure thing. They are still nervous at that end of the aisle, waiting for their brides to come to join them. I think it has something to do with the fact that at this moment, you could run away and no one would be able to stop you."

Marnie was just in time, looking beautiful in a deep red and gold-trimmed velvet bridesmaid dress. She was practically jumping up and down in excitement. She gracefully picked up Adira's train, gave the King a curtsy, and took her position.

As Duncan stood at the altar, everything went beyond what he thought was possible. The King went all out for their wedding; he chuckled to himself. Small wedding indeed.

Everything was covered in gold or silver sparkles; at least ten Christmas trees were also done in primarily gold and silver sparkles, and fairy lights were everywhere. Someone magically made snowfall from the ceiling; it never landed on the floor though, it was only magical.

A red carpet was going down the center of what looked like a sea of chairs made of sparkling snow. There was light music playing though Duncan couldn't pinpoint where it was coming from.

He was there with Marco at his side; Duncan was happily surprised when Marco showed up with Marnie. He told Duncan he wouldn't let his best friend get married without him. That was that, and now here they are waiting.

The chairs were filled, and the music became louder as they heard the main doors to the hall begin to open; everything but the music was silent.

There she was on the arm of the King; it was as if time had stopped. There was no one else there but Duncan and Adira. Apollo had to remind him to breathe. She was a goddess, his goddess. Till death do they part and beyond.

Adira was in a state of awe. It was everything and anything you could ever want for your wedding and so much more. She gave the King's arm a little squeeze of thank you. When she looked down the aisle, there he was, her Duncan.

Everything else faded away; time no longer had meaning as she looked into his loving eyes. The King leaned in and whispered, *"Just Breathe."* in her ear and she smiled brightly.

They slowly made their way down the aisle to Duncan. The High elder asked, *"Who Gives this Bride?"*

The King spoke in a very firm and loud voice...

"I do." He then reached for Duncan's hand and put Adira's hand in it. He stepped back and went to his seat.

Duncan and Adira only had eyes for each other; they would answer the questions when asked. It was time for them to say their vows. Duncan went first.

"Adira, you woke my heart from a winter's sleep,

the flames of my love are yours forever to keep.

I will always protect and love you till my dying day.

I am your rock; always I will stand, never will I stray."

Adira looked at him with happy tears in her eyes; they shone like diamonds. He felt their bond grow even more than he thought was possible.

"Duncan, I am your other half; forever be I here.

We are facing all our troubles and facing all our fears.

My love for you will never be broken or end.

My prayer they did hear, for you they did send."

Now they spoke the last lines of their vows together, while holding hands.

"Together we are tied, as before all we stand,

We are blessed, and it is by the goddess's hand.

On this day till the end of days, our love will be,

Forever and beyond, it's just you, and it's just me."

"The elder spoke again. Your highness, lords, and ladies. I now give you Alpha Duncan and Lady Adira of the Storm Crow Moon Pack. First bound by Love and now by Law."

"You may now kiss your bride."

Duncan pulled her in for a deep passionate kiss, not caring who was watching. Hoots and whoops were heard coming from the audience. Adira was bright red as they walked back down the aisle and out into the hall.

Once the doors closed again, Duncan picked up Adira and swung her in the air as they both laughed in happiness. She pulled his head in close to hers for another kiss. Deep kisses came one after another as their satisfaction consumed them.

"I am the luckiest wolf in the world right now. You are so beautiful I feel there isn't a word created that would do justice to describe your beauty."

Duncan carried Adira to the banquet hall, kissing and laughing all the way there.

Marnie and Marco followed from behind, taking pictures as they went, but the couple was completely unaware that it was going on, making for some great images.

The banquet hall doors opened, and trumpets sounded as they entered; the King himself announced their presence. Everything was decorated just like it was at the court Ball. Except for the chair for the bride and groom, it was a love seat in red and gold velvet. Duncan sat down with Adira on his lap. They were not letting each other out of sight as they fed each other.

That was how they spent their last night in the castle, in each other's arms.

CHAPTER THIRTY-NINE

Lily was in unfamiliar territory for herself; she had been going through some very intense therapy sessions. The more she remembered and had things pointed out to her, like how Michael groomed her from an early age.

As she got older, things that should have never happened to a five-year-old, were made to seem normal. The ultimate manipulation. She had been exhausted lately and was glad that she had her room as a retreat of sorts, she was allowed a TV, and now she could watch movies.

She was also treated a lot better now by the guards and servants. The guards even got her snacks now and then. The nightmares still come at night; they are not as long-term anymore, she has them, but she can also calm herself down. If they are particularly bad, Zinnia steps in and helps her.

The door outside isn't locked anymore; she still has one guard through at night; it was a suggestion from her therapist. It was to help her feel safe at night and help her if she started sleepwalking again.

At first, she didn't like the idea of a strange male hanging around with the ability to enter her private space. Over time they managed to gain her trust, especially after one night of sleepwalking.

She left her room; the guard on duty, 'George,' called her therapist and followed her outside; she went up on the castle's ramparts.

George got incredibly nervous because she kept getting closer and closer to the edge. She came to a part that had a step-down shelf. He went under her on the shelf and when she jumped; instead of falling to her death, George had caught her in mid-air.

She woke up at once. At first, she struggled until he calmed her down enough for her to look and see where she was. When she did, she grabbed onto George with a death grip. He grunted at the pain but walked her to her room, where the therapist was waiting.

Since then, George has been on duty most nights, and the nights he is not, there is someone he vouches for.

She keeps her door locked from the inside to help with the sleepwalking. Her therapist thinks that her sleepwalking might be an extension of her subconscious, where she wants to die to be with her mate.

Last night though, she had a different nightmare, a memory she had pushed away to the back of her mind. She was ten years old; Alpha Michael held her hand as they walked down a long hallway; it was like a hospital.

People in white lab coats looked at her as she was put on a table. They strapped her down, and she was terrified. They poked her with needles and scraped her skin till it bled.

It was a lot harder to track her as she got older, so first, they used her parents to drug her food. After that, she stopped eating and drinking things her mother gave her. They resorted to hunting her down with tranquilizer darts.

They stopped suddenly, though; she wasn't sure why, except Alpha Michael was worried they might force her into drastic measures or their secret getting out. He could only threaten someone for so long before it would no longer matter.

There was always this one guy in the shadows, he wasn't one of the doctors, but he was always there; she could always see his eyes glowing gold; he always gave her the creeps; she called him the Lurker.

Valdis Cessair hated shifters even though he was one. He was tall, with an olive complexion, dark hair, and golden eyes. Most women would consider him handsome until they spent any time with him.

He was not one to settle down and have a family; he preferred to hunt, kill, and eat his dates. It was a great sport and a stress reliever.

Waiting for this informer was a pain in the ass; he was the only source of information he had, so wait, he did. When he saw a flash of light, he got out of his car and headed into the woods.

He never saw the informer, but he could smell him a mile away. He was a rogue. The longer they are rogue, the stinker and crazier they get. From the smell of this guy, he was most definitely crazy.

Val was waiting for the day he could kill this piece of crap. He hated rogues more than anything else in the world. There will be time when he outlives his usefulness, and Val can have his fun.

Val waited for it to start talking.

"There are two packs in this mountain region; One is the Storm Crow Moon pack; the other is the Bear Mountain Clan. Werewolves and Werebears, if I were you, I would leave the bears alone, they are assholes, there are some that have never returned when they went into their territory."

"The Storm Crow isn't anything to take lightly either; it's a warrior pack. Their Luna will be back soon, and it's rumored

that she is carrying their first pup. That means that the group will be even harder to infiltrate."

"That is all the info I have; I will try to get more for now, but the two packs you asked about are the worst for rogues to go near."

Val walked away back to his car. So werewolves and werebears too. The bears being together in a clan is something unique and dangerous. It is a temptation he couldn't resist. If he could get both Werewolf and Werebear specimens, then the secret society of Science would get off his back.

It's funny that those arrogant scientists never discovered that he was a shifter. Then again, he suspected they knew, but he was more beneficial to them in getting their specimens than being one.

He would also make sure to get children and adults this time, they will pay a premium for both, but they love the kids the most—something about them being more resilient against pain and experimentation.

Time to get his extraction groups together for some recon and training. First, though, he called in two of his best to scout the territories and see how far they could push in without being discovered.

Duncan, Adira, Marnie, and Marco returned to the Raven Moon in a lengthy line of black SUVs. The King was not playing when it came to security. He made sure that no one would attack them on the road.

He also assigned all the security that went with them to stay, adding to Duncan's already impressive force.

Marnie and Adira were in the back seat going through baby names and baby store sites online. Duncan mind-linked to Marco.

"Our pup will be spoiled rotten before he is even born," Marco laughed.

"Wait till you see what is waiting for you both at home. You don't honestly think that they were not going to throw a party, did you?"

Duncan laughed,

"I know, and I look forward to it; Adira never got much chance to meet the pack. This will be ideal for her; soon, she will not have as much mobility."

"I just hope everyone is on board with their new Luna; she wasn't officially recognized or given the official Luna acceptance ceremony."

"Don't worry, Duncan. I had a ceremony of sorts, and everyone was on board and loved their new Luna."

Duncan couldn't help it. He was uneasy; something was stirring in the air and hiding in the shadows.

Sigh, he hoped it was just because he was tired. Still, he wasn't going to ignore the feeling. Once things are settled down, he will have a meeting with all his warriors.

"Marco, after the party tomorrow, I want a meeting with all the warriors and those sent by the King. I will not be caught with our pants down."

"Yes, Alpha. It is good to have you home again. Now I can get some sleep."

He was going to see about expanding his territory a little bit; there were no other packs near him except for Jacks. With all these extra's, he could have a guard every ten feet on all his borders and still have plenty leftover.

On the following day that Jack was home, one of his border guards informed him of some unusual tracks, they didn't go far into their territory, but they did get inside it. Jack went with his second in command to investigate.

Once they got there, Jack could smell the faint scent in the air, and looking at the tracks; he knew instantly that it wasn't good.

His second was right there with him; he also knew what they were dealing with as he sighed.

"Great, things just get settled down, and now we have to deal with fucking werecats. Not sure which type we are dealing with; the scent is too faint. It doesn't matter; they are all tree climbing, asshole jerks with a superiority complex."

Jack nodded his head in agreement, he met a few werecats in his time, and he even had one that was a good friend of his; to be honest, though, most werecats were assholes and bastards to deal with. So what is this one up to.

That Rising Moon crap is still floating around even after burning it. That pack wasn't werewolves, they cockroach shifters eating shit and spreading disease. Wolves would have died by now. Not these nasty bastards; they just keep popping up like daisies.

Jack was tired of this crap; it was time to call in his friend, the werecat, and his pride to see if they could nip this in the bud. The time for having fun with your enemy is over. It is time to get serious and no more playing. Time to bring the pain.

He also made a mental note to call Duncan to be on the lookout for sneaky kitty cats.

Chapter Forty

The pack was settled down; the party was a tremendous success. Luna Adira was resting and hanging out with Marnie. Adira told her all the details of the things that went on while at the castle. Marnie was making sure that she took it easy from now on.

Marnie had taken up as Adira's personal female guard, but also the King sent three personal guards for her and Duncan. Duncan liked that Adira had extra security, but he hated it for himself.

He decided since it was still a too little early to sleep, he and Marco would go patrolling together along the borders. Of course, his three shadows also had to tag along; one good thing about them is that they stayed out of the way.

Duncan had a great run with Apollo; it was what they needed the most. A good run in their territory. They were heading to the western border when both wolves stopped in the alert. They could sense that they were not alone and were being watched.

Duncan and Marco shifted back, grabbing shorts from a nearby stash. They stopped and pretended to talk and catch up with each other, moving closer and closer to the source of the energy they were feeling.

Duncan mind-linked his three shadows to come from different directions to the tree they were standing by.

A very loud snarl could be heard; it was a big werecat. Duncan and Marco looked at each other; Marco started walking around the tree, taunting the cat. "*Here, Kitty, Kitty.*" It was working. The cat didn't like bullying. They never did.

Just as they thought that they would catch themselves a cat, it leaped with an angry growl onto another tree, then another, till it was gone. They didn't bother to give chase since it was no longer in their territory.

The werecat did expose itself long enough for them to get a good look at it; it was a leopard shifter.

Everyone marked the smell of its scent to share with other guards and warriors. They also armed themselves as well. Cat shifters tend to like playing dirty. It's best just to get them at a distance and kill them. Otherwise, you must change into Lycan form.

Either way, werecats are a pain in the ass. Duncan didn't like that this one was so close. Usually, they get a drifter now and then. They will stay the night and then move on.

A few of them were great guys and relayed information on rogues. Some were loners passing through. Occasionally, you get a real asshole and must put him down.

Duncan's mind-linked all his warriors, telling them what they found and that there would be extra training for those who hadn't dealt with werecats before.

He would have to give Jack a call and tell him that they had a stray cat problem.

Val sat in his office listening to his spies; they were not happy to be sent into bear territory. No one is ever happy to go into bear territory, not even other bears.

They had been gathering human specimens; they were easy pickings. Humans with unique abilities were coveted by their buyers. He wanted the real prize, though.

"Sir, are you sure you want to do this? These two packs will be a lot of trouble, if not deadly. We couldn't even get far

into the werebear clan's territory before a fricken grizzly came out of the bushes to investigate."

The werewolf clan was in some ways worse; his spy there couldn't get inside the territory at all and was almost captured. Werewolves have one advantage over werecats. Werecats can mask their presence and their smell. Werewolves have one annoying ability, though, they can sense their energy.

Bears can smell them even when they mask their scent. The only way into their territory, would be a gap in their security; that isn't going to happen there; that clan is much too large. They would have to wait and see when they left the safety of their territory to see if they could ambush them.

As for the werewolves, he would have to produce a huge distraction to deal with them. Dang, he hated this kind of shit. Dealing with weak or corrupted packs was easy pickings; dealing with these two, however, was going to be a challenge.

He might have to call in some backup on this one. He would rather not because it was less of a payday for him. However, if he were dead, he couldn't enjoy the money anyway.

Lily couldn't stop that damn nightmare; it would repeatedly play every time she shut her eyes. It was getting frustrating. It was like her mind was trying to find something but couldn't, so it repeatedly played the same memory until it did.

Her therapist was trying to help her figure it out; they even tried hypnosis; again, it was the memory of that moment and those damn golden eyes. She was starting to feel that she was close to figuring it out; it was staying just out of reach.

Even if it's painful, she vowed to discover the whole memory.

Jack and Duncan met at the little coffee shop in town; they discussed the things happening and tried to figure out this next puzzle.

They picked up a local paper and found a link; several human girls and young boys had gone missing. Cops can't find any suspects or even a hint of a clue. The town went into lockdown. No one went out after dark; they never went anywhere alone during the day.

It slowed things down; no new cases had been reported. That just means they are lying low, waiting for their guards to drop so they can continue again.

Jack decided it would be a clever idea to give the town some added protection; since they both now have extra warriors; they were going to assign some of them to the city itself.

They figured it had to be a small group of cats; werecats are the worst for getting along, especially males. They only form groups if there is a family connection.

Stray females they will take in; males, though, are killed on sight. Any lone females that have young tend to stay away in fear that their cubs will be murdered.

Sometimes though it is rare, a group of stray males will group. It makes it easier to take over other family groups. When they attack, they kill all the males and male cubs. They keep all the females.

Depending on the type of werecats, the females can be more deadly than the males, especially if they have young to protect. Jack had heard stories of one female weretiger that killed a whole group of wereleopards that tried to take her daughter.

Marnie was sitting in her room, looking at designs on her computer. She was put in charge of designing the pup's nursery. She enjoyed herself; she loved Adira like the sister she'd always wanted.

Still, though she was getting lonely, it seemed like forever waiting for her mate to show up. In truth, she'd given up after a couple of years passed by. At first, she hoped that it would be Marco, but it wasn't. Still, she hoped.

She had been practicing her magical skills with the Mages. She can create fire and throw it. Her other magic skills, though, are lacking. Still, it was something she could depend on and her fighting skills; she was a formidable fighter, and in that aspect, she was badass.

She'd been feeling restless lately, not even going for runs with her wolf. Myan had tried to help, but her wolf was restless too. She should arrange for her and Adira to go shopping in town. Nothing elaborate, just a little outing.

Yes, that is just what she needed; Adira needs it too. She is getting bigger, and soon, she won't be going out too far to do anything. More baby clothes or some comfortable maternity clothes.

She jumped up from her room and skipped down the hall to her brother's office. It was time to see if her brother would allow Adira out of his sight for a couple of hours; not like we would be alone anyway, not with all the guards as their shadows.

Duncan was just finishing some reports when his sister came barging in. He smiled to himself; what is she up to now.

"Duncan, I want permission to take Adira on a shopping trip, just into town. Not the city or big malls. Just some small shops and have lunch. Soon she isn't going to be going too far; she still needs some maternity clothes and some small things for the pup."

"Sooooo, can we go?"

She was giving him those puppy dog eyes she had used since they were kids. However, Duncan wasn't sure if it was such a good idea. Things were calm right now, and the borders had been silent. Still, he wasn't sure.

"Alright, you can go, but you will not only take her guards, but you will also take six of our warriors along and a driver."

"You will keep your cell phones in hand; if anything goes wrong, I want you both gone; let the guards and warriors handle it."

"Also, Marco and I will be meeting with Jack; he is bringing a friend of his to help us with a new issue. You will be on your best behavior."

"Understood?"

She stood up and hugged him, then saluted him before bouncing out the door.

CHAPTER FORTY-ONE

Val had placed spies throughout the town, staying away from the werewolf and werebear territories. This small town was still considered under their protection, but it wasn't guarded as much; from what Val saw, it wasn't guarded as well as it could be, mostly though he still had to be careful.

He found an older house on the outskirts of town. It was perfect as a base for him. It was hidden by a long drive, trees, and overgrown bushes; it was an ideal location for him and for hiding anyone who comes and goes from the property.

There were many rooms, and the basement had only one way in or out. He found several strange things in the house that made him wonder about the previous owners.

Some rooms had locks on the outside of the doors; the basement even had shackles and chains still hooked up and ready. It goes to show you never know what goes on behind closed doors. This house had to be one of Alpha Michael's or one of his client's hideaways.

Who would have thought that the one weakness of those two packs was this charming small town filled with humans? Val had two more aces up his sleeve, he wasn't entirely sure about them, but he knew he could buy them for a fair price.

Now all he had to do was wait. One thing Val knew was that he was good at waiting. The art of the ambush was in his blood, and waiting is the anticipation builder of the game.

Duncan and Marco waited on the deck of the packhouse as two cars drove up, escorted by Jack on his motorcycle. Duncan always laughed when he remembered how Jack hated riding in a car; he looked uncomfortable and grumpy.

Duncan watched as they all got out of the cars and walked up to them. Only one of them stood out to Duncan; he was a big guy with long sandy blond hair, muscles everywhere, and gold eyes. Duncan knew the second he caught his scent.

He was a Werelion. Rarest of all the shifters and the deadliest. You didn't want to piss a werelion off; it would be a painfully long death. Werelions have been known to eat their kills slowly while the prey was still alive.

All their guests gave small bows to Alpha Duncan. Duncan, in turn, he gave them the same respect. He had to admit that there was a certain primal power emanating from these three.

Marco spoke, *"Good afternoon and welcome to the Storm Crow Moon pack, Gentlemen; if you follow me, I will take us to the Alpha office, where we will have some refreshments and talk."*

Duncan left them, to go to his office first, ensuring everything was in order. He sat down just as Marco and the guests came in.

After everyone was seated, the meeting began. Duncan began...

"As you all know, we have a problem with werecats. Though they were only detected once on both Stone Mountain and Storm Raven borders, I do not think it is the end."

"A few of my elders believe it was just a scouting mission to evaluate our security. That once they found it unyielding, they gave up. Perhaps, looking for alternative routes."

"Some of my warriors think that that was the end of it."

"I think this kind of thinking is dangerous and naive. I have seen too much of this stuff turned into a full-blown attack, so I am not letting it go."

"When Jack told me that he was calling a friend, I had hoped that not only will they help you, Jack, but perhaps you would also consider helping my pack as well."

"I know that the history between our species isn't precisely a friendly basis. This pack has never had a problem with Werecat prides."

The three newcomers looked at each other; the largest of the three nodded.

"My name is Archer Bennet. These two behind me are my twin brothers, August, and Ashton Bennet. As you by now know, we are Werelions. Our numbers are smaller in comparison to other Were species."

"We keep our true numbers secret for our own good reasons, which I might discuss later. We wish to be taken to your borders, especially where you detected the presence of the werecats."

"Even if the trail has gone cold, we can still detect a few things about them. Things that your species might not pick up. This will tell us what type of werecat they are, if they are loners or in pride."

"This will also help us with what we might be dealing with and develop a strategy. There are rumors in the cat prides that some loners are making their own prides."

"They are not behaving like normal cats either; they are into all kinds of nefarious activities; they are hunted just like your species hunts the rogue because of the things they do; one of their favorite hobbies is trafficking other species."

They decided it was best to go to the borders and hope they could find something that Duncan and Jack couldn't.

Archer Bennet didn't like dealing with other species; it was rare for a werelion to have friends other than other werelions. Jack was the exception, and because of Jack, he now has some werewolves as allies; he had to admit that he liked Alpha Duncan, and some of the things they thought about wolf shifters were wrong.

One of the gifts of being a werelion, especially a King was that you had a sixth sense; you always know two things about who you are dealing with; the first is you always know when they are lying, the second, you can tell the integrity of the individual.

So far, he liked who he was dealing with, straightforward, honest, and not some stuck-up, self-important idiot. It is plain to see that his pack is running well and that its members respect the Alpha and his Luna.

He wondered where the Luna was, though; he thought she would be greeting them as well; with her being pregnant, they are keeping her away from any potential danger. Three unknown werelions would be considered dangerous.

Archer was also impressed by the relationship between The Alpha and his beta; you could tell that they are close; if it came to a fight where both fought together, he would hate to be their enemies.

They were at the site, and Archer and his brothers started to check the area; it didn't take long before he picked up a scent; it was faint, but it was still there. He let out a low rumble of a growl.

"Weretigers."

Marnie and Adira decided to go shopping; they took two SUVs. The first was security; the second had more security with Marnie and Adira.

They also had two more security males riding motorcycles. They decided that the motorcycles had more room to maneuver into key positions, should something happen on the road.

They were excited to get out for a bit, though having all this security was causing some anxiety. Though most of the guards they knew, there were two they did not know. The two were of the group the King had sent.

They insisted that they ride with Marnie and Adira. Marnie wasn't sure about them yet; Adira agreed. They both decided to be wary of them but not let it ruin their trip.

Their first stop was for pizza; Adira had a craving for pizza with extra mushrooms and bacon. After spending an hour with the two new guards, they decided they were ok guys. Adira wasn't sure, though; she wasn't sure if it was intuition or hormones.

So she stayed close to the other guards instead. There were three stores in the town; one was a small mom-and-pop shop that sold a little of everything, clothing, and accessories. The third was for children and baby clothes.

There was a grocery store as well as a gas station. It wasn't a huge town, but it had a well-rounded supply of stores because it was isolated. They even had an antique store/electronic repair shop.

They also had a small diner and a bakery. Both were good.

Their first stop was the baby shop; they were excited when they saw all the homemade clothing, blankets, and other baby accessories. Adira picked up several handmade items and a beautiful hand-carved highchair.

Their second stop was the clothing store, to which they picked up a couple of outfits for Adira and some loose comfortable stuff to wear after the pup comes.

They decided to go to the antique shop last; it was small, so only two guards came in while the others waited outside. They browsed for a while when Adira noticed that the clerk was no longer with them in the shop.

When she looked out the big shop window, she noticed all their guards were lying on the ground. There was a fog surrounding them.

Marnie started to growl; three males were in the shop beside their two guards. Without them realizing it, they were herded to the back of the shop. Marnie and Adira managed to Mind link Duncan and Marco with three words....*"Ambush, antiques, HELP!...."*

Just as Adira turned around to look at Marnie, she felt a sting like a bee at the back of her neck; as she was starting to fall, she could see Marnie being caught in the arms of one of the guards.

Everything went sideways then to black as she knew no more.....

CHAPTER FORTY-TWO

Duncan heard the low growl of the word, Weretigers...then in an instant, he heard Adira and Marnie screaming in his mind link, *"Ambush, antiques, HELP!"*

Jack noticed first that Duncan and Marco both had empty looks in their eyes as they held entirely still; Archer, August, and Ashton saw that something was wrong; just as they were going to refer to Jack about their findings, both the Alpha and his Beta let out a horrible deafening howl. In the distance, they could hear several hundred howls answer in return.

Jack motioned for the three werelions to step back from the group and move in behind him, he wasn't sure what was going on, but he knew it had to really bad.

The sounds around them were getting closer and closer; Jack whispered to them, stay still, don't make any sudden or aggressive movements. Something has happened, and they are all about to go into a blood rage.

It's odd, though; I have only seen this behavior once when the Luna was attacked. Jack tried to mind link Duncan to no avail. When he tried a third time, he finally got a response.

As Jack had feared, someone had kidnapped their Luna, and now they were out for blood. A pack of solid warrior wolves out for blood is not something you want to get in the way of. He could only hope that Duncan and Marco would keep cooler heads.

All four bystanders looked on in horror as more and more wolves came through the trees; they were everywhere and angry. When they looked back at their host, he was now in a huge golden enraged Lycan form.

The only words that Jack could form in his mind were *"holy shit."*

Marco, however, didn't shift, he put a hand on the golden Alpha Lycan, and it calmed him down. Marco had a blank look, indicating that he was mind linking and talking to all the wolves.

The wolves had finally calmed down; all of them lay down with their heads on their paws; it was as if they were waiting for orders. The Golden Alpha, on the other hand, looked ready to kill.

Marco mind linked to Jack. *"Will you change into your bear form and try to talk some sense into him. I would, but to do so, I will have to shift into my wolf; That small second, I will lose my hold over the other wolves and Duncan, and things will go from getting under control to a shit show in less than five seconds."*

Jack shifted into his bear form and walked up the Alpha making chuffing noises. Jack continued to walk around him in a circle, making the noises, till finally, the golden wolf's eyes changed; Jack could feel Duncan was there now.

He quickly shifted back into his human form, sinking to the ground with a wail of pain. Yelling out, *"THEY'RE DEAD!!!!......... EVERY LAST ONE OF THEM...ARE..DEAD.......NO TRIAL... NO... MORE.........I..AM......GOING TO KILL.....THEM ALL!!!!.... IF THEY SO MUCH AS...LAY ONE FILTHY...FINGER ON HER.....I WILL GIVE THEM...THE MOST PAINFUL OF DEATHS....!!"*

At that moment, all the wolves that were surrounding them were now circling their Alpha. Marco knelt next to him, trying to keep Duncan from going Lycan and storming the town.

Marco called out; *"I want all the guards gathered up, every last one especially those that guarded the Luna. I don't care what is going on. I want them all here now. In one hour, I want any evidence, camera footage, and eyewitnesses on the*

Alpha's desk. I want our trackers out there picking up scents and directions. NOW!!!"

All the wolves gathered in groups and took off in different directions.

Marco looked over at the twins, August, and Ashton. *"I want to know if you are willing to help, and I need to know it now."*

The twins looked at Archer. He nodded his ok, and they turned back to Marco.

"What do you need us to do?"

"I need you to go down to the town and do your investigation, keep an eye out for traitors amongst my pack. If you find anything, let me know instantly."

They nodded and took off in the direction of the town.

"You two come over here and help me get the Alpha back to the packhouse."

{Pointing at Jack and Archer}.

"Till I know he has control; he will be dangerous. I must keep him from going into a blood lust frenzy. If that happens, no one is safe. He will not recognize friend from foe, nor will he care."

Adira woke up with a pounding headache; she tried to sit up but soon realized she was tied down. Her hands were tied above her head; she was kneeling in a cage. She looked around, and she found Marnie in a similar cell.

She could hear arguing on the other side of the door; whoever was yelling sounded pissed! They were not on the list to be taken; they were too high profile. They were supposed to get werewolves lower in ranks so they wouldn't be missed as easily.

"I DON'T CARE IF YOU WANTED REVENGE; YOU ARE FUCKING MORONS......"

"YOU IDIOTS!!! YOU THOUGHT THAT BY KIDNAPPING THE PREGNANT LUNA AND THE ALPHA'S SISTER, NO ONE WAS GOING TO NOTICE?!! IDIOTS!!!!"

The rest she could no longer hear because they were walking away. She looked around; it looked like a basement, an old cellar. She tried to mind link Duncan, but nothing happened. It must still be the drug in her system. She would have to wait a while as it moved out of her system.

She tried to whisper to Marnie, but she was still out. Adira then went to her wolf Artemis, but nothing. What is going on? Could it still be the drug, or is it more going on? She hoped it was just the drug.

Her position was uncomfortable; she thought about yelling out but wasn't sure she wanted anyone to know she was awake.

She felt like she would pass out again; her last thought was that she hoped Duncan got her previous message. Please, Duncan, find me.

Val was livid; those two morons had ruined it all because of their stupid need for revenge. Now I will have a whole pack of angry wolves out looking for her, and it won't take much for them to find this house.

He decided to take Luna and the alpha's sister to the scientists; indeed, a female werewolf and a pregnant wolf would fetch him a reasonable price. Enough anyway to put this shit behind him and start over far away from here.

He decided it was best if he and his two loyal guards took the girls out of there, it was best to leave the rest of these morons as cannon fodder. It was what they deserved after fucking up his plans.

He called his two guards and discussed the plans; they were to get two females of similar build and coloring to take the place of the female wolves. It would not fool anyone for more than a second, but none will have more than a quick look at them.

It was to delay the idiots from discovering Val's deception. It would be too late when their small minds figured it all out.

Marco, Jack, and Archer were in the Alpha's office. Duncan sat on the couch, as the Doc gave him something to calm him down. He was still showing signs of losing it.

"Marco!"

"Just for an instant, I could feel them, Adira and Artemis. It was very faint, as if they were far away. I think they are drugged."

Duncan stood up and looked around the room; Apollo had finally calmed down and let Duncan have control once again. They were saved from going into the Killing Rage, but Duncan still wanted blood.

He would find Adria if he had to rip and tear apart the whole lot of them to get to her. There were going to be no reports to the King, no trials. As soon as he had a trail or idea of where they were, he would go.

Jack and the other guy were looking a bit unnerved at what was going on; he was sure that they had no idea this thing could take place in a wolf pack. Still, his friend Jack kept his cool, which was good. Had they made one unintentional wrong move, it could have led to the group killing them.

Duncan had enough; no more; they wanted a war then a war they were going to get. It was time he showed these evil assholes what kind of hornet nest they thought they could poke.

He looked at Marco; *"I will get Adira and Marnie back. No matter how small, I will kill every last asshole who had anything to do with her kidnapping. If one hair is hurt on her head, I will pay every pain back to anyone who touches her."*

"I WANT THEM ALL.......I WILL HAVE THEM ALL. I AM DONE PLAYING NICE, I AM DONE PLAYING AT ALL!!!"

At that moment, not caring what anyone thought, he used his Alpha voice on his whole pack.

"FIND HER."

Jack and Archer watched in awe and a little fear as they could hear every pack member near and far let out a howl simultaneously in answer.

Chapter Forty-Three

Lily was trying to go to sleep when the memory hit her. Alpha Michael always called him the shadow; what was his real name? I know this........

Then it hit her like a bolt of lightning, Valdis Cessair. He was the one that always took only specific individuals for experimentation. She kept searching her mind; she saw it in one of the ledgers. It was so frustrating to have it on the edge of her tongue.

She decided to take a long hot shower; sometimes, it helped relax her body and mind. She let the waterfall on her and took deep cleansing breaths. She was just staring at the water when it hit her.

Octo Corp. that is where he sold them. She got out of the shower and went to get dressed in a hurry; she had to get the message to the King so he could tell Alpha Duncan and Luna Adria so they could finish cleaning up this horrible mess.

She wasn't sure why it was vital that she relayed this information; she felt it was essential and urgent. She ran faster to the King's chambers hoping that he was there and that he would receive her at this late hour.

Marnie and Adira were both awake, the drugs finally wearing off. They were in the back of a grey van; they were still tied up. Though this time their hands were in front of them, and their feet were tied together. So neither Adria nor Marnie could runoff.

There were two males in the back with them, there was a driver, but they couldn't see him. Adira had a very ominous feeling about where they were going and what they planned to do with them. If she had to guess, it had to do with money.

She remembered hearing rumors about some of their pack members being sold for science. She just assumed that it was like organ donor stuff like when you die. Still, not too many in a shifter pack just dropped dead.

She did have other things on her mind, like working on escaping. She hoped that they were not selling them for science or the other possibility, sex slaves.

She tried to move, and so did Marnie. The two guards moved closer to them, *"You two will have to stay quiet, or we will drug you again. It would be fine for this one, as he touches Marnie's face. However, I don't think you will want too many more doses in your condition."*

Adira did the only thing she could, glared at him. After returning to their side of the van, Adira tried to contact Artemis again. She could hear a little this time, but it was as if she was far away. Taking a deep breath, she tried to mind link, Marnie.

Success! *"Are you alright, Marnie?"*

"Yeah, a few bruises and an ass-kicking to my pride, but I will be fine; I can't say the same for these jokers, though, once Duncan catches up to them."

"Are you ok, Adira? Is the pup all right?"

"We are doing alright; I don't want any more drugs; I don't know what they will do to him."

"We need to figure out where we are, we need to tell Duncan where to find us, when the drugs finally leave our system. I just don't think we will see much till this van stops. So when it does, and they take us out, look for anything that can tell us our location."

"Also, a while ago, when we were still at the castle, Duncan insisted I carry pepper spray that works on

weres. They didn't search us that well because I can feel it still strapped to my leg."

"I think I can feel my knife on the inside of my boot, Adira. So we are not completely out of resources. Unless they try to make us strip off our clothes or do a more extensive search."

"Marnie, can you mind link Duncan at all?"

"No, it is like my wolf or anyone in the pack is just too far away. It has to do with the drugs they gave us. Also, it could be a combination of distance and the drug."

"If the distance becomes a problem for me, it won't work for you because your link with Duncan, you're his mate that makes the link much stronger than mine, Adira. Once the meds wear off a little more, you should try again."

"Either way, Adira, I will not dance to their tune. I would rather die."

"You will if you have to; Marnie, Trust me; you will dance when it comes to survival. Just remember that it isn't you that they are attacking. Keep yourself with your wolf. They can't touch you that way."

"We will get through this; they won't touch my pup. If that happens, Artemis might go crazy on their asses, and I will let her have full control. We can't shift into

Artemis's full form, but we can switch to the Lycan form without hurting our pup."

"For now, Marnie, we wait, and we watch. Take note of everything and anything. Never let them see that you know anything or are planning. It is always best when the enemy thinks you're stupid."

With that, they both went quiet and waited.

Duncan and Apollo were keeping themselves in check; it wasn't an easy thing. Finally, Marco mind linked him that they had all the guards assigned to the Luna, all but two.

Each had a cell in the dungeon waiting on the Alpha's pleasure. Duncan decided to let Jack and his friend Archer talk to them first; they can weed out the good, and then he will deal with the bad. If he went down there right now, he would kill them all just for failing to keep the Luna safe.

Marco came back up to be with Duncan; he was just as agitated as Duncan, only keeping his cool for now.

"Don't worry, Duncan, we will find them; they will be alright. Soon we will have them within our borders again.

Unfortunately, we won't ever allow them to leave again. But that is a fight for another day. We will find them and bring them home."

There was a knock at the door, and in walked Archer; he looked at them for a minute. He was a strange kind of guy, tranquil, but Duncan felt that he would be a force to be reckoned with if provoked. He could see why Jack and Archer were friends. They were made from the same stuff and moral code.

"Alpha Duncan, my two brothers, are following a van now; they are unsure if it is your Luna and sister, but they know that two females are in the van. They will see if they can't get a closer look to see if it is them."

"They will Link with me when they know more. I told them if it is the Luna and your sister, they are to stay with them and report their destination to us before trying to rescue them."

Since all this started, Duncan finally felt hope take over him for the first time. He prayed that those two had found Adira and Marnie. Tell them, if you will, that I want at least one of their captors alive and not harmed too much.

August and Ashton were in their Lion forms following a grey van; they were going the speed limit, which wasn't that hard to keep up with. They stayed within the tree line so they wouldn't know they were there.

They could smell the females; they weren't sure if it were the Luna and the sister, but they would find out. Either way, they were taken against their will and would get them back to safety; they hated anyone who abused females of any species; they were the lowest forms of life, just above those who harm children.

Wherever they were going was way off the beaten path; they kept going down a long gravel road. They were now, at a guess, at least three hundred miles away from the town; they only stopped twice. Once for gas and then food. They never left the van unattended.

The driver of the van looked like he was the one giving orders. He must be the leader, which meant they had to take out the guards first, so the slimy bastard didn't use them for protection or distraction. He would also make the perfect gift for the Alpha.

They hoped they would stop for good soon or at least the night; they were getting a little tired though they were determined. They ran silently through the forest with nothing but the stars as a witness.

Valdis wasn't the type of guy to lose control; he always prided himself on his power. He kept feeling that this was going to be his last sale. It was not because he planned on giving it up. His plans changed because of the two in the back were of high importance. That kind of shit always led to trouble.

Those idiots just had to go and take the two most essential pack members, nothing like inviting death to your door. Fucking idiots. Now he hoped that he would be able to sell these two, before some scout got a good whiff of what it in this van.

He knew the scientists would be interested in these two, especially the pregnant Luna. If he doesn't do this fast and correctly, then no money in the world will do because he would be too dead to spend it.

He didn't like stopping for the night. However, it was still another two hundred miles to go; if they didn't stop, they took the risk of not being at their best should trouble find them. They were about half an hour from a tiny village; let's hope they have a rest area or a motel.

Val knew that time was running out and stopping would bring trouble; if it came to that, he would abandon this mission and take off, leaving his two guards to deal with what was coming.

Still, his mind was going on how he could still profit if he had to split up their little group.

CHAPTER FORTY-FOUR

Duncan, Jack, and Archer were all running to the location of Archer's brothers. With them were twelve of Duncan's personally trained elite warriors. They knew they might not make it before sunrise. However, they would see where the girls were and where they stopped.

If they stop, it gives them more time to cover more ground. Duncan didn't care. He would go on and on till he caught up with them; Adira would not be harmed, because he wouldn't give those bastards any more time with her. He felt he should have never agreed to let them go shopping; what a stupid thing to allow.

Archer admired their determination and stamina as he ran alongside a werebear and a pack of angry werewolves. He wondered if the three weretigers who took the Luna and Alpha's sister understood what was coming.

Val pulled up to the motel; he wasn't happy about needing to stop. He was tired, and they had a pregnant female with them. The place didn't look like it would stand up to a strong wind. There was a light on in the office.

When he approached the window, there was a significantly overweight, greasy-looking guy with beady eyes. Val was repulsed by his greasy smell and way too much cheap aftershave. He rented a room, what condition didn't matter to him.

He went to the van and opened the back doors; his two guards jumped out.

"I will bring the Luna brought to the room; leave the sister in the van. Get what you need because both of you are sleeping in the van. One will stay awake while the other sleeps; I want someone on guard the entire time we are here."

"Hey, boss, come on. No one followed us here. I think it's safe enough for us all to take a break."

Val stared at the idiot until he became uncomfortable.

"Have you ever watched a nature show, you moron? Ever watch how long it takes for the wolves to sniff out their prey?"

"How about a whole fucking pack of these assholes? They are not normal wolves, you idiot; these are shifters. Which

means they might already be on our trail. We might be a few hours or a day ahead, but I can reassure you moron that they are coming."

"You might argue back that we as weretigers could take out a pack of wolves if they were just wolves, then yes definitely."

" These are not simple wolves, you idiot. They have a form that is unique to werewolves. It's called Lycan. That is something no one wants to face, and I can assure you that they will not only arrive in that form but will also be pissed off."

"They are a seven to eight-foot-tall wall of muscle, claws, teeth, and attitude. When you see them in this form, there is no bargaining, no reasoning. You are fucked; you can't even outrun them; all you can do is shit your pants and cry like a little bitch."

"What do you think will happen when that drug wears off completely? Then they will be able to contact their pack again. We don't have any more tranquilizers to give them. So it will be like turning on a locator beacon, like the fucking bat signal, saying here we are.!!"

"So you know what this means, right?"

"IT MEANS YOU STAY UP AND WATCH AS I TOLD YOU TO.!"

August and Ashton stopped upwind inside the tree line, watching the leader chew out one of his guards. They watched as the leader carried the Luna into the room. That meant the two guards and the Alpha's sister were still in the van.

They decided to wait for things to settle down, let them get comfortable. The leader was awfully familiar with where they were going. That meant they would have to stop them before they reached their destination.

They mind linked their brother Archer to tell him what their plans were. They settled down in their Lion forms and waited.

Marnie was left alone with the two guards; the leader took Adira to the room. That meant she was now out of danger from what Marnie was about to do.

She let out a muffled scream as the guards watched her get bigger and bigger. The bonds all broke as well as the gag. Marnie and her wolf were fully awake and joined to become Lycan; she laughed as she changed, making the guards stare in horror.

She was seven and a half feet tall, leaner than a male but heavily muscled just the same; there were places where she was almost human, and there were places where she was dark as a raven wing fur.

Her eyes glowed like two burning coals as she took up all the extra space. The two guards were in shock; the first one was an easy kill for Marnie and Myan. The other one managed to make it into the driver's seat; a quick clawed furry hand pulled him back headfirst.

His neck snapped like a twig. Now it was time to get that other asshole and get Adira out of here.

August and Ashton looked on in a little bit of horror when they saw what jumped out of the violently rocking van. It was, they thought anyway, the Alpha's sister.

"August, is that who and what I think it is?"

"Yup, looks like the Alpha's sister is walking on the big bad wolf side tonight."

"Should we lend a hand? After all, she has been through a lot."

"That, my dear Ashton, is why we will stay here and watch for a bit more. That is one pissed-off female Lycan and she is on a rampage. No way am I going to mess with that. I like my balls where they hang."

They watched as the female Lycan sniffed the air, then she turned and looked right at them with a snarl on her face. Both August and Ashton held their breath. She turned again and ran straight to the room where her Luna was taken to.

She broke down the door and rushed inside, it went silent for a bit, and August and Ashton were starting to stand, just in case they needed to lend a hand.

The most god-awful roar was heard, and things started flying out of the room; whatever was happening, she was tearing that room apart. The two brothers looked at each other, wondering what was going on.

They saw a pissed-off Lycan crash through the window and into the drive. She changed instantly in exhaustion. Both brothers approached her hesitantly; Ashton shifted back; one important thing about being a lion shifter is that you don't have to worry about losing your clothes.

Ashton went up to the female, wrapped her in his shirt, and picked her up. He could see that she'd spent too much of what energy she had left.

She cried out as if in pain; *"Luna, where is my Luna?"*

"She is gone; he took her; there isn't a scent to follow. She is gone." Marnie passed out after that.

August and Ashton looked at each other, *"Well, which one of us will relay this message? I am starting to develop a healthy fear of the Lycan form."*

Archer was unsure about relaying this latest information to the Alpha; he went to Jack instead for advice. Upon hearing what was going on, Jack let out a hiss, Fuck! They had to tell Duncan, let's hope he keeps his cool.

Jack went up to Duncan and relayed the information that Archer had. Duncan's eyes glowed a bright orange color. Jack took a step back; he opened his link to Duncan. It was absolute silence. All that could be heard was the deep breathing of a very pissed-off Alpha.

"Duncan, please keep it together a bit longer; we can't have you running off in a fit of madness! I promise when we catch up to that piece of shit, he is all yours. Just keep it together."

Duncan was still silent; he was calming himself down. He stood up, looking like a vengeful god of war about to rain hell down on the earth. Although they continued running through the dark forest, the glow of orange never left his eyes.

Jack thought it would only take one more of the smallest snags, and they would lose the Duncan side of things. Jack wasn't in any shape to take on a thoroughly enraged alpha Lycan. Jack hoped that Adira would be all right when they found her. Otherwise, shit would hit the fan, and a whole lot of ugly was going to be splattered all over the trees tonight.

How did that fucker disappear and take the Luna with him? He had to of had this planned. The asshole knew he was being followed or would be followed. He had a contingency plan waiting in the wing. Let's hope he is now out of hidey holes and escape routes.

Fucking weretigers are sneaky and clever assholes; you never knew how their attack would come; they are silent as the grave and quick as the wind. Their only weakness is ego and their temper.

Let us hope that this weretiger is not an elite grade. He didn't have that smell when he was in the house. That didn't mean much because they could mask their scent. Sigh. Please let the Luna be alright because Jack wasn't sure he could or would stop the storm.

It could be coming anyway; Jack knew that Duncan was at his limits of being messed with. Taking an Alpha's pregnant Luna was a death sentence.

CHAPTER FORTY-FIVE

Adira woke up in the back seat of a car. The last thing she remembered was being carried into the motel room. He gave her a shot, and that was the last thing she knew. She was getting tired of this; she tried to reach Artemis; she could hear her a lot better this time. They would have to devise a plan; the drug was almost gone, but they would stay pretending being unconscious.

It was time to take matters into their own hands. Whoever this guy was, he was particularly good at detecting slight changes. She was done giving him the advantage.

She went inside herself to meet up with Artemis. Together they would come out of this faster and have their link back in working order. They were planning; let's see if that jerk will see this coming.

So long as he keeps looking at the road and not back at us. He is so egotistical that perhaps it will be a good thing. Let him think we are weak and too scared to do anything against him.

Lily finally saw the King, *"Your Highness, I have a memory that I think will be important."*

"What memory is that Lily? Are you sure it's accurate?"

"Yes, your Highness, I know this one is for real; you have to warn them immediately. His name is Valdis Cessair. He is a weretiger; he was the third partner in the operation. He is the one that would take certain shifters and humans to a lab for experimentation."

"I am not sure, but I remember Octo Corp's name. It is the business front for these scientists. I have never been to their site, I think it is in the mountains, but that is all I know. I know it is a massive facility, and they pay top dollar. He is worse than the Alpha ever was; he had no trouble taking small children."

"They never returned from wherever he took them to. Sometimes bodies would show up in the lake, and Alpha Michael would order the gammas to fetch them out and burn them, so there wasn't any evidence."

"Valdis Cessair can know when trouble is coming and hide in the shadows to the point he is invisible."

Lily wasn't sure that the King believed her till he called for his guards. He ordered three of his guards to track down Jack or Duncan and relay this news. Lily let out a sigh of relief and hoped she was quick enough to do some good.

Duncan, Jack, and Archer arrived with a dozen wolves at the motel. Duncan was quiet, which worried Jack. The calmer he gets, the more unpredictable he will become, when he took his sister from Ashton's arms. He used his Alpha voice to wake her wolf gently.

Then they shared a mind link, and after it was done, Duncan used his Alpha voice to send her into a deep sleep. He handed her back to Ashton.

"You are now her guard; if anything happens to her, you will be held responsible."

Ashton felt honored by the Alpha's order; if it came down to it, he would protect her with his life. He also had a slight crush on she-wolf; he wasn't sure why.

Ashton put the girl in the van's front seat and drove back to her pack territory, with him were two of the twelve warriors traveling with them.

Jack had the best nose out of all of them; he was sniffing for anything they could use to follow that bastard or where he went. Duncan joined him because he was most in tune with the scent of his mate. Together, they picked up the faint smell of both tiger and the Luna.

They all joined in, with Jack and Duncan in the lead; they followed the trail to an old gravel road where they lost the scent. He had to of had a car or something here waiting for him; he knew he would be followed, so he used a backup plan, leaving his men as bait.

When Archer started to follow the tracks, they were easy to find because of the nature of the road and because it wasn't used much or at all. Duncan was getting impatient while Jack did his best to keep him calm.

"We will get them soon, don't worry. When we catch up and the Luna is safe. I will let you go all crazy wolf on their asses; I will even have popcorn to watch the show. For now, you must keep your head in the game, ok?"

Duncan nodded, calmed himself yet again, and continued with tracking, sending a silent prayer up to the sky.

"Please keep her safe till I can reach her."

Val wasn't sure who was following him, but he had that old nagging feeling and knew it was time for a backup plan. He had the feeling back at the house when those idiots decided it would be an excellent idea to kidnap the Luna and the Alpha's sister.

He knew the area, enough for his plan to work; he drove a stolen car to the spot. He needed to have it waiting for him and shifted to run back to his house.

As soon as both females were in the van, he felt the feeling again only stronger and knew he had to make a diversion to get out alive. As soon as he entered the motel room, he was out the window on the other side. It wasn't easy with the unconscious Luna, but this wasn't his first rodeo.

He masked his scent and tried to do the same with the Luna. Once he reached the car, they were off to the lab. They better pay him a hefty price for this bitch. From here, it was only another hundred miles to his destination. It was a shame he had to sacrifice two of his men for this. That was the risk they knew was there when they signed up.

He investigated the back seat. She was still sleeping, so he didn't have to hurry too much; going down this mountain area road could be dangerous.

Still, if he'd taken more than a glance, he would have noticed that the Luna looked more hairy than usual and bigger. She was doing it slowly in the dark, so he wouldn't see what she and Artemis were up to.

They had to take it slow not to hurt their pup; their pup was the utmost priority. It wouldn't have been possible if their pup had been at full term. He is still tiny enough for this to be done safely. She could sense that it would be harder to escape once they arrived at their destination.

At the same time, they mind linked Duncan and Apollo; they told them of their plan and that they were in a car, but there wasn't any way for her to tell them exactly where. She did notice a stone marker and some outcrop of rocks, but that was it. She said she would give them a signal as soon as they stopped.

All Adira and Artemis had to do was go slow with the shift and wait for the right moment.

They were all running the trail of car tracks when Duncan stopped. All the other wolves had stopped as well; they were standing there. Jack told Archer that it was a pack mind link.

They waited until they were all back; they seemed much happier now, almost energized.

"Well, Duncan, will you tell the rest of us?"

"Adira, she is alright. She plans to get away; she and Artemis couldn't do anything before because of the drugs in their system, but now they have worn off."

"She said the guy who has her is smart but arrogant; she made him believe she was still asleep. She said she has a plan and will try to give us a signal."

After that, they wasted no more time; they all started running down the road as fast as possible. If anyone came across the scene on the road that night, they would think the end of the world might be coming, or they were going crazy.

Faster and faster, they went up the mountain road; soon, they would catch up. Jack soon realized that the wolves were no longer in their wolf form; they had changed into Lycan forms and spread out into the forest while keeping along the road.

Jack looked at Duncan just as he watched him change from a golden wolf to a golden Lycan. It was something worth seeing, if you are not on the other end of those teeth and claws. He almost felt sorry for whomever they were about to meet. Almost.

CHAPTER FORTY-SIX

Val pulled up to the gate; the armed guard let him in. He went down the drive to the delivery door. He looked around the area; he never fully trusted these creeps; they always smelled strange and felt like they were all various forms of insanity. Thankfully, it was the last time he was going to deal with them.

He got out of the car and went to the back, opening the door just in time to be rushed at by a werewolf. She snapped her teeth at him but was in too much of a rush to stop for anything else.

She bolted into the yard, and with momentum, she easily managed to jump the seven-foot barbed wire fence. There were guards, but they were human and not fast enough. Val shifted to his Tiger and went after her. He did have little trouble clearing the fence; his more oversized frame just made him go slower over it.

Val knew it was important to find her quickly, she couldn't outrun him, but she could outlast him. If she were to get a big enough head start. Indeed he had underestimated the Luna; it wouldn't happen again.

He was happy she ran; he hadn't had a good chase in a long time. He relished catching up with the Luna; it would be satisfying to teach her a lesson. He knew she was in her Lycan form, but she was also pregnant. A couple of threats to her stomach area should subdue her long enough for him to get the upper hand.

Artemis and Adira were running but not at total capacity; being pregnant, they didn't want to use all their energy. Artemis knew they couldn't outrun the weretiger in a race but could win if it became a distance run.

Adira mind-linked to Duncan as soon as she cleared the fence; she told him which direction they were heading and where she ended up. Duncan gave their location to everyone giving chase, and Artemis turned a little south to catch up with Duncan and Apollo before the tiger caught them.

Still, Artemis kept her nose in the air to pick up any scents that may be a threat, especially feline. She could smell something faint about a mile behind them; they put on a little more speed.

Still, they can't overdo it, or it will cause harm to the pup. Artemis stopped for a second and turned to sniff the air. That weretiger was closer than they realized; he was masking his scent, so we couldn't tell how far he was behind us.

Artemis let out an earth-shattering howl and took off running again. They heard an angry roar behind them; they both smiled when they heard a chorus of loud howls in front of them—just a little further.

Duncan put on another burst of speed; shortly behind him was his Lycan pack of warriors and Jack and Archer. Duncan was far out front; once he heard Adira was being chased, he put all his anger and rage into his running. He leaped over fallen trees and bushes. At the same time, Apollo pushed faster, so they could get to their mate and pup.

He heard her howl ahead of him; he cried in answer. He also heard a roar; no way in hell was that bastard ever going to get his hands on his little wolf. He isn't going to use his hands ever again, because he was going to rip them off.

They scented their mate before they heard her running full out to meet them; just as they were almost to each other, a weretiger pounced out of the shadows, aiming straight for Artemis. Artemis dodged as she ran past Duncan and Apollo in their Lycan form.

{{So things don't get too confusing, I will refer to Duncan and Apollo's Lycan form as just Apollo. As well, as Adira in her Lycan wolf form will be just Artemis.}}

The weretiger snarls at them and launches at their head; Apollo dodges and grabs the tiger by the tail and whips him around like a carnival ride, letting go at the last minute, tossing the tiger back deeper into the woods; a loud crack was heard as the tiger crashed into a tree.

Artemis ran straight to the other Lycans as they formed a circle around her, protecting her from any further attacks.

Jack and Archer took flanking positions on either side of Apollo. Neither would step in unless Apollo asked or got into trouble and needed help. Otherwise, they were there to ensure the tiger stayed in the fight.

Apollo wasted no time going after the tiger; loud snarls and growls were heard, the trees moving violently as they were crashed into. The tiger came up behind and latched his jaws onto Apollo, going for the throat. Instead, his bite landed on the shoulder; Apollo let out a growl of pure anger.

378

Apollo shook off the tiger; blood ran down his torso from the bite. The tiger came at him again. This time Apollo was ready for him and dodged at the last second, at the same time reaching with his other hand full of razor-sharp claws and tearing open the tiger's belly.

This went on for about an hour, till finally, the tiger showed signs of getting tired. Apollo was still running on adrenaline and pure rage. They didn't feel tired or in pain. The tiger tried to run past Apollo to the other Lycans trying to get to the Luna.

Jack met him head-on and pushed him back into the fight; Apollo grabbed him by his back legs and dragged him back away from the others.

Val was getting tired of all this; it was time for him to either end this fight or escape. Damn, Werebear had the guts to get in my way; how dare he. He had fought plenty of werewolves in their natural wolf form; he had never understood the Lycan form till now.

He didn't like how this fight was going, but the bastard kept coming at him; why wasn't he getting tired? He managed to get a little more energy, enough to get up and fight again; his tiger form was healing fast but not fast enough.

Perhaps if he lets the Alpha think he killed him, he can play dead and when their backs are turned, I will make my run for it. Yes, that is what I will do. As he leaped out toward the Lycan, landing on Apollo's back.

Apollo let out a roar when the tiger landed a scraping blow with its claws. This, however, just managed to make him even more pissed off. Perhaps the tiger was hoping to make him so mad that he would start making mistakes. Apollo chuckled to himself. Good luck with that strategy. Lycans are at their best when they are fed by rage.

Apollo dodged another blow, this time, he sunk his claws deep into the tiger's side, holding on and then slamming it to the ground. The tiger lay just a few feet from him as if dead. It wasn't. That's when Apollo realized that the tiger was playing dead.

Apollo pounced onto the tiger, clamping his heavy jaws on its neck, holding, and suffocating it while shaking him back and forth violently till the tiger's neck gave an audible snap.

Apollo wasn't finished, though; the giant tiger was still alive. Apollo ripped out his throat and then beheaded the tiger, grabbing the tiger once again in his heavy jaws and whipping the head at his Lycan warriors' feet.

They all let out a howl of celebration.

Duncan shifted back. He was naked, and blood covered his chest and hip. He didn't care; he ran over to Artemis. He held her in his arms, and Artemis was licking his face and giving out whimpering noises as their minds linked.

One of the warrior Lycans was carrying a backpack. He shifted out of sight, coming back into the circle wearing jeans. He handed the Alpha a pair of pants and a long robe for the Luna.

When Jack and Archer shifted, they were already clothed. A benefit of being they're kind of shifter. The Luna wasn't changing back. This had everyone worried until Duncan explained that she would change back, but she had to do it slowly, so she didn't hurt the pup.

Either way, Artemis would not let go of this form until they were safe inside their pack borders again. She is very possessive of Adira and the pup. Apollo spoke up in the link; he agreed with Artemis. That she will not change till they are safe.

Duncan then went into another mind link; this was far off and took all his concentration. He motioned for two of his Lycan warriors that hadn't shifted back to come to him when he was done.

What was said next shocked Archer and Jack?

"I want you two to escort your Luna three miles to the south, where Marco waits with the second wave of warriors. They will take your Luna back to our territory; when you have handed her over to Marco, I want you to come back and catch up with us."

He sat down for a minute as another warrior saw his wounds; Apollo was already healing them so they didn't hurt or bleed much anymore.

He motioned for Jack and Archer to come to him; with a smile, he said.....

"It is time to end all this evil shit; what do you say, boys? Let's have some fun; it's time to go hunting."

CHAPTER FORTY-SEVEN

$\mathcal{D}$r. Devon Taylor, head research scientist for Octo Corp.; was ecstatic about what Mr. Cessair was bringing them, a pregnant Luna. He was already going through his mind the things that could potentially be discovered and created with this new specimen.

He knew the guard had let him in the gate; they were ready and excited to receive the female. When Cessair never came up to the door, he checked the camera footage, and to his horror, he saw Mr. Cessair changing into a weretiger and going after the escaped female.

Mr. Cessair has been keeping a secret; too bad he is so good at getting them specimens. Dr. Taylor put it down in a new file labeled Cessair weretiger. When Mr. Cessair stops being helpful, we will have another role he can play for the Corporation.

He will wait for Mr. Cessair to return the female; they have gotten away before, and it's never a problem either way, alive or dead; they are all useful. However, he did hope that the pup would still be alive; they are more viable for the experiments when living.

For now, everyone went back to work on their other subjects; it's a pity they don't last all that long. Still, their body parts are helpful as well. They can also be sold for a profit if you know where to find the right buyers.

The corporation heads all were excited about their new hybrids. However, they didn't know was that they were not as successful, as Devon had promoted them.

Some were plain uncontrollable, while others were a success in the breeding, but they were more like vegetables in mind. You could tell them to do something, and they would go to do it, but then they would get distracted by something as simple as a leaf or a blade of grass.

With this pregnant Luna, though, they could use the offspring's DNA and other cells to manipulate the pup in the womb, thus eliminating some of the unnatural ways they reproduced their hybrids.

Marnie woke up feeling warm and safe as she snuggled into the warmth a little deeper she was feeling worn out, and her muscles ached. As she was slowly waking up, she could hear something; what was that sound, purring?

She opened her eyes fully to see that she was in her room at the packhouse; she could feel the vibration of the purring on her back. She turned and stared at the handsome god in her bed.

She couldn't remember how she got back home or this male in her bed—deciding to get out of bed and find out what was going on. Was Adira ok? Where was Duncan? Who is this in her bed?

God, his scent was intoxicating though it was strange to her. A combination of an herb-like sage and an earthy aroma that was all male.

She took off into her bathroom and shut the door, locking it.

Ashton opened his eyes. He was still purring, thinking to himself. Well, it seems that the big bad she-wolf is my mate. This is going to complicate things a bit." He recalled reading about some legends where Werelions mated with other species, but those were usually humans.

He would have to do some research and find out about this complication; he was already in love with her even though he didn't even know her; that was enough to tell him that she was his mate. Wow, the universe has a messed-up sense of humor.

It doesn't matter. She is mine.

Marco sat in the back seat with Luna's head on his lap; they had an escort of two other SUVs full of warriors. Luna Adira was slowly changing; he could see the subtle changes. At the rate of change, he figured she would be back to herself in a day, maybe a little less.

The pack doctor would be there as soon as they pulled into the drive. He had everything set up in Luna's room. So he can monitor Luna Adira and the pup while the change happens. It is hazardous for a she-wolf to shift during pregnancy. It wasn't a rare thing, but still, I could kill or mutate the pup if not done right.

Marco suspected it had to do with the fact that she was a Luna and that they did it slowly. He wasn't about to let her out of his sight, not until Duncan came home and personally took her from his care.

Marco hoped that Duncan and the rest of the warriors wiped out all that evil shit for the last time; he wasn't stupid. He knew that evil would continue. He just wanted it out of his neighborhood. It's had enough time to fuck things up. Time for it to move on.

Marco had sent a dozen more warriors back with the two that brought Adira in. Also, August wanted to be with his brother Archer, hoping that they would rain hell down on their stupid asses.

Duncan, Jack, Archer, August, and all the now three dozen Lycan warriors had a small meeting to produce a plan. Jack and two warriors scouted out the facility; it was a rather large place. However, the buildings were small, so he suspected that they went underground.

There was just one guard shack which held two guards. There were also cameras monitoring the outside of the buildings. There weren't any though along any of the fencing.

They all thought that it was a bit lax in security. They were a top-secret operation, perhaps they took their protection from not being known. Still, they were all to be attentive at all times.

They split into three groups; group one would handle the guards and leave two warriors to guard the gate for any unexpected visitors and those trying to escape.

The other two teams would approach from the east and west sides of the compound: no need for the north end. It was a sheer cliff.

Duncan had one team, Jack another, and Archer the third. They sent August and another warrior off to scout for another way into the compound, going further down the mountain just in case there might be a back door. Jack figured they had to have another escape route, other than the one door.

They also thought that they had to have some sort of security inside the facility. To have just two guards was laughable and foolish, and he doubted that even these egotistical assholes were that stupid.

Jack decided that his team should go in first, take out the guard shack and see what was inside. Also, they would take out the outside cameras. When they finished those tasks, the other two teams would join them, and they would all go in together, leaving a few more outside as backup.

As they stealthily went through the door, an alarm sounded, and the lights went from white to red. They started to make their way through the corridors; it was empty at first. Mostly storage rooms with boxes.

They reached an elevator at the end of the corridor; it would open if the correct keys were entered. One of Duncan's warriors walked up, tore off the panel, and opened a kit. He bypassed the codes, and the door opened.

They decided that they would split into teams, so they could split up the floors, since there were fifteen of them, all going down. Once a team cleared a bed, they would join the next group until everyone was at the bottom. None of them were prepared for what they would find.

The first couple of floors mainly were technology and other labs. The scientists on those floors were rounded up and guarded by two Lycans. When they reached the fifth floor, things started to change.

Living beings in cages, it was hard to tell which were shifters, humans or even what race they were from; some looked like pure misery, while others just stared on with empty eyes. There were two, though, that were violent. They put them all out of their pain. It was the only thing left for them.

The scientists on this floor were horrified at the mob before them. One female scientist was holding a syringe full of some kind of liquid. When they asked her what she would do with it, she babbled and said she would inject one of the violent subjects.

When asked what was in it, she wouldn't answer till Archer twisted her hand behind her back hard.

"It's battery acid."

The room went eerily quiet no one dared speak. Then Archer walked up to the woman and injected her with the battery acid right in her neck. She started to scream, but then it became all garbled. She fell to the floor, dying. The other three scientists had their heads snapped off.

It was too easy of a death for them, but they were under the clock here, so they eliminated the threats trying to help those they could and put down the ones that were beyond hope; every one of the warriors wanted to take the time to punish someone personally, but they would have to wait.

The next couple of floors were more of the same; one was an actual morgue, but instead of slabs and lockers, they were hanging on meat hooks, body parts were tossed in corners. Each pile was for a separate part of the body; one pile was just bodies without heads. The heads were not in the cold storage room.

With each floor, everyone started to get angrier and angrier. Finally, they all met up on the next to the last floor. What they found there made their hearts drop to their feet.

Someone was going to pay.

CHAPTER FORTY-EIGHT

Dr. Taylor was beyond excited over his latest subject; he'd obtained it accidentally. They had set out traps for any rogue shifters. Instead, they got an even bigger prize. It killed two of the guards just getting it here. Right now, he had it drugged. He wasn't so sure how long the sedatives would last, though.

The average amount you would give an elephant didn't do the job so they had to double it. Still, even in its drugged state, it was a smelly angry asshole.

It didn't matter much, though; he had it locked inside a solid cage. Now he was ready to do his first experiments; these were just standard tests. To see what its blood and DNA were, what it was. X-rays and a CT scan if he could get it to fit inside the machines. He wasn't sure how they were going to do that.

He was so excited to have a new specimen that he had a hard-on; it was uncomfortable. The more excited he was about his experiments, the less he could keep it down.

Dr. Taylor wasn't a big man, only 5'6 with a balding head and sweaty skin. Even when he was a child, he loved experimenting with various animals and insects. His parents thought he was doing it to become a great scientist of the time. He was doing it because he loved to watch his subjects in pain.

Over the years, he managed to find other like-minded scientists, and they started to form a club of sorts. When Dr. Taylor got into a secret government program, he was allowed to pick his team, so naturally, he decided everyone in his club would come.

Now they were all doing what they loved to do most. Create new life while destroying the old life. The more painful it was for the subject, the more the scientist wanted. Some got off on creating mutations.

It was a perfect operation to oversee. Though they were running low on specimens, they would be thrilled to know that they would have a pregnant Luna. Finally, an unborn to experiment with and a Luna. That will keep them happy for a long time to come.

Adira was halfway through her shift; they had her on a hospital bed, giving her fluids to help ease the change on the pup. Everything was going fine. The Doctor said he had never seen anything like it before. Usually, once a she-wolf is pregnant, they don't shift; it can cause significant harm to the pup, even death.

Adria wasn't speaking to anyone; she maintained the link with the Duncan, something only mates can do. Marco was linked with her, so he was connected with Duncan. Once he saw what that so-called scientist did to all those poor victims Duncan found, he contacted all the doctors he could find.

Even calls to other packs and others shifter species, telling them what was happening and to be ready to go in. They were already organizing teams and supplies as well as transportation.

Two hours later, Luna Adira was back in her human form again. When they let her go back to the packhouse, the first thing she did was take a shower. Then she laid down on the bed and continued with the mind link.

Duncan tried a few times to block her from seeing some of the things he saw. She just told him they would face this together, and it would be better for her to see everything so she could help with the preparations and sending of supplies and medical help.

She was finally getting tired and fell asleep with Duncan still in her mind through the link; once he knew she was sleeping, he cut the link; no way was he going to let any more of this touch his Luna or their pup.

He would spoil her rotten for the rest of her life; it didn't matter whether she liked it. She had been through enough. It was time for her life to turn into happier times.

Ashton was with Marnie as she went to Luna's room to stand guard. She went inside and found the Luna in a deep sleep. Marnie sat down on the rug before the bed. She became a sentinel; Ashton sat next to her, two sentinels in the night.

They were both wondering what was going on with the scientific laboratories they found.

Ashton looked over at Marnie; she was the most beautiful female he had ever seen. Her scent was driving him crazy, not to mention her body it was perfect. She was a strong and crazy female, but she was so wonderfully full of energy; her spirit was bright and out for all to see.

He wasn't sure how he would go about winning her as his mate; he wasn't even sure it was possible. He was going to try his best, though. Fate and the heavens are praised for giving him this gift. He just hoped that he could hold on to it.

August and Gavin, whose name he had just found out, were searching for another entrance. They came upon a weird-looking rock wall; they investigated and found a hidden switch. Once they released the button, the rock wall slid to the side.

Behind it was two double doors that were locked by a keypad. Gavin, the werewolf warrior, mind linked his Alpha, telling him what they had found. Their orders were to stay there; two more would join them shortly to help guard the door.

August and Gavin were glad that others were coming to help; something about this place gave them the creeps. They heard a rustling in the distance, and sure enough, it was the other two who were sent to help.

Just as they were about to decide what position they should each take; a roar shook the walls, knocking down rocks from the sides of the fake door and plaster from the walls.

All four looked at each other, that sound came from deep within the ground, yet it was so loud it shook the floor and the walls. All four of them took positions away from the doors. Mind linking; they said at the same time...*"What the hell do they have in there?"*

395

It was absolute terror; the thought of anything doing this to other living things is unthinkable. It was a massive room; it might be as big as a city block. It was wall-to-wall cages, set up like a maze. Each cell had living creatures; each had a nightmare inside.

Some were easy to see what they were, with others there was no way to know. Most of them were children, some only toddlers. All of them had wires or tubes coming from them; each cage had a chart for tracking changes in the experiments.

Some were crying out in pain; most were just huddled as far as they could to the back of their cages. Some had more than two eyes, others only one or none. There were others still who had too many arms and legs; it was like a human, who also had animal legs growing out of them.

There had to be hundreds of cages. The smell was a cross between blood and death, it was overwhelming.

They had to walk the maze to find the scientists running this horror show. It hurt their hearts to pass all these children; until they could get some doctors in here to ascertain their condition, it was best to leave them where they were for now.

The further they went; the worse things became; most at this point were beyond help. Jack was about to go bat-shit crazy on their asses; the only thing keeping him in check was the poor souls in the cages. The last thing they needed was him unintentionally scaring the crap out of them.

These monsters would have given Josef Mengele a run for his money. They were going to suffer for this. Death will not come fast for these bastards. Oh, no. Jack would make sure they suffered every day for as long as he wished them to do so. If he had to build an enormous dungeon, so be it.

Finally, they reached the center or the heart of this madness. There were at least nine scientists here; they were so involved in what they were doing that they didn't even notice what had walked into their circle.

There was no signal, all the warriors and their leaders were so enraged that they just ran in and started grabbing them one by one. Duncan took one out and ripped him apart. He was about to rape a little human girl; she didn't look to be more than ten years old.

Only a few that they took lived, to hell with the punishment, what they needed was extermination, the subjects in the cages that could understand what was going on, would cheer wildly. It was almost painful in that vast underground room; it was so loud.

Archer knelt next to one of the scientists, with a growl in his voice...

"Tell me, Monster, where is your leader?"

He didn't say anything at first until Archer, with his barbed tongue, licked the side of the scientist's face, taking off skin in the process. He screamed in pain and pointed at a set of double doors.

Duncan, Jack, and Archer went and opened the double doors. They could not believe the lack of security in this facility. It was like they didn't care or were so arrogant that it didn't matter.

On the other side of the doors was a long hallway. It didn't have any other entries, just the one at the end. The smell coming down the hallway was something new and it burned their senses it was so strong.

They heard a loud crash from the other end of the tunnel door. A man was yelling while more crashing was going on. Then before they opened the door, they heard a terrible angry roar that shook the walls and the door.

All three looked at each other, minds linking. They said, *"**What the holy hell was that?!**"*

More warriors had joined them, they all stared at each other waiting to see who would be brave enough to go first.

CHAPTER FORTY-NINE

Adria woke up to early morning sunlight on her face and to something that sounded weird; at first, she thought it was snoring. When she looked around, she found Marnie and a male at the side of her bed on the floor, who had himself wrapped around her. She raised her eyebrow at this new development.

He was the source of the loud noise; he was purring; she couldn't help herself. She giggled a little when she realized what was happening.

It looks like Marnie has taken in a stray kitty. She looked at Marnie's face; she seemed so happy and content; Adira wished she had a camera.

She wondered if they would be compatible as mates; she shrugged. If they were not compatible with each other, then they wouldn't be mates. When fate has decided what tune she wants to play, all we can do is dance to the music.

Odd as it was to hear, the purring was comforting. Adria found herself sinking back under the covers and going back to sleep. Ashton opened his eyes while still purring; he smiled when he saw that the Luna had gone back to sleep.

She needed it; when they'd checked on her earlier, she still had dark circles under her eyes. He knew the effects of his purring, especially on females. He always calmed them right down; he put his arm back around his mate, kissing the top of her head, taking in the scent of her hair, smiling; he went back to sleep.

Dr. Taylor stood horrified at the creature that just bent the iron bars on his cage like they were wet noodles. It was pissed, Dr. Taylor looked for the tranquilizer gun; it was across the room. He would have to go by the creature to get to it.

The only other thing he had to protect himself was the gun in his desk drawer. The beast let out a roar. It shocked Dr. Taylor to his knees in fear. He crawled to his desk and reached inside his bottom drawer.

He grabbed the gun and stood up to face the beast before him; with shaking hands, he aimed the gun and pulled the trigger. Nothing happened; he tried again, still only an empty click. The beast turned his head and looked at him with a glowing red-eye gaze of hate.

Before he could even think or react, the beast was on him; he felt a terrible sharp pain down the middle of his body and an awful wet ripping noise.

In shock, he watched in the reflection of the glass partition as he was ripped in half. The pain was unbearable, but no scream came out of his mouth, just blood. Then he was no more, a much too easy death for that monster, but fitting.

Still pissed off, the beast picked up both halves of the Doctor and violently shook them before whipping them in different directions. Letting out another ground-shaking roar, it started to destroy the room looking for a way out.

Duncan, Jack, and Archer decided they should see what was going on, though none were too eager. Still, curiosity is a bitch. All three of them went through the doors slowly, cautiously.

What they saw on the other side was beyond their imaginations. Blood was everywhere; half of a man lay about three feet in front of them; no one could tell where the other half was.

What they saw looking back at them made them all stop in fear.

Duncan knew what he was seeing; he had an encounter once with one. Nothing like this, though. He'd never seen a pissed-off one. It had blood dripping from its fur, and the look on its face was pure rage. Its smell made all their noses burn. Its eyes were glowing red as it watched them.

Jack mind linked Duncan and Archer...

"Is that what I think it is?"

Archer was a little more worked up about it; he almost seemed happy excited.

"Holy shit, is that a fucking Big Foot.?"

Duncan's mind linked back as they all just stood still...

"Yeah, that is what we call the Wild Man. We don't bother them and they don't bother us."

It just stared at them, breathing heavily. You could tell it was still under the influence of whatever they injected him with. It turned and ran to the other side of the room; there weren't any doors, but it didn't matter. He made his own.

It broke through the heavy wall with two hits of its body, and then it was gone down the hall into the darkness.

They could hear banging at the end of the other hallway and then a crash as the doors gave in, and they could see the creature silhouetted in the light from the outside. Then it was gone.

August's mind linked his brother...

"Holy shit, is that what I thought it was?" Archer answered..."*Yes.*"

"Holy crap, Archie, what else do they have hiding in this area? A fucking Big Foot! I thought those were just make-believe."

August and the warrior went outside and sat down on a log and lit a cigarette. August didn't smoke as a rule, but he lit it up when the warrior handed him one and took a nice long drag. Both he and the warrior just sat there and listened off in the distance; they could still hear the Big Foot letting out howls of rage and crashing through the trees.

As they all looked around the lab, they found the other half of the scientist. They also found a whole computer full of nothing but logs and experiment results. It was a terrible account of what went on in this place and for how long. It made them a little sick to know that this was going on for so long, right under their noses.

Collecting all the data and pictures they could, they left the room and went to join the others.

"Soon, various teams will converge here to investigate and check out all these beings, to see if any can be saved." Duncan gave out a big sorrowful sigh.

Jack and Archer looked at Duncan.

"Duncan, why don't you head on back to your Luna? We know you have thought of nothing else, and your mind is only half here anyway. We will take care of everything here. Once this place is empty, we will set it on fire and then blow it to hell."

"The remaining scientists will be dealt with and delivered to our dungeons by this evening. So go back to your pack and Luna, reassure yourself that she is doing ok, and get some sleep and spend time with her. You and Apollo have expended a lot of energy. Do you need us to set you up with a ride home?"

Duncan didn't need to be told twice; he didn't even answer them; he just shifted and ran off; though the distance was pretty far, they knew he wouldn't have too much trouble, and if he got tired, he could always contact Marco to send transportation.

Adira woke once again; this time, it was look like twilight. She looked at the clock, which said 9:35 pm. When she realized she could hear the shower running, she sat up for a minute. She was unsure. She went up to the closed door and felt the presence she had needed for a long time.

She opened the door, and there, standing in the steam in all his naked glory, was the love of her life. She ran into his arms and started to cry. He held her in his arms high against his chest. Kissing her everywhere he could reach with his lips. With a sigh of contentment, he rested his face on the silky softness of her hair.

"I was going to sneak into bed with you and surprise you that way; it looks like you beat me to it, though. God, I have missed you so much. When you first ran past me, all I wanted to do was take you in my arms and leave. Lock you away with me forever."

"I know my big bad wolf; you had things that needed doing. I was right here waiting for you, always and forever. Don't worry; I have been guarded night and day while resting; I have something to tell you later."

"Later?"

"Why yes, darling, after we get reacquainted again, it feels like it has been forever. I need to feel all of you, to make sure you're not just a dream."

"That is good because I have." to the same with you, I have all kinds of stuff to share with you. Later."

He put her down on her feet, taking off her comfortable clothes. Her breasts were the first thing he noticed; they were getting even fuller than before because her body was getting ready for their pup. He would be a little jealous that he would have to share them soon.

She started to lick the droplets of water off his chest, swirling with her tongue as she made her way downward. She swallowed his member whole, then started to suck her way back and forth; it drove him over the edge, and he came to his climax with a roar. She greedily sucked every drop from him.

He picked her up again, this time straight to their bed. He very gently lay her down on the sheets; he was in heaven, her scent enveloped him, and the rest of the world was gone, only her and him.

He lay behind her while she lay on her side; he pulled her closer to him, relishing her warmth, skin softness, and scent. The sheets were soaking wet now, there was nothing else on earth like her, and she was all his.

Adira was in heaven or in a dream. She didn't care; everything that had happened was now completely gone with his touch.

When Duncan laid his hand over her swollen womb, he was surprised; his son kicked him. He pulled his hand back with a grin on his face. He looked lovingly at his Mate. He just stared at her in wonder and love.

He kissed her passionately, with all the longing and worry gone, replaced by the joy and passion of being with his mate. Being in her arms was epic; his kisses moved down her body as she started to moan, the most beautiful music he would never tire of hearing.

Once he drove her over the edge twice with his tongue, he moved her up against him, spooning her, gently putting her leg up over his hips, and in one thrust from behind her, he was in. Finally, he was home. He reached around her and held onto her swaying breasts, absolute heaven. His movements became wild, and they both screamed as they were overcome with ecstasy.

As the whole pack could hear them, they were smiling because that meant that both their Luna and Alpha were where they belonged and were happy.

August talked to Marnie about pack rules and the hierarchy of werewolves' lives just two doors down.

Suddenly, he heard screaming and roaring coming from down the hall.

"Marnie, what was that?"

"Don't play dumb, Mr. Kitty." Her new name for him, you know what those sounds were as she turned a bright shade of red. Those sounds mean that my brother is now home safe and sound."

He wondered what she would sound like when he brought her to her climax. Baby steps, Ash, Baby steps.

CHAPTER FIFTY

Marco was looking at the email, at a complete loss for words. Everyone has been through enough crap, figuring out where all the survivors will go. It was sad, but they couldn't save most of the mutated ones; ninety percent of them couldn't be moved, or they would die.

They blew up the facility and covered it in rubble, then they set more charges and turned the wreckage into a solid pile. No one will ever know its existence; sentinels were placed around the cleared area, all that was left outside the facility was the small pile still letting off smoke. They waited in the shadows to see if anyone came looking.

They are also discussing a multi-shifter task force that could look for this kind of stuff—trained to see it and know where to look—putting an end to the ignorance in the shifter communities; nothing like this should ever get a foothold ever again.

Children would also be taught about some things to look for and be aware of those who would manipulate or abduct them and keep an eye on the younger ones.

Marco was still looking at another damn email; he would have to prepare some rooms. The first order of business was to tell the Alpha of his upcoming guests after today. No way was he going to disturb him right now; he liked his head where it was.

Adira enjoyed having Duncan all to herself; they had breakfast and lunch in their room. They talked, laughed, made love, and watched a movie here and there. It was pure contentment. Duncan even listened to their pup as he moved around.

Around three in the afternoon, there was a knock on the door, and three-pack members brought in all kinds of flowers, bouquets of roses of every color, daisies, and iris. It was a cornucopia of flowers.

All of them were for her; most were from her mate. There were three bouquets of mixed flowers that were from the pack. All of them dumbfounded her. She smiled brightly, and that was what Duncan wanted to see. No more tears for his Luna.

He gave instructions to all pack members not to disturb them at all unless the place was on fire. He set it up to have their meals brought to them. As well as chocolates and flowers. She is going to be spoiled and pampered today and tonight.

He had already growled at two members for mind-linking him. He never answered their question; just growled.

Adira decided to tell Duncan about his sister, hoping he would be open to the idea. She didn't see anything wrong with it as long as they were physically compatible. She supposed that if they couldn't have their pups or cubs, they would be wonderful adoptive parents.

"Duncan, I have something to talk to you about; I want you to keep an open mind."

"What is it, little wolf?"

"Do you know that Marnie and Ashton are developing a relationship? I think they are mates."

He chuckled…*"Yes, love, I know about their budding relationship. I have no trouble with it as long as no harm comes to Marnie and it makes her happy. I don't know what kinds of things they will face amongst the pack or the pride; I like to think no one will have problems with it; if they do, they can bring their concerns to me and I will set them straight."*

Adira smiled at Duncan.

"Why are you smiling at me?"

"Because my wolfie, you just added another reason for me to love you. You add them every day."

Duncan pulled Adira to him for a kiss.

"Duncan, what were you wanting to tell me.?"

He started to laugh....*"You are not going to believe this, I'm not sure I do, and I saw it with my own eyes. When we reached the head scientist's lab, He had been killed by what he had locked up. It was a Big Foot."*

"What!!! No way, you are playing with me."

"Nope, my little wolf, I speak true."

"What happened to the Big Foot? Did you let it go?"

He started to laugh louder...

"Are you kidding? It made a hole and escaped all by itself. It was so pissed, that there was no way anyone was stupid enough to step in front of that nightmare."

Ash followed Marnie around like a lost puppy. She was annoyed, especially when he waited outside her bathroom door while doing her morning ritual.

In truth, she thought Ash was hot; she fell for him the first time she saw him. They were two distinct species, though. Would it work? What if they are not compatible? She felt sparks between them when he carried her the other day; that could only mean one thing.

Oddly, her wolf Myan had been strangely quiet about all this. Whenever Ash was around, she would go all shy and reserved.

"Come on, Myan; you're a warrior, not a shy giggling schoolgirl. I could use some advice on this."

Still, she had to see if she could lose Ash for a little while so that she could ask one of the elders. She decided that the best way to do it was to wait till he started eating; it was the only thing that could drag him away from her.

She decided to go the kitchen and talk to the chef about making some delicious dishes for their feline guests. The cook joked back saying that she would make them a fancy feast.

Lily locked herself in her room; she was so angry with herself for all the shit she'd done in the past. Now it is coming back to revisit her. That stupid drug they used on her for so long had side effects; they were giving her herbs to help clear it out. Not fast enough, though.

She was going into heat again. Sighing, she sat on her bed and began to cry. What was she going to do now? She didn't dare leave this room. At least this room had a tub she could fill with icy water. It does help to lessen the fever and pain.

It does nothing to stop the need for mating, though. This crap was only supposed to happen to mate females, so their mates could take care of them. She had her mate, they mated that first time; now, he is dead, and she is stuck with this endless punishment.

She started to cry even more when she remembered her handsome mate's face and gentle smile. She would kill for just one more night with him. Then the image of his last moments went into her mind, and she cried out in pain. She managed to calm herself down and start a cold-water bath.

Tomorrow it will be awful, she was supposed to go to her therapist, but that wasn't going to happen.

She picked up the in-house phone and dialed her female helper. She told her what was going on; there was no sound on the other end for a little bit. Then in a burst of speech, Molly, her helper, started to bark out orders to some other women.

She was ordered to keep her door locked and stay inside. They would bring her things she would need to help ease her through the process; she was only to unlock the door if it were Molly on the other side.

With a sigh, she sat back down and started to laugh.

At least it isn't in front of shit load of crazy biker bears this time.

The King was restless all day and well into the night; what the hell was wrong with him? He hadn't felt like this since his eighteenth birthday, and he met his mate that night.

Ever since Lily came to him to tell him about her last memory, he couldn't get her scent out of his head.

It made his mouth water; it reminded him of the warm summer sun and gardenias. He has been roaming the castle in his restlessness. He came to a stop.

Lord God above and goddess of the moon sure have a sense of humor. He knew then what was going on; Lily was his second chance mate. It would not be extremely easy, but it could be done. If he claims her as his mate, she would be his Luna; she couldn't be Queen, perhaps in name only, because of her history.

Still, though, why was he so restless? It could only mean one thing.

She was in heat!!!

Thorn, at that moment, started to howl in his head, *"She is alone, unprotected, and in heat. A locked door is all she has between herself and all the male wolves in the castle. You have to go to make our mate safe; then we claim can her."*

He called his servant to remove all guards from inside the castle until he tells them to return. He looked at his King like he'd lost his marbles.

"I SAID GO AND REMOVE THE GUARD FROM INSIDE THE CASTLE NOW!!! "

He explained that he needed to remove a female who unexpectedly came into the heat in a calmer tone.

The servant ran from the room, telling the guard his instructions. Ok, now all he had to do was get his mate out of her locked room without scaring the crap out of her. Thorn wanted to break down the door, toss her over his shoulder and run back to their chambers.

The King had other plans; sometimes, *"Thorn, you must be more diplomatic and charming to get what you want, not ram it down their throat."*

"You will be on your best behavior; I know the heat will drive you crazy; think about the scared wolf and what she has been through. We've got to take this a step at a time. I never thought we would have our second chance, mate; I know she didn't either. She wanted us to kill her so she could be with him."

"Now we show her that she is worthy of one more chance, and we will make sure she forgets her first and turns to us for the rest of our lives together. As far as the rest of the world, they can stick it up their uptight asses. Let him, without sin, throw the first stone."

CHAPTER FIFTY-TWO

Just after dinner, Ash waited for her to come back; he knew that she had given him the slip. He sensed though it was something she wanted to do alone. Yeah, he had to admit he was smothering her a bit; he couldn't help it; everything about her captivated him. He was hooked, and he liked it.

He hid in the trees just outside the house she was visiting; he could listen to the conversation, but he felt he should let her have some privacy; his Cat scoffed, *"You have not given her one ounce of privacy since you first met her. If I were her, I would have taken a swipe at your silly ass by now."*

"Ash laughed, really, and it was me alone that has been all over her; who purrs every time he wraps himself around her?"

Ash could almost hear Linus's eyes roll in disdain. Seriously though, he was just as gone on Marnie as he was.

She was coming out of that house; he hid on the other side of the tree; along the path she would have to take. She looked happy but lost in thought. A semi could roll up alongside her, and he didn't think she would notice.

As she was about to pass the tree, Ash reached out and grabbed her, pulling her tightly to him. He got his hand behind her head and pulled her in so he could kiss her. She didn't resist, so he deepened the kiss, taking over her sweet lips, parting them. He then took complete possession of her mouth.

When she pulled away, he put a finger to her lips to stop her from talking.

"Don't say anything; if this has to end, then so be it; if it means that you will be safe, I am ok with it. Just for this one moment, let me hold you. For just this one glorious moment, pretend that it is just you and me."

She pushed him away from her and, with a smile, whispered to him…

"We do not have to pretend, Mr. Kitty. I talked with the elders; they said our being together isn't as unusual as we thought; we can be together as mates. You will do this right and ask my brother for permission, then meet me in my room afterward."

"Marnie, are you sure? Is this true? Can we be together? Umm….wait, what if your brother says no.?"

He picked her up, twirling her in the falling snow as he laughed joyfully. Putting her down, he straightened his back and started to walk to the packhouse; he turned back to Marnie...

"Well, go and get ready for me to come to your room, my big bad she-wolf."

She giggled..."*Don't worry about my brother saying no; Adria would skin him alive if he did."*

Marnie ran off to her room as Ashton went to see the Alpha.

Marco was surprised when he received yet another email. The meeting would be postponed until the King cleared up some personal issues. He promises to be in touch soon.

He read the following email. It was from Jack; all was going well. They managed to find places for the survivors, and five found their actual families. Also, that horrible facility was now nothing but some rubble amongst the trees.

Marco let out a sigh, *"Well, at least for some, the torture is over."* He wondered how much more was going on elsewhere in the world and if there was any closer to home. He promised himself that he would be much more watchful in the future.

He also intended to teach others what to look for in the pack. To investigate and report it to him. They will determine what to do with a full investigation. No more assuming the world is all good just because they were.

Lily was going crazy with being in heat; everything they tried didn't work or it didn't last very long. She would find herself after each attempt worse than she was before. She started crying out of frustration and pain.

Crying out to the walls...

"Why isn't this going away by now? It usually always calms down after a few hours of an ice bath."

When Zinnia started acting crazier than before, she rubbed and pranced, making little whiny noises. Lily got frustrated with her.

"Stop that; you're acting like a slut; you know we are alone in this. There is no way I will go out of this room; you want me to give us to the first male that comes along?"

When she heard a loud and long howl coming from somewhere in the castle, it sounded close. Zinnia started to prance again, saying in a sing-song voice, *"It's our mate, our mate."*

"Zinnia, you know our mate is dead; he will never come for us again. Stop that right now."

"NO."

Lily was shocked; Zinnia never spoke to her like that.

"Lily, you don't understand; that is our second chance, mate howling for us. He wants us to join him; we need to shift to my form and run with him."

Lily sat there stunned, a second chance mate; who is he? Why is he here now? Is he one of the guards? Thoughts raced in her mind; the heat wasn't letting her think. Still, the howling went on, making her excited and scared at the same time.

She wasn't sure she could just run off into the night after a stranger in a castle full of guards; Zinnia was acting like a total hussy. What if she went looking but got jumped by another male—thinking of all the what could happens, made her start to spin.

"Oh, god, Zinnia, I don't know if I can do this again. Not with some stranger, and what if another wolf jumps

us? I can't go through that pain again; it still hurts today."

"Go to our Mate, little one; he will ease our pain and bring us happiness again. We deserve a second chance. Trust me, Lily, just one more time. He isn't a stranger to us; GO NOW, HE CALLS FOR US!"

Lily walked to the door and opened it; she took off her clothes and shifted into Zinnia. They ran off into the night, following the howls of their mate. Instantly she felt different and stopped at a small pool in the garden and almost leaped back in surprise.

Zinnia was not a brown wolf anymore; she was now as white as the falling snow.

They found their mate further into the King's Garden; he sat in the middle, waiting for them. He didn't move toward them. He was being considerate, letting them make the first move.

He was a giant golden wolf; he was magnificent, and his scent made them forget what was going on for a minute. He was glowing in the moonlight; he looked like an angelic creature amidst the snow. Then it hit Lily that the only ones that glowed in the moonlight were gold royal shifters.

She gasped,

"Zinnia, we can't do this; that is the King.!"

Zinnia was no longer listening to Lily; she walked up to him and started to rub herself all over his fur; they could feel the sparks shooting up between them, the pain of the heat was starting to ease.

"Zinnia, you hussy, stop that you're embarrassing me, stop it this instant!"

"You said you would trust me, Lily, so trust me. This is the King's wolf. His name is Thorn. He won't harm us; he will protect and love us."

Zinnia ran off into the snowy garden with the golden Thorn giving chase.

Adira sat in her window seat, looking into the snowy night; she had her hand over her belly as she smiled at their pup movements. Soon this little one will be joining us; everything is ready for you, little pup. All you must do is come and join us.

She thought back to her life before and the dreams she had to escape. They say, *"Tell God your plans, and he will laugh."*

She cringed when she thought of how it could have happened had she not found Duncan on the floor that night.

Artemis spoke up…

"What could have been is no concern of ours; what is now is. We have a wonderful mate, a home, people that love us, and soon we will have our pup as well. No more sad thinking; enjoy the here and the now."

With that, Artemis curled back up and went to sleep. We are leaving the past where it belongs, in the past, she smiled and said to her sleeping wolf.

"Yes, indeed, Artie, I will do just that."

Just then, Duncan came into the room with a massive smile.

"You look like a very satisfied wolf. May I ask what has happened?"

"Well, my little wolf, it seems that Ashton and Marnie got some good news; they are compatible. Ashton came to my office just a few minutes ago to ask my permission to be joined as Marnie's mate."

"You said yes, of course." She gave him one of her 'you better of had', looks he loved.

"Yes, after a little bit. I didn't want to make it too easy for him. I Made him sweat for a minute or two; then I gave my permission."

"I told him he was welcome in our pack or if they wish to go to his pride, that is fine too as long as Marnie is happy. I also informed him that if he ever hurts Marnie, I will show him what a pack of wolves could do to a certain part of a lion's anatomy."

He scooped up Adira from her window seat, twirled her in the air, and took her to bed.

CHAPTER FIFTY-TWO

Lily found the experience of being in her wolf exciting, especially when Zinnia would tease her. This was getting painful; their heat was taking over, and Lily would lose her mind if she didn't get rid of this pain.

Lily took control, and they ran back to the castle, unsure where to go or what to do. What if she encounters other males?

She stopped at the door, unsure if she should go in; that was when the golden wolf took the lead. She could hear Thorn and Zinnia talking; he would lead them to where they needed to go, without having to worry about being ambushed by another male.

"Zinnia, we need to get to our room and into the ice-cold water. I can't take any more pain."

"Lily dear, ice-cold water isn't going to help us anymore; we need to fight fire with fire."

That was when Lily decided that she would have to trust Zinnia, let this, whatever this is to happen. In truth, she was tired of being alone. The heat and pain were making her crazy and lonely.

The Golden wolf led them to the King's bedchambers; Lily was amazed at all the gold and blue silk, the velvet curtains, and the sheer size of the room.

She couldn't take it anymore, and Zinnia shifted as another wave of pain hit them hard this time. She lay naked on the Kings floor, screaming in pain, and she felt like she was on fire. That desperate feeling was coming over her, the one where she is so far gone she isn't going to care anymore.

The King came up to her in a hurry, when she started screaming,

"Little one, you are burning up!"

She looked at him in all his glory, and holy sweet goddess, he was gorgeous. His eyes captivated her; they were glowing like beautiful sapphires. When he picked her up to bring her to the bed, she was moaning in pleasure of the sparks they were giving off.

His scent drove her over the edge; he smelled like a pine forest warmed by the sun and the fall air. She couldn't stop when he laid her down on the bed; she reached out for him and pulled him onto her.

She grabbed his golden hair and pulled him down so she could kiss him. Oh, God, he tasted so good...He let out a low growl of pleasure. He was just as lost as she was; she hoped that this didn't lead to rejection in the back of her mind thinking now that would be punishment.

He took control; he kissed her, taking everything she could give; it was wild and sensual. It was beyond a pleasure. He kissed her neck right where he would mark her; he lingered nibbling on the skin, driving her insane, and she let out a long moan.

He took hold of her breasts; one hand was toying and lightly pinching it, teasing the nipple. While his tongue on the other one, sucking and licking, made her heated skin blaze. She arched her back and let out short little moans of pleasure. She couldn't catch her breath.

He growled again, this time a louder one of pleasure. She couldn't take anymore; she wasn't above begging.

"Please....pl..eas.e..."

"You'll have to tell me, little one, what you want. What do you need, my sweet little one? Perhaps you should call my name; I have three, Alexander Callen Liam Breckenburg."

"Please!"

"Is this what you want?"

He moved lower until he was lightly teasing her clit with his tongue. Lily arched her body; she had the sheets in both fists as he stopped licking and began to suck on her. He chuckled…

"Well, now, I can't decide which pair of your delicious lips I like kissing more."

He began again. He would lick and suck, lapping up her juices like the most wonderful honey he had ever tasted. Lily was burning up inside. It was too much. He was taking her too high; she had never felt like this before, she climaxed three times in a row, and still, her body wanted more of him.

"Please, I need yo..u inside..me!"

He wasted no time; he put himself at her entrance, again teasing her as he moved easily with her juices. She screamed in her frustration, trying to impale herself on his massive cock; it was huge she wasn't sure he was going to fit. She didn't care. She needed him to try. She let out little mewls of pleasure and frustration.

He bent his head, licked the space between her breasts, and left another mark on her. It excited her that he was marking her all over. She couldn't get enough of him; it didn't matter who she was or what she had done anymore.

431

It didn't matter that he was the King and that there could be all kinds of trouble afterward, including him rejecting her.

Just when she thought she was going to go crazy with the waiting. In one violent thrust into her wet heat, she let out a scream of pleasure; Lily felt like she was split in two. The pain soon gave over to intense joy.

He didn't move at first, just letting her body adjust to his size; she wrapped her legs around him to signal that he should start moving. He chuckled…

"So impatient little one. Don't worry; I will take you to heaven with me many times this night."

He began moving slowly at first, then faster as she started screaming Callen, Callen repeatedly till she was screaming Cal, Cal, Cal as she was moaning and crying out in the song of pleasure beneath him.

"Can you take more?" He asked in a raspy pleasure-soaked voice.

"Yes, more." Was all she could manage; she was beyond forming logical thoughts or words.

He grabbed the headboard, causing him to go deeper and deeper. Going almost out and then slammed back down to her core as his thrusts became faster and faster. As the bed banged against the wall over and over.

He came with a roar as he bit down on her neck, marking her as his. She came so hard that final time; it was so intense that she passed out as she reached heaven with him.

She was in a huge canopy bed lying on her side when she woke up. He was awake watching her as he gently stroked her hip and thigh with his fingers. He was smiling at her. His eyes were still glowing, though not as intense.

She turned to beat red; why was she so embarrassed? It wasn't her first time. Not like she didn't know what it was. Still, it was intense with her first mate, but this was on another level.

Not to mention that she didn't know his real name to start. Usually, you talk a little first before she knew it was screaming out Callen, one of his middle names. Not sure why she chose that name, it just sounded right to her.

"What are you thinking, my sweet little one?"

"I was trying to figure out why I chose to call you Callen."

"Are you worried that I wouldn't like it?"

"Well, yes, you are the King. Oh, God, you're the King!!"

"I understand if you want to reject me, I cannot be the Queen. Not only that, but it would be an embarrassment for the

royal family and the court. Please wait till morning; let me have this wonderful memory to take with me."

She buried her head into his shoulder as he began to chuckle. She is so cute; why hadn't I noticed before now? It doesn't matter; that is all that matters, and I am not letting her go; she is mine. Thorn spoke up.

"Ours."

He pulled her tightly to him…

"There will be no rejection now or ever; I am not giving you up. As for the royal family and court, they can kiss my ass, you could never embarrass me. Does that set your mind at ease now, little one? If you need more proof, reach up and touch your lovely neck."

She reached up and touched her neck in disbelief.

"You marked me."

"Yes, that is usually what happens when we claim our mates; you still have to mark me. I will let you decide when you wish to do that. I will take it as your full acceptance of me and all this."

He waved his hand in the air indicating all of his castle.

"Just so you know, in public, I am still your highness or my King; in private, I want you to call me Callen unless you

are in your pleasure, then I insist that you call me Cal. I can't say how wonderful aroused my name on your lips makes me."

Lily could still feel the heat within her; it was now less than before but still there; they were in for a long night or even a couple of days. She didn't want to think about all the royal rules and what this would mean for her right now.

She wanted only one thing; from the look in his eyes, he would give it to her repeatedly.

He licked in one stroke from the beginning of her butt all the way up her back to his mark. She heated right up again.

"Don't worry, my sweet little one; we will discuss everything you need to know and more; tonight and the next couple of days, we will get more acquainted. Remember the first time we met? I know everything about you. Everything."

"Now, through our growing link, you will know all of me. Because of the intensity of your heat, I couldn't go as slow as I wished."

Late into the morning, they were both asleep, exhausted. The King opened his eyes slightly as a maid brought in breakfast and other snacks for the day till dinner. She also dropped off what looked like some of Lily's clothes. He smirked; she won't be needing those for a while.

When the maid left, he locked the door again and slid back into the bed, pulling Lily close to him as he went off into a blissful sleep. Already he could feel her body heat getting hotter.

CHAPTER FIFTY-THREE

The King was at his desk taking care of some daily reports and expense logs, it was the fourth day since the initial heat, and Lily was now exhausted and sleeping safely in his bed; her heat phase was over. Already the council had been trying to reach him.

He ignored them, letting them sit and stew for a while. He would talk to them in his time, not theirs. It is time he updated the council. Time for some of those old horses to be put to pasture. Let some new blood take over.

Ones with fresh ideas and more open minds than the one's now sitting. Yes, he would start the petitions and see who applied.

He heard a small sigh coming from their bed; she was dreaming. He was a little ashamed when he saw that he left every inch of her covered in marks. Yet, at the same time, he was proud of it. No one will question what they did in here or that she is his.

She let out a whimper as if in pain; he went and sat on the side of the bed next to her. Her face was scrunched up as if she was in pain as well. She is having a nightmare. He had hoped it wouldn't happen; her abuse left deep scars.

He put one hand on her forehead and held her hand. He entered her nightmare when her mate had died, and she was still in the room with his body. She was tied to a chair, her mouth was gagged, and tears ran down her face.

 Her eyes were empty, unseeing the corpse before her. She was cold to the touch. The door opened, and there was that piece of shit, laughing at it all. He wished he could rip him to shreds; though he could touch the dreamer, he could not do anything else. His heart bled for her; he knew what she was feeling. He went through the loss of his mate.

This was different; his mate died from cancer, and her wolf couldn't fight anymore.

This was brutal; his face was destroyed, his dignity gone. She was forced to watch as he took his last breath, then tied to the chair, having to sit with the body for days as it started to rot. Cruelly, she was not able to look anywhere else or allow herself to grieve. Then they commit the worse sin they could and killed her unborn pup's.

It was her hell. He had to wake her and comfort her. Thorn was going nuts with not being able to do anything. He wanted her out of there, now.

"Do you think she feels guilty now that she is our mate when she never really got a chance with her first one? Do you think she feels like she is betraying him?"

"I don't know, Thorn; I imagine she has all kinds of emotions right now; I don't feel any remorse from her or her wolf. We must get her out of this nightmare and onto a better life. Show her that she is lovable and worthy again."

He let go of her hand and wrapped himself around her; He gently started to wake her. She opened her eyes, but she was still not with him.

"Come back to me, my little Lily flower; nothing is left for you there. He rubbed her back as he held her, whispering into her ear. You are mine now, let that pain go; he would not want you to linger there."

She let out a gasp as she came back to her senses.

He held her closer to him, so she could breathe in his scent and know she was safe. She held to him tightly as she started to cry. He never let go, just rubbing her back and saying soothing words to her as she cried out her pain.

Marco was informed from the front gate that they had a visitor coming. They said that it was a female, and she was here to see Werelions. Leaving him clueless, he did manage to find August and have him greet their guest with him.

As a black SUV pulled up, the driver stepped out and went to the back door. The first thing that Marco noticed was the red high heels. The next thing he thought was that something wasn't sitting right in his gut about this.

She came out all in red, her light blond hair in a fancy up-do, blue eyes, and red lipstick. If truth were told, if she were trying to enhance her beauty with the red lipstick, she failed; all he could focus on was her very red lips.

When she approached them, August had a scowl on his face and crossed his arms when she reached out to greet him. In a low growl, he said.

"Hello, Felicia."

"Marco, this is Felicia Mathews; she is a member of our pride. Felicia, this is Marco. He is the Beta of this pack, second only to the Alpha."

She turned her nose in the air at Marco with a look of how dare you to be unimpressed with my presence.

"Well, I never have been so insulted in all my life, August. I should not have been greeted by this, whatever you call it. Is your Alpha so important that he can't greet an important guest?"

August gave out another growl, this one more menacing.

"There is nothing important about you, Felicia Mathews."

Marco spoke up and the icy tone in his voice, almost made August gleeful as he watched the bitches face.

"I am sorry you are so offended, Ma'am; I was not informed of your importance. Even still, it is custom in packs that the Beta will greet anyone of lower rank first before the Alpha."

She looked at Marco as if he had just punched her.

"I am sure that August can find you somewhere for you to freshen up and do whatever you came to do, Unfortunately, if you have to stay overnight, you will have to stay at the inn in town. If you excuse me, I have other more important business to deal with. He gave a curt bow and left."

August had all he could not laugh as he looked at the pride whore before him, wondering what she was up to now. Probably trying to get into either Archies or Ash's pants again. August hoped he wouldn't have to deal with her again, once was enough.

"Come on then; I will take you to where Archer is staying, and he can deal with you."

He started to walk across the pack grounds to the guest cabin, where Arch was, but she didn't follow. When he turned to see what the matter was, she was just standing there in shock.

"What is your problem now, Flea?" August said with a sigh.

"I've told you several times not to call me that! For your information, I will not go tramping around in the woods in these heels!"

"You will not be going into the woods, we follow this path, and it goes right to the cabin next to the woods."

"I can't; you will have to carry me."

August laughed.......

"Flea, if I were to carry you into the woods, it would be because I will be looking for the next cliff to drop you off of. Now I suggest that if you want to see Archer, you better follow me; otherwise, I will call back the Beta, and he can tell you where you can go."

He walked off, not looking back. Felicia followed taking off her heels. August could tell she was pissed off at what he said. He didn't care; she was a greedy, snobby, and a pride whore.

She had been trying to sink her claws into Archer for years, and he wanted nothing to do with her. So she tried Ashton when he wouldn't even look at her, she went to him. He didn't want her either; she even tried to accuse Archer of getting her pregnant.

Hard to get pregnant when you don't bump fuzzies first. Still, she was the daughter of one of the Pride's Elder founders; he was rich, so she always seemed to have resources. He wondered what her plan was now.

After Ashton talked to August about the unexpected gift, he wasn't happy. He didn't like Flea. She hated that nickname, but it was the best description that could be made in one word.

When she hopped on you, she would suck your body dry. All she wants from you is to have the power to go with her money. She is mean and nasty. She thinks the world owes her everything. Heaven above only knows how many with which she has slept. She should have been born a vampire.

He was going to warn Marnie before she should happen to meet the bitch. I hope the Flea doesn't do anything stupid to provoke the wolves. OK, he wouldn't be heartbroken if she got her ass handed to her.

Still, he didn't want anything to harm the relationship that Archer had built here either. The Alpha is a kind and fair person, but he expects respect for all his pack members no matter their rank and good adherence to the rules.

He has been in other wolf packs before; this one has a really good feel; they work together for the good of all. Some rules must be followed; they are fair and mostly just plain common sense. Whether you're Alpha or Omega, you have responsibilities to your pack; everyone works.

Everyone is respected and protected; is this pack perfect? No, it isn't. Nothing ever is, though.

Ash thought he wouldn't mind living here in this pack. He was going to take Marnie home with him so she could meet his folks and friends.

He loved his home, but he wanted to live here with her; it felt right. First things first, though, got to tell Marnie about their guest.

CHAPTER FIFTY-FOUR

The King and Lily had what they assigned as the day of talking, asking questions, and getting to know each other on a more logical and practical level of understanding. It was their last day of being away from the world; tomorrow, they would have to face the council and others about their relationship. Not that either one gave a damn what others thought.

Sometimes fate deals her hand, and that is that, if you're smart, you will jump on the ride. Experience everything life will give you; if that means you must experience the bad shit too, so be it. That is the way it is, not everything is sunshine and daisies.

You just have to make sure that all the good experiences and memories you make far outweigh any bad ones that come into your life. If you go through life pushing all the people away because you don't want to experience the pain of losing them, then you will never know the joy of having them either.

He looked at Lily as she sat in one of the chairs in front of the fireplace. She looked like she was miles away. He went and sat down in the opposite chair.

"Lily, what has taken you so far from me? A penny for your thoughts, little flower?"

"I was thinking of the past, not the abuse. I was just wondering if Adira will ever forgive me."

"Little flower, if you don't ask, you will never have an answer to your question."

"I just keep thinking about her stupid stuffed bear."

"Stuffed bear?"

"Yeah, she made a bear from all the stuffed animals I would tear apart in anger. I wonder if she still has it?"

"You will have to ask her, Lily; once all the commotion of all this die's down, we will go and pay a visit to Duncan and Adira; it's time that you both had a sit-down and get it all out."

She let out a sigh.

"Back to our talk, now I know what happened to your first son; I thought you had two sons?"

His face went from concern for her to a darker shade of sadness. Almost one of intense pain. She leaned forward and put her hand over his.

"It's ok if you don't want to talk about it; I can see it is causing you great pain."

"No, it's ok. I will have no shadows; between us will only be truth and love."

"My second son wants nothing to do with any of this life, nor does he want anything to do with me as his king or father. He hated it so much that he had me disown him, he even took another name; he is married and wants his family never to know his birth family."

"My two oldest sons were as different as night and day; Adam was the firstborn, so, unfortunately, he was spoiled rotten by myself and everyone."

"My second son is brilliant and excels in every academic. He wasn't the playboy prince like his older brother; in fact, Adam hated him. Since they were small, he would torture his younger brother. It was one of the reasons that my second son had left for good."

"Unfortunately, I was so busy being the King I had forgotten how to be a father. When my second son announced that he had gotten married to a commoner and would have their first child, I wasn't sure what to think; I didn't care that she was a commoner."

"I didn't listen to my second son, Jason, though, when he told me that Adam was trying to kill his wife Karen and their unborn child. I wrote it off as their usual bickering."

"Adam was indeed trying to kill them, I didn't know it then, but I know it now. My second son never forgave me for not believing him, so he left and never returned. When I started to inquire about my grandchild, he sent a letter informing me of his wishes never to be known by my world again."

"Very few in the kingdom know that I had a third son. His name was Christopher. He was like sunshine, never cried, always the giggling baby. We were not sure what happened, but he died in his sleep, they said it was SIDS, but it never sat well with me."

"I know it sounds horrible, but after all I learned about Adam, I think maybe he had a hand in Christophers' death."

"I think that was also the reason my first mate died."

"Yes, she died because she lost the battle with her cancer, but Christopher's death helped it move faster. My first wife did have a wolf even if she was also half-human."

"It wasn't advertised out into the world because the council thought it would make me look weak. I was a fool for agreeing with them. I was young and stupid."

"After my first mate died, I and Thorn, we kind of lost our will to go on. The council covered it up and ran all the day-to-day activities. I should have been there for my second son."

"Jason is a lot like Adira's husband Duncan; Adam hated him passionately. Had I paid even the littlest attention to the

situation instead of trying to ignore the world, things might be different today."

"I know parents are not supposed to have favorites; Adam was my first mate's favorite. He was always a little off, and the other children didn't want to be around him; my mate always covered up his cruelties to the other children, or she would pay the parents off."

"I found out after my son's death many things that were not known to me before, and it breaks my heart that a son of mine would do those things; those poor children he tortured, he was insane."

"As far as Jason goes, I don't hear from him much. Only that they are expecting their third pup; it's a girl. After Adam died, I asked Jason if he would be willing to come back and take my place someday, and he said no. He was happy with how things were and would not change it for the world."

"That is why I wanted Duncan and Adira's firstborn to be my heir, but I don't think they want anything to do with the throne. They are there for me in the compacity of friendship only."

"Callen, you know I can't have children. I have been messed up for too long."

"My little flower, didn't you notice that your wolf Zinnia had turned all white?"

"Yes, I noticed, but I didn't know what it meant, and when I asked Zinnia, she just giggled and told me that I would know soon enough. She has been nothing but smug and mysterious lately; it's almost impossible to get a straight answer out of her."

"I love reading old texts of history and events; I believe, my little flower, that when your Zinnia turned all white, it was a sign from the goddess that you were forgiven. I do believe that it means you are whole and healthy."

"Furthermore, I believe we have already made our first pup, at least, according to Thorn."

Lily looked at Callen in shock as a giddiness filled her heart; she jumped from her chair into Callen's lap and kissed him all over his face and neck. She couldn't stop herself; when she reached that spot where his neck and shoulder met, she bit down hard, marking him.

He let out a growl of pleasure and happiness. Finally, he was mated for all and good. Things are going to change now for good, he hoped.

He picked her up and carried her to their bed; if there were a chance she wasn't pregnant with their pup, he would make sure she was when he was done tonight. This time, he will have a happy family, and there will be heirs for the throne, whichever of their pups suits it best.

Archer was enjoying the quiet of his cabin. It was a welcome change from the rat race he usually had to deal with. Life in a Pack is quite different from Pride, at least his pride anyway.

That was when he heard a shrill voice he hoped never to hear again. Felicia! He went from at peace with the world to chaotic frustration. He wished his parents weren't such good friends with Felicia's parents. They had been trying to get one of their sons to mate with her for as long as he could remember.

It wouldn't be that hard; she is rather pretty. That was until she opened her mouth. She was also under the impression that sex would get her anything she wanted. She is mean-spirited and arrogant; she thinks she is better than everyone.

She believes that her presence is a blessing for all to be thankful for. She is only tolerated because of her parent's money and status.

He looked out the window at the shrew walking up the path bitching all the way; he did get some satisfaction seeing her barefoot in the snow.

He did wonder whose pants is she trying to get into this time. She was determined that one of them had to mate with her. She had money, but she also wanted power over others as well.

Something she had better get into her head, is that it's never going to happen. Everyone looks at her as one of the pride sluts, and that is all she was ever going to be if Archer has his way.

He just hoped she didn't try her high and mighty crap with the pack members; the rules are a little different in this pack. She will be expected to, at the very least, be respectful of everyone—no acting like a queen here.

If she does end up causing trouble, he will let Duncan handle her punishment. That way, she doesn't get off easy because of dear old dad's money.

He sat down at his desk, putting her in her place right from the start. It's time, miss high and mighty, to learn some humility. He should have dealt with this sooner, perhaps being here will be a bonus for him; she can't just run off to daddy to fix her mistakes.

She isn't sleeping under this roof; she can either stay in a guest cabin or get a hotel room.

Still, something was bugging him about all this; she isn't the type to go traveling unless it's a million-dollar a night room and a string of parties. So why is she here now?

Felicia came into the room in a huff; she didn't look happy that she had to walk fifty feet to reach him.

"Well, Felicia, what do we owe the honor of your presence once again? Truly, you'll spoil us by gracing us with your angelic presence."

As Felicia looked at Archer, she could tell he wasn't happy to see her. Perhaps she had overplayed her hand this time. Then again, he always looked at her like that.

In truth, she had given up on Archer after a while; he lived like a monk and was not interested in her. He always gave her a look that said keep your distance. Even her daddy got off her back about him and told her to focus on the other two.

August played with her but never gave her any inkling that he would go further or that she could manipulate him to do as she wished.

She thought Ashton was the shy one; he was always watching her. He was the one she wanted this time, and this time she would get what she and her daddy wanted. Even if she had to travel to the middle of God knows where having to be around all these low-life stinky mangy mutts to do it.

Looking around at the cabin he was staying; she hoped that he didn't expect her to stay here in this dump; as soon as she could, she would get a good hotel room, or this fucking wolf pack would let her have the Alpha's bedroom.

CHAPTER FIFTY-FIVE

Marnie wasn't particularly happy with what Ash told her about this new female. She decided if push came to shove, she would do the shoving if that is what it took for this chick to get the message.

She doesn't have time for this drama queen crap, Adira is close to her time, and she wants to do all the things aunties get to do. She couldn't wait for the little pup to be born.

She was spending time with Adira and Ash. That is all; if this trashy girl wants to have a go, she can wait in line. She was on her way to Adira's room when she heard the loudest high-pitched yell, coming from the downstairs. She stopped on the landing of the stairs and waited to see where it was coming from.

This time the voice was accompanied by a loud bang, if this were to get any louder, it might upset Adira. If it upsets Adira, it is really going to upset Mr. Expecting Dad the Alpha. Sighing to herself, she went down to take care of the problem.

When she got into the kitchen, she was surprised to notice that it was trashed, the poor cook was in the corner crying her eyes out.

Marnie was instantly pissed, no one messes with the cook or the kitchen.

In a loud commanding voice.

"WHO THE HELL DID THIS?"

That was when Marnie noticed that there was another woman in the kitchen, she was holding a rolling pin like a weapon. She looked nuts.

"Who the hell are you, and what the hell are you doing in here.?"

The woman had a smirk on her face, putting her nose in the air, sniffing it like she smelled something rotten. She then threw the rolling pin at the cook's head.

Unfortunately, for this unknown bitch, she didn't manage to dodge Marnie's fist as well as the cook dodged the rolling pin. Marnie landed her right on her ass, and a look of total rage came over the woman's face, she was pretty before, but now she was positively ugly.

The change stunned Marnie for a second, she couldn't resist giving an insult, though.

"Wow, not only are you a bitch, but you also fell out of the ugly tree and hit every branch on your way down. Damn girl, you are ugly!!!"

Felicia was pissed, this low life not only touched her but hit her in the face. Now she was insulting her, how dare she call her ugly. She was going to die for this, how dare she, come in here and demand to know who she is. She was about to find out.

Marnie went over to check on the cook, *"Are you ok? Did she hit you with this rolling pin before I came in?"*

The cook was so upset that all she could do was nod her head yes. Before Marnie could stand up again' she was attacked from the back by the lioness. Marnie felt blood running down her back and burning pain.

Marnie was pissed, so was her wolf Myan. They shifted instantly into their Lycan form. They turned on the big cat and tossed her against the wall with a very loud roar. The lion landed with a thud and then slid down the wall.

Ashton was in the Alpha's office, discussing housing options for him and Marnie after they were married. When he felt a burning pain going down his back. He stood up but couldn't see anything, that was when he realized it was Marnie.

Ashton and Duncan hit the stairs at a run when they heard a very loud, angry roar. Duncan was trying to mind link his sister, but all he got back for a response was, red.

Duncan grabbed Ash to slow him down.

"Listen, Ash, Marnie has changed into her Lycan form, it makes her unpredictable. Marnie and Myan are really good together, and the Lycan form is their specialty. When you go in, don't make any aggressive moves."

"Because you are Marnie's mate, you will be in charge of calming her down and getting her out of there. Take her to your room and wait there."

They went into the kitchen slowly, what they saw was not what they were expecting, the place looked like a war zone.

There was flour and food everywhere mixed with blood, the cook was sitting in the corner. She pointed a shaking hand at the back door, which was standing wide open.

They ran outside, and there, in the front yard, were two figures fighting. Duncan recognized Marnie in her Lycan form right away, the Lioness; he had no idea who she was.

Archer was out there standing between Marnie and the pretty beaten-up Lioness; the snow was covered in blood spatters; it was a macabre sight to behold.

Marnie crouched down into an attack position; Duncan yelled to Archer not to make a single move. He turned to his sister, taking off his clothes, he changed into his Lycan form and went to stand before of Archer.

What they didn't understand as shifters of a different kind was that Marnie, in her own right, was also a Luna. If there was something done to her or her pack members, she will see it as a threat, she will have the right to the blood also known as, fight to the death.

Duncan, in his Lycan form, had to mind-link Marnie and Myan with his commanding Alpha voice to get her back down.

Marnie shifted into her complete wolf form and bolted for the woods. Ash ran after her.

Duncan also changed back, put on a pair of jogging pants that Marco gave him, and asked Archer what the hell was going on.

"I have no idea, I got here just in time to stop your sister from landing the killing blow."

Archer kneeled down next to the Lioness, she was unconscious but other than a broken wrist and bruises, she was going to be fine in a day or two.

Archer ordered her to change back, she did and awoke to scream swear words he never knew existed. He picked her up.

"Want to tell me what was going on?"

"I didn't do anything; she came out of nowhere and started to attack me. I was just defending myself."

Archer smirked.

"Are you sure that is how things went down? You do know they have security cameras everywhere, right?"

She became shrill, *"WHY DON'T YOU EVER BELIEVE ME!!!"*

"I don't ever believe you, Felicia, because you have never given me a reason to."

With that, Archer carried her to the pack hospital. So they could help this stupid bitch heal faster. Thinking to himself, maybe he should just find a really big snowbank and toss her in.

Ash shifted into his Lion so he could keep up with Marnie's wolf Myan, she was really fast. She ran until she came across a river, she jumped in and swam to the little island that the river went around.

He swam across, shifting upon coming out of the water. He could see that she was back in her human form. She was wearing a robe; she must have stashed it here at one time or another.

When he got closer, he noticed that there was blood soaking the back of the robe. He ran the rest of the way to her. He grabbed her by her shoulders and stood her up, so he could take off the robe to see what damage was done.

What he saw pissed him off, that whore is going to get a piece of my mind, and I am going to see that the punishment sticks this time. No daddy buying her way out or friends doing the punishment for her.

There were four deep lacerations, they went from Marnie's shoulder all the way down to just above her hips. He could see where her wolf was trying to heal her, the thing about werelion claws, is that they have not only a type of poison to subdue their prey, but they also have a type of nasty fast-acting bacteria.

He went to the river and soaked the robe in the icy water and put it back on her, then he picked her up

461

gently. He was tall enough to wade back, he carried her all the way to the pack hospital.

When he walked in, he heard Felicia screaming her fool head off, he was met by a nurse who took one look and showed them to a private room. The doctor came directly after her, demanding what was going on.

When he explained why the wound was not healing, they went into action. Duncan came running into the room, wanting to know what was going on. That got both Ash and Duncan pushed out into the hall, to wait.

Ash was pissed, he knew that for that poison to be injected, meant that it was a deliberate act. Felicia could not claim self-defense; not only was it a sucker punch move, but the poison also must be consciously delivered. Ash told Duncan everything, he also suggested that Felicia be punished according to pack rules. Since they are on pack grounds.

Duncan agreed, but he still had to take it up with Archer, since he was the head and had the final say on what should be done with one of his pride members.

Ashton smiled a wicked smile; he already knew what his brother was going to say.

CHAPTER FIFTY-SIX

Marnie woke up to the sound of beeping; looking down, she saw that she had an IV in her arm. She was feeling almost perfect, Myan must have worked her tail off to heal us.

Marnie mind linked Myan.

"Hey there, Myan. Are you ok?"

"Yeah, I am just tired. Going to need some sleep for a bit, that's all. That nasty cat had poison in her claws, I wish I would have got another swing at her ass."

"There was also a nasty bug in the poison, she probably got that from not cleaning out her litter box."

With that, Myan went back to sleep. Marnie smiled; Myan had always been her best friend. For a long while there, Myan was her only friend. Looking around, she didn't see anyone.

She reached down to her arm and gently pulled out the IV, holding the cotton ball on it while she taped it. She then got up, she was a little dizzy at first, but it was fine after a bit. She looked around but couldn't find any clothes.

She peeked her head out of her room door, and there in the hall was Ash, sound asleep in a chair. She didn't see anyone else. She hated hospitals, she tipped-toed past Ash.

She pushed the elevator button, and just as the doors were opening, she was grabbed from behind. She recognized his scent right off; it was Ash. He picked her up and carried her back to her room.

"You are not going anywhere till the Doc says you can, I don't care if I have to sit on you."

"As a matter of fact, I have a way to make you stay."

He slid in next to her on the hospital bed. Wrapped his arms around her and started to fall back asleep. Marnie gave a sigh of contentment, turning her face into his shoulder; she decided that she could wait a little longer.

Archer, August, Duncan, and Marco were in Felicia's hospital room. She was fully healed, she was putting on a show, though. Marco looked bored and Duncan looked pissed. Archer and August just rolled their eyes.

"You have to listen to me! She came at me first; I was just defending myself."

Archer, in a low and tired voice...

"I told you the rules of the pack, you were already told that you were a guest only. You have no authority, if you need something, you ask politely. If the answer is no, then you leave."

"Further-more, I find it insulting that you think I am that stupid. The wounds on Marnie's back were from an attack from behind, a sneak attack, not self-defense."

"The fact that you used your poison claws, also proves that your attack was deliberate. You cannot use the poison unless you consciously put the thought to your cat."

"Which leaves me to believe that your intent was to severely hurt or kill Marnie, a Luna of this pack. Not to mention your actions have put our pride's relationship with this pack in jeopardy."

"With all the evidence on the cameras, I would say you don't have a leg to stand on. This means that your punishment has to be decided by Duncan, the Alpha of the pack."

"It is in his territory, in his pack house, you were informed of the rules, you intentionally broke the rules. Now you will be punished."

"During your punishment, you will not be allowed to shift into your cat, if you do, I will have no choice but to have you banished from the pride. Before you say that I can't do this, keep in mind, that I can, and I will. I will be informing your parents as soon as I leave this room."

With that, Archer turned to August.

"You will stay to oversee her punishment."

August acknowledged that with a nod, and Archer turned and left room.

Duncan looked at the female with a blank face. Inside he wanted to slap her from one side of the pack grounds to the other. Instead, he was going to follow protocol.

"Ms. Felicia Mathews, you have beaten my cook and destroyed the kitchen. You intentionally tried to hurt, if not kill, my sister. You will be staying here in this pack until you've repaid the debt."

With a sneer, Felicia gave a little laugh; *"Just let me call Daddy, and he will send you the money to pay for everything."*

"You don't seem to understand, you will not be paying for the damages with money. You will be repaying them with work.

First though, since you did attack both my cook and sister, you will spend the next five nights in the dungeon."

"When your five days are up, you will then report to the very Kitchen you destroyed and will work as a servant for an additional week."

"You will not be allowed to talk to anyone, nor will you go anywhere in the pack house, that is not the kitchen or your room. You will not be allowed any form of technology, nor communication with any others during your punishment."

"Any infractions against these rules, will add on weeks to your sentence. Any infractions. It will be decided by Marco should this happen."

He waved to Marco and left the room as well. August grabbed Felicia by the arm and stood her up.

"Time to go, Flea."

"Wait, you can't do this to me, at least let me get dressed and out of this hospital gown!!!"

"You are dressed well enough for where you're going."

August dragged her out of the room, as Marco followed. Neither one said another word till they reached the dungeon doors. Felicia, on the other hand, screamed until her voice was nothing but a rasp.

Duncan sat at his desk, and in another chair was Archer. Duncan was pissed, when he saw the video from the cameras, he couldn't believe that someone could be that vicious, she had to be insane.

"Please don't tell me, Archer, if that woman is the rule in your pride? If that is so, then I am afraid I will have to decline the offer of a relationship between my Pack and your Pride. I am sorry, but we do not allow that kind of behavior here."

"It is not the norm in my Pride, in truth, her behavior has gotten erratic of late. I suspect that her father is pushing her to catch one of us. Had I known she wasn't even going to try to behave, I would have sent her on her way."

"Is our punishment of her crime going to cause problems in your Pride?"

"No, I will see that it doesn't. That is why I asked for a copy of the video. She won't be able to lie or cheat her way out of this. When she gets home, she will be punished again."

"Her parents are friends of our parents, that is why she has been able to go on for as long as she has. With this last action of hers, she will have no choice, she is going to have to sleep in the bed, that she has been making for a long time."

"Very well, her punishment starts immediately in the dungeon, then on to working as a servant, if she controls herself, she should be done in two weeks."

Felicia sat on the dirty floor of the dungeon, there was no light, other than what came down from the other side of the hall.

She was pissed, not only was she sitting in this nasty place in nothing but a hospital gown, but they fitted her with a type of shock collar, that will not only cause her great pain but also alert them should she shift.

How dare they do this to her, wait till she sees her Daddy, he will make them pay for this. She let out a scream of rage. That was when she realized that she wasn't alone down here. There was a smell in the air that wasn't just the dungeon.

She heard the laughter that gave her the chills, then it went to growling.

"What's the matter, little bitch, don't like your room, wanna come and stay with me? It's just you and me down here right now, my little bitch. Oh, I bet you're a tasty morsel. Who knows maybe I am to be your punishment."

He started to make strange moans, she realized that he was pleasuring himself, it was sickening.

"I saw you when they brought you down here, you are a sexy little bitch, one of those who always been too good for me girls. It's just you and me now bitchy poo, oh, I bet you have wonderful tits too. Too bad we can't share a room."

He started laughing and moaning again as he reached his climax, he started laughing even louder and didn't seem to stop.

She sat in silence, too terrified to speak, he just laughed and laughed, as she sat there, unable to do anything in her silence.

CHAPTER FIFTY-SEVEN

Christmas was quickly approaching, Adira had the whole pack house and grounds decorated, there wasn't a place left forgotten. She'd never had a real Christmas before, so she went all out. Duncan looked around and was pleased, the pack house hadn't looked this good since he was a pup.

He had decided that he was going to make sure she was spoiled rotten, besides the normal gifts she would receive from the pack. He had also brought her a special gift as well, his family's diamond and sapphire necklace, earrings and bracelet set.

He was now taking a tray up to Adira for lunch. She was so close to her time and was having problems with her feet and ankles swelling, the Doc put her on bed rest. This of course, was making her a bit restless and cranky.

For the last two days, she had been getting increasingly uncomfortable. So he had been dividing up his time with her mostly and then pack issues; Marco had been taking care of everything else. Thank God for Marco, his best friend since their crib days.

He also wondered what it is going to be like to be a Dad. Wow, he never had the time to give it much thought until now. He started to smile with thoughts of his little pup running around the house.

He got up to their door while juggling the tray, he managed to open the door, and there was Adira doubled over on the side of the bed. Clearly in pain. He dropped the tray and ran to her. She looked up at his face with a painful smile.

"Duncan, I think it's time."

Felicia was still pissed two days later, she was given a blanket, a pillow, and a bucket. The rogue in the other cell went quiet again.

She sat there staring off into the dark, planning her revenge. That little bitch of a wolf is going to pay, how dare she do this to her. Her plans were all of murder and betrayal. She was going to get her revenge one way or the other. Two more days, and she was out of this hell hole.

Once she was in the pack house again, she would start putting her plan into motion. Then they will all be sorry for what they had done to her. Perhaps Daddy will force Archer to marry me, as some sort of compensation, for what he allowed to happen to me.

Though right now, she wasn't sure she was going to stand the smell the dungeon for the next two days, the stench seemed to be in her hair and skin.

"What the hell is that smell!? Then it hit her; that smell was death, that was why that rogue went quiet? Oh, God, did they leave her down here alone with a dead body?"

"GUARD!!!!!!!!!!!!!!!!!!GUARD!!!!!!!!!!!LET ME OUT OF HERE, HE IS DEAD!!!!!GUARD PLEASE!!"

The only thing her screaming got her was more silence, she started to cry. They will have to take him out of here when they bring her once-a-day meal. Oh, god, she was so hungry, but how could she eat knowing what was rotting two doors down?

She curled up into a ball on her blanket, plotting a few more nasty things she was going to do when she got out of here. Crying, she was never going to get that smell out of her mind. She did have one hope, though.

I hope they let me take a bath...

Lily was sitting on a stool next to the King, while he held court. Everyone was looking at her in curiosity or with a scowl. To be honest, she didn't give a shit. One good thing about going through all that abuse, is that it gave her inner strength. She stopped caring a long time ago what anyone thought of her.

It was fascinating to watch her mate hold court; it was also quite boring. Most of it was legalities and land contracts, things of that nature. Once it was all done, the King then introduced his mate to the council.

Lily almost giggled at the looks on their faces. She managed, though, to stand tall and regal. Some were just surprised but happy for the King, others were quiet, and others still were out-right angry.

"As your King, I have the right through the Mate Law, to choose my own for when my true mate comes. Lily is my second chance, mate, and I am hers. I understand that she can't be an official queen and that she will be queen in name only."

"However, She will be given the respect that is her due. I will also allow her to have some authority to make laws, regarding women and children. These laws will pertain to their treatment and rights to be protected and to seek justice."

"She will be given the people and the resources to do these things, she will only have to seek permission from myself. Since the Queen, even if it's in name only, still only has to answer to the King."

"She will travel to all the packs in our care, no longer will the royal family stay within the walls of this castle alone. It is time to go out into the world to make sure what we are being told is the actual truth."

"It makes me sick that something as evil as that Pack, was able to get such a big foothold on us. From now on, my Queen and I will do everything in our power to see that it never happens again."

"I will no longer hold to the old stuffy and blind traditions of the past. Anyone here now who disagrees with anything I have said today, may step down and leave."

With that, he turned and kissed Lily deeply and possessively, sending his point out loud and clear.

Marnie was finally in her own bed, she was fully healed now, and no side effects were left from the poison. She wasn't alone in her bed either.

Ash was still with her, tighter than a tick in a butt crack. She didn't mind it, though, she was coming to love it. Her wolf Myan loved it too, though she was a bit unnerved by the loud purring. When he would make Myan grumpy, she would tell him to go cough up a hair ball, which in turn made Marnie laugh.

She rolled onto her side to get a better look at the sleeping Mr. Kitty. When she looked at him, he looked so handsome asleep, like he was a young cub again.

"Liking what you are seeing, my naughty little wolf?"

Startled, she blushed, when she realized he was awake the whole time she was staring at him. He didn't say anything more as he pulled her to him and kissed her possessively, she didn't think that a simple kiss could turn her on so much, her panties were getting wet just the same.

"I can smell your arousal; you smell so delicious. I want to lick all that wonderful cream; I want to know what you taste like. I want to feel myself inside you as we become one. I want to know what you sound like, when I bring you to the climax of your passion."

"I want your everything, and I want you to have my everything. Forever."

Before she even knew it, she was naked and under an equally naked Ash. He was sucking on her nipples; his hands were everywhere. He moved his mouth slowly down to her center.

His tongue did things she wasn't aware they could do; he licked all her cream and then slipped his tongue inside her to get more. She was screaming in her desire, arching her body to get closer to him. When she finally came, she thought for just that moment in time, that she had left the earth for heaven.

Once she came back to his arms again, he positioned himself between her thighs.

"Now, my love, we will ascend to the heavens together."

In one swift move, he joined them together in bliss. It was like nothing she had ever thought or was told it would be.

It was so much, much more.

It was right at this blissful moment that Marco popped into her head.

"Marnie!!! It's time, Adira is on her way to the pack hospital to have the pup.."

Marnie, to Ash's surprise, flew out of their bed and started to put random clothes on, all the while, in a happy sing-song voice, she kept saying, *"I'm an Aunt, I'm an aunt."*

She looked over at Ash as he was just watching her, "Come on, Mr. Kitty, we got to go. We are about to be an Aunt and Uncle. Get a move on!"

With that, she was out the door running down the stairs, while he was still putting on his shoes as he hopped out the door after her.

CHAPTER FIFTY-EIGHT

$\mathcal{D}$uncan wanted to go in with Adira, but the nurses all said no. He was out in the hall with Marco, August, and Archer, along with half the pack out in the main waiting area, keeping vigil.

Marnie came running in dressed in miss-matched clothes, and Ashton wasn't far behind, he looked like he was still in the process of getting dressed.

Duncan, despite his worry, laughed to himself. It was plain for all to see, what those two were doing or were about to do. From the look on Ashton's face, it didn't go as far as he wanted it to.

They wouldn't let him in yet, not until the doctor had a look first. Duncan was a bit miffed, he had to look first. What does the Doc think, he was going to see something that he himself hadn't already seen before?

Marco seeing how his friend was coming unglued, decided to track down a nurse and see if they would let The Alpha in with his Luna.

Before too long, a nurse took Duncan to Adira. No one else was allowed, that saddened Marnie but she understood. So now they wait for a new life to come into their world.

The pack started to fill in the outer waiting room area, it was like some sort of party. They were just as excited to have a new pup as the parents were.

The King was sent word that Adira was going into labor. He smiled and couldn't seem to stop. His godson would soon be here. He looked over at Lily, wondering what their pup's would be like.

He decided to wait to make the trip to Duncan's pack for now, until Adira has safely delivered their pup and everyone is settling down again. Lily and Adira really needed to have a talk face to face. He didn't think that it would go bad, it was just what they needed to do to put it behind them for good.

He also decided to make a strict law, against those who were found abusing, sexually, physically, or mentally anyone. Especially children, will have a trial; if found guilty, they will be put to death.

Because really are they not murderers themselves, they are killing whoever that person was or who they would have been. Also, sometimes the abused become abusers themselves as well, thus going on to murder others that could have been something special.

Giving the victim a lifetime of pain and mental issues that will affect the life, they now forever must live.

He didn't think it was too harsh at all. He even went as far as to make it the responsibility of the pack, making sure the victims get all the help they need for as long as they need it.

Knowing Lily had opened his eyes to a world he wished didn't exist, a world he will now live to eradicate. No more. This far, no further.

He couldn't imagine abusing his own children, sadly though, the parents are more often than not to blame for the abuse and neglect.

Lily noticed that pensive look on his face, putting a hand on his shoulder, saying...

"My love, do not stare at the tree of bitterness too long, it could make you fall into despair."

He smiled at her...

"My love, I could never fall into despair with you at my side, it is like a brilliant sun shining down on me from the

heavens themselves. No shadows can touch me now or ever again."

They went outside into the sparkling snow, where the King kissed his Queen without a care in the world, if someone were to see them, let them look.

August started to grumble, *"How long does it take to have a pup?"* Marnie looked at him, she wasn't happy with him right now.

"For your information, idiot, a pup comes when it comes, the first one is always a little messed up. I have seen some females go into labor for well over 32 hours. A few that I know, were only in labor an hour."

"Doesn't matter which way, I can't say from experience yet, just so you know, it's exhausting, painful work. Try to show some respect, if you don't know what you're talking about, then keep your mouth shut."

Ash looked back at August; instead of being mad about getting the smack down, he started to laugh.

"She is perfect for you Ash; she is going to be a big surprise to the parents too."

Nine hours later, a very stressed-out Duncan came out of the room to let everyone know that little Alexander Marco MacPatton, was eight pounds, three ounces, and sixteen inches long, had been born into the world.

The newest member of their pack, he has a head of dark hair and a good set of lungs. Adira is exhausted but doing well. If all goes well, she will be home in the morning.

Marnie jumped into Ashton's arms as he twirled her around happily, everyone was smiling it was a wonderful moment in time.

Duncan went over to Marnie after Ash put her down, hugged her, and mind linked that he needed her to do him and Adira a favor. She gave a smile and ran out of the hospital, taking a very confused Ash with her.

Marco went on down the hall to inform the rest of the pack of their new pup. Soon he will have his welcome to the pack ceremony. Marco was so touched that they used his name for the pup's middle name.

After he informed the pack, he went outside and texted Jack to let him know that the pup was born, and all was well.

Marco looked around him, it was a full moon and lightly hit the snow, making it look like diamonds. The air was crisp and clear, the perfect night for our little pup to come join us, he thought. With a wide smile, he went back in to be with Duncan.

Jack Dawson wasn't much for social activities. He gave a small thankful smile though, to the God above for letting nothing happen to Duncan's sweet Luna. They deserved all the happiness that life could give.

His clan was still sorting the victims, most were either brought back to their families, or found new families in either the packs or in Jack's clan.

There were just a couple of kids left, Jack decided that they would have them stay with his own clan members. They were three boys, brothers at that. He decided since they were nine, eleven, and twelve; that they would be good foster children to live in the clan house and learn from the males about being men.

He had plenty of money, and so did a lot of their clan. If those in the clan didn't have as much money for what they needed, then another clan member helps them out. It is just the way this clan worked. The first of its kind.

He gave out a sigh, looking out over the snow-covered ground, wondering if someday he would find a mate of his own, something like what the wolves have. A soul mate. It happens in the Werebear world, but it's becoming a rare thing anymore.

Most of the time in his world, if it was a bear female, aka 'sow'. She would go into her heat, and it would be the best male would win the prize. He would be with her for a while and then be gone. Sometimes love would follow, but it was rare.

He listened to the quiet of the night, with a sigh, he went on to bed. Perhaps he should just give up on that dream. He was a werebear, after all, not a werewolf.

He smiled when he remembered, what he got the little Alpha for his welcome to the pack gift. His very own motorcycle. Jack would have him over to his clan to learn to ride. As soon as he was old enough.

It was a dirt bike, that would be his learning bike; then for his sixteenth birthday, he was going to get him a real motorcycle.

Ten minutes later, Marnie came back holding what looked like Frankenstein's teddy bear. It was the ugliest teddy bear that Marco had ever seen. Marnie was carrying it like it was the most precious item in the world.

Duncan took the bear to Adira's room, he placed Max beside his son in the hospital crib, and then climbed into bed with his wonderful mate. He made a mental note to himself, he was going to ask the Mages to make their magical cabin again. He was going to get some alone time with his Mate and pup.

Pulling Adira close to him, spooning, she snuggled into him, and they were both asleep. A nurse came in to check up on the mother and son, and she found that the whole family unit was sleeping.

She got an extra blanket and covered her Alpha, checking on the little pup. Turning off the light, she left with a happy smile on her face.

Felicia was eating a delicious meal for a change. Usually, it was plain bologna or peanut butter and jam sandwich, with a small glass of water. This was a great meal, even if it was a bit cold. Steak and potatoes with a piece of white cake dyed blue.

She asked the guard why she got this meal; he was so happy that he forgot not to speak to her.

"The Luna has given birth to our first Alpha pup; it is a celebration."

He stopped himself before saying any more, gave her an angry look, and left. He didn't leave the light on, that light at the end of the hall was her only light, now she was eating in the dark. Good thing she had night vision, or it would become unbearable.

So, the Luna has had a pup, isn't that special? One more thing for me to destroy when I get out of here. She enjoyed the cake and lay down on her blanket again to bide her time.

CHAPTER FIFTY-NINE

Adira was ready to go the next morning, she was so happy that her son was healthy. She couldn't stand to be away from him. Duncan was hovering around them both in pride and protection.

She looked down at her son, *"Well, little one, it is time for us to go home."* He squeezed her finger in his little fist as if in agreement. She was amazed at his skills, and he was barely a day old. He was wearing a little blue hand-made hat with the A sewn onto it. He was wrapped in a little baby quilt that the elderly ladies of the pack had made him.

She then realized that she would never be alone ever again. She was complete.

Duncan told Adria everything that had been happening, even how Marnie and Ashton looked when they came into the waiting area.

He told her about Felicia and what she had done. He told her the punishment she would have to carry out. He also said he didn't trust that female any further than he could toss a semi-truck.

He and Marco had upgraded the pack house security system. Extra locks on all their doors, especially in the nursery and their bedroom since they were connected now. They also added a panic room off the nursery, just in case.

Cameras were added in the hallway and inside the nursery for their protection. They would send video straight to Duncan's and Marco's phones and computers. They would know right away if someone meant them harm.

He also assigned guard duty to the younger warriors as part of their training; they would walk the halls in shifts. Morning, afternoon, and midnight. They will do rotating shifts, keeping it random.

Duncan and Marco also have put guards, two male, and one female, on Felicia, for when she gets out of the dungeon. One must be always with her, including in the bathroom.

Her room is in the basement, she will be locked in there. The only time she would be allowed out was when she was doing chores. Only the guards are allowed to interact with her, making sure she kept separated from everyone while she was doing chores.

She will have shock and tracking bracelets around both her ankles. If she gets out of line, the guards have permission to shock her and lock her back up, till she can behave herself.

She will also only be allowed on the first floor, in the kitchen and dining room areas only. She will be given a gray outfit to wear. She will be allowed to clean herself once she is out of the dungeon. It will be the only time she will be able to wash.

Archer and August have also taken a personal role in guarding her as well. They will be an extra pair of eyes if things get out of hand. Also, Archer had talked to his pride, although Felicia's father was having a cow. Even her mother had agreed that this punishment was harsh but fair.

Archer also stated that if she should not behave while in the pack house, he was going to take her back to the Pride and she'd be publicly punished there, then Felicia would be kicked out of the Pride.

It seemed a bit harsh, but Duncan had seen this kind of behavior before, rich, spoiled, and entitled. He had nothing against the rich, after all he was one himself.

It's the attitude that has to be corrected; he wasn't even sure it could be. He didn't like the vibes she was giving off at all.

She is a snake hiding in the grass.

Marnie and Ash were back in her room again, this time, they just snuggled and watched some TV. Right now, they were solving a mystery with a group of cold case detectives.

He loved the feel of Marnie's room. It was feminine and warm, but it also had an edge to, just like his mate, gorgeous and a little sharp. Push her too much, and you will get cut. He loved that she was a bad ass. For so long, the only females he was around, were the salad nibblers that were afraid to break a nail.

No, his mate, she was beautiful and unique. She was smart with great intuition. He could watch her every day for the rest of his life, she was the flame to his moth.

He was thinking about some more bedroom play time but just being with her like this was something he wasn't willing to give up yet.

He intended to tonight, Adira will be home soon, and he knew that he was going to lose Marnie to Adira for a while. A newborn pup was tough competition.

That little guy is too cute, he is going to be breaking hearts before he knows what a heart is.

Felicia decided to play nice for now, today they will take her to the next stage of her punishment. She couldn't wait to get out of here, she did wonder if that other prisoner was removed yet. She wondered if she would see his body. She was fairly sure that being in this dungeon had messed with her mind.

Sure enough, they came for her, she was given a set of grey jogging pants and a baggy shirt to put on. With her hands tied and her feet in what looked like silver shackles.

As they walked her down the hallway, she looked in the cell where that disgusting guy was, to her surprise he waved back to her. Oh, my God, he looked like a zombie. Why did he go silent? It was then, just before the guards yanked her away, that she realized that he didn't have a tongue.

"What happened to his tongue?"

The guards looked a bit surprised that she would ask. The bigger of the two shrugged, and in a calm voice like this was some sort of dinner conversation, he said.

"He ate his tongue, right after he ate his dick."

Felicia thought she was going to be sick. What kind of sick monster was he to do that?

"Why?"

"Well, when a sicko like him goes against the wishes of his wolf, doing nasty things the wolf doesn't like, well, the wolf leaves, leaving the human to go insane."

With that, she was pulled along to the outer door. She was blinded, because of the sunlight on the snow, and had to stop to adjust her eyes. That just made her guards drag her rougher than before. She was walking barefoot in the freezing snow; they should cut her some slack at least.

She was aware that she was being watched by others that were lined up to watch her, it was like she was the float in the parade.

When they reached what looked like a small shed, the guards handed her over to another set of guards. What is this, she wondered. Wasn't she supposed to go to stay at the pack house?

She decided to keep her mouth shut and just play along, for now, to see what the situation was. Looking for any holes in the security or lapses.

She did scent another Lion, though, she looked around and there leaned up against a tree was Archer, he was watching her with his cat eyes, they looked like they wanted her to fight or run, so he would have a reason to rip her to shreds.

Archer was still really pissed at Felicia and for what she did. She had to be partially insane or something to do that kind of shit. Destroy a kitchen and beat the cook because the dinner wasn't going to be ready for another hour.

Then the sneak attack on Marnie, because of the poison, it was a deliberate attack. Then to claim it was in self-defense. Did she think they were idiots?

No matter what she does here, he was going to personally see to it that she doesn't step one toe out of line, if she does, he will claim it was self-defense. Only he will take much more care to ensure no evidence was left behind.

He had also decided it was time to tell his parents and Felicia's parents that they do not rule the Pride anymore and must step down.

No more power-hungry idiot's manipulating from behind the scenes. He will find his mate, or he won't; either way, it is up to him to decide.

Seeing how Duncan's pack was run, he decided to adopt some of his pack's ways, it was time for a substantial change to his Pride. He was certain that not everyone would embrace this new thinking; however, he was certain that they would all benefit from it if they gave it a chance.

Look at how Felicia acted here at this pack, he can't take another chance of making enemies with other species. He needed new bonds to make them stronger, the Lion line of the shifter world was slowing down. They needed some new blood into it to make it stronger. If those in his Pride are not up for the changes, then they will have to either get with the program or get out.

CHAPTER SIXTY

Adira and little Alex were sitting by the pack Christmas tree in the Luna room. It was Christmas eve. Elderly pack members were around her while the young pups played with their new toys.

The pack tree was different from other personal trees, it had all the twinkle lights and a star at the top. However, all the pack pups made its garland. There was a train under it going round and round.

Each pack family also made an ornament to hang on the tree. The rest of the ornaments were old-fashioned glass stars, moons, and nativity scenes. The rest of the Luna room was twinkle lights from the ceiling, holly around the hearth, and evergreen garlands.

It looked old-fashioned, warm, and welcoming. The two Luna's made Christmas cookies, with all the pack's pups for the Christmas Eve party.

There was also a huge bonfire in the pack square, they were popping popcorn on the cob and roasting nuts, this was for all the pack as well.

For Christmas eve dinner, everyone had pizza and snacks. Everyone was getting a sugar buzz from all the cookies. The kitchen was a buzz with activity preparing for the huge feast that they would have on Christmas Day.

Little Alex was sound asleep in the arms of Selma, the pack's head elder. Adira and Marnie were playing with the children, making sure all were happy. While the males of the pack hung around the snack table.

It was a peaceful and happy Christmas Eve. Tomorrow there will be a feast and then the Christmas Ball. Adira was like a kid in a candy store, all of this was new to her. She made sure she enjoyed every minute of it. While Duncan watched over them with a happy smile.

Felicia was not a happy female at all, she was allowed to take a ten-minute shower with lukewarm water. Then she was given another grey jogging outfit to wear, her hair was covered by a grey bandana.

She sat in her assigned room; it was grey as well. It had a small cot in the corner with a plastic milk crate for an end table. The cot didn't have any sheets, just a wool blanket, and a pillow.

The floor was just dirt, cold, damp dirt, but it did bring a little contrast to the room, though.

There were no windows only a light hanging from the ceiling. There was a small shelf on the wall, it was empty except for a couple of small booklets on manners and protocols for meeting new people, what to expect when visiting other were' packs.

There was a small room off from hers, she assumed it was the bathroom only because it had nothing but a bucket in the corner with a lid, and beside it was a cheap roll of toilet paper.

There was a shelf on the wall in this room as well, it had a bottle of hand sanitizer on it. That was it, so this was going to be her life for the next week or two.

There was a tray of food on the milk crate, it had two slices of cold pizza and a Christmas cookie, with a small glass of milk to wash it down.

She was told that was for her Christmas present this year, she would not be working till the day after Christmas, she will then be assigned to the clean-up crew.

It was Christmas Eve; she should be out with all her friends, dancing at all the best parties. She had a special gown made, just for the holiday. Now she is sitting in grey, doing nothing at all. Feeling sorry for herself, she laid down on the cot to cry out her angry tears.

What does it matter anyway? Really, it's not like any of them were real friends. It wasn't like her mother or father really cared about how she felt. Even her Lion is pissed at her for forcing her to attack the she-wolf.

Seriously, what was there for her back at the Pride? Nothing, nothing at all. Perhaps she should just take off for a while and just be herself.

The King decided that he was going to go to Storm Crow pack this year for Christmas, a surprise to all in the court. He decided that things needed to cool down a bit, so he canceled the Christmas festivities for the crown.

Instead, he loaded up an SUV with all the presents for his Godson, Alpha, and Luna. As well as a present for each young pup in their pack. He was going to play Santa this year.

Lily was both excited and nervous about going, it was time for her and Adira to have a long talk. She wanted to see her nephew too. It wasn't right what happened to them. That didn't mean, though, that they had to continue on the same way.

It was time they both led the lives they were meant to lead. The past is in the past, and there it will stay.

She too bought a gift for Adira, something special. As for little Alex, she didn't really bother, her mate bought everything he could find. There was nothing left for her to buy him.

They went out to their motorcade and were off into the snow and wind. The King held Lily's hand in comfort and encouragement. She laid her head on his lap and decided to take a nap. She always hated long car rides.

They would arrive there at around three in the morning, she wanted Callan {aka the King} to call ahead and give them some kind of warning, especially since they would arrive so early in the morning. He assured her that it would be ok.

Duncan and Adira were in their room for the night, they checked on all the preparations for the next day.

"Duncan, have you heard from the King lately?"

"No, I haven't actually. I suppose he is still getting things straightened out. Also, he has to attend all the holiday dinner parties and balls. Diplomats trying to gain his favor, I didn't really expect to hear anything from him."

"I don't know, Duncan, maybe it is my Luna intuition or something, I just feel that he might be coming here for Christmas. I had some extra rooms made up, and I had another cabin freshen up, just in case."

"Little wolf, that is really good thinking, if he shows up, we have the room. If he doesn't, then there is no harm done."

One of the best things for a female werewolf is that her body heals fast. So, no bleeding and all the weight that she gained was now all gone. She was happy because the gown she chose would knock Duncan's socks off. She had been very secretive about it.

For some reason, he asked if he could make one request about the gown. His request was that the gown would be a deep blue color. Adira wondered why but decided not to say anything.

After checking on little Alex in his homemade cradle, Duncan got into bed. They were both exhausted; between little Alex and all the prep for the parties, they were both too tired to do anything but sleep.

Jack Dawson was not much for the holidays, sure, he enjoyed watching all the cubs having fun. Heck, he even played Santa one year. He just felt more alone during this time of year. Though he is always busy with clan business and arranging the big holiday celebration and parties.

He just felt alone, he needed his mate. He had all but given up on that pipe dream, though. She would have to be rather unique in order to live with him for the rest of her life.

He tried to picture her in his mind, as always though, it was just a fuzzy out-of-focus picture. The snow all around him was twinkling with the moonlight. He walked through it with unseeing eyes. As he walked the grounds on patrol.

His bear Brutus was also feeling a little down. He was more positive about the whole finding your mate thing. He was starting to lose hope as well, they both decided to let it go, see what happens. Just continue on with clan life as usual.

He might, though, after the holiday season, go on a walk-about. Single male bears tend to get restless when staying around others. So occasionally, they go on what is called a walk-about; you go off into the woods to be just yourself and your bear.

Jack always found it to be relaxing, nothing but you and nature. There are several what they call hidey holes for the males, they contain some supplies for camping along with some canned goods for food. It usually depended on the time of year as to what was in them.

Jack had his own private ones that he used, especially on rainy days. Brutus doesn't like getting rained on, he will swim and play in the lakes and rivers, but he doesn't like rain. He never bothered to ask why, though. Brutus likes what he likes.

He decided that it was time to stop and go play with all the clan's cubs. Join in on the party in the main room. It was all decked out in holiday fashion, the cook, holy crap, can she make the best holiday dinners, Ham, and Turkey with all the sides, deserts all over the place.

He was especially fond of her lemon and honey cakes; she always baked him one. It was always just for him to have. She would get mad if she caught him sharing it. He chuckled at that thought and turned his way to go home.

It's Christmas, after all.

CHAPTER SIXTY-ONE

Three in the morning, there was all kinds of noise, lights, and singing at the front of the pack house. Everyone was running down to see what was going on, Marco was trying to mind link Duncan, and Duncan was trying to mind link the front guards.

All the front guards would say is that it is a Christmas surprise.

So everyone was down at the front of the pack house, staring in wonder at all that was there. It was, for the lack of any other thing, Santa Claus. He was in a big red suit; he was everything that the books said he was.

He was sitting in his sleigh that was pulled by eight reindeer. It was magical; Duncan went up to him.

"Who are you really?"

"Santa Claus leaned forward and winked at him, that was when Duncan noticed the eyes. He smiled; it was the King."

Then the King let out a jolly, *HO, HO, HO!!* Duncan looked out over his pack grounds; all he could see was the pack's pups running as fast as they could to get to Santa. There was even magical snow falling on top of the real stuff. It was all light and full of sparkle.

The Pack gathered all around with the pups all over Santa and his Sleigh. He had a present for each child and the adults. He must have had a mage help him; his big present bag just kept on giving.

The pups had awe and wonder in their eyes. Their excitement was all around. Once, everyone, had a present, Santa's Sleigh started to move, saying to the crowd as he pulled out of sight, Merry Christmas to all and to all a good night.

As Duncan was holding his and Adira's presents, the King Mind linked Duncan as he was leaving, telling him that he was off to the Werebear clan to deliver gifts; there would be a motorcade coming with twenty people, including Lily, with all the other presents from the King.

He will return once he has visited a few places, he said not to worry about him, the sleigh is magical if there is some sort of trouble, it will magically transport him to safety.

Jack was just coming back from patrol; it was four in the morning, and everything was so serene and quiet. He was about to enter the house when he heard what sounded like little bells.

His eyes looked up to the open sky, as he saw what at first he thought was his imagination running away from him, no...It can't be. His bear chimed in, ***"That is what you think it is. I can see him clearly; that is Santa Claus in his sleigh being pulled by eight reindeer."***

The bells got louder, and soon everyone was out looking to the sky as Santa Claus landed in the middle of the clan houses. Jack walked up to the sleigh with disbelief in his eyes.

"Who are you behind that beard?"

Santa Claus only winked and smiled at him as he reached around and pulled a present out for Jack. Jack recognized his eyes; it was the King.

Jack smiled, and mind-linked his entire clan to bring out all the cubs, for Santa Claus was here to bring them gifts. It was a very magical experience all around; the cubs needed this, especially all the abused ones they adopted into the pack. There wasn't a cub there of any age, that didn't have a look of wonder in their eyes and the biggest smiles.

Everyone was given a present, from the old to the youngest cubs. It was special and wonderful; the King knew just what his people needed. All the abused children for the first time had hope back, they were all laughing.

If Santa weren't the King, he would have given him a hug. Not caring if he lost his man card. Jack looked down at the present in his hands; it was a small little box. He opened it, inside there was a note.

Dear Jack,

Do not worry, what you wanted for Christmas could not go into my bag.

She is out there, and you will find her.

Just go on your walkabout this spring.

She will need your help, although at first, it might not look like it. Her name will be of the stars.

You will find her; it is your destiny.

With Love of Christmas,

Santa Claus

Jack just stared at the note as he watched the King, aka Santa Claus, drive his sleigh high into the air. Everyone in the clan was standing there in awe and laughter. Some of the warriors got toys. It was awesome. They were like kids again.

In a happy carefree tone that none in his clan had heard in a long time, Jack said…

"Merry Christmas, Everyone!!!"

Felicia was surprised when her door opened and there were three girls and Luna Adira coming inside. They all had something for her. A tray with all kinds of different foods on it, a bag with toiletries and socks.

When the ladies had left their gifts, Luna Adira sat down on the bed next to Felicia. She just looked at Felicia, Felicia was getting uncomfortable, it was as if Luna could see right into her heart.

Felicia tried to look away, but something didn't let her, she felt warm all over her body. Her anger was gone, she suddenly felt transported to another place. She was sitting next to a wolf on a cliff, the wolf was beautiful, all white with black tip paws and tail.

Her eyes were just like Luna Adira's only somehow more. She looked around again: over the cliff was a beautiful forest, and the sky was in vibrant shades of oranges and pinks.

When she looked back at the wolf, she started to hear a voice in her mind. It was the wolf.

"My name is Artemis; the Luna and I are one. This is my sacred place; I have brought you here to have a heart-to-heart. In this place of times moments, only truth can live, you cannot lie to yourself or to me."

"I have come with a warning, if you choose to harm my family or my pack in any way, I will not hesitate to kill you where you stand. Your law's do not matter to me, nor do I care about power or money. It is that simple; you harm, you die."

"Why are you so angry?"

"Where is your Lion?"

"Who are you?"

The questions just kept going over and over in her head, and she realized that she didn't have the answers. Her Lion refused to talk to her since she forced her to attack that other female.

She didn't know why she was angry all the time, she did accept that she was, though. As for who she was, she didn't have an answer for that either. What was going on here?

The wolf shifted into a beautiful woman; she was wearing a white gown, and it changed color to lighter shades of the rainbow when she moved.

"Tell me, Felicia, are you angry because your parents don't love you as they should? Your father seems to only care about how you can give him power; your mother only cares about what she can brag about."

"Who loves Felicia?"

"The answer, Felicia, is no one loves you, not even you."

"You are dying to be who you truly are, yet no one lets you. You are manipulated into obeying the wishes of others only for their gain. It has made you so hateful of yourself that you are lashing out at anyone and everyone."

"It doesn't have to stay this way. You can change, if you wish to."

"You don't even have to go back home again; start over somewhere new. Get to know people again and make new friends. Find yourself and love you for what and who you are. Not for what others deem as worthy, just for their own purposes."

"It isn't easy, you didn't get this way overnight, nor will you heal yourself overnight. If you want it, though, you have to embrace it."

"You will stay here for tonight; you need time to reflect and decide who and what you are. What you want to be."

"It is up to you."

With that, the Luna disappeared into the stars, leaving Felicia to ponder on her life. She looked around, there was a tree in the distance that looked like a good place to rest and think.

As she was sitting down, another figure came into view; she was gorgeous; she had silver hair that shimmered like moonlight. Her gown was a dark blue; it sparkled like it was made up of stars, and her eyes were blue but glowed like they were giving off a blue fire.

"Who are you?"

" I am the Moon Goddess; you are not one of my children. You are here because you need a second chance, you have burned all your bridges however, one of my children has spoken for you. Because she worries about her family and your life, that is why I have come to help you if I can. I can only help you though, if you wish me to do so, you must ask for my help."

CHAPTER SIXTY-TWO

The King, aka Santa Claus, delivered presents to all the children in the two orphanages that had taken in the human survivors of the scientists.

All the children got a present, and the orphanage's got a huge donation, not only in money but in needed items. Contractors were coming after Christmas to fix and upgrade all their electric, water, and sewer systems. Also to add on additional rooms as well.

Then when he was finished, he went back to Duncan's pack house, just like Cinderella and her pumpkin, everything changed back into only the King. The King decided he was going to make that a tradition every Christmas, unless, of course, the real Santa showed up and wanted to kick his butt.

Lily was waiting for him; she was nothing but glowing smiles these days. A change he was happy to be part of. He could tell that she was still a little nervous, about seeing her sister again. He put his arm around her and pulled her in for a quick kiss.

"Let's go and get some breakfast, the sun is now up, and I am not only needing a nap, but I am starving."

Playing Santa Claus for the night was very rewarding and exhausting at the same time."

They went into the pack house; breakfast was in the huge pack dining area; it was served buffet style. They were not lacking in anything for breakfast today. They even had a make-your-own waffle station.

The King loaded up on everything; when he sat down with Lily and a few of his guards, he was happy to note that although everyone knew who he was, they didn't pay him that much attention. It was refreshing to be just one of the pack again.

Marnie was up and getting ready to go down to breakfast when her bedroom door opened. There was Ash holding a big tray, filled with anything and everything. Most important, though, he also had on the tray a carafe of coffee with two mugs.

"Good, you are not dressed yet. Why don't you climb back into bed, and we will have breakfast in bed."

She didn't get into bed though, instead, she went over and sat on the couch by the windows. She patted the spot next to her with a half-sleepy smile. He took the tray and sat it down on the coffee table and went to her side of the couch.

Picking her up and then sitting on the couch, he put her on his lap. She giggled at that, he poured them each a cup of coffee, two creams, and some sugar. Just the way she liked it. Once they had some coffee, Ash began picking things from the tray to feed her.

She would let her lips linger on his fingers; she loved the cinnamon roll; it was so sticky. She would suck on his fingers when he brought her some. She would look into his eyes and see them grow darker with passion. She loved to tease him.

Every time she would see that look on his face, she would tingle all over, and she would also be affected by it as well. It was a wonderful Christmas morning.

She couldn't wait to give him his present later on after the ball. The whole Santa Claus showing up was something she still hadn't given much thought, sometimes, it is best to just go with it. She was mystified though when she opened her present.

It was a little raggedy Ann doll she had when she was little; she had lost it in the forest when she was six years old. How did he know? She guessed it was like the magician; showing his secrets would lessen the magic.

Though the road has been a bit rough lately, Marnie was happy that it turned out to be a great Christmas. She couldn't wait to wear her new gown; it was super sexy in a really fantastic way. It was cherry red silk that hung in all the right places to show off her assets.

She was going to blow Ash's mind.

Adira was waking up to Duncan singing softly to his son. It was one of those moments in time, that will stay till you die. She lay there watching them together; he was still too little to do much; when you looked into his eyes, you could tell he was taking it all in.

When he noticed that she was awake and watching him, he grinned from ear to ear. Bringing little Alex over to her so she can give him his breakfast. Now it was Duncan's turn to watch and take memory.

He waited for his mate to be finished with their pup, once he was sleeping again, Duncan reached into his top drawer and pulled out a long box and a square flat box. He wrapped them in gold paper and bows.

"This, my little wolf, is for you, Merry Christmas."

She opened the first box; it was a necklace and matching earrings of diamonds and sapphires. They were gorgeous. The smaller long box was next, in it was the matching bracelet to the set. She was dumbfounded. They were gorgeous.

Duncan was a little worried because she had gone so quiet. Then she started to cry. She jumped from her spot on the bed, straight into his arms. Duncan, they are simply the most wonderful and beautiful jewels I have ever seen, they make me feel like a queen.

"He chuckled in relief; they are the pack's, Luna gems. They have been worn by my great grandmother, grandmother, and my mother. Now they belong to you. Someday if we have a daughter, they will go on to her."

"That is why you wanted to pick the color of my ball gown for tonight, so that I could wear these."

"Duncan, I didn't have time to go shopping for you, though, what could I give you that would equal this?"

"My sweet little Wolf, you already have given me my present, something that cannot be compared or equaled to. You gave me your trust, your love, and finally, you gave me our first pup. No jewels can compare to that."

He pulled her in for a long passionate kiss, she could tell he was going to want a lot more. It was unfortunately going to have to wait till later after the ball.

She pulled back with a smile that held promise, then she started to back away.

"We cannot go any further than that for now, there are just too many things left to do, and now the King is also here. Not to mention the neighboring packs."

They invited the Werebear clan, but they declined; they wanted to have a clan only celebration instead because of all the victims they took in. Give them something happy and a bit less chaos and people.

So we have to get a move on, Sally their sitter/nanny will be watching little Alex tonight, along with her little sister. She will also be with several of the pack's babysitters as they all watch over the pup's tonight, the ball is only for the adults.

After the big potluck feast, everyone settled down for a while to just enjoy the day. Until it was time for the ball.

All was set, everyone was all dressed in their finest. They will all proceed down one at a time or as mates. When they reach the bottom of the stairs, they will be announced. The Alpha and Luna will be the last to arrive, as is tradition.

The first down was the single males, followed by Marco, Archer and August all dressed in tuxedos.

Next were all the single females; Marco stood to the side of the entrance to make sure all was going smoothly. Checking on security and the wait staff.

The next down was the King and Lily, the King, though, wasn't wearing his usual royal attire, he was wearing a tuxedo with the insignia of his house on the pocket. He was just like all the other males, in his clothing at least. No one would be fool enough to mistake him for anything other than royalty.

Lily was beautiful, she was wearing a light golden dress, her hair was up with little white jewel lilies sparkling in her hair. She looked regal.

Next was Marnie and Ashton, Ash was wearing a similar tuxedo to all the other men, Marnie, on the other hand, surprised Marco, she was in a silky red dress, her hair was done up beautifully with little rubies in her hair. It was truly the first time he had ever seen her in a dress.

He couldn't help but smile and be happy for her. Ash was a great guy and perfect for her.

Finally, the Alpha and the Luna came down, Duncan was dashing, of course, but The Luna, she looked like a goddess. She sparkled as she walked, she was wearing the

Luna gems. Marco smiled in approval. Finally, their pack was complete.

The ball went off without any problems, and everyone was having a wonderful time. Packs were getting to know each other better, and the King was also enjoying talking to them as well. Everyone, though, let the King and Lily be just like the rest of them.

Just as they were about to have the last dance for the night, a loud shriek and then the sound of children crying came down from upstairs. They started to rush up the stairs as smoke came down towards them.

CHAPTER SIXTY-THREE

Adira was the first to arrive, as she tried to make sense of the scene before her. It was Felicia, somehow, she managed to get out of her room, and it looked like she was trying to burn down the door to the nursery.

Felicia didn't look like herself at all, she looked crazy. The kind of crazy you don't come back from.

Felicia noticed Adira watching, and with a yell, she came close to her, that was when Duncan stepped in front, closing Felicia's access to Adira.

She screamed in anger repeatedly. Banging her fists on the floor. She was truly gone.

"I TOLD YOUR BITCH OF A GODDESS, NO. SHE LEFT ME ALONE THERE IN THAT PATHETIC WORLD."

She started to cough because of the smoke, then she started to yell again.

"WHEN I WENT TO LEAVE, MY LIONESS WOULDN'T GO WITH ME. SHE IS GONE, SHE LEFT

ME. SHE SAID I WAS NO LONGER WORTHY OF
HER!!!"

"YOU BITCH, YOU TOOK MY LIONESS AWAY
FROM ME. I AM GOING TO KILL YOUR SON AS
PAYMENT!!"

Felicia, in a fit of crazed rage, launched herself at the
on-lookers. Before she could make contact, though,
Archer stood before her. He was pissed.

"You leave me no choice Felicia, for this transgression,
after the Luna tried to help you by pleading with her goddess.
You know Pride law. It doesn't matter if you don't succeed; if
you try to kill an innocent, it is death."

August and Ashton grabbed Felicia by her arms, and
they dragged her out of the pack house, all the while, she
was kicking and screaming in rage. Archer followed
behind till they reached the edge of the forest.

August and Ashton dragged her into the night of the
forest, Archer shifted into a huge Lion. He leaped into the
forest after them. In a couple of minutes, Ashton and
August reappeared on the edge of the forest, standing
with heads bowed.

A mighty roar shook the night as a scream was heard,
then all that could be heard was the silence in the
moonlight, snow, and wind.

The King went out to meet with Archer about what had happened, he told Archer that he was a witness to her crime and would testify if there was a need. Considering her parents and all.

Archer was touched, he hated killing as a rule. He has had to do it from time to time to protect those that he loves and his Pride.

Still, he wondered what had happened to her, was it something that happened suddenly, or was it something that happened over time?

They buried her burnt ashes right there in the forest. Which will remain Unmarked and Unknown. Her parents will never see her again, nor will they have access to her remains. Let her be free of them, at least in death.

Duncan looked at Adira, he could tell she was upset about Felicia. He went over to her and wrapped her in his arms.

"Why Duncan, I gave her a chance of a lifetime."

522

"Sometimes, little wolf, not everyone can be saved or in this case, wants to be saved."

The fire didn't touch the children nor the smoke. The quick thinking of the helpers moved the pups far away from the door as possible. They opened the window's closest to the door to draft out the smoke.

Though they were a bit scared, they are all doing fine, with no aftereffects yet. Adira wouldn't let little Alex out of her sight. Even Artemis was acting possessive.

Duncan had to go and take care of all the pack business and talk to the King and Archer. To tell them that this incident didn't hurt their relationship. He needed to be in contact with Marco as well.

Adira placed little Alex on the bed, she then stripped and shifted into Artemis; Artemis jumped up on the bed and wrapped herself around her pup. Duncan could feel Apollo's approval. He was a proud wolf right now.

Duncan left and hunted down the first of a string of people he needed to talk to.

Lily knocked on Adira's door. She thought it was a little strange that she heard *"come in"* inside her mind instead of the normal way. She opened the door and went inside. Looking around the room, she soon realized why it was a mind link.

There, on the bed bigger than life, was Artemis. She had wrapped herself around her pup. She watched Lily with knowing eyes. Lily could tell that the wolf before her was all Artemis. Adira was not there, where she didn't know.

Zinnia spoke up...

"Lily, let me take this, it has to be all me, though, so you will have to wait for me, in our place inside."

Lily got undressed and shifted into Zinnia, she then left for the other world of Zinnia's.

Zinnia stood before Artemis...

"So it is a Queen Luna before me now, I see you are now white, when before, you were dark. Tell me, are you healed now? Does your soul still bleed?"

"We are healed now, goddess wolf. We have found our true mate and are happy again. Lily wishes to be a true sister now and aunt. If that is possible after all that we had done."

"Well, Queen Luna, it is possible. Adira is a very forgiving and kind person; she will accept you again as a half-sister. So Queen Luna, do you know that you carry your own pup within you?"

" I do."

"Good then, remember what you have learned, do not let that abuse continue on into our family line. It must end in the past."

"Would you like to see your nephew?"

Artemis unfurled her tail, and there was the face of a little angel. Zinnia stepped closer and took a sniff of the pup's scent, then she licked him. She got up on the bed with Artemis, and together they wrapped their bodies around their pup.

Lily and Adira still had to bring things out into the open to heal again. Lily found herself not within Zinnia's personal world but another's instead.

It was so vast and beautiful that she wasn't sure where to go exactly. That was when she noticed the goddess sitting next to a pool. Sitting with her was Adira.

Lily walked up to the pool, and she was greeted with smiles as the goddess patted the ground next to her. Lily, of course, sat down. They stayed silent like that for a little while or a long while. Lily couldn't tell; time felt different here.

The Goddess finally spoke to both of them.

"Well, my children, it is time that you speak to each other, I will not stay here for this; it is between the two of you. Stay here

525

in my garden; your wolves protect the pup. When you have finished, just think of home, and you will be inside your wolves again."

With that, she walked into the pool and was gone. Adira and Lily stared at each other for a little bit. Till finally, Lily spoke.

"I am sorry for how I treated you and for all the things I did to you. I was so angry and miserable that I wanted everyone else to feel that way too."

"Oh, Lily, I don't hate you, I forgive you for what you had done. The truth is we were both abused horribly. Neither one of us really had a choice in the course of our actions. How could we? We couldn't see what they were doing; that was intentional on their part."

"I know Adira, but still, some things I did do willfully. It is for those that I seek forgiveness."

Adira smiled; *"Then you are forgiven, so long as you promise to be my sister from now on and never my enemy again."*

"That is an easy promise for me to keep. I want to be your sister; I want to know what a real family is like."

The King and Duncan went in search of their mates, and what they found surprised and pleased them. Not only did things look like they were patched up, but Artemis and Zinnia were also on good terms and at this moment on a united front.

Both of them backed out of the room slowly; Duncan motioned for the King to follow him downstairs for some Christmas leftovers. They met up with Marnie and Ashton as well as Archer.

They entered the Kitchen on a mission, time to make a raid on all the treats that were left over, Duncan had his eyes on more ham. They all just relaxed for the rest of the day, the King, Duncan, and Marco sat down for a football game.

Others were outside, either training or just playing in the snow. It was an enjoyable day for the King. He was just another pack member here.

Which he knew wouldn't last, but he was going to ride this horse all the way to the stable. The time is coming for him to completely clean house. Change is coming, not everyone will embrace it.

Both Adira and Lily laughed happily, then they hugged for a long time while crying out the pain of the past and happy tears for the future.

When they were done, they willed themselves back into their wolves and stayed in their form wrapping themselves around the pup, while taking a nice lazy nap.

CHAPTER SIXTY-FOUR

Mr. and Mrs. Mathews just found out about the death of their daughter. They were not mourning like normal parents would, they were pissed. They were not pissed because of the way she died. They were pissed, because she was the last chance they had to gain power over the Pride.

Further-more, the Bennet's are no longer speaking to them, whatever that nasty brat of theirs told them. Made them shun them in the Pride. They are going to have to leave the Pride by morning or pay restitution for what their daughter did.

They tried to start a petition with the King, that was until they found out that the King was witness to the whole thing.

They were about to leave their house when a loud knock came from the door. They both looked at each other, wondering if they should open it. Perhaps it was one of their friends who had a change of heart.

When they opened the door, there stood Archer with all of the Prides elders.

"May we come inside?"

Mr. Mathews was at a loss for words; he motioned for them all to enter. The elders didn't waste any time.

"Mr. and Mrs. Mathews, you were already informed of the death of your daughter; information has also come to us that you have been trying to whore out your daughter for years. In order to gain higher standing and eventually take power over the Pride."

"This kind of behavior, as you both well know is not tolerated in this Pride."

"We have found evidence that states that once your daughter was married to one of the three heirs, you and your wife would slowly kill off the high family, thus making yours the only blood left."

"You know the rules; if you wish to challenge the king of the pride, you do so directly. You don't plot behind the backs of others. This, as you know, is considered an act of treason, this crime carries the death penalty."

"What do you have to say for yourselves?"

Mr. Mathews was turning a deep shade of red; he was pissed. Either because he was caught or he thinks himself above the laws of the Pride.

"You have got to be kidding, we are friends of your parents. Felicia loved you, that was all, perhaps she was a bit misguided, but she was young."

"Whatever she said or did, was because she was in love with you. You are the one who should be on trial; you're the criminal; you killed her without cause. I demand that you step down as our Prides King!!"

"Oh, really, Mr. Mathews, and who should take my place?"

"It should be given to our family, it is time for some new blood, the Bennet family has had too much power, it is time they step down and let the Mathews family take over."

Archer gave Mr. Mathews a dark look. One of a predator stalking its next meal. This visibly shook Mr. Mathews.

"Are you asking for the leadership challenge, Mr. Mathews?"

"No, there would be no way I could beat you in hand-to-hand combat till the death."

"So instead, you decide to use your daughter, to try to seduce me. When that didn't work, you went on to my brothers. When that didn't work, you wouldn't let up, you just kept pushing her over and over, till she finally snapped."

Archer motioned for one of the elders to bring a laptop over to the table.

"Let's watch a little movie, shall we?"

When it was all done, Mr. Mathews was visibly about to pass out, Mrs. Mathews just cried in the corner. Neither was willing to talk anymore after watching footage of their daughter and footage of them talking to other pack members about a power grab.

The 'Movie' had excellent video and sound. Nothing was left to speculation.

"Mr. and Mrs. Mathews, you will have a public trial and sentencing. I will let the elders decide your fate. I am too angry to do so. If I do it you would already be dead."

With that, Warriors came in and took them away to the Pride dungeon, where they were to await their trial.

Adira was watching her handsome mate hold his pup. It was at this moment that she realized that she no longer was The Spare. She didn't feel like she did before. She was stronger, confident, kind, and she hoped, a generous Luna.

Those days alone, always hiding, never able to make friends or even talk to anyone. No more waiting in pain, alone in the dark of the night, for the next day to come. No more losing hope or trying to fight the despair.

No more, it was gone. Replaced by the Love of her mate, Pack, and pup. It felt like it was so long ago when really it wasn't even a year. Artemis started to rub up against her mind.

"You are who you were supposed to be. It may have taken a dark and lonely road for us, despite all the bad, we have made it just the same."

"We have mates that are forever, and we will have many pups to keep us busy for years and years."

Adira smiled as her Mate brought their pup over for his afternoon meal. She wasn't a fool; there will be hardships, sadness, and danger. There will also be times of plenty, joy, and peace. That is the way of things, and she was so glad to be a part of it.

Duncan had long since banished her nightmares, now, she has dreams of the pups to come. She has also set up a charity/company that rescues and helps victims of all kinds of abuse. No matter their age, sex, species, or creed.

Duncan, with the help of Marco, Jack, and Archer, have continued to locate and find business, packs, or homes, where there was abuse and trafficking, and putting a stop to it.

They even have the backing of the King, as well as extra warriors and elders; that will also help them track them down to put an end to them for good.

Duncan knows that evil will always exist, but that doesn't mean that you sit on your butt, in your quiet happy little life, and do nothing. Doing nothing, when you know that there is something going on, makes you just as responsible as those who commit the sin.

Marnie and Ashton announced that they were going to have a wedding, even though they were already mates. Marnie didn't really care about a big ceremony; she just wanted a big party afterward.

As a wedding gift, Duncan and Adira gifted them with their very own newly built cabin. It had six bedrooms and four and a half bathrooms. With a large inner gathering room and a kitchen.

Ashton looked at Duncan with a smile...

"It is just the two of us; why so big?"

It was Marnie that answered.

"Duh, Ash, it is for all the pups or cubs we are going to have, I want a big family."

Adira and Marnie were like bee's buzzing around planning for the wedding and party afterward. There were so many guests that Duncan was starting to get a little worried and had to have the two Luna's taper it back a bit, they were going to end up with all kinds of people sleeping in every corner.

Marco finally decided to help them, so the many species of guests don't end up fighting. He prepared lists for them of who's who and the basic rules of their pack, clan, or pride.

He also arranged the menu and seating arrangements. As well as where they will all be sleeping. Some of them were only coming for the day, so that was a tremendous help.

Luna Adira arranged for the entertainment of the younger adults and pups, so they won't be causing too much mischief.

Finally, Duncan looked all over for his Luna, he even mind-linked, but with no response, he found his lovely mate in his office, sleeping deeply at his desk. He gently lifted her up in his arms and carried her to bed.

Just as he was about to lay her down on their bed, she wrapped her arms around him, giving him a kiss on her mark she gave him. He almost dropped her because of the surprise and sensation it made.

She didn't stop, he put her down on the bed and started to remove his clothes, but she stopped him.

"No, let me unwrap you, I just love unwrapping my gifts. There is so much anticipation and the joy of what is inside."

Before he knew it, she had him naked, the evidence of her efforts was plain to see. She kneeled in front of him and licked up his shaft with a naughty giggle. He about came out of his skin; it felt so good.

She continued to tease and stimulate him with her tongue and her mouth. Driving him crazy. Even Apollo was there with him. He couldn't stand it anymore.

He ripped off the little nighty that she had on, backed her up against the door, put one of her legs on his hip, and slid his way home. She was wild by his third thrust, and he was crazy by the fifth. It didn't take long for them to find their pleasure.

They stood there catching their breath when a loud knock pounded on the door. Then Marnie's voice was yelling at them.

"Gross you two, use the bed; that is what it is for. I don't need any images of my brother doing what he is doing. I know he does it, and that is all I need to know."

They started laughing.

They went to their bed and continued showing each other their love for one another.

Chapter Sixty-Five

On a majestic winter day, New Year's Eve, to be exact. Marnie was putting on her mother's gown. It wasn't a normal everyday gown, though.

It was an off-the-shoulder, tea-length dress of a very delicate fabric that seemed to flow with her movements. It was White with tiny white and crystal flowers. They sparkled brightly no matter what kind of light they were in.

Her hair was up in an elaborately braided half up half down style. With little white flowers woven into the design. She wore her mother's diamond necklace and earrings. Her shoes though made Adira sigh with laughter. They were bright red silk sneakers with diamond accents.

Adira decided to wear a red silk organza dress; to compliment Marnie's sneakers. When they were all done and ready, Duncan knocked on the door to walk his sister to her groom.

He looked dashing in his tuxedo and red tie. Another thing Adira added. Adira took up the front, holding Marco's arm. They walked to the main dining room, which was transformed into a ballroom.

In the center of the room surrounded by white roses and crystals. Stood her mate, her forever love. Ashton was standing with his best men, Archer, and August.

All of them wearing black tuxedos with red ties. The highest pack elder stood with them, waiting for the bride to join them, they were all smiles as well.

There were pack members that were friends and family, but that was all. Marnie wanted a small ceremony. Even though it was small, the pack decorated it with every white flower they could get. When they got closer to the alter, Ashton looked like he was going to cry.

Marnie had a huge smile on her face, she was radiant as she came down the red-carpet aisle to Ash. Duncan put his sister's hand into Ashton's to tell everyone that he approved of this joining, and then stood next to Adira and Marco on the Brides side.

Their hands were bound together with silver and gold cords. Representing the moon and the sun and all that is between. Making their vows of love for all the world to see.

The ceremony was beautiful and perfect; Duncan even arranged for a photographer to come in from town to take pictures. Once all the formalities were done. The bride and groom went upstairs to change for the party, and no one said anything when they didn't come back down for two hours.

The Party was huge; there was a large bonfire outside. The main party was inside because of the chilly weather. Dancing and drinking, all had fun. Marco was happy, everyone was getting along as they counted down to the new year.

After that, the party started to slow down, and it was time for the newlyweds to go start their honeymoon.

When the party was over, and the guests had all left, the bride and groom were to go to the bridal cabin in the woods. Everything was provided for them; they would stay there for three days. Then they were going to go to Ash's family for a little bit.

What they didn't know was that there were several pranks waiting for them when they arrived. For one, their clothes were all gone, and someone thought it would be funny to decorate one of the bedrooms like a bordello, complete with a vibrating bed.

They managed to find them all, except one. They did find it, just not before it found them.

Ashton and Marnie were halfway into their passion when Marnie turned back the covers because they wouldn't need them for a bit. Ashton backed her up to the bed, and together they fell to the sheets. Marnie gave out a squeak as Ash started to move her into position.

Stopping, Ash looked at Marnie, and she started to laugh. He was a bit confused, that was until she got up and took the sheets off the bed. Someone put extra coarse sandpaper under the sheets.

Once all the pranks were taken care of, the happy couple were finally able to make love, not only as true mates but as husband and wife.

Though Ash vowed to find the one who thought that the sandpaper would be funny.

Marnie was over the moon happy, explaining to Ash why there were so many pranks waiting for them; he still vowed to pay back for the sandpaper. Marnie didn't have it in her to tell him that there was more waiting for them.

She left him naked on the bed while she went to the bathroom to get changed into a surprise for Ash. It was something that Adira got her for her bridal shower, Marnie thought that it was a bit too much away from her comfort zone, but she trusted Adira.

She came out wearing a red lace corset, with red lace garter holding up red thigh-high lace stockings. Her hair was down, she didn't wear any panties. She was bare just for him. She could tell that he liked it, his eyes started to glow a golden color.

He was already under the covers; after he watched her walk around the room and do a little dance just for him, he pulled back the covers to show her the results of her teasing.

She put one foot on the bed and slowly rolled down one stocking, then she did the same to the other one. It was driving him crazy. He was so hard right now it was becoming painful.

When she stood up to start taking off the corset, he pulled her to him by her hips. He ripped off the corset leaving her bare for him. Her eyes went dark as she watched him; he could smell her desire.

She never felt more beautiful and sexier than she did at that moment. It was just her standing before him. He loved her no matter what; she loved him the same.

He gently pulled her to the bed and into the arms that would hold her no matter what, forever.

Duncan and Adira were laughing when they remembered their prank. Wondering how they enjoyed the extra coarse sandpaper in their bed.

Duncan was wondering if they had taken a shower yet. He had shut off the hot water valve in the basement. That should cool things down for Ashton, a little present from your brother-in-law, a nice welcome to the family.

It was Apollo's idea to turn off the hot water. Duncan was still laughing when they reached the Pack-house. It was their own fault for deciding to get married on New Year's Eve.

There was a long-forgotten tradition in the pack that those who get married on the eve of the new year are tempting fate. So as a counter measure, it is up to the pack to prank them as many times as possible on their wedding night. That way, they had already faced many hardships, before fate could throw any of them in their path.

Duncan knew that it was an old wife's tale, but when he was reminded of it by an Elder, his horns sprouted and the devilish thoughts overtook him. He shared it with Adira, and she shared it with the entire pack.

Wait till they get into Ash's jeep to go to his Pride. I think one of the pups left a dead fish under the seat. It is also filled with helium-filled rubbers for when they open the doors.

Pranksters had free reign to let their imaginations run wild. It was the most fun anyone in the pack has had in a long time. Even some of the younger pups were in on it. Mostly it was the elders.

When they were finally ready to leave to go to Ash's Pride, they would be running to get away. Unfortunately, Duncan had shared the information with Ashton's brothers, and they thought that since they were his brothers, it was their duty to make sure that fate didn't give them any more trouble.

Duncan and Adira sat together in the pack house. The living room was still decorated in all its Christmas glory. They enjoyed sitting close to each other while next to a roaring fire in the fireplace. They were talking through their mind link, sharing each other's thoughts and memories.

Sharing hopes for the future and the love for each other and their pup. Wondering how he will grow, after whom he will take. How he will be with his younger siblings.

They sat there watching the last of the pack members coming in from the party, they looked at each other and smiled.

Watching the last of the embers of the fire die down, they were happy, they were content. They knew that whatever fate had in store for them, they would come through it well, as long as they had each other and the pack.

After all the darkness and shadows, they were now living in the light and warmth of Love.

<u>Epilogue</u>

Adira and Duncan went on to have six pups in all, five boys and then one little girl that was the apple in her daddy's eye. Her name was Jaqueline; they called her Jack for short.

There were tough times and good times. Happy and sad. Through it all, they stayed strong and true as their pack grew. They still fought for those who couldn't fight for themselves.

The King and Lily had three pups, two princes and a princess. They didn't give them over to nannies or tutors. They raised them themselves, and their sons grew to be strong and stable leaders. Their little princess also grew to be strong and extremely smart. They, too, faced hard and good times.

Ashton and Marnie lived within Duncan's pack, they became great warriors and raised three sons. Two of which were werewolves, and the youngest was all Lion.

They were a rowdy bunch of little tricksters but responsible and loving.

Marco was offered a pack of his own, he turned down the offer. He was content where he was, he liked his place in the pack. He also found his mate. They would go on to have two sets of twins, boys, and girls.

All of the children were raised together in the pack, including those that were adopted. They were a handful, but everyone pitched in to help out. They all grew into responsible, smart, and happy adults.

They, with the help of all the other species involved, started an organization for the exploited and abused. It included every one of every species, from the youngest to the oldest.

Giving them help on all issues, medical, mental, and physical. No more taking a child out of a bad place and putting them into a worse one. They also established several halfway houses, transporting victims out of situations as quickly and safely as possible.

They also provided much-needed protection so that their abusers didn't come and cause them more harm.

The organization built extra living quarters for the older abuse victims and the children, pups, cubs, and so on; if they couldn't find their true homes, then they were taken to one of the Packs, Clans, or Prides and were treated like they were their own.

Besides what the King and Lily already started, they also expanded the watch organization, made up of warriors from other packs as well as royal guards.

They will be working in the shadows to hunt down the ones who do the buying and selling. As well as the corrupted politicians or higher-ranking royal party members.

There will be no buying their way out or going easy on them. They will be exposed for all to see their crimes and punished publicly.

As for Mr. and Mrs. Mathews, they tried to escape, killing a little old lady for her car. They were executed upon recapture.

Archer is still looking for his mate, he still has hope, but has put all his efforts into improving his pride. Making their pride the best one amongst all of them. He was a fair and just ruler. He had adopted two of the cubs that were victimized by the scientist.

He had a son and a daughter, and though both were permanently injured from their ordeal, Archer made sure that their handicaps did not define them. That they had all they needed to succeed in their lives.

August would go on to improve relations between pack, prides, and clans. Thus, minimizing ignorance between species by improving knowledge and traditions.

August also was waiting for his mate, keeping himself busy was key to him not being lonely. He was also a very protective uncle.

That just leaves us with Mr. Jack Dawson, a Grizzly Bear shifter. I cannot tell you anymore about Jack; you will have to get to know him more in the next story...."Just a Girl Alone."

He goes on his walkabout, only to find his Mate and trouble too. You will also learn the dynamics of the Bear Clan and all the things in between, that is for another time and place though.

I am a little sad to end the story, as they say, all good things must come to an end.

I hope you have enjoyed this book; it is my first published book. I look forward to you joining me on our next adventure.

{Thank you for reading.}

The story continues in book two,

"Just a girl alone."(Jacks Story)

Lori Ameling

Made in the USA
Middletown, DE
09 September 2024